The Lure of Song and Magic

Patricia Rice

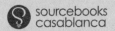
sourcebooks
casablanca

Copyright © 2012 by Patricia Rice
Cover and internal design © 2012 by Sourcebooks, Inc.
Cover design by Jamie Warren
Cover images © Stephen Youll

Sourcebooks and the colophon are registered trademarks of Sourcebooks, Inc.

All rights reserved. No part of this book may be reproduced in any form or by any electronic or mechanical means including information storage and retrieval systems—except in the case of brief quotations embodied in critical articles or reviews—without permission in writing from its publisher, Sourcebooks, Inc.

The characters and events portrayed in this book are fictitious or are used fictitiously. Any similarity to real persons, living or dead, is purely coincidental and not intended by the author.

Published by Sourcebooks Casablanca, an imprint of Sourcebooks, Inc.
P.O. Box 4410, Naperville, Illinois 60567-4410
(630) 961-3900
FAX: (630) 961-2168
www.sourcebooks.com

Printed and bound in Canada
WC 10 9 8 7 6 5 4 3 2 1

Chapter 1

HOLLYWOOD'S HOTTEST PRODUCER SEEKS FORMER TEEN sensation to find kidnapped son.

Dylan Ives Oswin grimaced as he imagined the gossip rag headline. The media would have a field day if they learned why he was parking his Porsche at the Little Angels Childcare Center instead of wheeling and dealing in his L.A. office. That he'd actually traveled out to the rural boonies reflected the extent of his determination—or demented obsession—to track every clue that might lead to Donal.

He did not like being made a fool, so his sources damned well better be correct. His time was too valuable to waste on hunting a spoiled, temperamental child star with a ridiculous name. If Syrene wasn't inside this cement-block building, heads would roll.

He'd left civilization behind over an hour ago. He was far into the coastal mountains now, surrounded by trees and shrubs tough enough to survive the arid conditions. A few miles farther east, on the far side of the mountain range, it would be real desert, but the town of El Padre was only halfway there. Why the devil would a former star rolling in dough live here?

Shivering in the chilly March wind as he climbed from the car, he concentrated on the tasks left undone back in his office rather than his current insanity. He had to finalize the Nathan contract that would keep his lease paid for the next year. He had a hot date tonight who might object to a threesome with his accountant if he had to stay late going over the numbers.

Right this minute, walking up to the door in the mountain-clear sunshine, with hope pounding at the locked doors of his heart, none of that mattered. Finding Donal was more important than an office or a date. The desperation gnawing at his gut would not allow him to ignore any clue, even the most freakish, even after all this time.

Clearly visible from these hills, the brown smog of L.A. covered the coastline as far as the eye could see. Up here above the palm trees, dirty snow from a freak spring storm still muddied the parking lot. The drive had taken him from the luxury of his high-rise Santa Monica office to rural oblivion. If he was on a wild-goose chase, it was his own damned fault.

His cell phone rang as he reached for the doorknob. Feeling antsy about his bizarre quest, he was almost relieved to flick the familiar headset back to reality. "Oz," he answered curtly.

"'No' is not an acceptable answer," he told his assistant after listening to his question. "If they want to play hardball, we can too. Call the network and tell them I'll pull all my clients if that's the way they want it. Send my calls to Carter until I get back, will you? I'm busy."

He took off the headset, tucked it into his pocket, and shoved open the day care door. His quarry was either here or she wasn't. If she was here, he'd figure out what to do about her then.

Oz strode in, expecting to enter a sterile foyer similar to the one where he'd occasionally taken his son on the nanny's day off. Instead of encountering a private reception desk and a locked wall preventing access to the children, he nearly stumbled over a munchkin dashing across his Italian loafers.

Before he could retreat, a cacophonous chaos of swirling children struck him—children the age Donal would be if he was still alive somewhere. The exuberance of childish energy shot a spear of agony straight to Oz's tormented soul.

He was six four, weighed in at one ninety—mostly muscle—and he'd faced hostile boardrooms and raging paparazzi with cool aplomb. Two dozen tiny toddlers stripped him bare, revealing the gaping abyss left by his son's absence.

Oz clutched the doorknob until the worst of the pain subsided, and his mind kicked in. Had the email from the mysterious *Librarian* led him here for a reason? Could Donal be here? He'd endure any amount of agony to find out.

Letting the door close, Oz suppressed all hope but narrowed his eyes and scanned the children. Would he even recognize his son after a year? Kids changed so fast...

But Donal's coloring was like his own—unusual. The boy's hair was lighter than Oz's golden brown, but his eyes were just as dark, more black than brown. The room teemed with dark-haired, dark-eyed children of Hispanic descent, combined with a number of fair-haired, blue-eyed Anglos. The only redhead in the room was a spiky-haired teenager in a far corner, reading a book to a circle of enrapt toddlers who swayed and sang when she showed them the illustrations.

A dumpy woman in a pink polyester pantsuit from the Dark Ages—or Goodwill—rose from a low table occupied by shouting, water-coloring children. Ignoring this evident figure of authority, Oz scanned the room again, this time in search of the woman he'd been told he'd find here. The teenager appeared to be the next oldest occupant. Her small audience was jumping up and down, blocking him from more than a glimpse of short red hair.

The person he sought was famous for her angelic, long, silver-blonde hair.

"May I help you?" the older woman asked as she approached. She looked harried and annoyed at his intrusion. She wore a Little Angels name tag with Bertha engraved upon it, and she was much too old to be the object of his search. Crazy as they were, Oz didn't want his sources to be wrong.

"I was told I might find Philippa..." He hesitated, trying to remember which way the fool female's names went. Her full name was Philippa Seraphina Malcolm James Henderson. The former rock star had used just one name—Syrene—but she had signed her contracts as Seraphina Malcolm. His private investigator had said the teen singer's former name wasn't known here, that she'd taken her other names when she'd dropped out of sight. "James," he concluded.

"Pippa? Who's asking?" Bertha asked in suspicion, presumably because he hadn't known the nickname.

"I apologize for not introducing myself, Bertha." Recovering, Oz smoothly offered his business card and a practiced smile. "Dylan Oswin. I produce children's television shows. I believe Miss James might be interested in my proposal."

"Television? Oh dear." Bertha looked even more flustered and glanced over her shoulder—at the red-headed teenager flinging colorful confetti over the heads of her laughing audience.

Philippa Seraphina Malcolm James—Henderson was her late husband's name—should be almost twenty-seven by Oz's calculations. She had gained fame as a tween singing sensation before she was twelve. And when she'd retired that life—a polite euphemism for crashing and burning in a fiery media frenzy—she'd apparently developed another career writing and illustrating children's books. *Writer* did not equate with *teenager*.

If the redhead was called Philippa James, she could not be the woman he sought, and disappointment once again tore open his aching wounds. Conan had found the wrong woman.

While Bertha dithered, waiting for the reading session to end, Oz eased closer to study the only other semi-adult in the room. From this angle, he could see that a purple streak accented the reader's spiky red hair. She'd painted a sparkling silver zigzag of a tear down one cheek. Enormous blue denim coveralls concealed most of her hot pink tank top. Silver glitter sparkled on her bare shoulders, and her fingernails appeared to be kaleidoscopic swirls of color.

Nine years ago, Oz had been busy building his client list, and Syrene had been much too young to come under his radar. Her pictures had been everywhere, though. The child singing sensation had worn her platinum blonde hair silky straight and down to her waist. Her image had been as squeaky clean as her music, appealing to the middle school set.

The kid in the corner was a psychedelic freak that in no way resembled the angelic image of the child singer.

Of course, nine years ago the teenage idol had metamorphosed into a belligerent wrecking ball, heedlessly destroying lives with her tantrums. Oz had driven up here expecting a rude, obnoxious prima donna. Recognizing—and dealing with—talent was his business, after all.

Preparing to confront a total stranger about his son's disappearance was a tougher task. He had no idea how she might be involved. The mysterious email had simply said, "Syren can find yr son." He didn't even know if Syren and Syrene were one and the same, much less if she was kidnapper or salvation.

This redheaded clown appeared to be neither, and his hopes sank. But he hadn't come here unprepared. Back in reality land, when Conan had told him Syrene was now an author, Oz had been struck with the concept of doing a series based on the work of the author Philippa James. It would be a damned good commercial idea. And if she really was Syrene, dealing with her over books might offer some clue as to how she could help him find Donal.

Well, at least he had a good cover for talking to the demented leprechaun.

As the redhead closed the book and the toddlers tumbled and laughed at some last instruction, Bertha abandoned him in the doorway. She crossed the room, stopping to wipe runny noses and accept grimy hugs in her progress.

Oz couldn't remember the last time he'd hugged Donal. He'd usually arrived home after the kid was asleep. Had he hugged him that last weekend before the boy had disappeared? He hoped so.

That he didn't deserve to be a father had often crossed his mind. But not knowing what Donal suffered kept Oz doggedly following every clue.

The spike-haired reader unfolded from the floor, revealing a surprisingly tall, slender figure who moved with a poise free of adolescent awkwardness. Oz revised her age upward.

He tried to compare Syrene's Alice-in-Wonderland looks to this bizarre redhead, but the images didn't compute. He'd fire his private investigator for sending him after the wrong woman, except Conan was his brother. *Damn.*

The redhead didn't look at him but vigorously shook her head at something Bertha was saying. Anticipating a bolt, Oz eased around the perimeter, posting himself between the two exits. People generally came to him, but he'd been known to hunt his prey when necessary.

She glanced in his direction, seemed to shrink backward, but then, acknowledging his proximity, straightened her spine.

Oz kept one hand in his pants pocket, adopting a casual, nonthreatening stance to lure her in. He couldn't pull off the oh-gosh-shucks farm boy look while wearing his usual uniform of a black silk polo and Prada blazer, but he beamed an encouraging smile, concealing the predatory white flash of teeth for which he was known in certain circles.

Lifting a weeping child wearing a pink pinafore as a shield, the redhead approached.

"Mr. Oswin," she said questioningly, wiping at the

child's tears with her colorfully painted fingernails and tickling her into giggles.

"Oz, please," he responded automatically. "Pippa James?"

She nodded, kissed the toddler's ruddy cheek, and returned her to the floor. Oz assumed he'd passed some test if she dropped her first line of defense. He was good at reading body language. His career depended on it.

"I have an agent," she informed him. "If you want to talk business, you should have called him. My editor would have given you his name."

She actually had an agent? *This* was really Syrene? If Conan was right about the child star becoming a book author, it would seem so. Oz hastily modified his preconceived notions.

Her voice was perfectly modulated, without emotion. It didn't suit her images, past, present, or otherwise. The child singer had exuded passion in every piercingly crystalline note. Even adults had wept at the teenage angst pouring from her soul. Her love songs had silenced screaming crowds to devoted tears. *Magical* had been the most used description of her performances.

Despite her impassive tone, the woman behind the clown disguise radiated a feminine energy that sucked him in. He could understand why she'd been a star. She had presence, even in torn denim and silver tears. And she was definitely not a teenager but a woman with jaded experience in her startlingly turquoise-blue eyes. Were those contacts?

"You're part of the package, Miss James. We would have to work together, so I needed to meet you before I made any offers." That part, he'd memorized. From here on, he had to improvise based on her reaction.

He had hoped that if she recognized his name and knew his son's kidnapper, he would see fear in her eyes. Donal's disappearance had been headline news for months.

She merely gazed at him with impassivity. "We can't work together," she asserted. "So if that's your concern, you may return to your office and write off the project. I don't need the money." She turned away.

Oz caught her elbow, meaning only to slow her down.

Without warning, she spun around, slicing the edge of her hand across his inner arm, a blow that might have broken bones had he held her tighter.

He rubbed the bruise as she stalked off with long-legged assurance, not even bothering to run.

He guessed that was a no.

His reputation for not taking no for an answer was legendary, for good reason.

Pippa took the well-worn dirt path behind the day care to her stucco cottage, fighting the tremors that hit as soon as she allowed herself to think. There were reasons she'd trained to act first and ask questions later.

But her training hadn't been necessary for so long that she'd hoped and prayed the world had forgotten her. Her books weren't Harry Potter bestsellers, just pleasant tales to amuse her and a legion of toddlers.

The stranger had called her by her author name. Did she dare hope he didn't know the other?

Pushing open the rusting wrought-iron gate to her

walled courtyard, she steadied her ragged nerves with a rush of pleasure and relief. Her home was her sanctuary.

Now that she could breathe again, Pippa realized she shouldn't have hurt the man, not because he didn't deserve it, but because sharks could be vicious. Prada and silk couldn't disguise the muscled grace of a predator. Despite Oswin's deceptive sheep's pose, she recognized a wolf when she saw one.

She was mixing metaphors. Closing the gate, she sank down on a wide timber bench and breathed deeply, inhaling the calming pine and sage scents of her garden. Curling her legs into a lotus pose, turning her palms upward on her knees, Pippa hummed her mantra until she calmed the raging tide of fear that threatened her whenever the outside world invaded.

This was her life now. Even constricted as it was, it was a far happier place than she'd ever been.

The rusty squeak of the gate shattered her tranquility. She jumped to her feet, clenching her fists as Oz entered. The ridiculous nickname didn't suit him. He ought to look like a wizard, not a lawyer.

At five eight, she was tall. He was nearly a head taller, broad shouldered, and muscled as she was not. The blazer concealed his physical strength in sleek lines, but in years of martial arts training, she'd learned to recognize muscular prowess.

She could take him, but it wouldn't be pretty. And she had to admit, his golden surfer boy looks were disarming—if she ignored the determination behind his deceptive smile. She did so at her own risk.

She had every right to protect herself against the way of life that had destroyed her. And he was blatantly part of that destructive existence. Keeping her anger and fear tightly leashed, as she'd learned to do through harsh experience, she warned, "You're trespassing."

"I do that occasionally," he admitted with seductive charm. "My brothers have tried to beat the habit out of me, but so far, they've not succeeded."

He had brothers. There was more than one of him. *Heaven forbid*. Accepting that he was human and not the monster in her mind, Pippa sat down abruptly and resumed her position. He couldn't seduce her with empty promises if she didn't listen.

"I'll admit, you're not what I expected," he said thoughtfully.

In overalls, wearing her Dorabelle clown face, she knew what she looked like to a snotty L.A. producer. She considered chucking a loose paver at his head until he spoke again.

"You're better, far more than I imagined."

Perversely, now that the insult had turned into the same old song and dance, she still wanted to chuck a brick.

"Because sharks don't have imaginations," she said dryly, forgetting her intention of ignoring him. She'd more easily ignore a prowling lion. He paced her courtyard, examining everything from the nearly bare jacaranda falling over the wall to the budding rosebushes protected by warm stucco and the garden gnome hiding behind the thorns.

And her. She knew when she was being checked out. She sat still in her bibbed denim, giving him no satisfaction, although her neglected libido trembled in expectation.

"I have enough imagination to know a market phenomenon when I see one," he said with amazing arrogance. "Admittedly, I'm not in the business of multibillion-dollar projects where a single meltdown could bankrupt me. I have employees who rely on their salaries, and I'm averse to unnecessary risk for their sakes. Instead I've learned to recognize the smaller, surefire projects. What I have in mind for you is almost pure profit with little effort."

Pippa closed her eyes so she didn't have to see his winning smile. She tried to find the focus inside her head, but his pacing disturbed the walled garden's tranquility. And hers.

"Talk to my agent about my books," she repeated. "I am not and never will be part of the package. There are plenty of starving actors who will work for peanuts."

"Possibly," he agreed, humoring her. "But I need you to approve the input. It's your style and charm that make the books successful. I'll need that to shine through in the show."

"No," she said firmly. "Please leave." She was afraid if he lingered, that the Voice, the Evil, the Bane of her Existence, would break through her resolve. Mr. Producer would end up crawling on his knees, which was much too tempting a scenario and the reason she hid from civilization. She'd sworn never to use that curse again, but she was weak, and the temptation to lash out and defend herself was strong.

Instead of leaving, he came dangerously close, close enough for her to smell the expensive aftershave that blended with his sexy male musk.

"I know who you are," he said silkily.

The threat untethered the last fragile bond of her restraint.

Furious as she was fearful, Pippa lashed out with her foot. Her heel would have rendered him incapable of procreating except this time, he'd expected the assault and dodged with the quick reflexes of a trained athlete. Her sandal merely slammed high above his crotch.

Undaunted, she brought both feet to the ground and, using the momentum of her motion, rose from a half crouch to jab the heel of her hand beneath his chin and snap his head back.

Despite his bruised groin, Oz grabbed her wrist and bent it backward before she could break his neck.

"We need to talk, *Syrene*."

She ripped her arm free of his grasp. Holding her ears, unable to fight the Voice any longer, Pippa collapsed on the ground, rolling into a human shield. Deep beneath the screaming banshee she became at times like this, her soul howled at the injustice of being exposed after she'd finally found peace.

Chapter 2

Just as Oz was wondering if Pippa's high-pitched keening was meant to prove she was insane, the fractious female shoved off the ground with an oddly muffled cry and almost took his nose off with her fist.

Had she been a man, he would have punched her lights out. Or if she'd been the usual hysterical actress, he would have left her screaming and walked away.

But there was desperation in her every blow, and damn, but she wasn't any flailing ninny, he realized as he dodged her knuckles and knees. She knew how to *hurt*. In a moment, she'd calm down enough to take out his throat.

Seeing no other choice, Oz ducked under her blows, grabbed her skinny waist, and used his greater weight to leverage her over his shoulder, where she silently beat the crap out of his back and did her best to unman him—again—with her toes. Fortunately for him, she was wearing sandals.

He was going with his gut on this one. He had no reason to believe this harpy knew how to find Donal, but she was too damned fragile to be left alone, and there was a story here. He was in the business because he was a sucker for a good story. He needed to know more.

Limping from a blow to his thigh, he crossed the courtyard and tried the mission-style timber front door. When it opened, he carried her inside. She continued beating him black-and-blue, choking on cries of fury. Plopping her down on a bed didn't seem safe or expedient. What he wanted was just where he'd hoped. He carried her through the airy, high-beamed front room and out the sliding glass doors.

The small teardrop-shaped swimming pool sparkled with crystal blue waters. Oz dumped his hysterical burden into the deep end. He didn't know if the water was heated or not. He hoped not. She needed to cool off.

He stood there long enough to make certain she didn't drown. When she popped to the surface doing the dog paddle and glared at him, he left her there. After that exercise in emotional exertion, he needed a drink.

The cabinets in her kitchen didn't contain anything more alcoholic than vanilla extract. He detested the juice drinks stacked in the pantry. Rummaging, he concluded she liked fruit. A blender sat on the counter. One of those smoothie things shouldn't be difficult.

He knew to take peel off a banana. He wasn't as certain about the lemon and orange, so he threw them into the container whole. Orange peel was supposed to be good for something. He whacked the leaves off a basket of strawberries, added the berries, and turned the whole mess on.

It still wasn't looking right when... What in hell was he supposed to call her? *Pippa*? Ridiculous name fitting a children's book author, but it didn't suit the dripping cyclone stalking through the house, presumably toward her room.

Oz checked the freezer and found mango ice cream. Perfect. He flung a few scoops into the pulpy gunk in the blender and buzzed the machine.

After running a shower, she returned to the kitchen wearing a straight, sleeveless yellow sack that fell to her heels. Oz could see every lithe, graceful move she made and gauged her bra size wasn't much larger than her skinny hips. He liked a little meat on his women, but he had to admit there was something primitively sexy in her lithe stride.

Her short red hair remained plastered to her shapely skull, and all trace of the clown makeup had disappeared.

"You look like a pencil in that piece of shit."

Her scrubbed face registered no reaction to the insult. Tantrum over, he guessed. Without cosmetics, her skin glowed with the translucence of fine porcelain.

"I made you a smoothie, and I promise I added no rat poison." He sipped his own to prove it was safe and almost gagged.

Apparently deciding what gagged him was good for her, she accepted a glass and sauntered outside, taking a lounge chair by the pool. Setting the glass down, she closed her eyes and turned her palms upward, absorbing the sun's rays.

Following her out, Oz rummaged in the cabana and dropped a tube of suntan lotion in her lap. "No ozone layer, remember. Redheads fry." He threw a towel over her wet head for good measure.

He was amazed at her self-control once she'd shed the hysteria. Any other woman on the planet would have blistered his hide. He probably deserved blistering. He could deal with that far easier than the silent treatment. Either way, he was determined to find out what she knew.

"What will it take to make you leave?" she finally

asked after tasting his unpalatable drink and grimacing. Her tone was dead neutral, emphasis on dead.

"What will it take to persuade you to work with me?" he countered. "Name your price. Everyone has a dream. What's yours?"

"World peace."

"Not enough money in the universe for that. How about a UN ambassadorship? I could pull a few strings..."

She lifted the towel from her head and shot him a stinging glare.

Shifting over a second lounge so he could watch her, Oz hung his blazer over the back, pushed up his shirt sleeves, and took a seat. He sipped his gawdawful drink. "Don't look at me like that. Senator Gordon Oswin is my grandfather. I have an uncle who does something mysterious and important on the UN Council. I have a fleet of aunts and great-aunts who know every senator and representative in D.C. Amazing what can be done when you know the right people."

"And what *you* choose to do is harass and threaten women?" she asked.

"No, I make deals. I'm damned good at it. Persistence is the key." He prayed it was the key that would unlock this inscrutable female. If he were a superstitious man, he'd almost believe she could reveal the mysteries of the universe. All he wanted her to do was find his son. So far, he couldn't see how that was possible, but giving up wasn't in him.

She began rubbing lotion on her long, slender arms, and Oz shifted uncomfortably. His bruised groin didn't need added stimulation.

"I have all I want," she informed him, keeping her

voice low and without inflection. "If you tell everyone who I used to be, then you'll destroy my career as an author, and I won't be of any use to you. I think that's a stalemate."

Pippa knew how to hide her fear. She'd been doing it all her life. She rubbed in the lotion and observed her relaxed tormentor through the corner of her eye.

He ought to have blood on his shirt front from where she'd smacked his nose, but the black silk knit concealed the stain. She suspected he would look preposterously sexy even with blood smeared ear to ear.

He obviously detested the fruity drink he'd created—for her? It was undrinkable, but if he'd done it for her, he got Brownie points for trying.

Despite her attempt to stifle the Voice, she'd thrown one of her fits in front of him—and he hadn't collapsed into a craven, quivering hunk of raw meat whimpering for her approval. Odd, that. She hadn't meant to have hysterics. She never *meant* to. They just happened, usually at the most inopportune moments. No one had ever thrown her in a swimming pool as a result, though.

Annoyingly, he accepted her verbal gauntlet with an amused curl of his lip. She'd just spent half an hour coming up with her brilliant argument—while struggling with the horror of losing her anonymity and being forced to start over. And he thought her terror was funny?

"You're looking at me as if I'm an ax murderer," he said.

He was more intuitive than she'd realized. That was exactly how she thought of him, except he didn't need an ax. He could destroy her life by simply speaking the truth. She might possess the wily cleverness of a trapped animal, but she lacked the wider resources of a shark who swam in an ocean large enough to contain senators and CEOs. She said nothing.

He tried his smoothie again, grimaced, and set it aside. "I have a children's network relying on me to fill a morning slot. I wanted Pippa James, the children's book author, to read books and interact with a select audience of children. When I learned you were Syrene, I knew you'd be ideal and hoped you might even sing kiddie songs. I gather that option is out."

"I have no need to leave this mountain," she informed him, hoping she could force him to listen even if she couldn't fully explain her reasoning. "I have learned that the more I have, the more I think I need, except satisfaction is never attained by possessing more. I no longer need or want fortune or fame. I repeat, speak with my agent about rights, find a good actress and singer, and I will happily sign whatever is necessary. Just do not include me in your plans beyond that."

She hoped he would heed her warning, but men like Oz never did—unless she unleashed the Voice on him. She'd sworn to herself that she never would again, but she wasn't a saint, as her earlier hysteria had already proved. He was lucky he was still functioning. Maybe the Bane of her Existence was rusty and merely pushed men to fix bad smoothies these days. She didn't dare test her theory.

"I can talk to your agent and hire an actress, a singer, and a dancer to take your place, which will reduce your profit percentage considerably, but you say that doesn't matter." He shoved his sleeves farther up his muscular arms, revealing more of his California bronze.

She stared in fascination at golden hairs glittering against brown skin and tried to shut out his rumbling, masculine baritone. She'd not felt attraction to a man in years. She didn't want to feel it now.

"But I will still need you as a consultant," he continued, as if she were agreeing with him. "Your musical talent reveals itself in your books. They need to be set to music. I don't suppose you can do that?"

She could. She already had the music in her head. And some in computer files. Even her editor hadn't noticed the rhythm of her stories. Scary that this man had. She shook her head no. "I see no reason to involve myself in the project at all. I would like you to leave now."

He studied her briefly, making her aware that she wore nothing beneath the thin swimsuit cover-up. It had been a long, long time since she'd felt like a woman, if ever. Her marriage at sixteen hardly counted.

She had no desire to be put through that hell again. She wanted him gone before all her pent-up misery escaped and someone else got hurt.

Blessedly, he rose with the athletic grace she'd noticed earlier. He'd probably played college football at UCLA. Or if he had family back east, perhaps he'd gone to an Ivy League school and played lacrosse. Or polo. What did she know of those things? Nothing. She had never gone to high school. Her GED had gotten her into community college.

"I'll be back tomorrow, Miss James. Think of what you most desire—something within reasonable reach—and I'll see if we can find terms that will suit us both."

He made a spectacularly poised retreat, throwing his

coat over his shoulder and strolling away with the confidence of a devil who knew he could have whatever he wanted. She wanted to heave the smoothie at him.

Instead, she assumed her yoga pose, found her focus, and slipped into a calming trance until she was certain he was long gone—and she could switch to the offensive.

Still rattled, she continued to take deep breaths as she returned to her office and dialed her agent. She put him on speaker so she could open her computer while she talked. She got his receptionist and agreed to wait, confident Reynolds would recognize her urgency since she'd actually called instead of emailing.

"What can I do for my favorite author on this lovely day?" Reynolds asked when he finally shook off whoever he'd been talking to.

"Dylan Oswin was just here. He claims to be a producer and wants to make a show of my books."

Oz had lied. While she'd sat here waiting on Reynolds, she'd Googled the website on the business card he'd left on the counter. He produced more than modest children's shows. His shows won Emmys.

On the other end of the line, Reynolds whistled at her mention of Oz's name.

Pippa's agent had never physically met her even though his office was only a few hours away. She used an unlisted number and a post office box even in dealing with her trusted, long-time business partner. Reynolds had seen nothing wrong or odd about that. Reclusive, paranoid authors were practically a stereotype.

"Why didn't he call me first?" was the first thing her perceptive agent asked. "And how the hell did he find you?"

Smart man, Reynolds. That was the reason she'd hired him. He knew she was hiding her real name behind a pseudonym, but still he protected her. Concentrating on her breathing, Pippa leaned back in her chair. "I don't know how he found me. He said he wanted to meet me before making the offer. Do you know him?"

"I know *of* him. I've never dealt *with* him. Oz was a legend before he was twenty-five. He has a reputation for striking gold where no one else has looked. His personal life isn't quite as successful."

Ah, there was the vibe she'd picked up before she had her fit and quit thinking at all. "In what way?"

Reynolds hesitated; probably deciding how much was safe to tell her if a lucrative deal was in the making. "You'll find it in the news files. His wife ran off with their son when the kid was an infant. She was killed in a traffic accident in Mexico. There are some who tried to say Oz arranged it, but it's *Mexico*. Who doesn't get involved in accidents surrounded by lunatic drivers? Anyway, he got the kid back, only to have him stolen again last year by the nanny. Word is, there was no ransom note, and the police can find no trace of the nanny. Gossip flies, but there's no proof of anything anywhere."

She knew about gossip. And the media. And the black cloud of suspicion. She almost—*almost*—felt sympathy for the big man who'd made a smoothie for her, had he been the least bit less confident of his ability to persuade her to do what she didn't want to do.

Fine then, she would simply have to undermine his damned confidence by demanding a payment he couldn't provide.

Chapter 3

Oz sat in his Porsche with the engine running, debating the wisdom of giving Pippa James a chance to run and hide. He still had the Nathan contract to finalize and a date to get laid back in the city. He didn't want to sit here, guarding the portals all night. But he didn't want to chase a madwoman down the mountain if she took a notion to flee.

Remembering her cottage had no garage or driveway, he got curious. Releasing the brake, he returned the Porsche to the road in front of the day care. Cruising the narrow two-lane, he located no side roads that would take him back into the area where she lived. No gated drives either. The house was completely invisible from the road. The woman was serious about hiding. No wonder Conan had only found the day care address.

Finally, he settled on a rutted dirt road that was little more than a wide hiking path. He'd bottom out the Porsche on rocks if he was fool enough to drive it. Parking off the pavement, Oz jogged through the piñon and sage, not caring if anyone saw him. He was banking on the lady not owning a gun, although that was probably a stupid notion on his part. Anyone with fists as lethal as hers knew how to kill.

For Donal's sake, he hoped she used her weapons for the purpose of good, not evil.

The path curved at a stone outcropping and then

descended at a rate requiring a goat or a helicopter. Oz stood on a boulder and gazed down the mountainside. Amid the rubble of rock and scrub grass below gleamed a white geodesic dome. He knew a music studio when he saw one. Syrene could easily afford her own.

The secluded, soundproof building would also provide excellent concealment for kidnap victims, but he wouldn't go there. The woman he'd met was a head case, but he wouldn't accuse her of crime. Yet.

He headed back to the car, pulling his cell phone from his pocket.

"Conan!" he growled when his brother answered. "I hope I'm interrupting something interesting."

"Wouldn't tell you if you were." Computer keys clicked in the background.

His youngest brother was a geek. Oz doubted that Conan ever did anything interesting.

"I've found Syrene, and I want to know more. Where did she come from? Who's her family? Boil down all the gossip into facts. She's a hot wire, and I need to ground her somehow."

"Why?" Conan asked, not unreasonably. "You can hire any number of other babes. Why a volatile bitch?"

Closer to Syrene's age than Oz, Conan was apparently more aware of her public image. Oz tried to find some way around the real reason for his fascination in the singer/author. His family would call an intervention if they knew his desperation was driving him to follow leads provided by email freaks.

"Just a hunch," was all he revealed. He had no other good reason for choosing a prima donna for a children's show beyond his stubborn obsession with finding his son. The day care aspect of Syrene's life held possibilities. Maybe she'd seen Donal there.

"She's still gorgeous, then," Conan concluded. "Wish you well. I'm going out to play now."

Conan wouldn't, of course. All Oswins were overachievers for a reason—their curiosity, intellect, and energy could not be contained. Conan would be at his computer, sipping black coffee and digging into Syrene's life well into the night, if only to figure out why Oz wanted to know about her.

Such aggressive competitiveness made for intense family gatherings, which might be the reason Oswins seldom bothered to gather. Alys, Oz's late wife, had attempted to reel his brothers in for the holidays the first year of their wedded life. The Christmas tree had ended up lengthwise on the family room floor after an impromptu football pass led to full-fledged sibling rivalry and a flying tackle.

He had belatedly remembered that their mother used to tie the tree to the wall and carried a fire extinguisher all through the holidays.

Alys had died the year after that party, so that had been the last time all the Oswins had been in the same house. He'd been a fool to try marriage, given his family's bad luck in the relationship department, but there for a little while, Alys had made a difference, and he'd had hope.

It was probably smarter that the Oswins each found a different coast or country to occupy than pretending they could live in the same space. Conan was making noises about moving to Hawaii. Their middle brother, Magnus, was currently in Alaska.

Oz made a few more calls before taking the Porsche back on the road. He didn't need Conan's report to know Philippa Malcolm James had trust issues. One of his calls was to hire a grunt to keep an eye on her movements.

His BlackBerry beeped before he turned on the engine. Oz glanced at the incoming message.

> Syren must sing Th...

The text cut off. Swearing, Oz checked the call back number, but it was blocked. He tried it anyway and got a disconnect. Swearing, he studied the text again. The sender had used a capital T, as if she was about to name a song. Ten bloody million songs began with *The*.

He couldn't curse away the spookiness of the message. Did the sender know where he was? Know he'd met with Syrene? Why had they cut off so abruptly?

He waited to see if another message would come through. The phone remained silent. Maybe the message was too long to text and the sender had given up and decided to email.

Oz checked his email online. Just the usual work messages. Nothing from the Librarian.

Apprehension niggled at his gut. The person who knew he was hunting Syrene had been interrupted trying to reach him. After these last few years fraught with disaster, disconnects left him itchy.

Trying to work out the knots of tension, he rotated his shoulders and rubbed the back of his neck. The damned black shirt was fine for the air-conditioned office but too warm for the sun.

Why would singing a particular song help find Donal?

He assumed that was what the Librarian had been trying to tell him. Would the song somehow lure the kidnapper from his lair?

His phone number and email address were on his website, so it wasn't difficult for every nutcase in the universe to reach him. But there was something more urgent about these Librarian messages...

Of course, part of the problem awaited him just a few yards ahead. Mothers were already slamming the doors of their SUVs, picking up their toddlers at the day care. The sight of all those tiny, helpless little kids had him breaking out in a cold sweat. Donal couldn't defend himself. That had been Oz's job. And he'd failed.

The images of what could be happening to his boy had given him ulcers and kept him awake at night. He'd never sleep until he knew Donal's fate.

The contract and his hot date could wait. Oz called the office and told them to let the accountants review the documents and he'd be in to sign them tomorrow. He left a message on Rita's machine and then blocked her calls. She wouldn't take kindly to being stood up, and he didn't have the patience for more tantrums today.

His hired grunt would go to work in the morning, keeping an eye on the singer so she didn't escape. Tonight, Oz would cover the bases.

Releasing the parking brake, he turned the Porsche onto the road, back into the tiny town of El Padre. He'd seen a B&B sign when he'd driven through earlier.

Tossed to the red mat in her family room, Pippa retaliated by lashing out with her heels. Lying with her back to the mat, she caught Park in the abdomen and tossed him over her shoulder with her legs. Her quads were stronger than her biceps.

As their instructor gracefully rolled into a ball and sprang back to his bare feet, Lizzy clapped. "You got some hostile mojo working for you tonight, girl!"

Park, their five-foot-four instructor, bowed in agreement. He was nearly seventy, but until Pippa's day from hell, he'd easily kept his students in line. "Miss James is ready to teach her own classes."

"Not me." Winded from the moves Park had put her through, she sat cross-legged on the mat. "I'm not trustworthy."

At Park's puzzled expression, Lizzy explained. "She's afraid she'll beat the crap out of her students if they don't behave."

Pippa enjoyed Lizzy's blunt honesty. Her friend's brashness could be painful, but Pippa always knew where she stood with her, and that made it easy to relax in her company. Liz was nearing thirty, divorced, mother of two toddlers, and thought she had life figured out. Pippa didn't disabuse her of the notion.

"My temper is not trustworthy," she amended, for Lizzy's sake. "And teaching a class would be a responsibility I'm not ready to assume."

"Like making a TV show?" Liz asked, feigning wide-eyed innocence.

Pippa threw one of her floor pillows at her. "Bertha doesn't know the meaning of quiet."

"Television pays very well," Park said, rolling up the mat. "But you are not an actress."

"You're a man who knows how to be polite." Pippa

unfolded from the floor and drifted to the bar where she'd left a prepared vegetable juice and ice cubes.

"But he's wrong," Liz said. "You put on a clown act for the kids, a sophisticated one for the mayor, a strong one for me and Park, and the list goes on. You were born an actress."

No, those were all hard-earned lessons—like not arguing with friends. Pippa sipped her drink and hoped the conversation would move on.

"Real acting requires exposing emotion," Park argued. "Dressing in costumes *hides* the heart. But why would a TV producer expect a children's author to act?"

"He doesn't. He wants me to read my books, but that's idiotic. I write books for toddlers. They would sound ridiculous on TV. Besides, writers weren't meant to be on stage. We're introverts."

"He's awful cute," Liz said suggestively. "You could at least talk to him over drinks, pretend you're considering the idea."

"You were at work today. How could you have seen him?" Pippa curled up on the sixties Danish modern couch she'd rescued from a garage sale. She'd had the upholstered cushions refurbished in bright sunset colors. She liked giving new purpose to old things.

"He was leaning against his Porsche in the parking lot, working his CrackBerry, when we came in." Liz added a swig of rum from her flask to her juice glass. Pippa's guests were accustomed to bringing their own alcohol. "Nice abs. I didn't think TV producers worked out."

"He's what?" Pippa slammed to her feet and strode to

the window, but of course, she couldn't see beyond her courtyard wall. "Now? He's out there now?"

Unusual for him, Park lingered after rolling up his mat. "He bowed to us. He has had training. Do you have reason to fear him?"

Yes, but Pippa couldn't say that aloud or she'd have to explain why. She paced between the two open rooms, swearing inwardly. "I told him no. I told him in no uncertain terms. He should be back in L.A. What is he doing out there?"

"Protecting his investment?" Liz suggested helpfully. "Bring him over to the Blue Bayou and let him woo you with pretty promises."

"So you can tell the entire town that a famous TV producer is here and have them all crowding into the bar?" Pippa knew her friend's ways too well. "And encourage drunkenness? Let me just give you the hundred bucks you'll profit. I don't need the bad karma."

"This is a farm town," Park reminded her. "Men like that have much money that would go far here."

"He doesn't want to film me here," Pippa protested. "He wants me to go to L.A. And I can't. I won't."

The very idea was sufficient to send her running for the hills. But she heard the longing behind her friends' words. Wealthy people might have homes hidden in the hollows and hills above L.A., but they rarely spent their time or money in farm towns like El Padre.

Liz shot Pippa an angry glare for the blow to her pride and ambition. She'd inherited the Bayou. It was her only income. Park didn't need money, but he had a large family who did. And they all had friends who were struggling.

Pippa was the only rich person in town, although most people didn't realize why. They just assumed writers made money. That was a joke.

"Talk to him, Pip," Liz urged. "Maybe he'd film here if you insisted. He could rent out the church hall during the week, and maybe they'd make enough to repair the roof. And his people would eat at Dot's and stay at the B&B."

Pippa wanted to tell her that wasn't how the entertainment world worked, but she couldn't tell her how she knew. Even her best friend didn't know about her Syrene past.

But Pippa had a feeling the good-looking surfer boy wouldn't give up, and she needed all the defenses she could summon—if only to keep from killing him for doing this to her. She'd already decided on the challenge she meant to present him if he returned. Adding another obstacle to his goals ought to really test his mettle. Why should she be the only one to suffer?

Draining her drink, Pippa nodded. "I'll think about it."

Chapter 4

OZ'S VIGILANCE WAS REWARDED THE NEXT MORNING when Pippa James emerged from her hideout and strolled down the town's main street to Dot's Café for breakfast. This morning she was wearing a diaphanous caftan of swirling pinks over a loose, white, ankle-length dress that might as well have been a burka except it had spaghetti straps. She'd covered her amazing eyes with rose-colored glasses.

After spending six hours in the B&B's rock-hard, antiquated double bed, Oz figured he deserved this prize. Instead of heading for his Porsche, he fell into step with her.

"Good morning..." He hesitated, hoping she'd supply the name she preferred. When she didn't, he smoothly continued, "Shall I call you Pippa?"

"That's my name," she replied curtly, not breaking her long-legged stride.

He refrained from arguing the point. "Do you mind if I join you? I have a meeting later, but I wanted to give you time to consider my offer."

"You have a pretty face, Mr. Oswin," she acknowledged, entering Dot's Café, "but you're slime underneath. I should have you arrested for stalking."

"I see you wake up snarling. Let me buy you some caffeine." Catching her elbow, he steered her away from the counter she'd been aiming for and toward a booth. He did so cautiously, ready to drop her arm if she whacked him again. "A double shot of espresso, maybe?"

"I don't drink coffee. Back off, Mr. Oswin, or I'll scream the house down. As you may have heard, I have a powerful voice." Fortunately, once she'd jerked her arm from his grip she didn't appear prepared to create a public scene. She slid into the booth and sat primly, hands crossed on the table, glaring at him through the ridiculous pink glasses that somehow worked with her red spiky hair.

"I apologize if I'm invading your space." He took the seat across from her and mentally prepared his arguments while verbally smoothing the waters. "We're a little more touchy-feely in the city."

He glanced up at the waitress pouring tea into Pippa's mug without being asked. Tea from a teapot, not a tea bag. She obviously ate here regularly, and they catered to her preferences. He nodded toward the coffeepot in the waitress's other hand, and she filled his mug without a word.

"The usual, Dot," Pippa said in the polite tones she reserved for everyone else but him. "How are the twins?"

"Doc says they'll survive to wreak havoc another day. O'course, I'm gonna have to feed the doc for free for the next year to pay his bill. Pity I can't do the same with the hospital." The waitress turned to Oz. "And what's your poison this morning?"

Assuming a Spanish omelet was out of the question, Oz ordered eggs over easy, bacon, and hash browns, keeping his eyes and ears open to the interaction between the two women and the other customers entering.

There were things to be learned by observing people in their natural habitat.

Every customer noted Pippa's place in the room when they entered. She acknowledged no one. Oz could attribute that to her being out of her usual place and curiosity about him. He supposed the buzz as people wandered about, gossiping, might be normal, but he was picking up vibes that said otherwise. Awareness in here was thicker than the coffee he was drinking.

"They all know what we're discussing, don't they?" he asked after Dot departed with their orders.

She tilted her head in curt agreement. "You're sitting there in a jacket that would feed their kids for a month while wearing a watch that would pay their mortgages for a year. And they're wondering how they can get some of what you have. It's human nature."

He hadn't brought a change of clothes with him and knew he was grubby and wrinkled. He'd bought a cheap razor at the drugstore and still didn't feel shaved. But the town had already seen dollar signs? Interesting.

She lifted her mug and sipped her tea with a half smile that was all cat in cream. That's when the message clicked. She knew what the town wanted already, and she was preparing a bombshell that every person in here probably already knew about. Oz hated surprises.

He did a mental tally of all the possibilities and hit the most likely one immediately. "You want me to film the series here," he stated without question.

He swore that her rose-colored glasses twinkled. She merely continued sipping her tea. "Rethinking your offer, Mr. Oswin?"

The computer he called a mind knew the numbers

could work, but people were the flaw in any math. The best people for the project weren't likely to spend half the year away from their homes, out of their sophisticated milieu in the city. Not for the shoestring budget the children's network expected.

Besides, how would staying in this Podunk town help him find Donal? He didn't mind ferreting out her secrets from the comforts of L.A., but his business would go south fast if he was stuck up here too often with no freeway to the office.

Yeah, he was rethinking his offer and resenting every minute that she forced him into this corner. But dammit, it was a good concept. And if she was as treacherous as she seemed right this minute, then she might very well know where his son was. He didn't have time to follow his logic while she wore that smug expression.

"If you will read the books so I don't have to hire an actress," he retaliated, "it might be doable." He disliked being manipulated. Let her be the one responsible for letting down an entire town if she refused him. See how she liked it.

The waitress brought a bowl of sliced lemons. Instead of dropping one in her tea, Pippa squeezed one with her teeth, as if it were an orange slice. Oz suffered an erotic vision of what else she might do with that lovely wide mouth and pink lips.

She didn't seem aware of the implication of her action. She stared over his shoulder, fondling a second lemon slice. "I come with a high price," she conceded. "I doubt that you can meet it."

He was actually anticipating her reply. He hoped she wouldn't disappoint by naming something trifling like a

Ferrari. "You're a very clever woman, Miss James. I'm interested in hearing what you want, since you claim it isn't fame or fortune."

Dot returned with their orders. "I talked with Brother Frank. He said the auditorium is available," the waitress said, apropos of nothing. "The church has a better sound system than the school. And Henry said he can operate it. He's been out of work since the radio station shut down."

She hurried to her next customer, apparently not expecting a reply to her enigmatic declaration.

Oz bit into his toast and raised his eyebrows questioningly. Miss Pippa's serenity didn't seem to be disturbed by Dot's announcement. He wondered if she had drifted to another planet.

He admired the flawless skin and distinctive high cheekbones she tried to disguise with the abominable pink glasses. Even the frames were pink. With seashells on the corners. Where in hell did she find rose-colored glasses?

Which was when Oz realized she was the *perfect* person to read her damned books. She *was* the characters she wrote about. He didn't know if she'd help him find Donal, but she was about to make him a shitload of money.

"I want you to find my family, Mr. Oswin," she said, without any inflection to indicate whether this was as impossible as joining her on whatever planet she was currently inhabiting.

"Your family?" He halted with his toast halfway to his mouth.

Her smile was beatific. "Exactly. I'm an orphan. I have

no idea who my parents are. If you cannot accomplish that, then you'll have to hire an actress. Either way, I'll only agree to the show if it's filmed here. Are we clear?"

She'd just kneed him in the groin and knew it. But he had an ace named Conan up his sleeve that she didn't know about. Oz loved negotiating, especially when his opponent was tall and gorgeous. Here was the jaded, bottom-line woman he'd originally expected.

"I already have this project approved. The network is desperate to fill this time slot," he warned her. "I work with them regularly, so they're willing to slot me in without a pilot. They trust me, which means I have to deliver, which requires filming now. I'll send my engineers up here to check the feasibility of using your auditorium and start hiring set decorators and script writers. But you won't get paid until the film is in the can."

"You can't put me on television until I'm paid," she insisted.

"We'll do your bit on green screen and substitute someone else if the deal falls through. Can I go back to town and call your agent?"

Whoops, he could see her eyes glaze over at that. He'd moved too fast. And brought up a topic she hadn't considered. So, she wasn't as experienced at this kind of negotiating as he'd hoped.

"I'll call him. We'll work out a deal," she decided. "I'll have him call you when he's ready. But you can't just foist off anybody as my parents. It has to be the real deal. I want documentation."

"Even if you won't like the result?" he asked warily. "What if they're druggies living in squalor in Hicksville, Alabama?"

"Even if they're dead and in a cemetery. But in that case, I want to know who their families are so I can try to talk with them."

"That's pathetic, you know." He took another swig of his coffee, but it was lukewarm. "You are who you made yourself. The sperm that created you only explains your eye color."

She removed her glasses and forced him to meet her eyes.

"These aren't contacts, Mr. Oswin. How many people have you ever met with eyes this color?"

No one had turquoise eyes, Pippa already knew. And she knew of no one who had a Voice that could kill and maim, either, but she wasn't about to reveal that nasty little bit of information. She needed to know if she was a true freak or if she had family out there who were just like her.

When she'd been little, she'd hoped people would notice her eyes and say they knew someone with eyes just that color, but it had never happened. When she'd agreed to go on stage and television, she'd done so in hopes of a phone call claiming she looked just like someone's niece or daughter. That hadn't happened, either, but she still hoped that was because of technology and not because her family was in a graveyard.

Some producers had said her eyes were freaky and told her to wear contacts. Most people didn't even notice the weirdness. They thought her eyes were green or blue and didn't see how the colors blended together.

Oz saw it, though. She watched his nonchalant

expression sharpen with interest. She had his full attention now. She didn't even need to mention her Voice as another means of identifying potential family.

"I thought they were contacts," he admitted. "That doesn't mean the color breeds true. The color could just be some genetic fluke."

She nodded acknowledgment. "I was three when I was left at a fire station. Someone might still remember me. The color doesn't come through on film, but if you can get me close enough to a place where my family lived, I can go from door to door if I have to."

"I'll admit I'm intrigued. Why haven't you paid someone to do the research for you before this?"

Pippa allowed herself a smile. "I have. They've all failed."

Finishing her last swallow of fresh orange juice, she rose from the booth and walked off, leaving him to chew on Dot's tough bacon.

Outside, she almost came apart at the seams, but she held herself together long enough to walk back to her sanctuary. She waved at people as if she were registering their presence, but she wasn't. She was shivering so hard she was barely functioning.

She'd just agreed to step on a stage again.

In the church, she reminded herself. The church was safe.

She would be Out There, in public. People might recognize her. Maybe remember the psychotic Syrene who had destroyed her husband and lives untold. The gossip sheets would have a field day. The paparazzi would be camped on her doorstep—

No, Oz would never succeed. He was no wizard. But

he'd have to come up here, spend money, help people until he realized that he would have to walk away without her. She was doing the right thing. Surely.

She bolted the gate behind her and settled on her meditation bench.

She hadn't hurt the kids at the day care with her Voice. That was her mantra. She hadn't hurt them. She wouldn't hurt them. She couldn't hurt them.

She wouldn't sing. She would just read. Calmly, carefully. She'd practiced. She'd be fine.

If she didn't fall apart. It all depended on whether she could tame the virago who lured men to destruction and keep her cool under stress.

Knowing nothing would come of her performance, she should be safe.

Safe, please, O Powers that Be. Don't let her kill again.

Chapter 5

Oz ran his hand through his hair, signed the Nathan contract, and shoved the papers over the desk to the lawyer. "We'll start scheduling the production next week. You have my assistant's number. Keep in touch."

Wearing Hollywood casual, the lawyer rose from the pedestal swivel recliner Oz provided for his guests. "I'm taking the client out for drinks this evening. Want to join us? He has some intriguing ideas."

Normally, Oz would have done just that. He liked knowing the people whose money he took.

But turquoise eyes and rose-colored glasses haunted his curiosity, and he needed to talk to pragmatic Conan before weird ideas of magical genies took root. "Another time. I've got a hot project almost in my hands. When that's settled, we'll talk."

The lawyer nodded and departed, leaving Oz free of accountants and lawyers and nagging Ritas. After a barrage of Rita's irate phone calls, his secretary had blocked her number from the office phone. The woman would probably come after him with a pickax shortly, but he still had time to call his brother.

Conan strode in before Oz could punch the call button. Tall and more lanky than muscled, wearing black-framed glasses, he still managed to fill a room when he entered. Oswins did not do meek well, no matter how techie they might be.

Conan threw a folder on Oz's empty desk. "Your girl could fill a filing cabinet. I reduced the file to her more dramatic moments."

Oz flipped open the folder, saw the first page was Syrene's very public meltdown, and closed it again. The photo of her grief and rage expressed in the twisted cry of her wide mouth, with rivers of mascara running down her cheeks, churned his stomach. "Do you have anything on her parents, where she's from originally?"

"What in hell does that have to do with anything? She's a big girl now. She doesn't need anyone's signature but her own. Did she agree to the show?" Conan took the chair just vacated by the lawyer and swung around, admiring Oz's trophies and the bank of fog covering the city view out the floor-to-ceiling windows.

"She's an orphan." Oz riffled through the folder. She was right. The startling color of her eyes didn't really come through on film. Interesting. She was still gorgeous, even as a teen angel with costume wings and long silver hair. "She wants to know who her family is."

"She was in foster care. Social Services can't tell her?" Conan grabbed the file and flipped the pages he'd obviously memorized. His whiskey-colored hair fell over his wide brow, and he shoved it out of his eyes. He produced a document and flung it across the desk.

Conan was thorough. He had a copy of the papers giving Philippa Seraphina Malcolm into the care of Patsy and George James for a nominal sum per month, which were dated over twenty years ago.

"They know nothing about her, not even her date of birth. She was found wandering around a fire station in Bakersfield."

"If they didn't know who she was, where did she get all the names?" Oz flipped through the next few pages, but they were mostly school records. She'd been a straight-A student while she attended public school. Hitting the stage at age twelve had required private tutors, and the grade reports stopped. The file included a copy of her GED diploma and transcripts from two years at a community college—both obtained after her public breakdown.

"Don't know. I didn't realize you were interested in toddler Pippa. I'll have to drive out to Bakersfield to research. This is just what I dug out online."

"Impressive." Oz pulled out a paparazzi shot showing a platinum-haired teen with an uncertain smile. "The eyes are wrong. She's wearing blue contacts in this. Her eyes are a weird turquoise. Her hair is red now. I didn't ask if that was natural."

Conan flipped through the file and produced an official-looking document probably hacked from a government agency. "Red hair, blue eyes. Some flippin' producer probably had her bleach the hair platinum to increase sales."

Since Oz was a flippin' producer and paying Conan's bill, his brother restrained his opinion of the entertainment industry.

Perfectly aware of what greedy money men could do to a child star, Oz hesitated before ordering Conan to dig deeper into her career. As these few photos showed, Pippa was damaged goods, so fragile that even he debated the wisdom of carrying through with this.

But then he thought of Donal, and he set his jaw. "Dig into everyone she ever came into contact with if you need to. There ought to be enough collateral damage willing to talk for a price. Try not to get too greedy on my dime, but I need to know who she is, or I'm out a lot more money than you'll cost me."

Not easily dismissed, Conan sprawled his legs across the pricey piece of modern art that Oz called his office carpet. "I know you, bro. You're not telling me something. There are ten dozen has-been teen sensations on the market. Why the bitchy, crazy one?"

"She writes the books I'm basing the show on," Oz said reasonably enough. "Now get out of here, so I can get some work done."

Conan didn't move. "You wanted Syrene before you knew she wrote books. Maybe it's about time you start treating me like an adult with a brain in my head."

"I trusted you enough to hire you and not some lame detective." Oz flung a stress ball at him. "No one said that requires telling you everything."

Conan caught the ball. Rising from the chair, he bounced it on the broad expanse of ebony desk. "It does if it affects the case. I hate puzzles with missing pieces."

"Believe me, what I know has nothing to do with what she wants. This is the only way I can bribe her to take the job." Oz knew he was being cryptic and probably driving Conan to bug his phones and intercept his email. That didn't mean he had to tell him everything. "I'm trusting you. You're going to have to trust me."

Conan nodded, only half-mollified. "She's a nutter. You'll regret going after her."

"Nutters do not write children's books so lyrical they can be sung," Oz retorted with conviction. "She's going to make me a stack of green."

"You'll earn every penny," Conan said cynically, heaving the ball across the desk.

Catching the spongy rubber toy and squeezing it as his brother walked out, Oz didn't dispute that.

Pippa was big-time trouble. He became a producer so he could deal with money and contracts, not make nicey-nice with the creative neurotics he bought and sold. He didn't like getting personally involved with the hired help.

But he was making an exception this time. He checked his BlackBerry for messages and then began his list of phone calls to find people willing to work in the outback of El Padre. While he waited on hold, he skimmed the file Conan had provided.

Until he learned why anyone would believe Pippa could help find Donal, he wasn't leaving the lady alone.

"I will not unleash the Beast," Pippa muttered her new mantra while carrying a tray of freshly baked cookies down the path to the day care. "I am a mature, responsible adult who does not need to have her own way, does not need to beat up annoying strangers, and does not shriek at imbeciles. I can handle this rationally."

She still wanted to pound the tray over the head of the man sitting in his inconspicuous gray Ford in the day care parking lot, rattling away on a keyboard while watching her every move. She wasn't stupid. Her manager had hired bodyguards when she was young and hormonal. She recognized a goon when she saw one.

She stopped at the Ford's open window and leaned

over to hold out the cookies. "I don't poison them the first time. I wait until you seriously begin to annoy me."

Wearing the lined, cynical face of a retired cop, the driver helped himself to a chocolate chip treat. "Some people are grateful for protection."

"I have a black belt and a secret weapon. I don't need protection, but you will if you don't move on. Tell Mr. Oswin that if he really wants my help, he'll leave me alone. I value my privacy."

The ex-cop looked noncommittal. "I'll pass on your message, but he's the one footing the bill. It's his call."

Be one with the breeze, Pippa, she told herself. *Take the anger where it belongs.*

She smiled, baring the teeth she'd painted with gold stars. "You may also convey to Mr. Oswin that neither you nor he will see me again until you're gone. Have a blessed day."

She strolled off, comfortable in her baggy overalls. She let no man have a piece of her these days, not even an eyeful.

Entering the day care's back door, she left the tray of cookies with the cartons of milk for the midday snack. She wouldn't disappoint the kids because the cowardly Beast inside her felt like running far, far away.

So she gave them story time as usual. The day care was an excellent place to test out new story lines, and the one about the little green pig was going over well. Afterward, she helped distribute snacks and clear up spills. Then, waving to Bertha, timing her departure to the daily supply delivery, she climbed into the back of the UPS van when its doors were open and remained there as the truck rattled back to the road.

"Just drop me off at the trailhead, Jorge," she told the driver.

He acknowledged her request with a wave of his hand. Half a mile down the road, he stopped long enough for Pippa to hop down, well out of sight of the day care and the hired goon in the Ford.

It had cost her a small fortune to have the studio built down the side of a mountain. At least there had been a road to the property at the time so the workers could drive their vehicles in and out. A small mudslide a few years ago had reduced the terrain to little more than a goat trail. It wasn't her favorite access but a useful one when she wanted to avoid people who knew about the front path.

She slid down the rocky slope and then trotted through sage and cactus until she reached the geodesic dome designed specifically for her purposes. She could explode a bomb inside the walls, and no one would hear it.

Her Voice could be more devastating than a bomb. A bomb killed people and put them out of their misery. Her Voice could cripple and leave them suffering for a lifetime. Bombs required mechanical devices and deliberate detonation. The Bane of her Existence required only an emotional trigger to explode without warning.

She used the keypad to unlock the entrance and reset the alarm after she flipped on the lights. The temperature was set at a steady seventy degrees to protect the equipment.

With the ease of familiarity, she set up the recording and sound machines, arranged the background chords, and switched on the computer. She'd once spent fortunes on technicians and musicians to handle the mechanics of the trade. These days, to maintain her privacy and protect the innocent, she'd learned to do it herself. There was something innately satisfying in taking a song from idea to disc without interference of others.

And the simple tasks gave her time to calm down, forget Oz and bodyguards, and focus on the Beast gnawing at her guts. Once she slid her earphones on and opened up the mic, the world went away.

She'd gone beyond the worst of the pain these past few years, which provided her with this small semblance of discipline. Poor Robbie was a ghost who still haunted her, a pathetic creature as lonely and tortured as she had been when they married. If she'd had any experience at all, she would have known he was weak, despite his macho bad boy image. But she'd been sixteen and in love. Her stupidity was excusable. And from the distance of time, Robbie's descent into adultery and addiction was predictable.

Killing him with tears was neither excusable nor understandable.

So she still cried with that long-ago pain and then wept out her heartache from the isolation she'd suffered all her life, the loneliness that stalked her, despite the friends she'd managed to cultivate. She had no family to miss or to miss her. She didn't regret losing her singing career. But she regretted the loss of the audience, the brief illusion of being loved, if only for a few hours.

She poured into the microphone her sorrow that she would never know love of any kind—parental, maternal, romantic.

And once she sang away her tears, she was free to let

her fury boil upward, to lash the scales, to destroy the harmonies, to scream and bang her head to the canned beat. She shouted. She shook her fists at the roof. And she let the Voice cry agony until it was raw. She could harm no one releasing it in here. No one would ever hear these discs.

By the time she'd emptied her soul and sent the recordings to her password-protected cyberspace library, her security camera showed it was dark outside, and she was starving. She texted Bertha, too depleted to attempt talking. Cop gone? she asked.

Dscvrd u missg few hrs ago. Cursed. Left.

He could be anywhere. She hoped he'd returned to L.A., but as long as the man was being paid, it wasn't likely.

She could give the hired bodyguard and Mr. Oswin a real panic attack. She didn't have to leave here until she knew the coast was clear.

Opening the freezer in her studio kitchen, she dug out a frozen meal and nuked it. She'd spent many long nights on the futon in here. She could occupy herself for days, if necessary.

Let omnipotent Mr. Oswin put that in a pot and stew it.

Chapter 6

A TEXT FROM THE LIBRARIAN ARRIVED JUST BEFORE Oz shut down the office for the day. The Silly Seal Song was all it said.

After an hour of Googling every possible variation of that title, when he should have been hunting dinner, Oz didn't know whether to curse or weep. There was no such title in any index he could locate. Maybe the Librarian simply hated him or thought he ought to give up having a life.

The title sounded like a children's song. Oz had bought CDs of kids' songs to keep his son amused when they were in the car. He and Donal used to sing along with them while stuck in traffic. The kid had crowed over his favorites.

Donal would be five in May. Would he still listen to silly songs? Or was he too terrified to enjoy silliness? Provided his son was even alive. Oz pressed his fists to his eyes, refusing to trek down memory lane.

Digging deep inside him to where the pain lived and clamping it down, Oz reached for the phone. Maybe this was the connection to Syrene the Librarian had alluded to. Maybe Pippa knew the song.

The phone rang before he could key in the number. Checking Caller ID, he answered curtly, "Yes, Bob?"

"She's scarpered," the ex-cop said without preamble, "just like she warned you. If she's in town, no one's talking."

Oz's fury escalated, multiplied by the frustration of this past hour. She was his only damned *hope*. He should be allowed one lousy little hope.

"They're her friends. They won't talk." He buried his hand in his hair and glared at the desk he'd spent the day emptying. "Go home. I can play this game too."

He'd lost any interest in playing games the day his son had been stolen. If Pippa James had any part in Donal's kidnapping, she would pay, and she would pay dearly.

Except even *he* was still rational enough to know that all he had was a hunch and anonymous messages to believe his son was alive. For all he knew, he was badgering the damaged singer for nothing. And yet, he meant to go on badgering her until he lost all hope. That was his idea of fun these days.

He'd skimmed her file throughout the day, looking for clues. Besides the devastating photos of a lovely child deteriorating into a half-starved, bedraggled hellion, it contained a familiar litany of offenses committed by the entertainment industry, none of them new or unusual.

Philippa Seraphina Malcolm James had been rescued from poverty and a foster home and given a life of hard work, wealth, and adoration, and she'd blown it all in a spectacular meltdown after her young husband's death. The only real news was that her management had never robbed her. She'd taken charge of her extremely healthy trust fund on her eighteenth birthday and disappeared.

He wouldn't let her fall off the radar again. If she held clues he needed, he meant to find them.

He went home, packed a bag, and flung it into an old Dodge Ram pickup he'd driven as a kid to carry his surfboard and gear. He couldn't remember the last time he'd gone surfing, but the truck had a lot of miles left on it. He saw no reason to throw it away.

Driving into the mountains, he left his headset and BlackBerry off. He'd spent the day lining up production people for the children's show. It was a simple, inexpensive concept that in the right hands would have the project in motion and talent lining up within a week. He had time to ponder the neurotic singer's vanishing act.

Pippa wasn't quite as fragile as she seemed, he was beginning to suspect. She'd broken when he'd revealed that he knew about her past. But she'd recovered swiftly enough to retaliate.

He based his career on knowing people, understanding their idiosyncrasies, judging how far he could push them. Pippa had the tensile strength of fine steel concealed behind that skin-and-bone facade.

Which meant she probably wasn't shivering in fear in some dark corner but carrying out her threat until he restored her privacy. He respected that.

But if she was the key to his son's disappearance, he couldn't let her out of his sight. He'd better hope he discovered something soon because it could get damned tricky sticking close to a devious madwoman who didn't want him around.

It was dark by the time he booked a room at the B&B. He'd flung an air mattress in the truck with his suitcase. He'd buy new mattresses for the lumpy beds in the morning. He was used to the finer things in life and saw no reason to accept less.

He'd had the drive up the mountain to develop a strategy. It wasn't much of one, but his patience was limited. After checking into the El Padre Inn, he strode across the road to Dot's Café and let the screen door slam behind him. Dot's customers stared as he stalked up to the counter still wearing his office attire of silk pullover and designer blazer, although today the shirt was white and the coat silver-gray. He could *aw-shucks* with the best of them, but tonight, he meant to make an impression.

"Coffee, black," he told the waitress behind the counter. She was young enough to be Dot's daughter. "And the biggest burger you can fry. A side of fries with that."

When she had the order, Oz turned with his back and his palms resting against the counter so he could sweep the room with his gaze. Old ladies in a corner booth glanced up at him and then whispered among themselves. A couple of old men at the counter pretended he wasn't there. A young Hispanic family ignored his posturing and stayed focused on keeping the toddlers fed and in their chairs.

Oz might never persuade Donal to eat his spinach again. Forcing down the familiar pain, he concentrated on the adults in the room now that he had their attention.

"I understand the church needs a new roof," he said in a mild voice that easily carried over the whispers and dying conversations.

"The whole town needs roofs," declared a wag wearing a billed cap bearing a tractor image.

"I'll be hiring shortly," Oz acknowledged. "Buy roofs with your wages if you want. But the only reason I'm here is Miss James. Without her, I go away. She doesn't like me much, so I'll have to rely on you to keep her interested in the project. Can I have your cooperation?"

He didn't hear footsteps behind him, but he ducked instinctively at Pippa's first words.

"You're a jerkwad, you know that?" she declared.

The remains of a lemon pie skimmed the top of his head, leaving whipped cream to dribble down his cheekbone. He wiped off a smear and licked his finger, turning around to admire the irate fairy who had flitted in from the kitchen. *Damn*, but he was good. He'd expected it would be morning before his theatrics would draw her out. Somebody at the B&B must have warned her of his arrival.

"You're a hysterical nutcase, but I can deal with that." He grabbed a handful of paper napkins from the dispenser to wipe down his blazer. His dry-cleaner would earn his pay.

While dabbing off lemon pie he kept an eye on Pippa. She'd painted her teeth today. The streak in her hair was gold, to match the glitter on her cheekbones. She looked like sunshine personified. Even the overalls were orange and gold, with a glittering sun painted on the bib.

"You're bribing an entire town to spy on me!" Hands on nonexistent hips, she looked as if she'd like to fling another pie, but she never raised her voice. Women usually shrieked when they threw things at him.

"I don't work with disappearing acts," he admonished. "You're the one who insisted I move the production up here. I want a guarantee my talent won't do a flit after I've spent a few million. Fair is fair."

"Now I remember why I left L.A. I don't tolerate insufferable asses." She spun on her painted Keds and departed the same way she'd entered, through the kitchen.

One of the old men at the counter left a dollar beside his cup and stood up. "I'll see she gets home okay."

And that was that. Figuring the entire town knew Pippa James walked a thin edge and needed looking after, Oz sat down and devoured a burger savory with triumph.

The insufferable ass was at Dot's the next morning, occupying the same booth they'd shared yesterday. Pippa aimed for the counter, ignoring him, until Dot waved Pippa's usual breakfast under her nose and carried it back to Oz's booth.

Cursing traitorous friends under her breath, Pippa considered walking out. Until those horrible months when she'd killed and maimed with her grief, she'd never learned to fight back. At twelve, she'd bent over backward in her eagerness to be agreeable. At sixteen, she'd simply walked away. At eighteen, she'd self-destructed. Since then, she'd learned calm acceptance and ignored that which could not be changed.

Calm acceptance and Dylan Oswin did not exist in the same universe. He simply tempted the shrieking furies of her Voice by his presence.

Today, he'd dropped the shark suit. In its place he wore a short-sleeved, blue cotton shirt. It had probably cost a few hundred to achieve that tailored, I'm-one-of-you-look. Except no one up here had highlighted hair styled to evenly brush the back of said collar. Or wore a half-grand art-carved gold loop in a pierced ear.

And damn if the result wasn't the sexiest thing she'd seen since watching Rhett Butler on the big screen when she was a kid. Oz hadn't worn that earring yesterday with his shark suit, she'd lay odds. This was his idea of laid-back and nonthreatening.

Which almost made her laugh. Almost. He held her life in his hands, though, and that wasn't a laughing matter. She slid into the seat across from him and let him admire the blue-green tears she'd painted on her cheek this morning.

"Good choice of color," he commented before biting into his bacon and regarding her critically. "The camera will love you. So will the kids. You're a natural."

"I'm about as unnatural as it gets. You'd better be lining up your actress because you're not getting me in front of a camera again."

"Reneging on our deal already?" He didn't seem fazed as he sipped his coffee and studied her. "I've hired a dead ringer for you as your stand-in, but Audrey will never be you."

She didn't like being studied. She hated that she found him attractive. Her skin felt two sizes too small under his scrutiny.

"I've tried finding my birth parents. I've spent a fortune hiring experts," she informed him after sipping her juice. "I don't exist. So you may as well quit tormenting me and resign yourself to using my material and my town but not me."

"Do you know a song called 'The Silly Seal Song'?" he asked out of the blue.

Her stomach dropped to her toes, and she stared at him as if he'd suddenly developed a crystal ball for a head. "Why?" she demanded. Her hands were clammy, and she didn't dare lift her fork for fear she'd reveal her trembling.

"You do," he said with satisfaction. "Do you have the lyrics?"

Either he was too perceptive by far, or she wasn't doing as good a job hiding with him as she did with others. She'd *written* the lyrics. They'd been her first tentative steps toward writing her stories into music. She'd sent them to her cyberspace library when she'd bought a new computer nearly four years ago. No one knew of the song's existence. How could he?

"If you want to know all my secrets, Mr. Oswin, you can discover them yourself. Why should I make it easy?" She returned her attention to her eggs as if he hadn't dumped another hot load of burning oil over her head.

He was the one who looked uncomfortable. It looked good on him. Pippa recalled all the smug, arrogant men who'd pushed her around, turned her into a walking, talking Barbie doll, and manipulated her and her music and her life, and she hummed happily to herself. Turnabout was fair play, even if Oz wasn't the cause of her original grief.

She liked having control for a change. It had been a precious commodity for most of her life.

Pippa could see him plotting, scheming to get what he wanted without telling her why. He'd soon learn she was no longer the easily influenced child she'd been. She'd prepared herself for this moment for years.

She would not—ever—go back to being Syrene.

Chapter 7

OZ GRITTED HIS MOLARS AND TRIED TO ASSUME A nonchalant stance when what he really wanted to do was reach across the table and strangle the self-satisfied elf eating her eggs and toast.

She knew the title of the song! Or she pretended to. Or he was reading things into her expression that weren't there in his desperation to find the connection between the annoying female, the Librarian, and his son.

"I did not *discover* the title of that song," he said slowly, watching her face, searching for clues. She refused to look at him. The paint tears down her cheek reminded him that she wasn't stable. He didn't want her curling up in a fetal ball and keening again.

It was a damned good thing he wasn't into fragile women, or he'd be trying to wipe away make-believe tears. "I received it in an untraceable text message."

The turquoise turtleneck she wore beneath a denim jumper concealed her body language, but he thought she grew still. He made no sudden movements, as if he were trying to capture a wild creature. He needed bait to entice her, except Conan hadn't had time to find the one thing she wanted.

"An anonymous message?" she asked coolly. "What could it have to do with me?"

Excellent question. One he wasn't prepared to

answer. He wasn't ready to tell anyone of his obsession with tracking down crackpots in his desperation to find his son. "I've read all your books. None of them have a 'Silly Seal Song' in them. Are you working on a new book that might?"

She finally looked up, glaring at him through turquoise eyes that appeared as translucent and mysterious as the ocean. "What difference is it to you? Are you in the habit of hunting down the writers of all the spam that hits your mailbox? You must be a very busy person, if so."

He didn't trust her. If he mentioned his son and she was somehow involved with his disappearance, she would run, and he'd never find her again.

"It's not spam," he said carefully, plotting as he went. "It's from an informed source, one who led me to you. Someone knows more about you than I do. Do you have any idea who that might be?"

He bit his tongue and prayed she had that backbone of steel he suspected, or he was about to be treated to another hysterical tantrum.

She had a redhead's pale skin, so he couldn't tell if her cheeks lost color they didn't have. She simply sat still, as if processing his information through a concealed computer. But her eyes were blank, and he was afraid he'd lost her.

"I don't think this person means harm," he offered. "I really think they're trying to help, but the messages are so incomplete that it's hard for me to tell who they're helping. They've cut off abruptly at times. I think the sender might be monitored."

"And they say *I'm* crazy," she replied noncommittally,

scraping up the rest of her eggs. "I don't suppose you write science fiction by any chance?"

Damn. She had a suspicious mind. He supposed he couldn't blame her. "Look, I'm trying to find your parents, like you asked, and I need to know everything about you. If you really don't want to know your origins, tell me now, so I can reboot this project. I have a lot of people relying on me to pay their mortgages, and I dislike letting them down."

"Why would who I am have anything to do with your crazy text message?" she asked with what seemed like genuine curiosity. "And feel free to kill the project anytime. It was your idea, not mine."

"The town is counting on you," he pointed out. "Do you really want to let them down?"

She glared and finished off her juice. "They'd survive if you quietly slipped away and never returned."

"Not happening. I've booked the show with the network. They're thrilled about you. Your agent is hopping up and down with glee. I've got a cameraman whose kid has cancer, and he needs the work. You want to blow them all off because you don't like me?"

"I don't like Syrene," she hissed, leaning over the table so no one else could hear. "I don't want her resurrected. She's dead and gone. I'm a writer of children's books, nothing more."

A little lightbulb lit, and Oz sat back in the booth so she couldn't stab him with her bread knife. "Syrene wrote the seal song," he declared.

"Yes, and that's all you need to know." She stood up and waved at Dot, who waved back. "I've got a bunch of little kids waiting on me. Have a lovely day."

He had no idea in hell where this was leading, but so far, the Librarian was batting a thousand. And Miss James didn't like it a bit.

Toweringly egotistical Hollywood baboon! Pippa screamed inside her head as she walked the path from the day care to her home after the morning reading session. The citrus scent of the Mexican orange bush growing in the sun at the back of the day care mixed with a whiff of jasmine from her courtyard. She'd spent years developing this low-key walk in the sunshine so she could relax to the sound of birds and the fragrance of herbs planted among the stones. But she wasn't relaxed now as she replayed the breakfast she'd shared with Oz.

How could he possibly know about a song she'd written in her studio nine years ago and sent to cyberspace with no other person anywhere involved? Was he *psychic*?

More likely, he had some hacker in his employ who had broken into her computer. The thought infuriated her even more, until she applied cold logic. Unless he meant to steal her songs—and she didn't think Oz was a thief so much as a manipulator—a hired hacker good enough to bust through her firewalls might find government records other investigators hadn't, records that might reveal her parents.

She could add more buffers to her system and keep it turned off so the snoop couldn't nose around anymore. But a hacker that good could be the reason Oz was so confident he could meet her challenge.

Which ought to terrify her. She had no intention of appearing on television as Syrene and driving herself over the brink of destruction again. She'd fought too hard to find the peace she enjoyed now.

But she really, really wanted to know who she was. Did her parents have weird eyes and weird Voices? Maybe they were from outer space. Why had they abandoned her at a fire station? Had she used her Voice even as a toddler and driven her real parents crazy? She was afraid that was the answer, but she wasn't afraid to find out. She needed to know. It was like living with a missing piece in her soul, not knowing who she was or where she came from or why she'd been abandoned.

When she walked into her lovely, tranquil house and saw Oz through the patio door, sitting beside her pool, typing on a laptop, she almost submitted to the urge to let the Beast free to scream. Oz had invaded her privacy one too many times. He *deserved* the worst she could throw at him.

But to do so meant throwing away years of practice at maintaining a Zen calm. She didn't want to deteriorate into the dangerous infant she'd once been. She would not let him destroy everything she'd worked so hard to gain.

She would not let him think he belonged here, either.

She emptied a tray of ice into the food processor, crushed the cubes, and calmly carried the pitcher outside. Absorbed in his work, he either didn't hear or ignored her approach. His gold-streaked hair rubbed his shirt collar, and his wide shoulders crushed the meager cushions of her lounge. He crossed his long legs at the ankle while he worked, neatly balancing the laptop on khaki-clad thighs. He looked much too comfortable in *her home*.

She upturned the pitcher of crushed ice over his sleekly styled hair and tailored shirt.

He didn't scream or curse or drop what he was doing. He merely set the laptop down on the tiles and, scowling, rose to his towering height to pull out the tail of his shirt and shake the ice out. She didn't fear him. She glared back.

Without a word or gesture of warning, Oz caught her arm and flipped her over his shoulder, into the pool. She hit with a splash and sank to the bottom, the denim jumper growing soggy and dragging her down.

When she fought her way back to the surface, he stood at the edge, glowering down at her. "If you've got a mat, I'll take you on. Let's work this out now before we go any further."

She didn't want to take him on. He was too damned physically attractive, and she was too hormonal. Sex-deprived. Whatever. Besides, a man who could react that swiftly without giving away his intent was a formidable opponent. But two could play that game.

Despite her hampering garments, she expertly flipped out of the pool. Squeezing water from her dress, she stood up, and with barely a hitch in her movement to warn him, she shoved him in, fancy Rolex, earring, and all.

"This is *my home*," she told him when he returned to the surface. Every cell in her body wanted to shriek with fury and frustration, but he'd already hit her with his worst, so she had no reason to lose her temper. Now it was just a matter of who was in charge here. "You are not to invade the privacy of my home. It's bad enough you're taking over my town and my friends and my life, but not my *home*."

She couldn't tear her gaze from the bulging biceps he used to pull himself out of the pool. This was no lazy studio exec who spent his gym time schmoozing. The thin wet shirt revealed Dylan Oswin's serious pecs. And she would not look lower to the soaked khakis clinging to his narrow hips. The chilly water should have cooled him off.

She turned away and headed back to the house. "Pick up your stuff and get lost."

"The inn doesn't have wireless," he shouted after her. "Or a pool. Or anywhere private to work. I'm brainstorming the project concept and thought you might like some input." He grabbed a towel from the cabana to dry his hair.

No one had ever asked for her opinion on a project. Pippa pretended not to hear him as she aimed for her bedroom and dry clothes. It wasn't warm enough this time of year to go around sopping wet.

When she returned to the kitchen wearing a lavender tie-dyed hoodie and purple capris, Oz was throwing her strawberries into a blender and ruining more fruit—while wearing no more than a towel.

She was going to have to kill him.

She could hear the dryer tumbling in the laundry closet off the kitchen. She pressed the heels of her hands to her eyes to erase the image of rippling abdominals, swung on her heel, and returned to her bedroom.

Next time she returned, she had a fluffy white robe in her hand. "Put this on. By Bungo, you're disgusting. And presumptuous."

"Yeah, people like that about me." He hit the blend button and watched the fruit concoction spin while donning the robe. "By *Bungo*?"

"I write children's books. I try not to swear, except in my head." She reached for the raspberry-banana juice in the refrigerator, stopped the blender, and added it to the container. Then she poured water into a teakettle and proceeded to make tea. "Bungo is one of my characters, if you'll remember."

"I'm trying to fix you something healthy to put meat on your bones, and you're drinking tea?" he asked in disgust, watching her. "I don't suppose you have coffee?"

He managed to look dangerously sexy even in a fluffy white robe that was too short for him all over. Maybe she should just shoot herself. "I don't suppose I do. And this is raspberry tea. It's warm. I'm not. There's a hair dryer in the bathroom."

If she could just keep this impersonal, pretend he was one of the kids, maybe she could survive without maiming either of them. Maybe.

It was pretty much impossible to pretend a six-four hunk of muscle was a little kid. The man was *huge*. Damned good thing she wasn't into huge men. They intimidated her. She liked her guys on the geeky side.

Not that she'd had many guys since Robbie. Sex was problematic for her unbalanced state. One uncontrolled shriek in bed, and she might drive a man to rob banks or leap off high cliffs.

Hmmm, there's a thought. She wondered which Oz would do.

He'd probably make lemon-banana smoothies and leave the peels on. With a sigh, she tested the blender concoction, added a scoop of yogurt, gave it another swirl, and filled two glasses. It wouldn't kill him to drink something healthy besides coffee.

By the time Oz returned with his flashy surfer-blond-streaked hair styled and wearing her hotel robe, Pippa had sipped her herbal tea and calmed herself as much as she was able. The dip in the pool had cooled any need to beat anyone up. She simply had to outsmart and outmaneuver a shark who probably brushed his teeth with minnows like her.

"You don't get the right to use my house as your personal office, got that?" she said before he even sat down. "You need an office, you can rent one. You want to work with me, you call and make an appointment."

"Renting an office comes out of your share of the profit. Until I'm sure you won't do a flit, I don't want to waste any more money than I already have. I warned you, I'm not a big budget spender. It makes more sense to expect me to be here when you get home so we can work on this together." He sipped the smoothie with suspicion and, apparently deciding it was potable, took a larger drink.

Rather than sit across the table from a man she wanted to murder, Pippa rummaged in the refrigerator, producing smoked Gouda, spinach leaves, a small loaf of brown bread, and salsa she'd bought at the farmers' market from one of the locals. "I have books to write," she reminded him. "I can't write with anyone around."

"I've talked to your agent. I'm paying you more than all your books combined earned over a lifetime. Get over it. You don't like me. I got that. I'll be out of your hair as soon as the project starts up. But for right now, this is what I do. I put all the pieces of the puzzle together and make things happen."

Had he been sitting there in his pricey shark suit, his white teeth gleaming in a practiced smile, she could easily have dumped the smoothie over his head for insulting the worth of her books. But he was sitting at her little mosaic-tiled kitchen table in a fluffy white robe sipping a strawberry-colored smoothie and scowling.

She trusted the scowl more than the smile. That he was able to still be his usual manipulative self while wearing a knee-length robe said he was so full of himself, so certain of his masculinity, that he didn't give a damn how he looked. She liked that even better.

"How many hours of my day do you need?" she asked. "I can only parcel myself out so many ways, and I won't give up the day care time."

"Three," he said instantly.

"Two," she countered. "You can use my wireless and pool while I'm at the school. I'll come here and give you two hours of my time. And then you're gone. *Sayonara. Auf wiedersehen.* Out of my hair until the next day. And I get weekends off."

"How about dinner? My treat. I hate eating alone."

"You're going to push until you knock me down, aren't you?" She carried her smoothie outside and arranged herself on a lounge chair.

She had a feeling Dylan Oswin was the ultimate test of Zen.

Chapter 8

Oz couldn't imagine why anyone called this woman Seraphina. There was nothing angelic or serene about the tense, vibrant female burning up the keyboard in the lounge chair beside him.

It had taken another hostile argument to persuade her to pull her chair next to his so he didn't have to shout across the pool at her. If it ever rained in California, he had a feeling they'd get no work done at all because she wouldn't share a space as small as a house with him. Working in the great outdoors was all she could manage.

While *he* was conjuring images of sharing a bed, even when she was wearing that concealing hoodie. Bad Oz. He knew better. He'd just never found someone so stubbornly resistant to his usual charm. Which forced him to study her more.

And the more he watched her, with her cropped red hair bent over the keyboard, her slender nape vulnerable, the deeper he dug his hole. He liked polished, sophisticated women who knew the score, women who used him just as he used them—mutual itch scratching, some newsworthy gossip action, a few good dinners where they could see and be seen, and then *sayonara*, as Pippa had so colorfully said.

So his attraction to the skinny elf with freckles on her unpainted face was confusing. And distracting. He kept checking out her slender pianist's fingers flying across the laptop's keyboard and wondering how they'd feel in his hair. Which led him to wondering if she had any curves at all beneath the ugly hoodie. Which led to more distraction than he could afford.

"Muppets are expensive," he warned when she went off on a creative tangent. "Besides, they've been done. And so have costume characters. Why should kids relate to talking ducks?"

Her wicked blue-green eyes glanced up from the keyboard to spear him with a frosty glare. "Kids need security, the comfort of the familiar. Half the *adult* population of this country dislikes change, so don't expect kids living in a world they don't understand to accept surprises. People even hate clowns. You don't want a children's show to be *too* original. Just original in a familiar way."

Her phone rang, leaving Oz to ponder original but *not*, while she leaned over to punch the speaker button.

The torrent of Spanish spilling forth ripped Oz straight out of his musing. He spoke fluent Spanish, but this flood of idioms and hysteria blurred to one clear topic—a child was missing. Why was someone calling her about a missing child?

His gut churned. The pen that Pippa had given him for note-taking, while she'd appropriated his computer, snapped between his fingers. He tensed, following her every gesture and word.

Fear for a lost child caused incoherent suspicion to buzz through his brain. It made no sense to connect Pippa with kidnapping. She had nothing to gain from Donal's disappearance but the notoriety she so blatantly avoided. But she was irretrievably linked with his son in his mind, and now she had some link to another missing child.

Instinct made him doubly wary because he *wanted* to trust her, but he'd learned he couldn't trust anyone. Not his late wife. Not Heidi, his son's nanny. No one. Which was why he hadn't even told his brothers why he was here.

"Slow down, Juanita. I'll ask," Pippa said reassuringly into the receiver. "I'll do everything I can. I'm sure Tommy is asleep under a tree somewhere. Let the sheriff do his job. Don't tie up your phone line. I'll talk to Oz right now."

She calmed the caller with soothing tones that left the woman weeping, grateful, and less hysterical by the time she hung up.

Oz was already picking up their equipment and notes and carrying them to the house by the time Pippa swung her long—gorgeous—legs from the lounge chair. She might be skinny, but she had great legs, now that she'd let him see them. Or part of them.

"What does she want us to do?" was all he asked as he dumped laptop and notes on the table.

"She thinks Hollywood producers can call in CSI. She's not thinking straight. It's her grandson, Tommy. He's autistic. She brings him to Bertha's for story hour because he seems to listen when I read. We can't tell if he's absorbing the story, but it gives Juanita a chance to relax and take some time for herself. Her daughter works in the city, trying to make enough money to pay counselors for his treatments."

She was throwing things into an oversize tote as she talked. Water bottle, sunglasses, a miniature copy of some of her books... Oz lost track. He pulled a floppy hat off a rack by the door and pulled it over her cropped hair. She didn't fight him on it.

He'd dressed again after his clothes dried. His dry-clean only shirt was wrinkled, but his khakis had held up. He was presentable enough for the public. "So, how do you look for an autistic kid?"

"Same as any other. It's pretty much desert out there, except with more vegetation to hide in. The town has trackers. Unless you know magic, you might as well go back to the inn."

Oz grabbed a bottle of water from her refrigerator and opened his BlackBerry as he followed her out. "No magic. Just contacts."

She nodded, apparently aware of the value of knowing the right people. She didn't look like a woman who would steal a child. She looked like a worried baby-sitter.

A worried baby-sitter had stolen Donal. Maybe Pippa was a sicko who got her jollies out of watching parents panic because she didn't have any kids of her own. A whole lot of psycho stuff could be traced to abandonment issues.

She definitely had abandonment issues.

When they reached the day care parking lot, she walked on past his Ram. Oz grabbed her elbow, felt her stiffen, and prepared to duck. But she reluctantly climbed in when he opened the truck door.

"Where to?"

"They're forming a search party at Dot's, but Juanita's hacienda is just outside of town. Don't drive and talk." She took the phone out of his hand.

"Headset." He stuck it in his ear and flipped it on. "Call Conan."

She found his brother's name on the menu and hit it. The phone was ringing on the other end by the time Oz covered the short distance to Dot's and maneuvered into a tight parking space between two dusty pickups behind the café.

"Got a lost kid," he told Conan as he switched off the ignition. "Where are you?"

"Driving back from Bakersfield. It'll take me an hour to get there. I've got equipment with me."

"Good. Alert the team. It may be a simple wandering case, but the kid is autistic. Did you learn anything useful while you were out?"

"Made some contacts. Nothing solid yet." Conan hung up.

He couldn't expect Conan to dig out Pippa's past in a day, but he was getting a little more desperate with each passing minute.

Oz realized she was looking at him strangely as they climbed out of the truck. He supposed she had a right to wonder about who he'd called and why. Donal's kidnapping had been all over the news, so his interest in finding missing children was no secret. That he'd formed a task force to find them was a little more private.

"CSI?" she asked dryly, leading him through the café's back door, the one she must have used the other night to sneak up on him.

The entrance opened onto a hallway with a public phone and restrooms, not a kitchen. The kitchen door was open, but no one was working. A voice barked with authority in the front dining room.

"Not quite. I just know people." He didn't want to explain and miss what was being said about the lost boy.

People glanced back at them as they entered, but the crowd was focused on the man in uniform at the front entrance.

"Sheriff Roy Bailey," Pippa murmured as they found places at the back. "Good man."

"We've got the horses meeting at Juanita's," Bailey was saying. "The search team needs a supply of water for themselves and for the animals, and horse feed if we're out there long."

Two men wearing battered cowboy hats and jeans raised their hands. The sheriff nodded in their direction and continued listing needs and taking volunteers.

When he seemed to be winding down, Oz spoke up. "Do you have an air crew?"

"Nope. You volunteering?" In crisp khaki, wearing a holster over his middle-aged belly, the sheriff sent him a hard glance.

"Tell me when you need it, and I'll get one here. If you need more dogs, tell me that too. I've got a crew coming in with night vision equipment in case it's needed."

People stared. Murmurs rose around the room. Pippa slipped behind him as if he were big enough to hide her.

"We'll take all the free help we can get. We ain't got money to pay anyone," the sheriff warned.

"My crew is free," Oz assured him. "You know the territory better than they do, so I'll send them to you when they arrive."

"Pippa, give him my number so we can keep lines of communication open." The sheriff put on his hat and nodded at the door. "Let's move 'em out."

Pippa preferred working quietly in the background, providing water, helping the women arrange food on the open fire pits to serve the searchers as they returned from their fruitless quests. People got lost up here, she knew. In the six years she'd been in town, tourists had fallen off slippery rocks, kids had lost their seats when their horses bolted, and hikers had lost their way a dozen times a year. Any number of minor events could add up to a missing persons report.

Even the media hadn't bothered checking out Tommy's story, it was so commonplace. Although they might later, if the search went on overnight. Or if it was a slow news day. But the town had no newspaper to alert a news crew.

Except a child who couldn't communicate was a different problem from more routine searches. Tommy would run and hide from the rescue teams. Pippa fretted about that knowledge, working up her courage. She had no notion that she could actually help, so she prayed they found him before she had to offer.

Besides, until they found a trail, she really couldn't help. Even if she knew it would make a difference—which she didn't—she couldn't broadcast over the twenty square miles a kid could travel in a few hours. She hoped he hadn't wandered that far, that he was close by and just hiding, but they'd found only a few footprints that might be his. The dogs had lost the trail half a mile down the path.

So she distracted herself by watching Oz. Probably a mistake, but she couldn't seem to help herself. Every time she looked up, his square shoulders loomed over the crowd—talking to the sheriff, introducing a tall, lean man who must be the mysterious Conan, handing hundred dollar bills to the women for food. He was just *there*, a presence felt by all, even though he spoke quietly and did nothing overt to attract attention—for a change.

Finally, when she ran out of busywork and his tense body language radiated a pain that even she could sense, she sidled up next to him.

"Is this how they searched for your son?" she asked hesitantly, uncertain whether to bring up the past he never spoke about.

He shook his head. "In the city, dogs and horses are useless. They sent out alerts and flyers with pictures of the nanny and Donal, checked security tapes around the neighborhood, went door to door. I didn't even know how long he'd been gone when I returned to find the house empty. They had to judge by the time on a security camera at the gate."

The sorrow and guilt in his voice said it all. He blamed himself. Pippa didn't know his story and couldn't tell if the guilt was justified, but she knew he didn't have to be here right now, sharing his hard-earned lessons.

"It takes a strong man to use his suffering to help others. You're doing a good thing here today. Juanita was hysterical, but you've given her confidence and calmed her down, which helps. She even remembered to tell the sheriff that Tommy had been playing with a dog before he disappeared. Every little bit of information can make a difference."

Oz didn't nod acknowledgment but shoved his

hands into his pockets and watched the next round of searchers return.

They'd found the dog but not Tommy.

A tall, lanky stranger with sharp cheekbones and eyes hidden behind wraparound shades ambled over to join them. He had arrived earlier, talked to the sheriff, and gone about his business in the same efficient, quiet manner as Oz, distributing equipment and men as needed.

As he approached now, he studied Pippa but didn't take time for introductions. "I've got the night vision goggles ready to go. It'll be dark in about an hour. Do I call in the air crew or tell them to wait until morning?"

"Morning," Pippa told him without waiting for Oz to reply. If Oz could face his pain for strangers, she could use him as an example to overcome her cowardice for a little boy she knew and loved. "The noise will scare Tommy. We'll do better to light bonfires and let him come to us."

Oz nodded silent agreement, and after sending him a look of concern, the other man wandered off to join his crew.

"That's Conan, my brother," Oz said. "He thinks it's his fault that his contacts couldn't locate my son. He overcompensates."

"He admires you, and he wants to help. That's not a bad thing. You're very fortunate to have family."

He cast her a look, no doubt remembering she had none. He shouldn't need reminding that he was a lucky man.

Before he could comment, a shout rang out near the front lines.

"A shoe! We found his shoe! Bring the dogs."

Excitement rippled through the crowd. With hope rejuvenated, people threw down their burgers, finished off their bottles of water, and prepared to set out again.

Pippa took a deep breath to steady her nerves. She didn't know if she could do this, but she knew deep down inside that she had to try.

"My turn," she said quietly. "Does your brother have sound equipment in his magic trunk, or shall I fetch mine?"

Chapter 9

IN THE END, OZ DERIVED A SMALL AMOUNT OF COMFORT from managing the production just as if he were back in L.A. While dogs and searchers took the path where the shoe had been found, he set Pippa up in a tall chair near a bonfire. He had Conan help form the crowd into a quiet circle far enough away from Pippa that they hid in shadows—for her comfort as much as Tommy's.

When the sheriff mentioned a reporter had inquired about the situation, Oz got on the phone and diverted him. The story wasn't big enough to risk landing on his blacklist, and the media knew he'd return bigger favors later. If that boy was to be found, they didn't need TV crews terrifying either Pippa or Tommy into running.

Thinking of Donal and how he loved hot dogs, he passed out more cash for food to be thrown on the grill so a hungry boy might follow his nose.

Oz did everything possible not to think about coyotes and rattlesnakes and treacherous mountainsides. He even admired Pippa's technical expertise in helping with the sound equipment. She shocked even Conan with her knowledge, forcing him to adjust his rich bitch opinion of her.

And then they baited the boy trap.

Opening and closing her fingers, Pippa looked nervous and uncomfortable as Oz fastened the microphone to her hoodie.

"I don't want them counting on me," she whispered before he turned on the sound. "This is just a shot in the dark."

"They're ready to place hope on the number of times a frog croaks right now. You can't change human nature. If this doesn't work, we'll think of something else. Pretend you're at the day care." He hated to shove her out there alone, but there was nothing he could do to make her more comfortable. She'd said children liked the familiar. His presence would frighten the child.

So Pippa took the chair by herself, a microphone clipped to her shirt, while everyone else hid in the shadows. After a momentary look of panic, she settled down to read from her books. She read slowly and surely, without the drama of an actress, although she changed the timbre for different characters. Her calmness sent a soothing message into the universe.

Oz stayed in the background, keeping an eye on the production. He heard a few people near the road scoff that she was grandstanding, but Oz suspected Pippa would rather be anywhere except here at this moment. She was simply doing all she knew to do—read because the boy liked it.

He admired her courage in waiting these long hours, dreading this moment. He'd learned enough about her need for privacy to grasp some small amount of her discomfort.

And still she sedately read the nonsense words about Tommy Turtle and Billy Bob Bat. Oddly, the crowd of adults quieted, concentrating on her reading just as if they were toddlers.

He didn't know how she did it. She was magic.

Tension drained from taut shoulders everywhere he looked. Even Tommy's family quit crying and settled on the ground, cross-legged, listening and praying. Perhaps the reading was a form of prayer.

A coyote howled in the distance. A dog barked. A nearly full moon began rising over the scrub-dotted hills on the horizon. The aroma of sizzling beef drifted on the chilly breeze, along with the crackle of the warm bonfire. And Pippa's voice droned through the landscape as naturally as the call of a night bird.

Despite the spell she cast, the crowd rustled uneasily when they realized she was repeating books she'd already read and Tommy had not appeared. People turned away and muttered among themselves. When Pippa's confident voice faltered with uncertainty, Oz wanted to break the circle and haul her out of the spotlight. He didn't think he had a protective bone in his body, but he wanted to shield that frail, fey female from a mob mentality that could turn on her at any moment.

Juanita and her daughter, Sara, hugged each other, weeping as they rose from the ground. Their neighbors crowded around them, adding words of hope and sympathy that no one felt.

Conan came to stand beside Oz, not tearing his gaze from Pippa. "She looks as if she'll shatter into a million pieces any minute," he said with the same concern Oz was feeling. "She's not what I expected."

Oz snorted, remembering flying fists and feet. "Don't tell her that, or she'll break your nose. She's been badly hurt, but I think this place has helped her heal. She's trying to return the favor."

"I want to know the story," Conan demanded, crossing his arms.

"Whenever you find the beginning and I learn the rest." *Maybe*, Oz amended, knowing Pippa's preference for privacy.

A gasp and a hush fell over a part of the circle farthest from the bonfire. Pippa continued to read, adding a little more emphasis than usual to Tommy Turtle's dialogue. Picking up on the expectation, the rest of the crowd quieted as well. A horse nickered.

"And then Tommy Turtle knew his mother loved him best of all," Pippa said into the microphone, breaking from the story she'd told earlier and inventing a new ending as a small shadow slipped from the sagebrush. "And he came home."

Weeping, Juanita and Sara rushed in to scoop up the little boy. He clung to his mother's neck but kept staring at Pippa. Looking tired and frazzled, Pippa climbed down from the chair and handed the small book to the lost child. She unsnapped the microphone so the crowd couldn't hear what she said, but the boy took the book and rested his dirty head on his mother's shoulder as she spoke to him. And then Pippa walked away.

Jubilation filled the air with shouts and whistles. A woman broke out of the crowd to hug Pippa. Others pounded her on the back.

She kept walking, past the ring of well-wishers, past Oz, down the road as if in a daze.

Oz punched Conan's arm in thanks and farewell and hurried after her.

He wished he knew what he was doing, but he had no idea what he was dealing with here. He caught up with her easily, tapped her shoulder, and pointed out the direction to the truck. With a blank gaze, she turned to follow his gesture.

He had no right to touch her. Didn't know if it would hurt or help if he did. He opened the truck door for her and offered his hand to steady her as she climbed in. She didn't even seem aware that she took it.

They drove back to her place in silence. Oz waited for some clue from her, but she offered nothing. He wanted to tell her she'd been brilliant out there, that he wished she'd been around when Donal had disappeared. Except, he acknowledged, even her magic couldn't have saved a boy who'd been stolen away in a car.

He allowed himself relief that one small child had been saved from disaster—because this frail woman had known what to do and put herself out there and done it. Not many people would put aside their selfish concerns to help another. He couldn't think of anyone he knew who would.

When they parked at the day care, she climbed out of the truck without his aid, but Oz wasn't ready to let her wander down that path on her own. He followed behind her, and she didn't object. The moon illuminated the barely discernible rocks laid out to form a walk, but the house was hard to miss once they were past the bushes.

She didn't object when he followed her inside. She wandered like a ghost to the kitchen and then stood there as if she didn't know what to do next. Oz opened the refrigerator, found one of her bottled juices, and poured her a glass. She took it and sipped.

He would have to start carrying a flask. He needed something stronger than vitamin juice.

He knew now that Pippa could not possibly have been involved in his son's kidnapping. It hadn't made sense before. It made less now.

What did make sense was the Librarian's admonition that she could *help*. He didn't know how or why or anything else, but Pippa had just lured a small boy back from the edge of disaster. Could she do it for Donal?

With "The Silly Seal Song"? It didn't seem credible.

"Will you be all right if I leave you alone?" he asked with concern.

"I'll survive." She didn't sound too certain, but she'd at least spoken.

"You've been doing little more than surviving for quite a few years, it looks like." Oz was suddenly angry with her pale face and listless attitude. "You *saved* that family back there from unimaginable heartbreak. Why aren't you part of the celebration?"

She glanced at him blankly and then headed outside to the pool. "It was a very small payment on a very large debt."

Grabbing the juice bottle, he followed her out. He needed something liquid, so juice it would have to be. "Explain," he said curtly. He wanted to know everything about her, but he knew nothing.

She shrugged and fell into the lounge chair she'd left earlier when she'd received the call. She didn't move it away from the one he occupied.

"Karma," was her explanation.

Oz made a rude noise. "Then I'd like to know what I did in a former life to deserve losing my wife and my kid. And what I can do to get them back, if it just takes paying some karmic debt."

For the first time since they'd left the crowd behind, she looked at him with a degree of interest. "You lost your wife, too? Are you sure your head is nailed on straight?"

"No, can't say that I'm sure, some days." He'd been shell-shocked at losing Alys, but driving to Mexico to recover Donal and trying to find out what had happened had kept his head occupied. He'd learned from that experience—stay busy. But some days... it didn't help.

"We can't stop living because someone else did," he told her. "I don't think there's any way I can pay back the universe for whatever in heck I did wrong. Personally, I think the universe owes me."

This time, Pippa snorted. "How have you improved the world?" she demanded. "Do your renowned skills of perseverance and negotiating bring joy to the unhappy or enlightenment to the ignorant? Or do you just put money in a lot of bank accounts?"

"Money in the bank brings joy to some people," he pointed out, not caring if she sniffed at his accomplishments. "It makes me enough money to finance the team you saw at work back there. Each to his own skill set is my take on it. I don't know what worm you have eating your brain that you let your talents languish, but I doubt that you're improving the world by doing so."

She shot him a look that sparked with anger—a sign that she was returning to normal.

"You have no idea what an improvement I make in the world by staying out of it," she announced. "It's the reason I'm not doing your show. If you think you're *protecting the talent* by hanging around here, you may as well go back to your happy life in the city. I don't need you, and you don't need me."

"I need my son, and you're the only key I have to finding him," he finally told her, although why he did so now, Oz couldn't say. But he was about to trust her with information that would have the whole world laughing if she revealed it to anyone.

Of course, he held her secrets, too, so maybe they were even. Maybe he could only trust when the score was equal.

She studied him quizzically. "I'm a key to finding your son? How do you figure that?"

He drove his hands through his hair and tried to coordinate his definitely unbalanced thinking. "Thank you for not stating the obvious. My family believes he's dead."

She waited, not offering sympathy or false encouragement. Oz rubbed his jaw and swallowed more of the nasty juice. He really needed a strong one to get through this. "My wife ran away with Donal when he was just a baby, leaving a note saying he was in danger."

That Pippa said nothing was actually calming. Oz watched the moon climb over the garden wall. "Alys made it as far as Mexico City, where someone sideswiped her car and drove her into a building. It was a freak accident. A sign on the wall fell through the windshield. She died instantly."

"Your son was with her?" Pippa asked quietly.

"No, that's what saved him. She'd left Donal with some woman she trusted. I have no idea why. Alys was from L.A., not Mexico. I don't know how she met this stranger. But the woman called me, told me it was up to me now, that I had to keep Donal safe. By the time I got down there, the woman had disappeared, and Donal was with the police."

She whistled softly. "I was at least left in this country," she murmured. "With a fire station. Thank goodness for whomever that woman was, or your son could have been as lost as I was."

"But he *is* lost," Oz insisted. "I was supposed to protect him. I hired security guards, installed alarm systems, hired the best nannies money could buy. And he still disappeared. The nanny carried him out one day and never came back. He's out there, somewhere, just like you were. I *know* it. And I have to find him!"

"And I can help you how?" she asked, astutely enough.

"I don't know," Oz groaned. "I have utterly no idea."

Chapter 10

DEPLETED BY THE ANGUISH AND GUILT SPILLING FROM Oz in waves, as well as her own exposure, Pippa sat back in the lounge chair and stared at the stars. Sometimes, she wondered if her real parents were up there somewhere, looking down on her, and if they approved of how she'd spent her life.

Other times, like now, she didn't think anyone cared what she did except her, and that was okay. She didn't want anyone depending on her, because she'd already proved herself to be a monster of irresponsibility. So this was good, sitting here, not caring, just watching the stars.

Because if she thought any harder, she'd know what she'd done tonight wasn't natural, and she didn't want any part of it.

So she pondered Oz's incomprehensible problem as if it were a math quiz. "*Why* do you think I can help you find your son?" she asked. There for a moment, she had feared he'd say he wanted her to go on television and beg for his son back. At least he wasn't totally insane. Of course, not knowing why he thought she could help him was near enough to crazy, but Oz didn't strike her as crazy. Just desperate.

She could understand his desperation to some extent. She'd never lost a kid, but losing Robbie as she had... had been a deciding factor in coming undone.

For Oz to lose his wife in such a weird manner would

certainly have unbalanced a lot of men. Why Mexico? Had his wife simply flipped out? Been paranoid? Or had there really been a danger to his son that Oz hadn't seen? Since the boy was stolen again, it did seem fate had marked him somehow.

"I'm desperate enough to follow any clue, and the very few I have led me to you," he said, sounding pained to admit it.

"Me? Me as Philippa James or me as Syrene?" Because she was two different people, whether he realized it or not.

"Syrene, although since you're the same person, I don't know if it makes a difference. The first message said *Syren can help find your son.* Syren, spelled with a *y* and without the final *e*. It took Conan a bit of digging to figure out the connection between the author and the singer."

"So you cooked up the TV show idea so you could come haunt me because some idiot wants to resurrect Syrene?" she asked in disbelief. This whole evening had been surreal. She'd thought this man had a head on his shoulders. She'd *admired* the way he'd taken the crowd in hand and twisted them to his will. She hadn't known many men with the confidence to command a crowd without raising his voice.

She didn't want to believe he had a head full of maggots, just like her.

"The TV show idea came to me after I read your books." He sipped his juice and stared at the stars, apparently suspending disbelief for the moment. "The nanny used to read to Donal at naptime. Some of your books were in his nursery. That's when I developed this crazed notion of putting you on TV where Donal might hear you, at which point I realized I had gone over the edge. But the TV show was a good idea. I meant it when I said you have a lyrical voice. I listened to some of your songs after Conan told me about you. You write a kind of mystical poetry in a simple language that harmonizes with your melody. Your music shines through in everything you say or write."

"That's not good," she muttered. "All the more reason to stay out of the public eye."

He shot her a quizzical glance. "Do I dare ask why having a recognizable voice is a bad thing? All good authors have it."

Her ego would swell to twice its size at knowing a man of his obvious intelligence and experience recognized her foolish words as talented—if she didn't know the very large flaw in the picture.

Pippa wasn't ready to reveal her ultimate insanity, because no one would believe her. She turned the question back to him. "So you found out I wrote children's books, but you realized I wasn't the Pied Piper and couldn't read your son back home. So why on earth would you believe I can help find him? Just because some wacko said I could?"

"The wacko knew you had written 'The Silly Seal Song,'" he pointed out. "It's not traceable anywhere on the Internet that I can tell, although I suppose I could set Conan to looking. The wacko calls himself the Librarian. Does that mean anything to you?"

No one knew she'd written that song except herself and cyberspace. Unless some long-buried alter ego had emerged from her subconscious to send messages to a man she'd never heard of until three days ago... She knew she was crazy, but she didn't want to go that far.

"I don't think I want to talk about this anymore." She rose from the lounge chair with her insides churning and her head doing loop-de-loops as if she were on some god-awful roller-coaster ride. "Thank you for seeing me home. I don't handle intense emotions well, but you've talked me back down. I'll see you in the morning."

Staying as loose as she could manage, Pippa strode into the house, escaping to her room and shutting the door as if she were a normal, sane person. She listened, waiting for Oz to depart.

She could tell he did so reluctantly. She didn't think he was the type to take advantage of a woman when she was emotionally vulnerable. She'd wager a charming hunk like Oz could have any female he wanted with a snap of his fingers, so there wasn't much chance that his returning here with her meant he had any interest in her as a woman. She had to believe he'd actually followed her home to make certain she was okay.

And that degree of sensitivity was damned dangerous. She didn't want him getting close or understanding anything.

But he wanted his son back, and if that poor boy was alive anywhere, crying for his daddy, being hurt by the careless monsters who thought kids were nuisances or punching bags or creatures to be exploited—she wanted to find the boy, too. She knew what it was like to be abandoned.

Tears crept down her cheeks as she leaned against the door and sobbed.

Pippa painted a cheery red smile on her face the next morning.

She didn't feel like smiling. Yesterday had terrified her on too many levels. But she had no reason not to look cheerful for the kids. They knew when adults were upset. Little kids might seem carefree, but they picked up vibrations and worried just like the grown-ups around them.

Her cell phone rang before she left the house. "Hey, Lizzy, what's up?" She slipped the strap of her small shoulder bag over her head and stepped into the courtyard. Warmed by the sun on the wall, one of the foolish roses was trying to bloom, and she pinched the bud off and slipped it into the buttonhole of her baggy denims.

"You might want to avoid the café today," Lizzy said. "They're all lying in wait for you. Why don't you bring the hunk over to the bar tonight so I can get some of that business?"

Pippa scrunched up her nose. "Why is anyone waiting for me?" She was so used to being anonymous these last years that it took a moment before the fear hit. "Not the media?" she asked before she could stop herself.

"Of course not, silly. El Padre is too tiny to rate even a blip on a radar screen. Your remarkable act of heroism will go unheralded by anyone outside of town. But every unemployed hopeful in the county is lining up at the café because that's where *he* is."

Relieved, Pippa laughed. "You said they were waiting for *me*. Oz is the one with the deep pockets, not me. I could sit on the counter and fiddle and no one would notice."

Lizzy snorted. "Oh yeah, right, like that would happen. What are you wearing today, cherries jubilee on your cheeks and the lemon overalls? They notice, all right. But that's not why they're waiting. Oz won't hire anyone unless you approve. So they're waiting on you."

Pippa said a very bad word, one that probably dented her karma for another few dozen years. "Okay, thanks for the warning. I'll see what I can do about sending him over to the bar tonight in return for the favor."

"And hey, just in case no one said anything yesterday, you're a genius and a maker of magic for luring Tommy out of the brush. I think Juanita's family is planning on building a shrine to your name."

Pippa laughed, momentarily pleased by her friend's inanity. This was why living outside her head was good for her. "They need to find a saint to repay Oz for the burgers that lured Tommy out when the kid got hungry. I just made an idiot of myself to pretend I was doing something."

She'd just about convinced herself of that over the last hours she'd spent lying in bed, staring at the ceiling. All she'd done was read the books, as she always did. It was just the dark and the moon and the bonfire and everyone praying that had created the illusion that she'd done anything significant at all.

And it was that kind of oblivious thinking that had killed Robbie. Fortunately, she'd learned control since then.

She turned around and went back inside, dropping her purse on a chair and aiming for the kitchen. She'd bake muffins for breakfast.

She would not worry that either someone had hacked

her computer or she had multiple personalities hiding in her subconscious.

She might worry if she thought one of those personalities had something to do with Oz's son, but she was pretty certain she wasn't that crazy, or her therapist would have told her so.

Oz caught up with her as she carried muffins to the day care. She opened the box and offered him one. "I ate breakfast," she informed him before he could chastise her for skipping the meal. It was a little startling and disquieting, realizing she understood him that well, but she could live with it.

He helped himself to a blueberry one. "You're hiding."

"Can't argue with that," she admitted. "Your show. I'm not accepting one whit of responsibility for who gets hired."

"Heard that, did you?" He bit into the muffin, murmured his approval, and followed her up the path. "My director will do the hiring. He'll be up next week. I just thought you might like some input."

"Nope. No input, no responsibility, no Pippa at all. Just the books. My agent says your contract is very fair. If you're trying to bribe me into helping you find your son, you're not succeeding."

"I had another message from the Librarian this morning," he said without warning, just as she was about to enter the rear door she'd painted with hot pink trim.

Pippa froze and refused to look at him.

"It just said *Ronan wants to come home too*." He waited expectantly.

Pippa thought she might lose her breakfast all over his pretty shoes.

"Ronan is the seal in a book I haven't published yet," she whispered.

Then, angry that he'd done this to her, she jerked open the back door, stalked in, and slammed it in his face.

Oz didn't use Pippa's swimming pool for his office that day. For one thing, the March wind had turned nippy, and he had no interest in freezing his nose.

For the other—he didn't like being manipulated, and someone was yanking his chains. And Pippa's, apparently. He hadn't thought it possible for her to be any paler, but she'd looked like a ghost when he'd told her about the Librarian's latest message. Not just white but translucent.

He was angry that he was doing this to her and angry that someone might know something about his son and not just come out and say it. He wanted to throttle anyone who got in his way.

In that frame of mind, it was easier to drive into L.A. and get some work done in a real office rather than torture himself or Pippa anymore.

Between signing off on disbursements and ordering his favorite wines sent to the B&B so he could at least have some alcoholic fortification when he needed it, Oz left messages for Conan to call him.

Conan. Ronan. Weird. Why would anyone write a book using a name like Ronan? While talking to the director he'd hired for the show, Oz Googled *Ronan*.

It was derived from the Celtic word for *seal*. Which made sense if Pippa knew that.

Conan was also Celtic, meaning *wise*. Oz snorted

at that and searched for Dylan—Welsh for *son of the sea*. Among the many stories she'd told her sons, their mother had claimed to be descended from Druids. Welsh ones, apparently.

And this was getting him nowhere, except for learning the Ronan/seal connection, and that had to be Pippa's doing. Why was she writing songs about seals with weird names, and why was the Librarian connecting them with Donal?

He snatched up the phone when Conan's number flashed across the screen. "Tell me what you found out yesterday."

"Yes, O Fearless Leader," Conan said mockingly. "I am at your command. I hope your secretary put a fat deposit in my account this morning."

"I just signed off on it. You won't starve anytime soon. Spill."

"I went to the fire station where the police report said she was found. I got the names of the men on duty at the time, and I've been calling all of them who are still alive. They're all pretty clear that they found her crying around midnight almost twenty-four years ago. She told them she was three and that her name was Philippa Seraphina Malcolm, but her mama called her Siren. Or that was their interpretation of toddler-speak."

"Siren, like on fire trucks?"

"Or like the fatal seductresses in *The Odyssey*," Conan said dryly.

Oz ignored his brother's cynicism. So the names were real. Siren. Syren. Oz felt a chill of foreboding.

"She said she lived on Hollow Road," Conan continued, "or that's what it sounded like to them. Except there is no Hollow Road in Bakersfield. The police speculated that a three-year-old couldn't pronounce the name correctly and checked variations and came up with nothing."

"A three-year-old who can enunciate three unwieldy names wouldn't have much problem with *Hollow*," Oz mused. "Did they ask her in what city? Maybe she wasn't from Bakersfield."

"She didn't know the city. I verified all this with the local police. They said their reports go out across the country. There are no guarantees that all of them get cross-checked with missing persons reports, but no one reported a match. No Hollow Roads. No missing Malcolms. The name is distinctive enough that someone should have recognized it. Nothing."

"Just like she said. She doesn't exist." Oz tapped his pen against the desk. "Social Services tried too?"

"They *really* tried. The state hates paying for abandoned kids. And she was cute and precocious, and even hardened caseworkers stayed awake at night, trying to think of new angles to try."

"Shit," Oz muttered. "She may as well have been dropped from another planet. No wonder she feels alienated. What next?"

"I'm running databases under all three of her names. I'm focusing on Malcolm as her original family name. Did you read the whole report I sent you earlier?"

The warning in Conan's voice said Oz should have caught something that he obviously hadn't. He flipped open the file, stumbled over the photo of Syrene with mascara-stained cheeks, and almost shut it again. "I skimmed it. How much do I really need to know about teenage singing sensations?"

"Read the police report on how her husband died." Conan hung up.

Chapter 11

NOT FINDING OZ WAITING AT THE POOL AFTER SHE WAS done at the day care, Pippa scowled, fixed a tofu taco, and carried it down to the studio.

She hated to admit that her heart beat a little faster in anticipation of seeing Oz's broad shoulders filling one of her boring lounge chairs. Whatever she was, she was female, and she appreciated a good-looking man, especially one with active brain cells.

But she darned well didn't need his accusations and implications and demands. She didn't need anyone.

That didn't mean she didn't enjoy his company. Unhappy with that acknowledgment, she unlocked the studio, reset the alarm system, and settled into her desk chair.

She'd set up new firewalls and kept the computer shut down since Oz had told her someone knew about the seal song. She was no computer expert. She had no way of knowing if her privacy had been hacked. She didn't even know where to go to find out.

Booting the computer up, she located the file labeled "Ronan." It hadn't been touched since she'd written it after Robbie's death over nine years ago.

At the time, she'd just turned eighteen and never written a book, never even thought about it. The story had simply appeared in her head, about the lonely seal with no family. She'd scribbled the words, sobbing all the way through the process, thinking she'd make a song of them one day.

She had written "The Silly Seal Song" later, just as she had for her other books. But this story had been too painful and personal to sell. She could swear she'd never told anyone about it, not even her agent. Ronan the Lonely Seal was her secret alone.

As were all the songs she'd written since Robbie died. She'd only sold the books—pages of text that the Voice couldn't ruin. Rubbing her forehead to smooth the wrinkles, Pippa stared at the silly words of the song. She supposed if there was a market for children's songs, she could sell these. She didn't have to sing them. Was that what Oz's weird messenger wanted?

Ronan wants to come home too. And the message had arrived after she'd brought Tommy home. The coincidence was too spooky. Was someone here in El Padre sending the messages?

Could one of her friends have broken into the studio and found the files? Maybe it was possible to copy them without actually opening them?

That made her even sicker as she perused the list of songs she'd recorded over the years. No one was ever intended to see or hear these files. They were her personal diary—her anguish and fears and sorrows. No one should be allowed to see inside her heart like that.

Much less blackmail Oz with them.

Because if it was someone here in town, that's what they were doing. They were teasing Oz with the impossibility of finding his son in order to get him up here and spend his money. And they were using Syrene to do it. If that theory worked, then someone knew who she was—someone besides Oz.

Angry now instead of sick, she shut down the computer and carried the server across the room to the safe containing everything that remained of her past. She'd shed most of the material things, but she had so very little from her childhood that there were some things she couldn't let go. Opening the heavy safe door, she moved aside the worn-out stuffed seal that had inspired her song and settled the machine on top of old gradeschool papers. Silly to keep them locked in a safe, but the box was fireproof, and she didn't want them lost.

She dialed the lock and hoped that would prevent any more theft. She didn't know what she could do to counteract what was already out there. Who would most benefit from bringing Oz to town?

Who among her friends might break into her studio?

She couldn't bear to believe it of any of them. They all needed money. Lizzy was constantly bugging her about bringing Oz to the bar. She'd be the most obvious suspect. Park was the one who had suggested talking to Oz. His family was large, and many of them were poor. Even Bertha had a son who wanted to go to college and a day care roof that needed repair.

The only alternative to believing her friends guilty was to believe someone had remotely hacked her files by some weird magic.

Magic. Oz had called her magical. Little did he know how close he had come, although her own personal word for it was *evil*.

Dammit all, she would have to reveal the existence of the files and deal with all his inquisitive questions just so she could ask about hackers. To ask anyone else would raise even more questions than Oz would ask. At least he knew her identity already.

She hated depending on others even more than she hated being responsible for anyone besides herself. She needed her independence. Scowling, she let herself out of the studio, reset the alarms, and jogged up to the house.

By the time she opened the back gate, she'd reluctantly accepted that maybe, just *maybe*, she needed to talk to Oz and see if they could puzzle this out together.

Responding to the message Pippa had left at the B&B, Oz found the Blue Bayou Tavern on a side street later that evening and sauntered in. He hadn't been inside a bar like this since college. He wasn't entirely certain the ones he'd visited then were quite this seedy.

The walnut bar looked as if it had been there since the gold rush. Battered, carved with initials, and worn in all the places where arms might rest, it needed a good restoration. The hard wooden stools pulled up to it looked damned uncomfortable, not to mention scratched by boots and tottering on lopsided legs.

The red and black vinyl on the booth seats was cracked, torn, and spilling stuffing. He kind of admired the oak separating the booths as opposed to the aluminum and chrome seen in all the new places, but decades of wear required a good sanding and polish. He'd probably find bullet holes if he looked hard enough.

Why the devil would Pippa want to meet him here? He didn't think she even drank alcohol. Or ate meat.

He'd had to buy Gardenburgers just for her when they were grilling last night. And she hadn't been happy with sharing the grill with red meat.

The tavern was nearly empty, even though it was prime happy hour on a Friday night. A grizzled rancher soaked up a mug of beer at the bar. A couple of motorcycle jockeys occupied one of the booths. No one paid much attention when Oz took a booth near a front window covered by black curtains.

A buxom woman with hair an unnatural shade of auburn emerged from behind the bar to take his order. Her smirk revealed she knew who he was, but she merely nodded at his request and retreated to the bar to pour it. At least he would get a drink out of this.

He needed it after reading the police report on the death of Rob Henderson, Pippa's young husband.

The kid hadn't even been twenty-one, but he'd had an alcohol level three times the legal limit when he'd crashed his Lotus off a cliff near Malibu. He'd also been pumped full of steroids and flying on coke.

According to witnesses, Pippa had jumped out of the car when it slowed down for a stoplight five minutes before it had gone off the cliff. Slowed. Not stopped.

The police had found her walking alongside the Pacific Coast Highway, stumbling over a rockslide in the pouring rain with one high heel on, one off. The other shoe had been in the car when they'd pulled it off the rocks.

She hadn't even been eighteen at the time.

Oz didn't read the newspaper accounts Conan had included in the file. He didn't even want to know what kind of breakdown Pippa had suffered after that.

That she'd suffered was all too visible even now, nine years later.

He sipped the beer the bartender handed him and checked his watch. Even though he faced the bar and not the door, he knew by some instinctive radar the moment Pippa entered on the dot of six. Timely—he liked that in a woman.

He did a double take when he turned and got a full view.

She was wearing a spaghetti-strapped baby doll tunic in turquoise and gold that actually complemented her red-gold hair for a change. She'd completed the outfit with skintight gold leggings cropped at the knee and sandals that wrapped and tied halfway up her shapely calves. She looked sexy as hell even dressed as an adolescent. He wondered if she'd bought any normal clothes in the years since her departure from the entertainment scene.

Her face lacked painted smiles or tears, but she'd bothered to darken her lashes and wear a shiny lipstick that had his mouth watering.

He couldn't tear his gaze from her wide lips when she sat down across from him. There was just something about her mouth that turned him on...

He dropped his gaze to her tunic top. She had breasts. Real ones, if he was any expert. Not huge, but plump and firm and high with just the right amount of cleavage. A pearl wrapped in a gold cage dangled there.

"Up here, Wizard," she said wryly.

Caught. Damn. He'd not been struck with lust like this since he was knee-high to a grasshopper, as his grandma used to say. Oz pinched the bridge of his nose, closed his eyes, and reopened them. She smiled like a mocking fairy. She'd put gold glitter across her nose and cheeks.

"Why here, why now?" he asked without filtering his words.

"Because Lizzy is a friend of mine, and because I thought you'd need a drink, and maybe because I thought you deserved a reward."

He nodded as if that made sense. "Lizzy, the smug-looking chick behind the bar?"

"That's her." Pippa leaned around the wooden bench and waved at the buxom bartender, who waved back and filled a glass from the soft drink dispenser.

"Why do I need a drink? And is that getup my reward?" Oz rested his shoulders against the high seat back, glad he hadn't worn anything fancier than jeans and a white shirt. He rolled up his cuffs now that he saw dress casual was the order of the day.

She waited until Lizzy placed the soft drink in front of her and departed to greet a new arrival.

"You need a reward because I'm going to tell you things you won't want to hear, and because the bar is about to fill with people looking for jobs. And yes, this is as real as it gets. I go back to being Dorabelle tomorrow." She sipped the Coke and waited.

"Can we do this over an order of wings and fries? I need protein to take bad news."

"Wings and fries aren't good for you." She signaled Lizzy again. The bartender held up a finger, and Pippa held up two.

Oz had to admire the efficiency of communication, if not the ambiance. "Are you going to tell me what I don't want to hear before or after the bar fills with job seekers?"

"It won't take long." She sipped her drink before launching into her story. "I wrote a book about Ronan the Lonely Seal when I was eighteen. Sometime after that, I wrote music for the words, sang them onto a CD, and uploaded 'The Silly Seal Song' to my computer. I backed up all my files to cyberspace storage before transferring them to a new computer, but they have not been opened since they were created." She watched him expectantly.

The dim light from an overhead bulb glittered on her nose and illuminated her damnable turquoise eyes, and for a moment, Oz thought that she almost looked eighteen: hopeful, eager, anxious, and worried. Very worried.

He considered the improbability of what she'd just said. *Nine years in a computer*. No one had ever actually seen "The Silly Seal Song" or a book about Ronan. It wasn't anything Donal would have known. Or anyone else—except Pippa.

Oz bit his tongue on a curse as the bartender returned and placed two vegetable pizzas in front of them. He glared at zucchinis and spinach and neatly sliced tomato rings.

"Cheese isn't protein," he grumbled, using his fingers to rip a slice from its mates and watch the cheese drip off the thin crust.

"Yes, it is. And Lizzy hides bean sprouts in it." She hummed in anticipation as she neatly sliced a bite-size piece with her knife and fork.

Instead of staring at the soggy mess in his hand, Oz watched as Pippa slipped the tiny bite between her expressive lips. Her eyes narrowed with pleasure, and Oz wondered if she made that purring sound in bed.

He was losing his frigging mind. He took a big bite of his slice and nearly burned the roof off his mouth.

He grabbed his beer, chilled his mouth, and sat back to let the rest of the pizza cool.

"Someone hacked your computer," he concluded.

She dipped her head in apparent agreement. Finished chewing, she added, "Or broke into my studio and copied the files. Is that possible without changing the date?"

"Probably. I'll ask Conan. He's the geek in the family. To what purpose?"

"To send you messages and lure you up here?"

She looked as if she feared he'd reach across the table and hit her.

She had a low opinion of human nature.

Oz glared at the pizza and thought about her suggestion. She was saying the messages were all about her and had nothing to do with Donal.

He didn't want to believe that.

Chapter 12

Oz preferred anger to pain. Sitting back in the bar booth, he punched Conan's number into the BlackBerry. He frowned as an elderly man tottered into the tavern wearing a black sombrero embellished with silver and little dancing balls around the brim.

"Pancho," Pippa whispered, leaning over the table. "He claims he's the Cisco Kid, whoever that is. Nice old guy." She lifted a finger at him, and the old guy nodded solemnly and cruised on to the bar, politely not intruding on their tête-à-tête.

Conan didn't answer his phone, which didn't mean he wasn't available. It just meant he didn't want to be bothered. Oz left a demand for him to call back.

The door opened, and a trio of muscular ranchers trailed in, nudging one another and glancing in Pippa's direction. Or Oz's. If the men had any brains in their heads, they'd be looking at Pippa, but they were probably married and broke and looking for work like Cisco.

Oz kind of liked the sombrero. Rubbing his forehead, he eyed the scalding pizza with disfavor, but it looked like it would be a long night. If the only reward he was getting was seeing Pippa in an almost-normal outfit, he'd better fuel up.

"Here come the Donner sisters. They sing in the church choir."

"Union cards?" he asked grumpily.

She smiled in their direction and turned back to Oz as if they were in deep conversation. "Of course not. They've never worked outside their homes. Their husbands have decent jobs so they're looking for excitement. And to show off."

"Would they wear chicken costumes?" He tried the pizza again. This time, it went down better. If there were bean sprouts, he didn't see them, but the oregano was nicely done. He should have brought a bottle of his wine.

Pippa giggled. She actually giggled. He looked up at her in surprise, and a smile was tugging that gorgeous mouth. He almost swallowed his pizza bite whole. Her whole presence *glowed* when she lit up like that. He'd give good money to see her smile again.

"Chicken costumes should end everyone's delusions of grandeur," she agreed with a laugh. "Have someone sketch up the costumes for the show, and we'll post them in a window. They'll scatter to the winds so fast you won't even see their dust."

Oz studied the sombrero and the little old ladies who jingled in wearing red cowboy hats and boots and spurs. Ideas spun inside his head, ideas he'd rather consider than thinking these people had conspired to bring him up here by using his son.

His cell played a few notes of the "Baby Elephant Walk," and he hit the button. "We have a situation," he said without waiting for Conan to speak—without giving a single thought to how much he would have to tell his brother.

"Bring it on," Conan replied.

"First, is it possible to copy a computer file without changing the date it was last opened?"

"Sure. Basic. I hope it gets better than this."

"Depends on whether I have to put my fist through your mouth if you scoff." Oz watched a Hispanic woman enter, shepherding twin boys about the age of nine. They'd been spit polished until they shone. She sent Pippa an anxious glance. Pippa gave her a thumbs-up, and the woman smiled in relief before taking a table in the center of the room.

The evening was making it blatantly obvious that Pippa wasn't a recluse. These people knew her and accepted her as she was. She simply needed a safe place and familiar faces to be comfortable. And anonymity from her former life. Oz filed that information in his mental banks while Conan protested his threat and implied insult.

"Pippa's computers files have been hacked without opening them," Oz volunteered when Conan wound down. "Someone has been sending me text messages with snippets of information from those files."

"Give me your CrackBerry, you friggin' asshole!" Conan shouted. "Why the hell didn't you tell me this earlier?"

"Because I need my BlackBerry?" Oz said with a hint of irony. "Bring me a new one, do your magic so my files get transferred, and you can have this one."

"I want more info than that. Where the hell are you? It sounds like a tea party."

"I believe the Donner sisters are warming up for an impromptu audition. And if I'm not mistaken, the Cisco Kid is taking a lariat off his belt. I can't decide whether to escape now or watch the show."

"I've got your GPS signal. I'll find you." Conan hung up.

"That went well," Oz said, sliding the PDA back on its clip and reaching for his cooling pizza. "How do I tell your friends that the director gets to do the hiring?"

"You don't." She shrugged slender white shoulders and turned to watch Cisco whirling a rope near the ceiling. "They're entertaining one another, and Lizzy's income is getting a much-needed boost."

"I like the old guy in the hat. And the biddies in red boots. Don't suppose you're thinking what I'm thinking," he asked.

She tilted her shapely head, and Oz noticed for the first time that she wore small gold and diamond musical notes on her ear lobes. In an evening gown, she'd be a knockout.

And every damned man in L.A. would recognize her. Even with short red hair instead of long platinum little-girl locks. Ten years had taken her from cute to stunning. Not beautiful. Her mouth was too wide, her cheekbones too prominent, and her coloring too pale. But she was too striking not to turn every male head in the room.

So much for hoping he could use her on the show without everyone recognizing her.

"You're thinking we can use real characters instead of costumed ones," she decided, in answer to his question. "That could work. Kids would relate to grandmas and grandpas. And to singing aunts and annoying little brothers."

He still wanted Pippa for the main character. She would light the show with magic. But he owed her for this intrusion into her world. He'd pay what he owed before working out how to make the show happen.

His hopes had been crushed before to the extent that he didn't have them anymore. Working was what he did best in the vacuum that his life had become. Someday, if he was really lucky, maybe Donal would become a misty memory of his past.

Sometime after Oz was dead and buried, maybe.

Pippa laughed until she cried at the impromptu comedy routine that followed Pancho's lariat roping two of the ranchers, followed by the Donner sisters singing louder and louder to cover the ensuing cursing. Maria had had to hustle the twins out of the bar. Realizing they were behaving badly, the ranchers fell to cracking jokes with Pancho. Lizzy turned on the music, and Pancho and the ranchers were now dancing with the red boot ladies.

Even Oz was smiling, although he radiated tension. She didn't know what he'd made of her hacking theory, but he wasn't happy. She couldn't blame him. Some worm had raised his hopes about finding his son alive, and now it was eating him from the inside out. She almost felt relief when Oz's brother finally showed up. He must have taken some hairpin turns at high speed if he lived in L.A.

Conan slid into the seat next to her, forcing Pippa to scoot over. Oz scowled but handed over his BlackBerry without argument.

Conan was about the same height as Oz, but he had a leaner build, with ropey muscles and a lanky swing of long arms as he scooped up the PDA. Apparently the sunglasses he'd worn the other day weren't an affectation. He donned dark-framed reading glasses now.

He had a long, sharp nose, and his hair didn't possess his older brother's golden salon sheen, but their tight-lipped smiles were identical. She knew Oz could apply charm when needed, but right now, they were both focused on business.

The excitement in the rest of the bar had about died down. Pancho and the red boot ladies were having a gabfest. The Donner sisters had gathered their scattered dignity after the lariat incident and called their husbands to join them for dinner. Lizzy was smiling as if she were in seventh heaven. She loved entertaining a crowd, even if the crowd didn't pay much.

"You can trace Oz's whereabouts from his BlackBerry?" Pippa asked in curiosity, when it became obvious the men didn't intend to talk.

"Cross-checking cell towers. Can't pinpoint exact location without better equipment, but it's hard to miss the bright lights that follow Oz," Conan said dryly, removing a new BlackBerry from his shirt pocket and then popping the back off the old phone.

"We call Conan the Bloodhound. He used to track us even without equipment. We've decided he has an overly developed sense of smell." Oz leaned outside the booth and caught Lizzy's eye, making a gesture that indicated he needed the tab.

Pippa wasn't certain how to take that. Brotherly ribbing, she supposed, although she had little experience with it. "How can someone hack my computer without opening a file?" she asked, trying to keep the subject impartial and not the devastating invasion of privacy it was.

"If you're connected to the Internet and someone

cracks your passwords, they can dig around in your computer's guts, but they can't read a file unless they open it. So someone had to have copied your files and opened them elsewhere." Conan talked as he apparently uploaded information to the Internet and then swiftly exchanged tiny parts from the backs of the phones. "Who has access to your computer?"

"No one. Ever. I had the place I bought it from transfer my data, and that's it. I keep it password protected and behind locked doors. The files accessed are over nine years old, as far as I can tell, and they haven't been opened since. They're not even important files, just personal."

"Where are your backup files? If you've had them for nine years, you're not using the same machine, are you?"

"I pay for Internet storage, so if anything happens to my studio, the files are still out there in the cloud." She kept up on her reading. She knew about cloud computing. She had no clue how it worked.

Both men sent her identical sharp looks. Pippa didn't know whether to preen or hide. Nervously, she clasped her hands around her water glass.

Lizzy arrived with the bill. "I wish the two of you could stop by here every night. I haven't had so much fun in forever. Hello, handsome, can I bring you anything?"

Conan looked up with a blank expression. "A beer, thanks." He returned to putting the phones back together as if Lizzy's dazzling smile was aimed at someone else.

"If your evenings are always this entertaining, I'll have to stop by more often," Oz said with a smile that made up for Conan's cluelessness and melted Lizzy with its charm. "The pizzas were fantastic. Do you have a menu?"

"I've never needed one," she admitted anxiously. "I could come up with one. The regulars just know what toppings are available."

"Experiment," he suggested. "Use fancy computer paper, and you can print up new menus whenever you want to change them. Open the curtains and let in some light, and you might get more families."

"What about the film crews?" she asked, narrowing her eyes and studying the tatty curtains. "Won't they want a dark tavern?"

"This isn't Hollywood, and I'm not filming movie stars," Oz explained. "My director is likely to bring his family up here whenever school's out. The camera crew is a husband and wife team with a toddler. A kids' show calls for people who like kids."

Lizzy nodded. "I can do that. I've got kids of my own. Thanks." She wandered back to the bar, her brow knit in thought.

"Thanks for that," Pippa murmured. "She's had a hard time of it since her ex quit paying support. I can't say I approve of bars, but this is all she has."

"She could turn it into a family restaurant that serves alcohol. No harm in that. But it would take money," he admitted, glancing around at the battered decor.

Conan shoved the new phone across the table, apparently oblivious to their discussion. "Details. What am I looking for on here?"

Oz looked unhappy as he punched up his computer menu on the new phone. "Look for the messages from the Librarian. One refers to 'The Silly Seal Song' that doesn't seem to exist anywhere except on Pippa's computer. And the other is a reference to a book about Ronan that's never been published."

"But you've backed them up to the cloud?" Conan asked, turning his sharp glare on Pippa.

"They're password protected," she protested. "Someone would have to know the website address, the email address I use, and my password to break into my library."

Oz's head jerked up from his keyboard. "Library?"

The Librarian had sent the messages. Pippa blanched and covered her mouth as she thought of all the files of anguish and sorrow she'd poured into her personal cyberspace library over the years. And a *Librarian* could access it?

"They can't, can they?" she whispered. "No one can read my cyberspace files, can they?"

Both men looked grim enough for her to believe that someone not only could but had.

Chapter 13

CONAN DROPPED THE OLD BLACKBERRY INTO HIS SHIRT pocket and turned to Pippa. "I don't suppose you'd let me play with your computer?"

Oz watched her freeze into the fragile icicle he'd first met. He reached over and clasped his hand around the ones crushing her water glass, instinctively reassuring her. That she didn't immediately jerk away said she was retreating into her cave.

"Conan is hunting for your parents," he explained. "He knows more about you than you do, is my bet, and he'd probably explode into molecules before revealing anything he didn't want anyone to know. But you don't owe him anything."

She nodded as if she understood, but her brilliant eyes were wide and unseeing as she dived into that mysterious abyss inside herself. What the devil did she keep in that computer?

"I'll need the address to the cyberspace library if we're going to find this scumball," Conan said as if he hadn't noticed anything wrong. "So I probably don't need your hard drive. I just wanted to see if he left cookies to scoop up anything in your personal files that aren't in storage."

Pippa looked as if she wanted to bolt in panic at that possibility. Releasing her hand, Oz reached over the table and hit the heel of his hand against his brother's forehead. "You're scaring her, doofus."

Conan batted him away and turned back to Pippa. "If someone has access to your computer, they've kept it quiet so far. I'll make certain they're permanently shut down."

That brought her back to life, Oz noticed with interest. She released the water glass and pulled her hands out of sight—and touch.

"How?" she demanded. "How can you shut down someone who has access to all my secrets?"

"We don't know that they have that kind of access yet," Conan reminded her. "For all we know, someone sneaked into your computer room one night, copied a few files, and never bothered looking at them until lately. Or we could be totally wrong, and there's a simple explanation for the messages."

"How?" she repeated. "If we're right and someone has hacked my cyberspace library, *how* will you stop them?"

Conan sent Oz a look asking how far he could go. Oz nodded his permission. Pippa needed to know.

Conan flipped out his wallet and showed her his ID. "Call me Cyber Agent 007. No one knows this, so now you know my secrets, too, okay?"

She studied the ID, rubbing her thumb over the seal to verify its reality. "You're the law? You can shut them down and lock them up?"

"I can find them, and the law will shut them down, if they're doing anything illegal. I'm unofficial, off the books, behind the scenes, but legit, and I know the right people in the right places."

Pippa glanced at Oz, and he could see her finally absorbing what he'd told her earlier about their family connections.

"Friends in high places?" she asked steadily.

"Cyberterrorism is high priority," Oz confirmed when Conan said nothing. "If someone is using cyberspace to steal your information, then they can also have access to information vital to this country's security. I still don't think we're dealing with any more than a mediocre blackmailer who stumbled across a few files, but it won't hurt to let Conan do his thing."

Pippa drew a long, slender finger through the moisture droplets on her water glass, meeting neither of their gazes. "If he couldn't find your son..." She let the rest of the question dangle there.

Conan shoved from the booth. "I didn't have federal clearance a year ago. I got official when I saw what a botch the cops were making of the trail. But you're right, I'm not perfect."

He stalked away. Oz let him go. Conan had his own problems. He was a big boy and could handle them on his own.

Pippa, on the other hand... Oz ran his fingers into his hair and tried to defuse the tension.

"Conan recommended the nanny I hired," Oz explained. "He performed a routine search and found nothing dangerous in her background. Since then, he's traced her all the way to her parents in Europe, but every trail is dead."

"Which is why you're both ready to believe these messages are part of a bigger crime than bringing you up here on a wild-goose chase?" She didn't look any more certain, but she'd at least returned from the brink.

Oz left a stack of cash to cover their tab, slid out of the booth, and held out his hand to help her out. "I don't want to believe anything. I just want to find my son, whatever it takes. In the meantime, I have to work, and this kid production has my interest. I've quit looking beyond the moment."

Which wasn't the total truth anymore. He was looking beyond the moment for an opportunity to take Pippa to bed, to lose himself in her luscious lips and slender curves and whispering need.

Even he knew that would be a mistake, but the production wasn't enough to keep him occupied this time. He needed more than just work.

"You don't have to walk me home," Pippa objected when Oz steered her past the B&B. "I have a black belt and could break anyone who tried to touch me."

She feared his company more than she feared walking in the dark at midnight. The big man's tension was almost palpable, and she suspected it was because of the topics they'd been discussing more than her.

Except she couldn't ignore the electricity that crackled when they touched. She wanted to tug his head down and kiss away his guilt and assuage her own needs at the same time.

She knew better. Oz didn't. He foolishly thought she was normal. Or just a little unbalanced. He didn't know the depth of her evil. She didn't think he'd believe her if she told him. Oz was above all else a practical man.

"I need to walk," was all he said, falling into step with her as she hurried toward home.

She nervously clutched her elbows, forcing him to keep his hands to himself. "You think I should give my computer to your brother?" she asked rather than let him bring up more personal subjects.

Oz shoved his hands into the pockets of his jeans. His white shirt gleamed against the dark silhouettes of buildings, emphasizing his straight posture and broad strength. He didn't seem aware of the impression of assurance he gave off as he considered her question.

"I don't know what you keep on your computer," he said warily. "But if you give him the address of your cyberspace storage, then he will have access to everything anyway. All your hard drive will do is give him clues as to who else might have tapped into it, I think. I'm not the geek."

"There are files on there too painful even for me to open," she admitted, trying to make them sound as if they were merely emotional experiences and not the destructive tools they were. How could she possibly warn these eminently logical men that listening to her Voice could cripple and damage them for life? She hadn't held back the anguish on those recordings.

"I don't think he has to open the files. Admittedly, Conan can be pretty ruthless if he's after a criminal, but he has no curiosity about what makes people tick, just computers. He works on the hidden files, and those aren't likely to be your personal folders."

"Could I take all my personal folders out before I give the hard drive to him?" she asked, knowing the answer but desperately looking for a way to avoid what he wanted.

"You could, but it wouldn't matter. There are echoes of them still on there, plus your online backup." He glanced at her with curiosity as they crossed the day care parking lot. "Unless you have files on there admitting your guilt in some crime, you're safe in his hands."

Pippa sighed. "He's not safe in mine. No one is. Unless I know he won't listen to any of those files, I can't turn it over. I just can't."

The flowers on the ice plants lining the walk had closed for the night. She hurried over the dirt and stones to the safety of her sanctuary, praying he wouldn't question, that he'd just leave her alone at the door. Even she knew that was a stupid hope.

His big shadow followed hers. The moon was still nearly full. She had memories of a beautiful moonlit night on a Mexican beach, a night when she thought she'd finally learned what love was about. A night with a beautiful boy who had made her heart sing. How had it all gone wrong when it had felt so right?

She knew, and it was all her fault.

Oz caught the courtyard gate before she could open it. Holding the tall planks shut, he glared down at her, meeting her gaze with controlled fury. "It's not all about you," he reminded her. "Is your precious privacy worth my son's life? Worth letting a kidnapper free to steal another child? Worth letting a freak invade our lives at will?"

Pippa wanted to hit him, to strike back, to shove his words down his throat, but he was right. For what little he knew, he was right. She just couldn't tell him that what she held secret was worse than cyberterrorism.

"It's not all about me," she murmured in protest, facing the gate, hoping he'd release it so she could escape. He stood so close; she could almost hear his heartbeat. She could smell the heat of his skin. Feel the slight distance between his chest and her shoulder blades. "I'm protecting your brother and you and anyone else who might accidentally hear the files." When he still didn't budge, she defiantly gave him the rest. "I killed Robbie with my Voice. I don't want to hurt anyone else."

She tried to say it unemotionally, but it was impossible to be nonchalant about tragedy. Her grief and anger raised her voice an octave, and the Beast roared. She winced when she felt his body respond with a jerk, waited for the bellow of pain or outrage or whatever her Voice instigated.

She got silence.

"You have bigger problems than I thought," he finally said, pushing the gate open but following right behind her so she couldn't lock him out. "I hope you're talking to a shrink about this messianic complex of yours."

"*Messianic?*" she asked in outrage, swinging around to glare at him in the faint light from her porch lamp. "What the hell is that supposed to mean?"

"The Messiah saves souls. You're trying to save ours. Ain't happening," he said with a shrug. "Just like in the fairy tales, if Conan ignores the warnings and listens to your files when he shouldn't, then it's his own fault if he fries his brains. You have nothing to do with it."

"You don't believe me," she said flatly. "You think it's a joke. That *I'm* a joke."

"I'm not a shrink. I can't give you the fancy name for what's wrong with you."

Astonishingly, he faced her without flinching, even though she'd unleashed her furious Voice.

"But if you've got a bee in your bonnet, believing what you do is responsible for the actions of others," he continued, "then you're wrong. Your husband died because he was fried out of his skull. Unless you physically poured the alcohol down his gullet, shot him full of coke and steroids, and glued his hands to the steering wheel, you had absolutely nothing to do with his death."

Pippa punched him. She balled up her fist and hauled her arm back as far as it could go and plowed her knuckles into Oz's flat, hard abdomen.

She nearly broke her hand. He didn't wince, just caught her fist and twisted it behind her back, so she couldn't hurt herself again. Then he frog-marched her up to the door, threw it open, and shoved her inside.

"He did all of that because of *me*!" she shrieked, not trying to restrain her inner Beast, her Voice, wanting to hurt him as he'd hurt her. Striking out as she'd trained herself not to do.

She waited in trepidation to see how Oz would strike back. Or if he would crumple to the floor or run off to avoid the dagger she'd twisted in his heart.

He merely stood there in the porch light, looking down at her as if she were a pathetic piece of hysterical flotsam.

"You could have horsewhipped him within an inch of his life," he said calmly, showing no effects from her anger. "You could have walked up and down his spine in spikes and broke his head, and *none* of that would have forced him to do what he did. What he almost did to *you*. Get over it. The fact is, you were better than him. Stronger. More talented. And he wimped out. Not you. You survived. That's what you are, a survivor. It's damned painful, being a survivor. But there's got to be a reason you're still standing here and he's not. Find it."

Without warning, Oz grabbed her waist with both hands, hauled her up against his wide chest, and planted his mouth across hers.

Pippa almost swooned at the intoxicating warmth of strong, competent human hands touching her, holding her up, absorbing her into his physical warmth as their mouths twisted, fought, and finally locked together. Oz's breath breathed life into her. His kiss renewed hungers she'd forgotten.

She fit against him as if she belonged there. She flattened her hands against his chest to push him away, but the heat of him beneath the thin cotton melted her frost, stripped her of the icy exterior she'd maintained all these years.

Oh, God, he was hard and strong and muscled, and she wanted to burrow into his arms and never come up for air. She needed him to take her away from herself.

The minute he took a step across the threshold, she panicked, shoved away, and slammed the door in his face.

Leaning against the heavy timber, she sobbed and choked on the pleasure she'd stolen, the pleasure she didn't dare share with anyone, the pleasure she craved and had never thought to know again.

Chapter 14

RUBBING HIS BRUISED NOSE AND BATTERED EGO, OZ stood outside the timber barrier Pippa had slammed between them.

She'd melted in his hands like a hot chocolate bar. She wanted him as much as he wanted her.

And they were both damaged goods. Okay, he got that. Who wasn't damaged these days?

If he were back in L.A., dealing with a shrew who'd objected to his advances, he would have walked away. Walking away was probably the smartest thing to do in this case too.

The problem with that thinking was that he believed Pippa had more depth of character than any shrew, that she contained mysteries he needed to pursue, and that she was hurting even more than he was. Ergo, he couldn't leave her alone. It wasn't a matter of his mother teaching him better, because while she was alive, she'd pretty much left his education to the schools he'd attended. No, it was because some deep down masculine instinct said this woman was crying for help, and he couldn't turn his back on her.

Okay, so he'd call his shrink when he got back to the city.

Oz let himself through the gate and took the narrow path between the house and the wall surrounding the property. She'd put walls up all around her house and not locked any of them. There was probably something Freudian in that.

Behind the house, he stopped at the patio door and looked in. She'd left a light burning in the kitchen but hadn't turned on any of the others. He saw no movement. Would he scare her to death if he walked in?

Probably. He scraped the lounge chair around so he could watch the door and made himself comfortable. Except for the cold, it couldn't be any worse than sleeping on an air mattress.

What the hell had she meant when she'd said she'd killed Robbie with her *voice*?

She was really and truly frightened of Conan listening to her silly children's songs. He'd listened to CDs of a few of her teenage love songs. Her voice rivaled the music of an angel's harp. It was a gift straight from heaven. Had something happened to it that she didn't want anyone to know?

She was possibly a real head case, and he ought to run away as fast as his feet could carry him, but his gut kept him planted in the chair.

He knew he was right for waiting when Pippa drifted to the glass sliding doors and opened one. She slid out like a bright flame against the dark. There were no lights back here. She ought to install a security lamp, but he wasn't the one to tell her that.

If he let his mother's Celtic ancestry rule, he'd believe she was a wraith drifting across the tiles to hand him... what? Hemlock?

He accepted the glass and waited to see what she would do next.

She took the lounge she'd left beside his earlier.

Except now instead of sitting side by side, she was facing him. He could see her pale features against the striped cushions, could reach over and wiggle her bare toes, but that was about it. He guessed the distance made her feel safer.

He still wanted to kiss her. That had been one spectacularly explosive kiss, and he wasn't about to give up a chance at another. So that was his real reason for being here, right?

He sipped the drink. Raspberry something or other. Instead of heaving him in the pool for his refusal to take no for an answer, she was feeding him. Maybe he was on to something here.

"Robbie was only two years older than I was, so yes, at twenty, he was probably weaker than you are now," she said in that toneless voice he was learning to despise, now that he'd glimpsed her passion. "Maybe if we'd met today, he would have been able to save himself. But I killed him before he had the chance to grow up."

Oz had already pointed out the flaws in her logic. He waited to hear if she explained them away.

"I know you don't believe me," she said flatly. "No one believes me. How could they? What I'm capable of is not real. That's what I thought, too, that it was all in my head. But every time I opened my mouth, someone got hurt. People went crazy. Men actually crawled on their knees when I got hysterical. You're sitting here now, why? Is this something you would normally do?"

Oz thought about it. "For Alys, I might have. But I was kind of young then, cocky and obnoxious and determined to have my way."

She snorted impolitely, and he grinned against the

darkness. Yeah, he hadn't changed much. He was relieved that she was smart enough to see that. He wasn't much of an actor and had never pretended to be other than who he was.

When she said nothing else, he continued feeling his way around her perfectly legitimate question about why he was sitting here. After all, he'd been asking himself the same thing.

"These days, I don't see many women worth wasting my time on," he admitted. "We get old, jaded, use each other as we've been used. But you're different somehow. I'm not in the habit of hurting women, but I feel as if I'm hurting you. So I'm just trying to sort things out. If men crawled on their knees for you, it's probably because they knew they had hurt you and wanted to make up for it."

He wasn't entirely certain he believed her version of events. Teenage girls often developed hysterical fantasies, and the business she'd been in would create a lot of stress. But he was willing to hear her out. Maybe he'd get to the bottom of the mystery and he could walk away with a clear conscience. When all was said and done, he was only here because of Donal. Pippa was simply a diversion to keep him occupied.

"I don't think *that* many grown men are idiots," she replied wryly. "I wasn't a little Lolita who drove men to drink with seduction and rejection. But one time, I got angry and shouted at a reporter to go soak his head. He did—in the pool. He couldn't swim. Fortunately, there were others there to fish him out."

She sipped her own drink, and Oz waited. If she wanted to talk, he was ready to listen. Paparazzi ended up in pools and sandwiched between cars because they were incurable pests and someone was always eager to swat at them. He figured this one got pushed.

"I don't know how it works, exactly," she murmured. "Experimenting is too dangerous. But looking back, I should have seen the problem long before Robbie. My first manager tried to seduce me when I was twelve. That should have been a sign right there."

Oz sat straight up, nearly spilling his drink in his lap. "I hope the police locked up the son of a bitch."

She waved a careless hand. "I hardly knew what was happening at the time. I'd just reached puberty and didn't even know what sex was. My foster parents had spent more time taking me to singing competitions than teaching me the facts of life. I thought Bill wanted to reward me for winning the contest. He hugged and kissed me and told me how wonderful I was. What lonely, unloved kid could resist that? I only panicked when he unzipped his pants and let it all hang out."

Oz thought the top of his head might explode if he contained the steam much longer, but he bit back all the scathing retorts and did his best to pay attention. He might be an obnoxious bully upon occasion, but he was skilled at listening.

"And you think it was your fault for not handling the bastard better?" he asked with what he considered admirable restraint.

"No, I've had lots of shrink time. As I said, I know I was no Lolita. I was scrawny and red-haired and petulant. I didn't know enough to encourage him. But when I sang... grown men wept. I didn't understand why. I still don't completely. Bill was declaring his abject love to me even after I shrieked until the hotel security guards broke in and clapped him in handcuffs. He didn't fight with them, but the guards still overreacted and nearly beat him to a pulp—until I quit shrieking. I should have learned my lesson then, but it was all much too confusing."

"Where were your foster parents?" he demanded. He could see fault in the actions of every adult around the poor scared kid she must have been. He just wasn't seeing why she blamed herself.

"Down in the bar celebrating the nice contract they'd just signed. They were a little ticked when Social Services threatened to take me away after that incident, but they stepped up to the plate better after that. I was never really mistreated, if that's what you're thinking. I had a good life. An exciting one that I thoroughly enjoyed. I love singing. I would have sung every minute of every day if I could have."

He heard the wistfulness in that last. "But you can't go back to singing because…?"

She met his gaze steadily, even though it was too dark to see the color of her eyes. "Did you notice what happened the other night when I read the book for Tommy? I tried very hard not to put my fear or hope into my reading, but it creeps out when I'm upset."

"I noticed that you brought that kid out of the brush when no one else could. You wanted the coyotes to get him?"

"Pay attention," she said impatiently. "I'm not going to recite my life history. What happened to the crowd when I read?"

"They got quiet. They listened to the story."

The tension and fear that had been there that day had drained away to a moment of perfect harmony for the waiting crowd. Oz didn't say that aloud because he thought he'd imagined it. The night had been crystal clear, like this one, with stars glittering in the heavens. Her simple tale had focused the universe on her for a few brief magical moments.

"An entire crowd of terrified adults got quiet and listened to a children's book. That's what I do. I cast spells. And don't look at me like that. You felt it too. It's probably why you're here. I've let you hear too much of my soul, and I'm probably infecting you just as I did Robbie. I don't want to destroy you or your brother. I just want to be left alone to live my life quietly, under circumstances I can control so the Beast doesn't hurt anyone else."

She really honestly believed she was doing something harmful. Oz puzzled over that, but he couldn't make any sense of it. "Women have given me strange excuses for not wanting to have sex, but I think yours might take the cake," he observed irreverently.

She flung the rest of her drink at him and started to rise, but Oz grabbed her ankle. "It's the truth, isn't it?" he demanded. "We got too close tonight, and you're scared. Maybe you believe your crazy little story. I don't know how a writer's mind works. But it's my business to read people, and I know when someone is backing out of a negotiation because they're scared. Because they're used to failure and shoot themselves down when they get too close to success. You're running from the best damned kiss I've ever known, and I've known a lot. If you want me to back off, that's fine. Just say so. Don't give me fairy tales."

"You really are the most impossible, arrogant, obnoxious piece of shit I've run across in a long, long while." She kicked her foot free from his grip, stood, crossed to his chair, and straddled his knees with hers. She seated herself on his legs close enough so that she could lean forward, grab his shirt, and plant her lush lips across his.

Satisfaction rolled through Pippa, followed by greedy hunger as Oz grabbed her waist but otherwise let her control their kiss. *She* wanted to be the one in charge for a change. All those needy years she'd let men tell her what to do and how to do it. They'd insisted she wear her hair long and her skirts short. They'd made the first moves, and she'd waited for them.

For just this one brief moment out of time, she got to plaster her hands against his hard chest, feel his heart thump, while she decided when to open her mouth and let him in.

The control was giddy-makingly awesome. The kiss... She could not begin to describe how Oz kissed. The world went away. All the stars in the heavens encompassed them, filled her with joy and need and urges she barely recognized as her own.

And he brought them to an abrupt halt by using his greater strength to lift her off him and set her to one side so he could stand up.

She wanted to punch him again, but her knuckles were still too sore from the last time. Sitting on the edge of the lounge, her lips bruised and aching, the rest of her screaming for the completion he promised, she buried her head in her hands and didn't look at him.

"I'm not the other men in your life," he growled. "I do not take advantage of hysterical, distraught, or otherwise vulnerable women. I want you fully sane and willing when we hit that bed. And I want you to be able to get up in the morning and look at yourself in the mirror and still agree to do this production with me."

He started to turn away.

He still wanted her. She could hear the thickness in his voice, had felt his physical response. Pippa couldn't bear it if he walked out now. For the first time since Robbie, she felt almost alive. He hadn't faltered beneath any of her assaults—verbal or physical. She wanted to assume Oz was safe from the Beast. He didn't believe she was dangerous, but she'd *warned* him. It might be the only time she was brave enough to speak of her fear. Like a genuine wizard, Oz made anything seem possible.

Maybe she could experiment on him. Could she *deliberately* keep him from leaving?

With brains addled by hormones, she summoned the sensual purr that had turned grown men into kittens. "I'm sane, Mr. Oswin," she drawled huskily. "I'm dangerous, but I'm very sane. You're the vulnerable one here."

When he turned back to study her, she rose with confidence and strolled up to him, took him by the hand, and turned her face up for the kiss he hungrily grabbed.

After a mind-swirling moment, she gently pushed him back.

"Take me to bed, Mr. Oswin," she purred in her best siren's voice. "And you can look in the mirror in the morning and tell me if you still want to work with me."

Chapter 15

PIPPA'S SENSUOUS PURR WAS STARTLING AFTER THESE past days of icy monotone. Oz thought he preferred the blunt woman to the sex kitten, but he was a man. Her blatant invitation would arouse a tree stump. He wasn't opposed to whatever she had in mind.

"Did you spike your juice?" he asked suspiciously when she tugged him toward the door. "I don't want you blaming alcohol in the morning."

She chuckled in a soft, seductive tone an octave lower than her usual soprano. He ought to be weirded out, but he was fascinated—and aroused. She was still Pippa, all graceful angles and luscious lips. Just Pippa without the snarly attitude.

"After what alcohol did to Robbie? What do you think? Are you feeling drunk?" she asked with interest, sliding the door open.

"I'm wary of the siren act, not drunk." Oz followed her inside, debating the wisdom of taking this further.

He had to decide if he was dealing with a psychotic or trust that she knew what she was doing. He wanted to trust her. And screw her. Definite conflict of interest.

"*Siren*," she laughed.

She actually laughed, in a full range of vocal chords that equaled the most melodious chimes invented. Had he ever heard her do that? Her eyes sparkled, and her mouth lost its grim tension. She looked almost as young as her teenage rock star images.

"Like Ulysses, you're going to crash on my rocks?" she asked playfully. "That works for me. Don't say I didn't warn you."

If this was about her evil Voice, Oz wasn't buying a word of it. He wanted her even when she didn't use the kitten voice. He wanted her when she said nothing at all. She was a leashed tigress, and he admired her strength, as well as other parts. Her laugh was pure joy—and erotic as hell, he had to admit.

"Since I don't have a faithful wife waiting for me at home like poor Ulysses, I can loll on an island with a beautiful witch all I like." He loved this new side of her. If sex made her happy, he was glad to oblige.

Instead of following her insistent tug, Oz grabbed Pippa's shoulders, crouched to scoop up her knees, and carried her down the hall. To his immense pleasure, she circled his neck and began nibbling and kissing anywhere she could reach. The new Pippa was a distinct turn-on.

Her bungalow wasn't large. He passed by a computer library lined with books and located the bed in the room at the end of the short hall. He deposited a handful of squirming curves and female scents on the covers.

Lying flat on her back, she shimmied out of her capris before he could make his next move. She wore skimpy pink underwear. She lay there tauntingly, one leg propped up, and he could see the frail pink barrier that was all that stood between his aroused dick and her tender flesh.

Heat surged through him. Focusing all his considerable attention on that patch of pink, he dug out his wallet, produced a condom, and threw it on the pillow beside her. She pushed up on her elbow to admire the show as he unbuttoned his top shirt buttons. Rather than deal with the rest of the fastenings, he dragged the shirt over his head and flung it on a chair.

"Surf boy!" she crowed. "You didn't get those muscles from lying about in tanning beds."

"Naturally brown," he corrected, kicking off his shoes and lying down next to her across the covers. "I don't have time for surfing anymore, but I have a gym." He slid his hand beneath her baby doll tunic to caress fine skin.

She tensed at the touch. Oz slid his hand north, and she grabbed the hem of her shirt and tugged it over her head.

A pink lace confection pushed her breasts into plump mounds for his delectation. In gratitude, he leaned over and kissed her parted lips.

Pippa twined her fingers into Oz's thick sun-streaked locks and held his head where her kisses could reach him. His mouth was firm and hungry, and the contact with his tongue incited small fires in her midsection. She hated that she'd used her Voice to tease him in here, but he wouldn't believe her otherwise. She thought he was strong enough to walk away when he finally realized what she was.

She *hoped* he was strong enough to walk away. He'd already said he'd found an understudy for her part who could read the books, so she wasn't destroying his project. Just driving him out of her life. But before he left, she'd have one night of finding out what it was like to be normal. Almost normal.

Oz was big and heavy and could easily make two of her, but he balanced his weight on one elbow while his free hand flipped open the front hook of her bra. His fingers encompassed her bare breast, and she bit back a groan of pure ecstasy.

It had been so very long...

She didn't think it was too evil to seduce him into what he wanted in the first place.

Tonight, she desperately needed what he had to offer, if only to clear her hormone-impaired head. So she arched upward, pressing her breasts against him to distract him, before pushing him backward into the mattress. He grabbed her waist and hauled her on top of him.

"He-man," she taunted, unfastening his belt while kneeling over his hips. Cool air caressed her breasts, but she was hot from an internal fire.

He slid his hand between her legs to finish unfastening his jeans with an expertise she didn't possess, rubbing her the way she'd been rubbing him, the friction arousing both of them. Together, they shoved the soft denim past his hips, taking his briefs with it. Muscles rippling, he arched to rub his erection against her panties, and she almost came undone right then.

"Siren," he countered, flipping her back to the mattress and kneeling over her.

While he grabbed the condom and tore it open, Pippa gave in to the wonder of casting aside all her control so she could freely admire the man on top of her. Not a shred of fat marred the bronzed muscular walls of his chest and abdomen. His shoulders weren't the brawny masses of cord and bulk that characterized men who spent too much time at the gym, but a smooth, tensile motion of muscle and bone. Mesmerized, she watched him open the condom and don it.

She was quite certain Robbie hadn't been that large.

She was so wet, she didn't think it mattered.

"Now, where was I?" he murmured, bending over to suckle at her breast.

Pippa nearly came up off the bed as heat and hunger engulfed her in a tidal wave of greedy need. She couldn't think about the dangers of this act, not when he was giving her everything she could possibly want. Her skin tingled as if electrified where he caressed her. She dug her fingers into his powerful forearms, and when he turned his attention to her other breast, she stifled her scream. She'd proved her Voice worked simply by using it for seduction. She didn't want to damage him with her cries.

Her muffled noises didn't appear to distract Oz. Could she actually relax enough to dare let her voice free as she did in the studio?

She rubbed her panty crotch against his arousal, driving him to growl and nip and finally to slow her down by running his hand beneath the thin silk to caress her bottom.

"Take them off," she urged, squirming beneath his weight in an effort to do so herself.

He complied, sliding the elastic over her hips and down her thighs. But instead of surging into her, he teased her curls with his fingers, stroking and opening until finally—she clung to his arms, unable to control her cries of release.

And still, he didn't fill her, even when she was weeping and quaking and demanding more.

He was supposed to *obey*, dammit. She wanted him *inside* her. Now.

Maybe she said it aloud. She couldn't remember with her head clouded with the bliss of a long-denied orgasm. She simply knew that one moment he was teasing and kissing and caressing, and the next, he'd driven the thick head of his penis straight up her narrow passage.

He hesitated. She didn't. She arched upward, driving him deeper, forcing him to unleash the raw passion he concealed beneath designer jackets and smooth charm.

And Oz obliged, pounding into her with increasingly deeper thrusts until she screamed again with exploding pleasure and wrapped her legs around his buttocks to squeeze out every ounce of joy. With a groan, he bucked and drove halfway to her heart before he gave in to the throes of his climax.

Even then, he leaned over to suckle at her breast and create new ripples of pleasure when she ought to be depleted.

She would regret her foolishness later, when her brain started working again. For this moonlit moment, she indulged in pure pleasure.

They had sex again later that night when they both woke and bumped into each other and discovered the delights of sharing a bed.

Later, Pippa woke to the twittering of wrens in the courtyard, mellow sunshine pouring through the shutters, and an empty bed. Weren't men supposed to be aroused and willing in the morning? She wasn't ready to give up the best sex she'd ever had in her life.

And that's what it was—sex. They weren't making love, she told herself firmly. She flipped over and recognized the sound of the shower and the sight of steam pouring from the bathroom. It was six o'clock on a flipping Saturday morning, and he was already up and showering?

A few moments later Oz turned off the water and paraded into her bedroom wearing a towel draped around his lean hips. She practically salivated at the sight.

She threw off the covers they'd finally turned down last night, exposing her bare breasts. "Let's not get hasty just yet," she murmured seductively, thinking her Voice had its purposes when the towel stirred with interest. "It's too early to be up and about."

He leaned over and kissed her tousled hair and then straightened and reached for his jeans—ignoring the temptation in her Voice. "I've got obligations. I need to head into the city. Want to come with me?"

No, she didn't want to go with him. She didn't want him leaving. Hadn't her Voice made her desire clear? She'd made men crawl when she'd purred. Perhaps she wasn't releasing enough of her emotion. After all these years of holding back, she was out of practice.

She wrapped a sheet around her hips and kneeled on the mattress while he hunted for his clothes. "Where is Ulysses when I need him?" she asked, pouring all her need for him into the sensual tone generated by her admiration of his superb backside.

"Ulysses is out of condoms and going back to his ship for more," he said, throwing her a laughing look over his shoulder while he pulled up his jeans. "Come with me, and we'll explore foreign shores. I'll take you to a birthday party. You can read to the kids while I talk to our director about the production."

Pippa sat down on her heels and stared at him. He'd told her no? He wasn't down on his knees, begging for more?

Now that she thought of it, Oz hadn't gone over the edge when she'd cried out last night either. Robbie used to get frantic when she urged him to go faster. A cry of pleasure would make him weep with his efforts to please her more. Not that she'd understood that at the time. Mostly, he exhausted her, which hadn't helped their marriage much.

But Oz was oddly resistant to her demands. Had she been denying herself sex for no good reason?

She didn't think so. She'd tested men's reactions to her voice while attending college. She couldn't think of one of them who hadn't come when she called. Or even when she hadn't. She simply had to talk to them when she was feeling horny, and they were all over her like white on rice. She'd learned to speak harshly to drive them away.

Oz was walking away even though she didn't want him to. Which said she'd gone beyond perverse into the realm of unreality. She'd been trying to get the man to go home all week. Now that she wanted him to stay, he was leaving.

She flung a pillow at him. "I'm not going into the city. Ever. Again."

Although, if her Voice had actually lost its touch... could she? She didn't dare risk it until she experimented more.

"Do you want to take my computer to your brother?" she asked, pushing her fear deep down inside her and summoning her stoic calm.

Buttoning his shirt, Oz turned to study her. "You've gone back into your cave again. I like it better when you're shouting and throwing things at me, among other things," he added with a lopsided tilt of his lips.

"You *like* it when I shout?" She tried to keep the incredulity from her voice, but she wasn't certain she succeeded. He was not only a wizard if he could resist her Voice, but he was a perverse wizard. She ought to shout him into a cowering kitten.

"Shouting is real. That monotone... not so much. Drive into L.A. with me. You can sing along with the radio and see if I drive off a cliff."

"You're making fun of me." Angry now, she dragged the sheet with her as she climbed out of bed. "Just because you're too thickheaded to be affected doesn't mean I'm imagining what my Voice does. My life may be limited, but I really don't want to end it like Robbie did."

"I'm sorry, I shouldn't have said that," he called after her.

Well, at least he was apologizing if not groveling. Pippa turned on the shower to drown out anything else he said.

He'd turned her quiet life upside down. Now she had to deal with this amazingly new perspective. Was her Voice dead?

Chapter 16

OZ KICKED HIMSELF THRICE OVER FOR THE STUPID crack about the cliff. But Pippa had been so enticing, sitting there in a pool of yellow sheets and sunlight, her luscious lips pouting because he didn't leap to do her bidding, that he hadn't been thinking straight. She must have led some freaking weird life to think men preferred that sex kitten act to the passionate woman she concealed.

But he wanted back in her bed again, so he had to make amends. She was obviously not experienced, but that meant she responded eagerly to everything he did, which could dangerously inflate his already brawny ego. But she was smart. And athletic as all hell. She'd catch on quickly, and he would have a hard time keeping up. He really enjoyed that idea. A woman who challenged him in bed was worth working to keep around for a while.

She certainly hadn't bored him yet.

So he rummaged in her freezer and found frozen muffins. He wondered if there was room in her tiny kitchen for a coffeemaker. He was dying for caffeine. But he poured juice while warming the muffins. He cut up fruit in a dish and doused it with yogurt. And he carried the lot into the bedroom on a silver platter he found in one of her cabinets.

She was wrapped in the fluffy white robe she'd loaned to him earlier in the week, drying her hair, when he entered. Oz took her look of surprise as reward for his efforts.

"Nick Townsend and I go way back," he said, setting the tray on the bed. "I'm godfather to his eldest. I can't miss the kid's birthday. And I promised to fill Nick in on what we're planning up here. His wife isn't too happy about him working away from home all week and commuting a couple of hours a day, so I have to pacify her too."

Recognizing the rising look of panic in her eyes, Oz stepped back, giving her space. Where had last night's tigress gone? "If people are going to recognize you, you might as well start with friends. It's a controlled environment. Just Nick and Mary and a few kids. You're used to kids, so they shouldn't be a problem."

She sipped the juice and glared at him through slitted eyes. He couldn't predict if she'd kick him in the balls, fling the juice at him, or try to seduce him again. And here he'd thought she was a passionless stick. So much for his boast that he understood people.

"People don't recognize angelic Syrene in my natural dorkiness," she finally said. "People see what they want to see, so I've established my author image here, and they don't look beyond it. But if I walk into your friend's house on your arm, they're going to expect to see some glamorous bimbo, so they'll be suspicious and look deeper."

Oz grinned. "I never take women to Nick's. Mary hates my dates. She'll like you, and that's all that matters. You can handle her and the kids for an hour or so. Then we'll go stand over Conan while he empties your computer innards. You can make certain he doesn't open any dangerous files."

That caught her attention. She sipped her juice and thought about it. "You really think there's something in my computer that might lead you to your son's kidnapper? It sounds pretty far-fetched."

"I don't know anything. I just take one minute, one minuscule piece of the puzzle at a time and try not to hope too hard," he admitted. "Shall I disconnect your computer and carry it out to my truck?"

"The one in the house is my business computer, not the one with the music in it. We have to go to the studio for that." She set the glass down, opened her closet, and pulled out several of her colorful overalls.

So she'd really meant it when she said she kept the computer behind locked doors, Oz realized. Breaking into her studio would be serious business. It was less and less likely that someone had copied files from her home.

He crossed the room, leaned over, and removed a filmy hot pink and orange sundress from a hanger. "Wear this, and you won't have to paint your face. You don't need to be a clown to entertain kids. And there's no point in hiding if you'll be working with Nick for weeks."

She shot him a look that should have killed and flounced off to the bathroom, slamming the door after her.

Well, that had gone well, hadn't it?

Any time she wasn't trying to rip off his balls was good, Oz decided.

Wearing the bright sundress, a floppy-brimmed straw hat, and sunglasses, Pippa ventured off her mountain for the first time in years. She told herself it was to protect the computer stored behind the truck's seat and to prevent anyone from harm if they got curious enough to listen to her dangerous emotional outpourings.

She suspected it also had a lot to do with wanting Oz in her bed again that night. One night was not enough to make up for the years of loneliness. She'd forgotten how marvelous it was to share space with another human being.

He hadn't run away or done any of the things she'd expected. Maybe she was losing her aberrant talent. Maybe he was impervious. She didn't dare hope for either; it was too dangerous. But she desperately wanted to learn more, and as impossible and annoying as it seemed, Oz was apparently the man who could help her.

He'd not been surprised by her studio, the bastard. He'd gone snooping and knew it was there. But he'd wisely kept his mouth shut as she'd removed her computer from the safe and allowed him to haul it out to his truck.

The prospect of actually being involved in his TV project loomed on her radar like a towering mountain that she didn't have the power to soar above. A crash was inevitable.

Well, she'd gone down in flames before and, like the phoenix, survived. What didn't kill her made her stronger? She tried to think of more platitudes, but Oz was too distracting.

After they'd removed the computer, Oz had gone back to the B&B and changed into loose linen trousers and a Hawaiian shirt, one almost as loud as her dress. Driving the big truck down the mountain with one hand draped over the wheel, his overlong hair blowing from the open window, he looked as if all he needed was a surfboard in the truck bed.

He glanced at her warily. She knew she was sitting stiff as the surfboard he didn't have, with her hands clasped in her lap as if fearful the truck would fly off the side of the road. The highway did have some spectacular curves and drop-offs, but his driving wasn't her fear.

"There are CDs in the console," he suggested. "I promise not to jump your bones if you sing along. Or I'll wait for a good place to pull off first."

She wanted to smack him for laughing at her fears. Just feeling angry could get them killed if she opened her mouth and said something. She took a deep breath, crossed her legs on the seat, and rested her hands palms upward on her knees. She needed to find her center and calm the Beast.

He slid an Anonymous Four disc into the player, and the haunting sopranos soared from the speaker.

She definitely needed to smack him, the irritating, nonbelieving man. But the lilting voices filled the cab and sucked her up until the music filled her, and she became the music.

Glorious, glorious sound, lifting her higher, spinning her around. How she'd missed the music!

Inside her zone, she hummed through "Wayfaring Stranger" and "In the Sweet Bye and Bye." When the CD came around to "Amazing Grace," she lost her control. It was one of her favorite songs, and she couldn't keep the words from her tongue, softly at first.

She sounded rusty even to herself, so she tried to blend with the voices, disguising her own to fit in. These were the songs she'd first learned, the ones she'd sang in church choir, before she'd been *discovered*. Childhood songs, without the painful memories of later.

She was weeping so hard before the song ended that she couldn't see the road. Oz was destroying *her*, not the other way around. These few blissful hours of freedom had set her soul gliding too close to the sun. How would she ever confine her real self again, after he left? She ought to jump out of the truck and run home and lock the doors and never speak to him again.

"Shit!" Oz shouted, startling her out of her morass of despair.

Terrified her singing had caused still another trauma, Pippa grabbed the door handle. Forcing the sobs back down her throat, she waited for the moment she'd have to fling herself out the door. She sent him a frantic glance.

Jaw tight, Oz stomped on the brake and competently swung the truck into a wide space on the narrow shoulder. The rear of the truck fishtailed, but he held the big machine to the gravel without sliding into the ditch nearby. He wasn't even looking at her.

Blinded by tears and fear, Pippa didn't know whether to fall out of the truck and run or stay and fight whatever had set Oz off. Without waiting to explain, he flung open his door and hit the road running. Robbie had almost driven her off a cliff. Had she driven this man to flinging himself off the mountain?

Finally realizing Oz was running down the road, she blinked the moisture from her eyes, still afraid she'd hurt him. No longer blinded by fear, she looked out the windshield and finally recognized what he'd seen—an abandoned car, a man and woman farther down the road.

The man was viciously dragging and beating at the furious woman while she screamed and fought.

Their car had apparently gone off the road—while arguing? The old Ford Escort teetered ominously on the steep embankment in a narrow stretch of the road farther down the mountain. Alarmed, Pippa watched a crying toddler climb from the precariously tilted car. Without another thought, she jumped out of the truck and raced in Oz's wake.

He was far ahead of her, his long legs carrying him directly to the grappling couple on the far side of the car. None of them were aware of the baby behind them. Pippa cried out a warning, but she was too far away, they were too angry, and the wind through the canyon drowned her out. She winced as Oz seized the man's shoulder, spun him around, and plowed a fist into his jaw. Assault and battery would look good on his record. Not. But she had to admire a man willing to step from his own comfortable world to take charge of a bad situation.

She couldn't possibly catch the attention of the adults. But she had to stop the little boy.

She threw her Voice as she had learned to do in church, singing whatever silly song came into her head to catch the child's attention. Children had sharp hearing. The mop-haired toddler looked up in interest. He'd heard her!

Loosened by her singing in the cab, her Voice rang out clearly. To her ears, it echoed off the canyon walls, but the adults still didn't notice. The wife beater had turned his rage away from his victim, intent on flinging Oz out of his way first. He was larger than Oz but slower. Oz's fast fists didn't allow the bully to get close.

Pippa was terrified they'd both go over the side, along with the car.

She slowed her song to a lullaby, singing sweetly now that she was closer, teasing the child with smiles as she'd learned to do in the day care, doing her best to look nonthreatening. Clad in a too-small T-shirt and a dirty diaper, he took a step toward her.

The shouts and blows of the men and his mother's terrified weeping distracted him into turning away.

Pippa forced the panic inside the strongbox she'd forged over the years. Panic would only exacerbate the anger and pain of the situation. Instead, she separated the panic from the music in her head, letting the song come out of its own accord, as it once had, before she'd discovered the danger. But this was for good. It was just a song...

"Sing, sing a song," she called, aiming for an audience of one. Her fright eased as the toddler swung back to her again. She added a teasing lilt, and he began clapping his hands. She made up lyrics to encourage him to continue clapping.

By the time she reached him, he willingly climbed into her arms and hugged her neck, and she could breathe again.

Only then did she realize that the boy's mother had also heard her song. Looking dazed, she abandoned the brawling men and walked back to meet Pippa, slowly clapping as well. Pippa switched from her made-up ditty to "Puff, the Magic Dragon," and the woman nodded and began to sing with her. The boy laughed and thumped Pippa's shoulders in delight.

She glanced up to see how Oz was faring, wondering

if there was any way on earth she could stop the fight. She'd never been successful in stopping the riots she'd caused before she quit the business.

Her Voice should reach them now that she was closer. She raised it higher, staying with the lighthearted song.

The bully hesitated, looking around and shaking his head as if to clear it. Unfazed by her Voice, Oz felled him with a powerful blow to the jaw.

The man didn't get up again.

Leaving the puking drunk beside the road where he belonged, Oz jogged past the beat-up Escort. Pippa's voice soared through the air with the ethereal power of angelic choirs and birdcalls at dawn. He'd known she was talented.

But observing what she'd just done, he was ready to believe she was enchanted.

She'd frozen a drunk in place. Oz hadn't made a lucky blow. The dolt had heard her, stopped fighting, and been diverted by a damned child's song. And now she had a bruised and weeping woman and a frightened toddler clapping and smiling and singing beside the road like puppets whose strings she pulled.

Siren magic.

Pippa raised her eyebrows questioningly as he approached but seemed to think it necessary to keep up the entertainment. He nodded, kissed her soft, golden-red hair, and murmured, "I'll pull their car back to the road. Take them away from the edge."

Like the Pied Piper, Pippa sang and clapped and led

her audience of two across the narrow mountain road to a grassy area where oncoming traffic wouldn't endanger them. By the time Oz had chains on the Escort, she had them sitting in a circle, clapping hands with one another in a three-way game of patty-cake.

He had to be imagining this. He'd seen the man hit his wife so hard, she shouldn't have a tooth left in her head. But here she was, laughing with the joy of a child—because of Pippa.

And she *hid* this magical gift of hers?

Magic. Yeah, like he believed in magic. Oz thought he ought to bang his head against the truck a few times, but he had better things to do for now.

After setting out flares in both directions, he returned to the Ram. Making certain the road was clear, he climbed into the cab, threw the shift, and carefully tugged the small car off its precarious perch and back to the road shoulder.

He returned the pickup to its original parking space farther up the mountain and then jogged down to see what his personal genie intended to do with her new fans-for-life.

He wasn't a fanciful man. As a kid, he'd preferred real stories about sports heroes to his mother's fairy tales, and as an adult he read histories and biographies. Magic was fantasy.

Pippa was real. And very possibly as dangerous as she claimed.

She ended the singing circle by taking her audience's hands. One last clear note echoed over the canyon, and peace descended with only the occasional rumble of traffic farther below.

"Will the Escort run?" she asked quietly while the little boy climbed into the woman's lap.

Oz watched the boy with a hungry pang, wishing it could have been Donal, wishing he could bash out the brains of the boy's father all over again. Which reminded him...

"The Escort will run. I think it will be safer if I load our friend down there into the Ram while these two drive on. Can you drive?" He threw the last question at the woman climbing to her feet with the boy in her arms.

She nodded. "He'll report the car as stolen, but I can reach my family before the cops find it."

"Then get going. I won't be too fast in delivering him to a hospital. He'll be fine, but the medics will keep him around for a while."

Oz watched the pair safely cross the road and return to their car as if they hadn't just been mesmerized by a voice from the gods.

Then, reluctantly, he turned back to the wicked elf standing with crossed arms in a stand of prairie grass, glaring at him defiantly.

Chapter 17

"I'll need you to sit behind the wheel while I load the bastard into the back," Oz said after the Escort drove away. He glared back at Pippa as if the problem was all hers.

"What, you don't want to clap and sing with me?" she asked mockingly, because that worry was at the top of her head. Why hadn't *he* responded to her singing? Was he really immune?

"I'll pass this time," he retorted. "Give me another chance later." He grabbed her arm and half dragged her across the road.

Fortunately, she had long legs and could keep up with him as he hurried back to the pickup. She kept glancing over her shoulder to the man sprawled in the dust, wondering how long before he got up and wandered into traffic.

"He's passed out," Oz said, opening the passenger door so she could climb in. "The alcohol fumes were enough to knock me over."

"I hope she goes far, far away and never has to see him again," Pippa said vehemently. "There ought to be vaccinations against alcoholism."

He snorted and started the ignition. "Or against stupidity, because chances are, she'll go back to him as soon as he shows up sober."

Pippa couldn't argue that. She'd spent almost two

years taking Robbie back every time he pulled a stupid stunt. At least he'd never hit her. He was far too busy being sick and groveling beneath the fury of her evil, evil Voice. As soon as she cooled off and shut up so he realized that he'd been behaving like a mewling milksop, his humiliation made him go out and get high again. It had been a vicious circle neither of them knew how to end. Until it was too late, and she realized the problem was her.

Oz parked the truck as far off the road as he could, and Pippa slid behind the wheel to keep an eye on traffic while he climbed out. Watching the rearview mirror, she could see him tote the heavy drunk as if he were no more than a sack of grain. She didn't think a lock of Oz's golden-brown hair fell out of place as he did so. And he didn't appear winded when he returned to reclaim his seat.

He wasn't Robbie by any stretch of the imagination.

She wasn't entirely certain Oz was real. Which worked out, she thought, remembering how he'd glared at her a few minutes ago. He wasn't certain her Voice was real, and her Voice was *her*.

A chasm wider than a canyon loomed between them. She was out of her mind to think of sleeping with him again. But she was.

And so was he, she was pretty sure. She'd like to bask in the satisfaction of knowing that golden boy wanted dorky *her*, but more than one night smacked of relationship territory, and she really shouldn't go there.

He darted her another of those wary looks as he hit the ignition. "You okay?"

"Fine," she said airily. "I used to sing to abused

women and children and drunks all the time. Usually, though, the crowd was bigger."

He chuckled sardonically and pulled back on the highway. "If you sang like that in front of audiences, they forgot they were abused and drunk for a few hours. Where in *hell* did that voice come from? You're good on CD, but in person, you're surreal."

She shrugged and then folded her legs into a lotus position again, taking deep breaths to calm herself before committing any irreversible act. Oz had seen more of her than any man since Robbie, and he wasn't running. Now was the opportunity to give him the chance to get the hell out of Dodge. Decision made. "In my nightmares, I dream it's my Voice that made my parents dump me at a fire station."

There, she'd said it, her worst fear. She could seduce and entertain with her Voice for only so long. Eventually, her temper exploded, her terror escaped, her sorrow poured out, and everyone was miserable with her. Who could possibly live with that kind of turmoil?

"Your foster parents didn't dump you," he pointed out, logically enough. "So chances are pretty damned good that loving parents wouldn't. And if your first experience with a man coming on to you was after puberty, it's possible that whatever…"

He hesitated, and Pippa hid her grin. He would have to admit that she wasn't just singing if he continued that sentence.

"That puberty gave you a greater range?" he finished with a nice save. "In which case, it's doubtful you drove your parents to abandonment."

She liked that idea. She happily absorbed it into her

lexicon of theories. "Maybe I wasn't abandoned but stolen?" she added, for good measure. She didn't want to be thrown away.

"That, I can believe. Can you imagine hearing a child prodigy, stealing her in hopes of making a fortune, then having her turn into a raging virago? A kidnapper would have dropped you, pronto." He grinned. "I bet you were a hellion."

"I wasn't an angel," she agreed. "I know that's the image my managers tried to promote, but I was an angry toddler, a sullen grade school kid, and a mean teenager. I knew I was being used and resented it, but I'd never known any alternative. The nobody-loves-me syndrome, I guess. I thought if I did what I was told, they'd learn to love me, so I tried to please. For far too long, I tried. But they only loved me when I was doing what they wanted. They turned away when I showed them my unhappiness," she said with the dispassion gained from the perspective of distance. She'd had lots and lots of time and therapy to understand the dynamics. And realize they'd never change.

"Wicked dangerous—beauty, talent, and temperament. It's a wonder you survived." He glanced in his mirror and muttered a curse. "Our guest is awake."

Turning to see the bearded passenger shaking his shaggy head, Pippa debated. They couldn't let him fall out of the truck if he tried to climb out. She was pretty sure she could stop a drunk with her Voice. She certainly had the experience. And she'd already stopped this one once.

Except Oz was driving. She didn't want to distract him or put him to sleep at the wheel. But so far, he'd seemed impervious to everything she threw his way. He'd unleashed her urge to experiment with his encouragement, and she had barely begun to sample the heady taste of freedom. She'd probably never be satisfied with the results of her research until she killed someone else, she realized bitterly. But the drunk was likely to kill himself if she didn't try something.

She slid the cab window partially open while considering her repertoire. She couldn't sing her Syrene songs without the danger of being recognized. She had to stick to standard fare.

She hummed a few bars near the window, watching to see how the moaning man reacted. He was unsteadily trying to sit while holding his jaw. She hoped Oz had broken it.

The man winced and tumbled over, bouncing with the bed of the truck. Oops. Her anger had escaped. Taking a deep breath, aiming for the control she'd so painstakingly developed over these past years, she sought a calming tune. She hummed a little louder. Their passenger quit cursing.

"You keep him down until we get him to the emergency room, and I'm going to have to start believing you," Oz warned. "And I don't want to believe you. I'm not feeling a damned thing except irritated that you're singing to him and not me."

Pippa almost smiled. "If you weren't so thickheaded, you'd fall asleep at the wheel. Mind the road, and I'll mind donkey brain back there."

She returned to the lullaby she'd decided on, singing softly. Maybe the drunk would think she was the radio. She had to keep one eye on Oz to be certain he wasn't getting sleepy too. But he seemed fascinated, casting glances in the rearview mirror far more often than he should as she put their passenger back to sleep.

She'd sung Robbie to sleep on many occasions. She didn't want to remember them, but the knowledge didn't go away. Back then, the lullabies had left her drained and even more alone than before, which had created some very unhappy music. She couldn't put herself to sleep.

But this time, with no emotion involved other than a need for peace, the song left her energized. For a change, she was being useful. The world's scariness went away when she knew she could help.

Oz followed a hospital sign off the highway and into a suburb. Pippa tried to concentrate on the song and not her jumpiness as he drove through unfamiliar streets of neat little houses. She'd distanced herself from the city and its enormous population for good reason. She needed isolation to prevent her roller-coaster temperament from being driven by too many people. She no longer knew how to behave among strangers, feared the noise and crowds and her reactions to them. She could feel herself shrinking into nothingness already, despite all the work she'd done to become strong.

She'd only practiced control among friends in a small, safe environment. And even then, she'd needed her studio to release all the pent-up rage and frustration hammering inside her some days. The city was too dangerous, too volatile. Too many bad things happened there. She had only to look to the past hour for proof of that.

Oz pulled up in front of the emergency doors, took

one look at her, said nothing, and climbed out of the truck, leaving her safely inside. Pippa was grateful that he didn't expect her to go into the chaos of the emergency room and find a doctor. A hospital would unbalance her of a certainty. She squinched down in the seat and threaded her fingers to hold herself together.

Their passenger woke as the medics lowered the tailgate, but she didn't dare sing with anyone other than Oz around. The bully came up fighting, but with Oz's help, the medics strapped him on a gurney. No more busting jaws. Oz returned to the cab, took another look at her hunched position, and reached for the ignition.

"I told them I found him beside the road. He's in no shape to know what hit him." He guided the truck out of the parking lot and toward the highway.

Thoughts and emotions all racing incoherently, Pippa tried not to glance too often at Oz's stoic expression. She feared his silence meant he was regretting bringing her with him, that he finally realized how damaged she was.

In that outrageous Tommy Bahama shirt, he lost some of his glitz and sophistication. He had dirt on his trousers from a collision with the gravel and a small cut on the corner of his lip from a collision with the drunk's fist. Instead of sophistication, he exuded frightening strength and masculinity. Even orange flowers couldn't take that away.

Maybe, if she tried to act normal... Could she be normal? For a day?

"Are you taking your godson a present?" she finally asked, just to break the unspoken conversation in both their heads.

He cursed at her reminder and swung the truck into a turn lane. Before she could catch the dash or panic, he asked, "Mind coming back to my place? I'll clean up and pick up the gift."

Yes, she minded, but it would be rude to say so. She was on unknown territory, afraid to put the wrong foot forward and trying desperately to behave as if she weren't psychotic.

She was trusting the damned man to understand and be patient with her! She had baloney for brains.

She nodded agreement to his suggestion, keeping her fears to herself.

Oz didn't worry that Pippa would turn up her nose in disgust at his bachelor condo. After Alys died, he'd moved here rather than deal with the house she'd so lovingly decorated. He'd brought Donal's familiar furniture to the condo, but he'd had a designer buy and arrange the rest of the place, adding the decorator touches women expected.

After Heidi, the nanny, had disappeared with Donal, he'd had to hire a maid service to keep the place neat. These days, he was seldom there except to sleep, so he hadn't left much of a mark on it. Pippa should be safe enough admiring his awards and his ocean view long enough for him to make a fast change.

He was more concerned about Pippa herself, but he'd been the one determined to haul her spoiled ass back to town, and now he had to deal with the result. Did he keep pushing or let her retreat up the mountain?

He had a feeling if he let her retreat, she'd never come

down again. And he couldn't help it: he was excited about her voice. Evil or not, it was amazing, and his curiosity knew no bounds. He hadn't been this excited about anyone or anything in... Since he'd married Alys. And that had worn off. So he wouldn't let himself get too involved this time.

Returning to his black-and-white front room wearing stone-washed jeans and a less enthusiastic blue print shirt, Oz halted in the doorway.

Pippa had taken the black cushions from his sprawling couch and arranged them in an acoustic shield around his stereo equipment. She'd turned off the surround sound, sat on the floor in front of the shield, and directed the front speakers toward her, so she had a perfect balance of resonance.

She was singing along with Michael Jackson's *Thriller* album. And she did it better than Michael. She was scary good.

And damn if she didn't look like a bouquet of orange and yellow tropical flowers brightening his chrome and glass decor. He hadn't realized how cold the room was until her red-gold hair warmed it better than a fire. He needed to install a fireplace.

He wanted to linger and admire, but they were already running late.

"Don't mind me, I only live here," he said in amusement when he approached, and she jerked out of her reverie.

She hastily began returning cushions to his couch. "I threw away all my CDs. I miss them."

"I hope you have a good therapist." He flung the rest of the cushions back and let her fuss with arranging the decorator pillows. "You are a living embodiment of music. Surviving without it must be like living without water."

She held up a photo of Donal chasing a butterfly that he'd had framed and left hidden behind his CDs. "Surviving without music may be somewhat akin to surviving without a son."

The pain around his heart crushed like a vise. He took the small photo and set it back on the shelf, sticking to the topic she'd tried to divert. "You have the power to bring back the music."

She shrugged her narrow shoulders and strode toward the door as if eager to escape. "You've not seen how I can destroy. Don't push me, Oswin."

"That's what I do best, push." Hand at the small of her back, he shoved her across the threshold into the condo corridor. "Nothing would ever get done unless some of us take the reins and lead. So, do you want to be pushed or led?"

She elbowed him with her sharp elbow and strode down to the elevator, avoiding his pushing hand. She stood straight and proud as any goddess. Guess that told him where he stood in the scheme of things.

Chapter 18

PIPPA UNDERSTOOD OZ'S HAWAIIAN SHIRT PENCHANT when he introduced her to Nick and Mary Townsend and their beach house. They were native Hawaiians, and elements of their history adorned every shelf and wall. A hand-carved canoe served as a mantel over a polished stone vent-free fireplace. Stone statues guarded the lush plants visible through the floor-to-ceiling windows off the terrace. Coral and turtle shell artwork blended with the casual but expensive wicker furniture and tropical pillows.

In the middle of the lovely oasis, bright red and blue plastic toys covered the bamboo floors, and Pippa relaxed a fraction.

While the adults talked, Pippa retreated to the children. Children were simple. They liked attention. All she had to do was admire their artwork, push their toys, and read to them. She'd even learned to allow her pleasure to seep through in her voice, so they tended to behave better when she was around—the reason the day care loved having her.

She didn't know how Oz was surviving with the devastation of losing that gorgeous little boy she'd seen in the photo. No wonder he was pushing her, even if thinking she could help him wasn't rational. Losing his son must be eating him alive.

As she played with the children, Pippa knew the

director was studying her and his wife was taking her measure, but she no longer cared. It was liberating to know that she didn't have to perform for anyone anymore—even if they figured out who she was. She no longer needed anyone's love or approval. And that went for the damned man analyzing her as if she were a Picasso he didn't understand.

By the time they left an hour later, she was in control again, or as much as she could be surrounded by city traffic, with a sexy but silent man at her side, while contemplating what they would find on her computer.

So, she wasn't exactly serene.

"Does your brother know we're coming over?" she asked when the silence had stretched too long.

"I warned him earlier. He'll be there. He's dying to figure out the puzzle. You ought to try singing for him and see if a human exists inside his robot mind anywhere."

Pippa tilted him a reluctant half-grin. "A Syrene song maybe? Want to see if he'll follow me anywhere?"

Oz grunted and cast her a look of displeasure. "You think you enthralled your audience with your voice? That they didn't buy your music because it was good but because you magicked them into it?"

"I'm not that crazy. I'm good, and they got their money's worth when they bought my songs." She sat back and folded her arms, staring at the eclectic array of houses in the neighborhood they'd entered. "But it does leave open the question of whether or not I'd be popular if it hadn't been for…" She hesitated, unwilling to name the evil. "This is a ridiculous topic. I can't talk about it. It is what it is."

"Do you have any songs that aren't about sex?" he

asked with interest. "Something that will make Conan clap and sing like you did with the woman and her kid?"

"Still don't believe me, do you?" she taunted. "And the truth is, I don't know. Different people react differently. I sing a love song, and one man hands me flowers, another tries to rape me. You don't seem to react at all. Lullabies are usually safe. You want to put him to sleep?"

Oz chuckled. "He could use some sleep. I'm inclined to try."

"Well, I'm not. He could fall so deeply asleep that he won't hear a smoke alarm go off, and it would be my fault if he died of smoke inhalation. I don't want the responsibility of any more lives. Period. The end."

Oz's phone buzzed as he pulled into the narrow drive of what would be called a faded blue fishing shack anywhere else but in California. Pippa figured the Realtors called it an adorable, authentic bungalow, and given the location not far from Redondo Beach, it probably cost five times more than her place in the mountains. There was no yard to speak of. A towering, modern blocks-of-glass townhome occupied the entire lot on one side. A shack more bedraggled than Conan's adorned a scruffy lot on the left. A bright red and blue parrot squawked from the tropical greenery on the scruffy shack's collapsing porch. Conan had interesting neighbors.

Truck safely parked, Oz pulled the vibrating phone off his belt, read the screen, and cursed. "Let's get inside and see if Conan can trace this."

Rudely leaving her sitting, he jumped from the cab and took three big strides to the blue house's peeling maroon front door. Not bothering to knock, he shoved past the door, leaving it open so Pippa could follow.

"Well, Pippa, my dear, you know your place in his life," she mocked herself, climbing out and pushing the seat up so she could retrieve the computer behind it.

Carrying the heavy equipment up to the porch, she decided she preferred a man who had his own priorities. She didn't want any more needy men clinging to her skirts. She enjoyed her independence and liked that he put his son first.

But she wouldn't be female if she didn't enjoy the looks of appreciation both men gave her when she walked in carrying a stupid box of metal. Pippa wasn't at all certain if it was her or the computer they were admiring.

"What?" she demanded, setting the box down on a crate after Conan knocked the books off it to clear space. "Am I wearing feathers in my hair?"

"You've got muscles," Conan said—idiotically, in her opinion.

"I have bare arms. I know how to use them. Get over it. This isn't the beach, and I'm not a bunny." She glared at Oz, who was fighting a grin. He dropped his BlackBerry on the table in front of his brother, distracting him.

"He's not groveling yet," Oz said. "Try harder."

She'd spoken with irritation. And neither man had fallen on the floor and writhed. She'd once sent a stagehand into epileptic spasms when she'd yelled at him. Huffing, she sought a place to sit.

And gave up. Conan's entire front room was devoted to equipment, books, files, and an incomprehensible clutter of mechanical and electrical parts. With his back to the front door, he occupied the only chair, the one in front of a bank of computers on the interior wall. Really bad feng shui, she observed.

Leaning against a wall as Oz was doing, Pippa met his gaze. She was learning to challenge the man. She was also learning he liked it. "What sent you dashing in here? Who is he tracing?" She tilted her head in Conan's direction.

Conan had already dived into the BlackBerry and was doing something mysterious with a piece of equipment hooked to his computer, no longer aware of her or her muscles.

"Librarian," Oz replied, losing his smirk. "New message. It only says, 'Santa Domenica.'"

"Never heard of it." Pippa glanced around, locating what appeared to be a dusty laptop on one of the shelves. She unburied the case from a pair of earphones, a diver's mask, and a broken pen.

Conan paid her no attention, but Oz was instantly at her side, carrying a chair from another room so she could sit and open the machine.

"Is this how his guests usually entertain themselves, or are we special?" she asked, opening the shell and turning it on to see if there was any battery.

"You think he entertains in here? If he's even got a girlfriend, I don't know about it. We're not the closest of families." Placing his hands on the back of her chair, Oz peered over her shoulder as she called up an Internet browser.

He smelled of a spicy aftershave that had her mouth watering. The hands that had brought her to ecstasy the night before were propped right behind her shoulders.

Heightened awareness wasn't good for concentration. She missed a key, and he leaned over to correct her spelling, hitting the right combination on the keyboard for her.

Would he want another night with her, or had she scared him off?

She couldn't care. She wouldn't allow herself to care.

"Santa Domenica, Italy. Santa Domenica, California. Want to take bets?" Still leaning over Pippa's shoulder, Oz hit Enter on the California link.

"Population 1500. Looks like desert. Not far from Barstow." Pippa rattled off the important facts as she scrolled down. "I'm betting two gas stations, a church, and a trailer park filled with scrawny dogs."

Fighting the need to yell at his brother to hurry up, to track the damned message, do *something*, Oz settled for tugging Pippa's hair. "Thou shalt not judge. If the Librarian lives there, one of those trailers contains some damned sophisticated equipment. It's not easy to remain anonymous. Do they even have Internet in the desert?"

It was easier to believe the messages were crank calls meant to manipulate either him or Pippa into something. If Oz let himself believe that the Librarian knew his son, he'd have to find a means of reaching through the phone and shaking him.

So he concentrated on the bright spot in Conan's dingy hut—Pippa.

Nick and Mary had approved of her instantly. Oz had known they would, especially when Pippa kept the boys wildly entertained. Mary was satisfied that her husband wouldn't be flirting with one of Oz's usual morally handicapped dates. Neither of them had recognized the former teenage idol, but then, she hadn't been singing.

"No idea what deserts have," Pippa muttered, attempting to call up Google Earth. But the laptop battery died, blacking the screen.

"I'll check it out," Conan said, breaking into the conversation as if he'd been listening all along. He tossed the new BlackBerry back to Oz. "Not a trace. Your caller is wilier than a coyote."

"We don't even know if it means Santa Domenica, California," Pippa said quietly.

Oz looked her over to make certain she was okay. Passive had not been her natural state all day. She was twiddling with the lock of hair he'd tugged, wrapping it around her finger.

"Santa Domenica can wait." Conan began pushing aside the collection of books and papers in front of his monitor. "I can't believe this Librarian is going to all this trouble out of meanness. He's either psychotic or providing clues." He produced a screwdriver from the depth of a drawer spilling with cables. "Give me your computer."

"I told Pippa she can stand over you and make certain you don't open any files, so let's make this fast." Oz carried the computer over and set it down. "You're not planning on dismantling the whole thing, are you?"

"Wanted to check for bugs." Conan glanced over his shoulder at Pippa. "What do you have in here, terrorist plots or something? I swear I won't touch 'em."

Pippa rubbed her forehead as if it ached. "Now that you mention it... If terrorists broadcast what I have in there, they might cause mass chaos and anarchy."

Oz smirked as Conan sent him a questioning look. "Don't ask, okay? Just leave the files alone. You've been officially warned of their destructive nature. If anything happens to them or you, it's on your head. We are no longer responsible."

Pippa sent him a disgruntled look at the cop-out, but Oz didn't really want to stand in his brother's hovel for the rest of the evening while Conan poked around inside the hard drive. He feared Pippa might just explode from nervous exertion or sensory overload.

"I'm more interested in the byte-size files hidden in temporary folders, so you have no need to worry. Did you stand over the guy who moved all your files from the old computer to the new?" Conan asked.

Good question. Oz looked at Pippa, who had dived into her cave again. She'd perfected the expressionless mask. No wonder she'd had to paint tears on her cheeks.

"I didn't know anyone was interested in my old stuff at the time," she murmured. "I just had Lizzy carry the old drive down and leave it at the computer store. She picked the new one up the next day."

Conan didn't bother hiding his opinion of that, Oz noticed. His brother sent her a black look of disapproval. "How did you dispose of the old computer?"

She shrugged. "The guy at the store promised to wipe the disks, update the hardware, and give it to charitable causes. That sounded better than a landfill."

"Three years ago, you said?" Conan asked sharply.

"Almost four," she said warily.

"What's the name of the store? Where was it?"

Even Oz understood the direction this was taking. Almost four years ago, a stranger had access to Pippa's songs. Four years ago, Alys had run off with Donal, but that seemed an impossible connection. It was equally impossible that the Librarian had led him to Pippa with information garnered from an abandoned hard drive. He was out of his territory here.

Pippa gave Conan the name and street of the shop, and he jotted a note. Oz was tempted to head straight over to the store, but those places came and went with regularity. Far more efficient to let Conan do the legwork.

"I'm on it. Why don't the two of you go get pizza or something?" Conan dived back into the computer innards.

"We could do that, or..." Oz turned to Pippa. "We could go to my place and call carryout from a restaurant with a little more class than pizza and research Santa Domenica."

He was skilled at negotiation for good reason—he knew what people really wanted, and he knew the right bait to lure them. Pippa wanted isolation, but she would cling to that damned computer unless he offered her something more important to protect—like his son.

She hesitated, glancing nervously to the box Conan had unscrewed, then locking her fingers together when he started hooking it up to his cables.

"How long will this take?" she murmured in that dispassionate voice she used on the world.

"Depends on how much crap you've got in here. If you've had the machine for four years, that could be a lot of cookies to trek through." Impervious to Pippa's reaction, Conan didn't even look up.

Oz felt her jolt of fear and exhaustion as if it were his own. He rubbed her tense shoulders and then offered his hand. "C'mon. If you can't trust a secret agent, who can you trust?"

She returned a wobbly smile and accepted his hand. "If he's a terrorist and the world dies tomorrow, it's on your head," she retorted, proving she wasn't oblivious to his machinations.

Chapter 19

SHE WAS SO *STUPID*.

Pippa gazed out Oz's wall of windows to the sun setting over the distant surf and wondered if it would be simpler to retreat to her studio and never come out again.

She'd unwittingly put her entire *life* in the hands of a stranger four years ago. And here she was, doing the same again, except now she didn't have the excuse of ignorance. How did she know Conan and Oz weren't planning on pirating her songs and producing them? She didn't.

While Oz had been ordering up dinner, she'd excused herself to wash up. And she'd pried. She'd opened the door to the beautiful nursery with toy truck murals and bright red and blue toys stacked neatly on shelves, untouched for a year. She was trusting a man who wouldn't give up on finding his son despite all odds to the contrary. Oz could be as demented as she was.

Standing at the window, she was still dithering over her next step when strong fingers shoved a beautiful handblown glass of raspberry-scented crushed ice at her. She accepted the delicate stem if only to admire the fragile facets reflecting a rainbow prism from the fading sunlight.

"It's nonalcoholic," Oz reassured her. "I might pollute your mind but not your stomach."

She wanted to laugh, but she was too frozen. "I could be contaminating Conan's mind right now," she said without inflection. "Who knows how many minds I've polluted? Do you really think there's a chance the guy at the computer store would have listened to my files? And that's how someone knows about 'The Silly Seal Song'?"

"I don't want to believe these messages mean anything except some idiot is conning me into a TV production I want to do anyway."

Oz sipped from an identical glass, but Pippa was fairly certain his drink of choice wasn't a virgin daiquiri. Wearing a long-sleeved black polo he'd donned earlier, he stood with feet apart, looking like a captain in charge of a ship.

He practically commanded an empire. She wanted to believe he had the power to protect everyone around him. Which was patently ridiculous, since he'd lost both son and wife.

Which meant she was on her own, as always. It was a lonely place to be, and she wished it could be different.

"A show I *don't* want to do," she reminded him. "So who is setting up whom? I think I'd rather believe some kid has your number and is texting inanities to annoy you."

"Santa Domenica certainly seems to be a wash," he agreed, standing close enough that she could inhale his musky scent. "But giving me your name wasn't. Even if the Librarian is batting fifty-fifty, I can't ignore any clue. I have tomorrow free. Want to drive out there?"

"To Santa Domenica?" she asked in surprise. "We've already established there's nothing there. Even if your son was, how would we find him? Go door to door?"

"I don't know." He lifted his big shoulders and took a

drink. "I just hate doing nothing while Conan is playing with his box of tricks."

His phone buzzed again. Hoping it was Conan with the answer to all their questions, Pippa sipped her drink while Oz checked his message. Supper had been lovely and elegant. She hadn't realized how much she'd missed the delicately balanced flavors of fine dining. Her own poor efforts could scarcely compare.

Oz swore viciously and fluently and showed her the phone.

The message on the screen read Urgent. Nothing more.

Her heart threatened to climb up her throat, but she was still paralyzed. "What does it *mean*?"

"It means I'm heading to Santa Domenica. It's all I have. That could have been Donal wandering in the road today. I can't take chances if he might be in trouble. You can stay here if you like, or I'll call a driver to take you home." Oz looked at her with regret.

His chocolate eyes held warmth that melted her icy shield in ways she shouldn't allow. Pippa knew what he'd hoped to do with the evening. She was guilty of similar thoughts. Her body was already humming with anticipation, wondering what his bedroom was like and if they could get any better than last night.

But now their minds were elsewhere, on an urgent message from the desert. It wouldn't be the same.

"I'll go with you. I couldn't sleep otherwise." She drained her glass and set it on a coaster. The sun had slipped into the ocean. They would be driving mountain roads in the dark. "I'll need a sweater. Should you call your brother?"

Oz leaned over and kissed her, a kiss of appreciation

as well as desire. Pippa's knees, and her resistance, weakened. She didn't want to go to the desert. She wanted to try his bed.

The desert was undoubtedly safer.

Oz talked to Conan while disappearing into the depths of the house to retrieve warmer clothing. Pippa listened to the classical music pouring soothingly from his stereo and wondered if she should take up an instrument. Perhaps a violin. Could she create havoc with a violin?

Not if she didn't know how to play it, she decided with amusement. Oz returned with an overlarge hoodie as she was smiling at her own fantasy, and he stroked her cheek after she took the giant pullover from him.

"Your smile lights the room. You should use it more often." He shrugged into a black jacket with elastic bands at the wrist and waist and zipped it up.

The hoodie fell to midthigh, and Pippa had to roll the sleeves up a dozen times to find her hands, but the bulk made her feel safe. "I smile at the kids all the time. It's adults I avoid."

"Make the world go away?" He caught her elbow and steered her toward the door. "You've been granted the talent to create joy. In a world of woe, you can provide hope. You're being selfish by denying your audience as well as yourself."

"Well, aren't we full of sermons?" she asked edgily, jerking away from him. "If I could also lead people off a cliff like lemmings, would you encourage me?"

"Could I choose the audience?" He took her arm again as the elevator opened in the basement garage.

Imagining what audience he would choose to leap off a cliff ought to make her laugh, but she was too nervous. "I don't know why I try arguing with you. I should recognize genius and bow before it." Pippa shook her head in dismay as they walked out of the elevator and he unlocked a sedate black Mercedes. "A truck, a sports car, and a sedan. Do you own a plane and a train as well?"

"Not yet. Haven't the time. But I can always call my rescue team if I need them." He held the door and assisted her inside.

She heard the mirth in his voice. He was being obnoxious to distract her, and it was working. Not that she needed a great deal more distraction once he slid into the leather seat beside her. His presence filled the dark car as he turned on the ignition and the dash illuminated.

"Has Conan found anything yet?" She tried to remember why she was here. It wasn't easy. Her gaze followed Oz's strong hands as he expertly swung the big car out of the tiny space and into the night.

"He has some software running on your computer's innards, so he's been hunting your computer store while he waits. It's moved a block or two from the original location and isn't open tonight. If he finds anything suspicious about the owner or management, he'll find a way in, but it's a long shot."

"Thank goodness I keep my financial information on the other computer," she murmured, looking for positives. "I don't think anyone could tie me directly to the songs on that drive. Maybe anyone hearing them will just assume I'm downloading from the Internet."

They were both avoiding talking about the Librarian's urgent message. Pippa could feel Oz's tension in the way he held his shoulders and steered the car. He hit the accelerator once they were on the freeway. The car shifted smoothly into high gear and purred past traffic.

There was nothing to be said about a meaningless message from nowhere. They were both keyed up and overreacting. But anything was better than doing nothing and wondering what they'd missed.

"Someone has connected the seal song and Syrene," he reminded her. "What I want to know is how they're related to Donal."

"And Santa Domenica. Are we driving into a trap?"

Oz smacked the wheel with his fist to vent his frustration. "I can't see how. So far, the Librarian has just provided information. You may feel threatened, but it's all been good for me."

Pippa sat silently and pondered that. He didn't regret finding her, didn't mind that she'd dragged in the town of El Padre and tortured him with hysterics?

"You are a single-minded man," she decided.

He laughed curtly. "That's a polite way of calling me an obnoxious bully. Dinner must have mellowed you."

"Or being out in the world again is going to my head. Be ready to box me in if I lose control. I can't always know when it's happening."

"Good topic. We've got over an hour's drive ahead. Let's explore your limits. What does it take to stop you once you—what was it you called it? The Beast? Once the Beast escapes?"

His deep baritone expressed no more than curiosity. She didn't hear mocking or doubt. His logical approach made more sense than her emotional reactions.

"No one has tested my limits," Pippa admitted. "If I'm sad, crying will ultimately choke me into silence.

You've shut me up by tossing me in a pool." She ignored his chuckle. "When people respond oddly to what I'm saying, I'll notice after a while and shut up. Keeping my mouth closed works best, but I'm not naturally mute."

"I noticed," he replied with humor. "I like knowing where I stand, so I appreciate your willingness to let me know. You realize you've had nine years to explore your self-restraint, and that without unpredictable teenage hormones to mess with your mind, you may be able to manage better now?"

"Providing I'm not PMSing?" she asked. "That's just your weird ability to be unaffected talking. You wouldn't say that if I knocked you over like I did the drunk earlier. Yes, I've practiced control. No, it doesn't always work."

She stared into the starry heavens above the hill ahead and tried to imagine a day when she could converse normally without fearing anything she said would cause people to turn against her or one another. One person at a time, and she might manage. An entire TV production? No way.

"Then we can stop the car on Main Street, Santa Domenica, let you out, and you can bring everyone running just by shouting?" he asked, prodding her sore points.

"I could sing a siren song and open every door in town, unless there are more like you. But if there's a villain of some sort out there, do you really want to lure him out in the street with the innocents?"

The angles of Oz's face were shadowed as he glanced in her direction. "Setting aside the impossibility of that feat, what's the reverse? If a villain appears and you have a shrieking fit in the center of Main Street and people are writhing in agony, do I have to throw you in a pool to shut you up?"

"Trying to disarm my Voice?" she asked in amusement. "To my knowledge, you're the only one who has ever succeeded. Once I lose control, I have no idea how to stop on my own. It's probably the reason I'm here. With you, I don't have to watch every sound I make."

Without Oz, she could shriek a man into suicide, with no way of stopping herself.

Scary, terrifying thought. They both stared out at the ribbon of highway ahead. Maybe now he understood.

She was a walking, talking time bomb.

Chapter 20

It was past ten o'clock by the time the Mercedes cruised the silent main drag of Santa Domenica, if a huddled group of aging buildings constituted a town. Pippa had been close to the truth, Oz acknowledged. The town had a gas station with an all-night mini-mart, a few deserted storefronts, a scattering of battered wooden shacks, a cluster of rusted-out mobile homes, and a pack of starving dogs running the street. A tumbleweed rolled after them.

"Now what?" his companion asked in a whisper, gazing at their dismal surroundings with the same dismay as him.

Pippa had tolerated his prying questions with remarkable good humor for the past hour or more. Oz assumed that just being able to talk freely of a secret she'd locked away for a decade had oiled hinges and opened doors. She was likely to slam them again any moment, but he had the keys now.

What worried him was this miserable excuse for a town. What if Donal was being kept here? Putting stark reality to his nightmares ate at his gut.

The Mercedes was conspicuous. Anyone watching would notice them. Oz pulled up at the gas station, trying to look innocuous. He wasn't certain he wanted gas polluted with sand in his expensive machine, but he needed time to think.

"I could stand on the roof and sing the seal song," Pippa said facetiously.

She looked too terrified to set foot outside the car. Even without her handicap—and he was starting to believe there was *something* compelling about her voice—he couldn't blame her. Desert rats were often armed and dangerous.

"I think the best we can do is be seen," he told her. "Maybe the Librarian will send us a text. I'm hoping we'll get to meet him." Oz climbed out and examined the rusting gas meter. It didn't take credit cards. He'd have to give the clerk cash. He leaned back in the car. "I have to go inside. Want to come with me or stay here?"

She hesitated and then opened her door. "Come with you."

She didn't explain, but Oz was relieved that she'd agreed. He was fairly confident that she could take care of herself, but he liked the idea that she trusted his strength more than her own. He'd examine that notion at some better time.

He locked the car doors and, with his hand at her slender waist, led them inside. In the bulky hoodie, she didn't look quite so frail. In the fluorescent interior, a scruffy teen watched them from behind a cage at the register as Pippa headed for the bottled water and Oz poured coffee. Without standing in the street and shouting as she'd suggested, he didn't know how else to let the Librarian know that they'd arrived. Provided that's what the note had meant.

He handed cash over to the clerk and told him he needed twenty dollars in fuel. He wasn't polluting his gas tank more than that.

"Don't look now, but there's someone at the corner of the building," Pippa murmured as they returned to the desert darkness, standing in the doorway with drinks in hand. "And there's a man coming out of the restroom."

Oz nodded and led her across the lot, senses on full alert. Opening the passenger door, he helped her in. She sat sideways, not letting him close the door. He wasn't too worried about taking on men with fists, but if they had guns, that was another matter. He'd rather she was inside. Pippa shot him a look as if she knew what was running through his mind, so he didn't argue. He hoped she could run fast. Or that her screams were as effective as she claimed.

The gangs in this area were notorious.

The man emerging behind them headed toward a nondescript Ford parked in the shadows on the side of the station. He stopped to light a cigarette. Oz stuck the nozzle in the gas tank and watched from the corner of his eye. He suspected the other man was doing the same thing, sizing him up.

If nothing else, the Mercedes was a tempting target. He should have stayed with the pickup, but the backseat was small, and he'd hoped... Damn, he should never hope.

It had been a long time since he'd had to face thugs. Unless Donal was involved, he didn't want to face this one now. It was too dangerous to the woman he was doing a damned poor job of protecting.

Oz straightened and stretched, letting the other man know he wasn't precisely a pushover. If there was only one thug, he'd slink away. Cowards preferred easy prey.

Pippa began humming.

Oz had no idea what the song was. He didn't even hear any emotion behind it. She was simply humming some pleasant tune that might make him smile if he wasn't so wary of his surroundings. Did she think the sound would carry across a parking lot?

Could he believe her humming was the reason the stranger climbed in his car and started the engine? Probably not. But if it made her feel better to think she helped, that was fine with him. The more confident she was of handling her surroundings, the more likely it was that he could talk her into the show.

Now, if only he could figure out why the hell they were here...

He kept an eye on the Ford as it turned onto the street and drove east, out of sight.

He'd almost forgotten the unobtrusive shadow Pippa had pointed out at the corner of the store. The figure had completely blended with the darkness, making no overt moves that he'd noticed. Hiding from the guy in the Ford?

It seemed so. Haltingly, a woman in a long, loose skirt stepped into the parking lot light, leaning on a cane.

The gas tank clicked off, and Oz returned the hose to the pump while Pippa's humming changed in a way he didn't quite grasp. If her voice was as magical as she claimed, he was definitely immune to it. He just knew the pattern of the notes changed.

And the woman stepped more boldly onto the pavement, crossing the lot in their direction with eagerness. Her stride was still halting. She was slender to the point of frail, even more so than Pippa, but the full skirt and loose blouse disguised the fact fairly well. Unstyled and pinned in a twist, her light hair captured the overhead glow as she approached. She wasn't tall but carried herself as if she were.

She halted some feet away from the car, leaned on the cane, and just stared, drinking them in as if they were an oasis in the desert or space aliens she'd long awaited. Her slender fingers lifted to cover her mouth, and Oz could swear she had tears in her eyes.

Nervously, he wondered if he ought to usher Pippa into the car and take off, but he was hoping the Librarian had sent them here for a reason. Could this be a messenger?

Pippa's humming stopped. The woman seemed to shake off her trance. Taking a deep breath, she limped forward. "Did the Librarian send you?" she asked in a voice of cool assurance.

At last! Oz nearly whooped his joy. "He did," he said, coming around the car so he could catch her if she decided to flee. Not that she would get far with that limping gait.

"She," the woman responded. "The Librarian is female, I'm pretty certain."

Well, shit. The Librarian had dragged him out here to rescue another female? A female librarian. A loony one. Trying not to reveal his disappointment that Donal wasn't here, he waited for her to continue.

"I'm…" She hesitated, and Oz knew she was about to lie. "I'm Jean Wainwright. I'm in a bit of a predicament. I know this sounds very odd, but could you give me a lift out of here?"

At Pippa's demanding look, Oz opened the rear passenger door and assisted the woman into the seat. He was officially insane. This could be some elaborate scheme for killing him in the desert and leaving his bones to bleach in the sun. He'd heard of worse.

He was *trusting* Pippa's instincts, which made his insanity even worse. He'd never trusted a woman in his life. Alys had come close, but he'd been young then. Alys had ended his ability to trust anyone to any extent.

But he was letting a lying stranger into his car as if it was a perfectly normal thing to do.

"I'm Dylan Oswin," he said gruffly, as she settled her skirts into the leather seat. He deliberately didn't introduce Pippa. Let her choose her own lie.

"Mr. Oswin, I'm so far beyond grateful that I cannot express it. I only hope I can return the favor someday." Her voice was low and articulate, suitable for a faculty meeting in any college in the country.

"People have helped me in the past," he replied. "I believe in passing it on. Do you have a vehicle here we need to lock up?"

"No," she said firmly, without the lie in her voice. "I had a driver, but he was an illegal and didn't feel safe. He abandoned me here."

He nodded curtly, closed the door, and strode around the car, suddenly eager to get the hell out of this hole. He hated mysteries for a reason. He wanted this one solved.

Pippa introduced herself as Pippa James as he buckled in. Their new passenger murmured a pleasantry in return. Did he imagine it, or was there a hitch in the woman's voice? He was attuned to nuances, but he preferred seeing faces before jumping to conclusions. Pulling from the station, he checked the rearview mirror, but their passenger had settled into a pool of shadow.

"Where can we take you?" Oz asked, turning the car toward L.A. He tried not to acknowledge his overwhelming disappointment at not finding Donal here. Or any clue to his son's whereabouts.

"Since my credit card has been stolen, you'd probably best drop me at a homeless shelter," Jean Wainwright suggested. "That would be safest."

Pippa cried out in immediate opposition. Oz thought Jean's suggestion more sensible than anything Pippa was about to say, but it was quite possible the woman had only said it to attract sympathy. He had to be suspicious for both of them, apparently.

"We should go to the police," Pippa said indignantly. "Who stole it? Your driver? They'll catch him. And then we'll find you a place to stay."

"I've already reported the theft to the credit card people, dear," Jean said gently. "I can't believe anyone is still looking for me after all these years, so I'm hoping that's all it was, petty theft. But it's always best to expect the worst. I don't believe the Librarian brought me back to the States to cause either of us harm. I think I'm supposed to explain what little I know."

That silenced Pippa, Oz observed. Trying not to hope that this woman might have the clues he sought, he checked the rearview again and spoke in Pippa's place. "We'll find a Denny's open if you'd like a bite to eat while we talk."

"I wish I could say I might be helpful, but the Librarian is very vague about what's happening. She simply asked me to return to Bakersfield."

Oz mentally reviewed his entire repertoire of curses but refrained from frightening the women with his opinion of the damned vague Librarian. The winding desert road was empty. If there were cops ahead, he'd suffer the consequences. He wanted to know where his son was, and the sooner, the better. He hit the gas.

"Does this have to do with Oz's son?" Pippa asked quietly.

He darted her a look to be certain she was okay. She was modulating her voice again, keeping it low and even. But her hands were twisting restlessly in her lap. She'd warned him that her pent-up emotion could explode without warning. But she was apparently wary of revealing anything to strangers. He wished he knew how his easy life had become mixed up in this craziness.

He clenched the steering wheel and waited for their passenger to form her careful reply. He didn't trust her further than he could see her, but if his son's life was in her hands...

"I think I may know something about the kidnapping," Jean finally replied. "But you'll have to understand that I don't have the answers, that I'm as much a victim as you."

"How are we involved?" Oz demanded, his attention fully focused at the word *kidnapping*.

The woman waited a long time before replying. "I don't know how much to tell you," she admitted. "I hadn't expected to ever meet you. And I'm afraid that the more you know, the more dangerous it will be."

Shit. Oz slammed down the accelerator, and the Mercedes flew down the dark road.

Chapter 21

PIPPA CLUNG TO THE DOOR HANDLE AS THE UNEVEN landscape flashed by. She didn't fear Oz's speed so much as her own uncertainties.

She was fairly confident that she had reassured Jean with her humming, that the woman had responded to her Voice. So she shouldn't be afraid of her. In fact, she was drawn to her in some manner she couldn't define. She didn't hear anything in the stranger's voice, but Jean's presence seemed to have a calming effect on the Beast. Might other people have weird abilities that could cause a connection?

It wasn't working on Oz. She darted him a wary look. If the car had been a rocket, they'd be on the moon by now. She suspected if Jean didn't speak carefully, he'd rip her head off in an effort to pry answers out of her.

She could understand his desperation. If there was any possibility Donal was still alive and this woman had a clue to his whereabouts, she was willing to rip heads too. She knew what it was like to be left abandoned and alone. She wanted no other child to suffer that loss.

"Speed limit sign," she said softly, jerking Oz back to the moment as they cruised into the outskirts of town.

"Having my card stolen was probably just a result of my carelessness. I don't think anyone is really looking for me. I've been gone a long time," Jean said from the backseat.

"Why would anyone be looking for you?" Pippa asked. She didn't know how she could be involved in any of this, except the Librarian had led Oz to her.

"It's an old story, dear. I'd thought it ended, but I try not to take chances these days."

Oz parked in the darker part of a Denny's lot, hiding the distinctive Mercedes as much as possible. Pippa waited for him to come around and open their doors. She'd feel safer with his broad body beside her.

Once inside, they settled in a corner booth farthest from the door, Oz with his back to the wall so he could watch anyone entering. Pippa sat beside him so she could look through the window—and because she needed his proximity.

"I can't believe I leave home for the first time in years and get involved in skullduggery," Pippa muttered as the waitress delivered their coffee. She hated coffee, but she'd spent enough nights on the road during her rocky career to know better than to order tea in a place like this.

"No one knew where you were," Jean said in response to her mutter.

Pippa blinked and stared at her in astonishment. "Me? Why would anyone want to know where I was?"

The woman's face looked lined and tired. She'd been pretty once, Pippa thought. She might be again if she got a good night's sleep and perhaps relief from whatever pain made her limp. Jean was probably in her fifties, and her skin was still taut, although worry lines crinkled about her eyes and lips.

"If I begin with my story, it might place both of you in danger, so forgive me if I sift through my thoughts to find the ones you need." Jean sipped her coffee and studied them from across the table.

That's when Pippa noticed Jean's eyes were a faded turquoise. Like hers, only older. She gasped and set her cup down so abruptly that coffee sloshed over the brim. "You have my eyes."

Oz stiffened and clasped his big mitt over her fingers, grounding her. "Similar," he said. "Not as vivid."

"No one has blue-green eyes," Pippa insisted when Jean said nothing.

"It's a family trait," Jean agreed wearily. "Don't make anything of it just yet. We're a very, very large family. Scattered. Perhaps for the same elusive reasons my car was deliberately driven off the road all those years ago and why Alys's son may have been kidnapped."

Deliberately driven off the road? Pippa's stomach lurched, and she cast Oz a glance, but he seemed frozen. She squeezed his hand, and he returned the favor.

"Go on," he rumbled when Pippa couldn't find her tongue.

"That accident killed my husband and put me in a nursing home for years," Jean said slowly, obviously sifting as she spoke. "When I got out about six years ago, I went to a website in search of the rest of my family. I immediately received a private message from the Librarian."

"What website?" Oz demanded.

Pippa would rather hear the rest of the story first, but she waited, knowing Oz had more at stake than she.

Jean waved her hand in dismissal. "If it's important, I'll tell you later. Let me organize this story as I think best. I don't want anyone else hurt."

The waitress returned for their orders. Pippa didn't know if she could stomach greasy eggs at this hour while under this tension. She ordered the fruit and hoped for the best.

"Oz is worried about his son," Pippa said when the waitress left. "Could you tell us if he's alive?"

Again, the woman hesitated before nodding. "I believe so. I think that's why we're here. I think the Librarian wants us to talk. I don't know why she can't. Or won't. Perhaps she's like me and hiding."

Oz's hand nearly crushed her fingers. Pippa covered their joined hands with her free one, wishing that humming would ease his anguish. She was amazed he didn't leap out of his seat, grab Jean by the neck, and drag her to the nearest police station. He was practically vibrating with the need to act. She had never learned the natural ability to comfort without her Voice. She tried stroking his hand in hopes that helped.

It felt odd thinking of the Beast in a positive manner, but she'd learned today that if she tried, she could gain a few moments' peace for others by using it.

She just couldn't help Oz if he couldn't hear her.

"Is Donal all right?" he demanded.

"I think so. I'm uncertain of the motivation for the kidnapping, but if..." Jean sighed as if she carried the weight of the world on her shoulders. "I don't see any other way of saying this. I wanted to protect you from the knowledge and myself from your skepticism, but I don't know how else to explain. Was your wife's maiden name Malcolm?"

Oz sounded puzzled. "No, it was Bryan."

Jean shrugged. "It doesn't matter. Somewhere in

her background, Alys must have believed she had a Malcolm ancestor. Your son may have been targeted because of this."

It was Pippa's turn to stiffen. *She* was a Malcolm. It was one of the names she'd given the firemen when she was three years old. How many people knew that?

Oz did. He began stroking her hand with his thumb, forcing her to focus on the conversation and not her panic.

"That's nuts," he said, flattening her fears another notch.

Jean nodded with a weary smile. "I fear that's the problem. No one believes us."

"You know who's behind Donal's kidnapping?" Oz asked in a voice that threatened mayhem.

"No. I've been bedridden for years. All I've done is made a few connections and run into the Librarian at that website. Once I recovered enough ability to use my hands, I filled my time with computer research, looking for family. There's a genealogical website that's tracking us, and it seems the Malcolms are prone to trouble."

"Why Malcolms?" Pippa asked in puzzlement, although in her heart, she feared she knew the answer. Because of her Voice. Because there were others like her out there, others who had to hide what they were.

Jean's blue-green gaze pierced her, and Pippa had to shut her eyes. Her guess was right. A very odd bubble of joy and hope swelled inside her at knowing she wasn't alone. If she believed this tale.

If she believed this tale, Jean knew who she was.

"Malcolms aren't normal," Pippa said before anyone else could.

Jean laughed lightly. "We're normal. We're just able

to access parts of our brains that others don't—and only then if we're trained from birth to nurture our abilities. If a child bursts into song at a table in a restaurant, she can be hushed—or she can be encouraged to access the gifts that song releases. If a storyteller isn't punished for telling tales but given a microphone and told to record them, she might produce childish fiction—or the tale could reveal secrets others would rather hide."

She turned to Oz. "A Malcolm boy who cries in sympathy with others should be encouraged to explain how he's feeling, because it's likely he has more empathic receptors in his brain than normal."

"Bunk," Oz said shortly.

Excited, Pippa ignored him. "I read about that study! It said empathy was physiological, that it related to receptors in the brain that register some chemical. The more receptors someone has, the more empathic they are. Which is why some people are concerned for others besides themselves, while the nonempaths seem self-absorbed—because they don't register the feelings of anyone except themselves. I bet if a child is rewarded for his empathy, he'd learn to use it even more."

She turned to Oz and poked him in the side. "It was on the news. And I read about it online. It's real. It's scientific."

His lip curled sardonically. "Fine. *Star Trek* lives. There are empaths out there. What does this have to do with my son?"

"If he's a Malcolm, he may have an extra ability you're not aware of," Jean said with a trace of sympathy. "And I know this sounds ridiculous even to me, but he may have been taken because of that talent. Alys registered his name on the website."

An extra ability?

The woman was obviously a basket case. She couldn't know anything about Donal. Oz clenched his fingers, desperately trying not to hope.

But the Librarian had led him to Jean. And to Pippa—who was a Malcolm and claimed to have a strange gift. He remained dubious until facts were proven, but... It looked like if he wanted to find his son, he might have to start believing in magic. Or psychics. Same difference.

"What website?" he demanded. He needed something concrete. Factual. If only to prove he wasn't losing sight of reality.

"Even going on that site could be dangerous," Jean warned, removing a pen from a small shoulder purse. "The Librarian watches it but apparently has no way of shutting it down. The home page places cookies on your computer. It's helpful for family members looking for family, but it's also available to those who think Malcolms can give them an advantage. As I have learned to my sorrow, power corrupts."

She wrote the domain name on a napkin and shoved it across the table. "I'd advise using caution before accessing it, especially if there's any chance you're related to a Malcolm."

Oz clicked on his phone and rang Conan. "What have you found out?" he demanded when his brother answered.

Pippa leaned into his side, and he lifted the phone away from his ear so she could snuggle under his arm and listen too. He would worry about the comfort of her familiarity later, when he wasn't ready to implode.

"I'm still tracing cookies," Conan replied, as if he'd tuned into their conversation. Pippa stiffened, and Oz went on alert. "There's an odd one on here," Conan continued. "I've isolated it, and I think it tracks to her online storage. If I'm right, someone knows how to access her account. No proof yet. I need more time."

Pippa growled, and Oz thought his hair ought to stand on end at the sound. He hugged her closer.

"So it's possible the computer is bugged?" he asked for clarification.

"Possible, yes. I'm thinking of paying the store a visit."

"I've got another lead, this time to Donal. It's a website. Get out your keyboard but don't access it yet." Knowing his brother kept notes on his computer, he waited for Conan to find a digital notepad before giving him the genealogy website address. "My source says someone may be using that website to track kids. And maybe worse. Don't use any traceable access."

Conan whistled. "Got it. You're good, bro. Don't suppose I could talk to this source?"

"Not yet. Just tell me what you find first."

Oz closed the line and dropped the cell back in his pocket, aware both women were hanging on his every word. He turned to Pippa. "Did you ever go to that website?"

Her eyes grew huge. "At one point, probably. Years ago, I tried to do my own search on my family."

"Back before you bought the new computer?"

She nodded, frowning as she tried to recall. "Back when I only had one computer for business and…" She cast the stranger an uneasy look. "The other. I was on an email list." She smacked herself upside the head. "I was isolated and looking for company, and the online community of Malcolms was the family I didn't have. I even asked where to go to back up my computer and how to transfer my files."

"So you went to a store recommended by someone on this website?" he asked in incredulity. "Use your head much?"

"Bite me, Oswin." She sat up straight and grabbed her cup.

He missed her breasts pressed into his side, but she was seriously messing with his mind. He needed distance to think clearer. Not that he wanted to think clearly as the puzzle fell together and gave him cold shudders, but someone had to use his head.

"You say the Librarian has access to the website?" he asked the woman watching them from across the table.

"And is very adept at tracking us," Jean agreed.

"And she may know where Donal is?"

Jean looked thoughtful. "It's hard to say. I think she wants me to help you find him."

"That makes no sense," Pippa protested. "She could just tell us what she knows."

Oz shook his head. "Not if she doesn't know any more than she's telling us or if someone is reading her mail. The messages I've been receiving are innocuous if anyone looked at them. She could be a mental patient in a hospital for all we know."

The woman with the faded turquoise eyes stared at him with hope, as if he could make magic. And his *empathy* knew who she was. It was written all over her anxious face.

No matter how impossible it might seem, they were sitting in a booth with Pippa's mother, who was afraid to reveal her identity—because she feared invisible villains might be tracking Malcolms like her daughter.

Malcolms, like his son.

Oz's great-grandmother on his mother's side was a Malcolm.

Chapter 22

Pippa picked at the slices of old melon the waitress delivered, but her head was too confused to care if she ate or not.

Somewhere out there, I have a family.

She was sitting across the table from a woman who had just opened a world she had desperately sought all her life—a family with turquoise eyes and weird gifts. One where she might fit in, one who might actually want her and accept her as she was, warts and all.

She didn't know how to feel. She'd spent so long teaching herself numbness that she was terrified to feel joy. She didn't trust happiness. She was one sick, pathetic excuse for a human being. Maybe, if she could believe this woman really was family...

Could that possibly mean that she had a mother somewhere who had trained her to access her Voice? Did that mean it wasn't evil? Or on the flip side—had her mother thought she was evil and that's why she'd been abandoned?

That was just the very tip of the iceberg of questions she sat on and the reason she couldn't jump for joy just yet.

She feared she'd choke on the subjects threatening to tumble out in confusion and that she'd say something that would drive this one connection to her family fleeing into the night.

"Conan can investigate the store and website," Oz said in that take-charge manner that would have irritated her, except she was too paralyzed to object. "We need to find a place for Mrs. Wainwright to stay. It's too late to check her in at the B&B. What if I give her the key to my room, and I stay with you?"

Not a choice guaranteed to jar her into action. She had one bed. He wanted to share it.

"You could go back to L.A.," Pippa managed to say in a dead tone that shouldn't drive anyone off a cliff.

"I'd rather not. It's late. Your place is closer. And by morning, we'll have a dozen more questions to share. I've got half the production crew setting up on Monday, so we need to work quickly."

His son. Oz wanted to find his son. She understood the urgency. If she made it all about the boy—she could do this. Wrapping her defensive shield tightly around her, she nodded. "Rest is good. Can Conan find some way of giving Mrs. Wainwright—"

"Jean, dear. No one has called me Wainwright in a thousand years."

"Jean." The name felt wrong, but Pippa tried to stay on track. Too many lions and tigers and bears lurked beyond the yellow brick road. Stick to the known. "Jean needs a new identity if she feels she's in danger." Another of those unasked questions. Why might she be in danger? Who had driven her car off the road?

"One of those things we need to consider. Let's go where we can talk privately." Impatiently, Oz laid a large bill on the table, caught Pippa's hand, and dragged her from the booth.

She wanted to shake him off or throw him over her

shoulder as she would have a week ago. But she thought he might be part of the road she needed to follow right now, so she stupidly clutched his fingers. Maybe he needed this grounding as much as she did. His emotions had to be as volatile as hers, but he expressed them with action. While she did the opposite. She almost smirked at that realization.

Oz assisted Jean from the booth and offered his arm for her to lean on. She declined.

"The doctors say the muscles are atrophied. I'm determined to exercise them." She walked with dignity through the empty diner, one step ahead of them, using her cane only for balance. What had happened to her?

So many questions… Donal. Stick to the boy. Pippa waited until they were back in the car with no prying ears to hear. "Do you know why the Librarian mentioned a song that doesn't exist?" she asked neutrally once everyone was in their seats and buckling up.

"The song exists if the Librarian knows about it," Jean said. "If you don't know it, then we need to find it. Perhaps there's a clue in it."

No clue that Pippa knew of. It was a song of loneliness and abandon, with a humorous ending for the sake of any child who might listen.

"The two of you are dancing around each other, playing games, while my son might be held by a lunatic!" Oz interjected angrily, hitting the gas and peeling out of the parking lot. "I understand Jean is trying to protect us, but until *all* the facts are on the table, we can't move forward. No one can hear us here. So let's get talking, ladies. Jean, how do you know the crash that harmed you was deliberate?"

"Quit bullying," Pippa muttered. "We don't have to tell you anything."

"I'm betting I know a damned sight more than either of you, and if I hadn't bullied you out of your cave, you wouldn't be this far down the road of knowledge," he countered.

"If I'd stayed home, I wouldn't be out in the desert fearing we're being stalked by maniacs!" Pippa knew that was irrational and that she was in danger of venting her Voice in the confines of a car. That could be deadly, as she knew too well. She shut up and fought her frustration internally.

Jean began singing "Amazing Grace" in a pleasant soft soprano.

Just those few bars, and Pippa's frozen shield dissolved, evaporating like a mirage in the desert. Some internal key unlocked, and she saw the world with the wonder of a child, memories of comfort and security tumbling free so vividly that they brought tears to her eyes.

Pippa hummed the last few bars with her eyes closed, tears rolling down her cheeks. The moment was so familiar...

"Let the bad feelings go," Jean sang with the tune. "Let grace lead you home."

"I always thought Grace was a nanny like Mary Poppins," Pippa said, without thought. Then covered her mouth in shock. Had *she* said that?

"I hope your bully knows what he's doing," Jean said quietly, her voice tired. "You loved watching *Mary Poppins*. It's the only movie you ever asked for."

How could a stranger know—?

The familiar voice, the beloved song—

Wrenched back from that brief moment of security, Pippa crash-landed in reality.

Jean Wainwright was not only a turquoise-eyed Malcolm, but her *mother*? Or an aunt. Family. She had known Pippa before... the crash?

The crash. The blazing fire against the sky—

Oh my God...

"Amazing Grace, how sweet the sound..."

The music was in Pippa's head, swirling around, crashing like breakers on the shore, crumpling, pounding—

"Oh God, oh, please, I can't—" Pippa keened, holding both hands to her head to quiet the screams that familiar voice and song now invoked. "*Nooooo!*"

At her cry, Oz slammed on the brakes and swerved the card to the side of the road.

Pippa heard the tires squealing. The frantic cursing. She shook with the force of the images flashing across her memory. *Fire!* Smoke! Belching black smoke. Terror—

Strong hands grabbed her, yanking her out of the leather seat and across the console in a masterful triumph over gravity. She couldn't hold back her hysterical, high-pitched keen. She was trembling so hard she couldn't fight him.

"Pippa! Pippa, it's okay. Let it go. Sing a lullaby." Oz's familiar baritone broke through the flaming film playing in her mind. He rocked her, pushing the seat back and holding her in his lap. Holding. Comforting. "Sing something!"

She didn't know if the order was for her or for—

She couldn't think it. Couldn't believe it. The fire! And screams—

She wept, trembling and burying her face in Oz's jacket, desperately blocking out the terrifying shrieks of horror and anguish. Only his arms around her held her together.

"Siren, honey, it's all right," the motherly voice soothed, not screamed. From her head? From the backseat. "Siren, baby, it's okay. Come back. I'm here."

Oz hugged her, holding tight so she didn't fall to pieces as the words seeped into the panic rampaging through her head. *Siren*. The heartbroken scream wailed her name. *Sirennnnnn*.

Her keening turned to sobs. She was Siren. Siren had died. Siren had died that awful night, in billows of black smoke and flame.

Syrene had died the same way, on a different night. No, not Syrene. *Robbie*. Robbie had died the way Siren had died. Crashing, tumbling, in an explosion of pain...

She wept so hard she didn't think she could stop. Didn't want to stop. Didn't want to face—

"Pippa, I'm about to bully you," Oz's voice warned from somewhere in the world outside her head. "The cops are going to check us out if I don't get this rig moving. Your mother is alive. You're alive. Whatever film you're running in your head now, replace it with *Mary Poppins*. Sing 'A Spoonful of Sugar' or something sappy. We need to get you home."

Despite his stern voice, he rocked her, comforting her like a small child.

Pippa choked on a sob and a laugh as "A Spoonful of Sugar" piped from the backseat. The fiery images receded, replaced by the solidity of Oz's arms. She locked the horrors inside their box, rested her head against his broad shoulder, and decided she'd never be able to face him again. She was a coward who couldn't let go. She feared the images would return.

"I'm so sorry," Jean whispered, faltering over the words to the song. "It's been nearly twenty-five years, and I still see you as a toddler. I want to hug you and hold you so much—" Her voice broke with tears.

"I think you've got some catching up to do. C'mon, sweetheart, let's get you buckled in again."

Pippa reluctantly released him when he tried to lift her. Clumsily, she scrambled back to her seat, wiping her wet cheeks with the back of her hand, fumbling for the seat belt.

"I'm sorry," Pippa murmured. "I saw—oh, God." She scrubbed her eyes again, refusing to look in the backseat. "I can't say it. You're a ghost. You can't be real. I've finally gone around the bend."

"Nah, you're just a natural-born hysteric," Oz said with a hint of humor as he pulled the car back on the freeway. "You'd be a great actress if you could harness that passion and use it."

"Mr. Oswin!" Jean shouted, shocked at his rudeness.

Pippa almost smiled, amazed at how quickly he could recover from drowning in tears. "It's all right. He's being a bully again. He does it for my own good, I think. If I take my rage out on him, I'm not hurting myself or anyone else."

Which was an amazing freedom in and of itself, she realized. She could scream all her fury and fear at Oz, and they rolled right off his back. She couldn't kill him with her pain.

"Nah," Oz objected. "I do it because it's fun. And if you hit me, I get to call the shots later."

In bed. She blushed. If Jean Wainwright was really her mother... She punched Oz's bulging bicep. He didn't flinch. It was a weak punch anyway. She was still too shattered to function.

"He understands then?" Jean asked dubiously. "I learned to shield myself from your cries, but my grandmother had to teach me. Your father... Your father never learned," she finished with a sigh of regret.

"I drove him away?" Pippa asked, suddenly frozen in terror again. "It was my fault—"

"That we drove off a cliff? Horrors, no child! You were sound asleep in your car seat. A semi rear-ended us. Your father tried to accelerate and get away, but the driver kept ramming us. Your father was a policeman who caught drug dealers. This time, they caught us. We didn't have a chance. I've been hiding from them ever since I was released from the nursing home."

"You think they may still be after you?" Oz asked warily. "Why?"

"I'm hoping they've forgotten me by now," she answered wearily. "But Jordie and I worked as a team. I lured the dealers with my Voice and helped my husband trap them. It's not wise to let criminals know what I can do, although I'm not anywhere as talented as Siren."

The disembodied voice of Pippa's long-lost mother rising from the backseat was disconcerting enough without adding the experience of riding in a luxurious car sailing down the highway, past shadowy boulders and a barren nightscape, speaking of drug dealers and weird gifts. It was too surreal. Like a dream from which she couldn't wake.

"Your name isn't really Jean?" Pippa asked, straining for a memory—and normalcy.

"Like you, I have a lot of names. Your father called me Gloria. Gloria Jean Wainwright Malcolm. We met at a family reunion and were distantly related, but he was all logic and science."

Her father. She'd had a real father.

"Don't think about it, Pippa," Oz suggested. "You've had too much for one night. We'll be in El Padre shortly. Sleep on it."

"But what about Donal?" She found the yellow brick road again, found her footing. The bears might still be out there in the night, but they hadn't caught her yet. Oz was at the end of the road. She muffled a laugh at the fantasy conjured by his name. She ought to write a book.

"I can't tell you where Donal is," Jean—Gloria—said sadly. "Four years ago, I heard the seal song. That's the reason the Librarian thinks we can help. That's why I've come out of hiding. The seal song is what my grandmother called a siren song. And it's designed to call children."

Silence fell inside the car as they digested this unreal and explosive new suggestion.

"No arguing," Oz told Pippa after he'd settled Gloria Jean into his room at the B&B. The older woman had been too exhausted for them to torture her with more questions. He steered the Mercedes toward the day care. "I'm not leaving you alone tonight, and I'm not asking any more of you than a pillow for my head."

It was costing him to say that. He wanted to drag her to a microphone and set her loose with that damned song in front of an audience of every child in the country to see what happened.

But the steel-spined Pippa he'd come to know looked so broken. He'd have to be more of a heel than he already was to push her more. He didn't know what in hell had happened back there, but he'd been terrified he'd almost lost her.

And it mattered. Losing her mattered big time. Oz didn't want anyone or anything to matter again, but Pippa had somehow grabbed him by the throat. She was this beautiful gossamer work of art that currently occupied his sky, fascinating him, and he didn't want her dashed to the ground.

So he was taking this one cautious step at a time, keeping an eye on the prevailing wind until he had her safely reeled back.

"Do you think this is all some elaborate hoax?" she whispered.

"Could be. Doubt it, though. Did you have some kind of flashback when she started singing?" His heartbeat still hadn't settled down after that terrifying moment when she'd begun keening and shaking. She'd done that once before, when he'd first called her Syrene. This time, she hadn't come up fighting. And that's what had terrified him.

He could scarcely see the pale patch of her nape above the hoodie as she stared at her hands in her lap. He could almost *feel* her pain. He grimaced at recalling Gloria's pointed message about empathy. The woman had to be a witch. Even he'd never consciously realized he could sense the emotions of others. It might explain a lot, if he thought about it. But Pippa came first.

"I saw the car exploding."

She spoke so softly he barely heard her, but the words were enough to send his mind reeling. "You *saw* it? How old could you have been? Three?"

"I guess. I don't know my real birthday. But I remember. I remembered the song, the way she changed the words, and it was like unlocking a box where I'd stored all the memories, the good ones and bad ones both, because I couldn't handle the bad ones, the smoke, the flames, the horrible..." She shuddered. "The screams. I don't know how anyone could have survived."

"You can't remember accurately after all these years. Gloria said you were rear-ended. There might have been time for everyone to escape before the gas tank burst. Cars usually don't explode like they do in movies. We'll have to ask her in the morning."

"She's real, isn't she? I'm not imagining this? I do that sometimes when I'm writing."

"You imagine talking turtles when you write?" he asked in amusement, parking the car near the walk down to her house. "Do you need to go to your studio, or are you wound down enough for bed?"

Her head snapped up, and her luminous eyes nearly glowed in the dark. "I'm okay," she said in wonder. "I think I'm okay. You have no idea how long it's been... Let's go to bed."

Exactly what he wanted.

Exactly what he shouldn't do—get mixed up with another whacked-out woman who thought villains were after her.

Chapter 23

Fighting his doubts, Oz unzipped his jacket as he followed Pippa inside her bungalow. He dropped it over the cushions of her flowery orange couch, decided the black looked out of place against the feminine colors, and looked for a place to hang it.

Pippa sailed toward the bedroom, disregarding his discomfort. Women generally hung around him, taking his coat, offering him drinks, looking after him. Pippa—Siren?—just assumed he could take care of himself. She was right, but the experience was a little disconcerting, especially after the evening's pyrotechnics.

Finding a tiny closet off the hall, he hung up the jacket and then used the guest facilities, giving Pippa time to herself. Finding her mother in the desert had to be difficult emotionally. He already knew she had problems dealing with emotion. If her memory of that night really had come back, the trauma had to be overwhelming.

He probably shouldn't be here, but the instinct—or empathy—he relied on to build his business said she shouldn't be left alone.

His crass logic wondered if Gloria Jean counted as his finding Pippa's family so she had to do the show. More than ever, he was realizing he needed Pippa, not some substitute, if he meant to find Donal.

Receiving no signals one way or another from his hostess, Oz wandered back to her bedroom and heard the shower running. Which immediately conjured images of Pippa, naked, that steered his course of action. They both needed a good dose of reality, and there was nothing more real than sex. He flung off his shirt and began unfastening his jeans. Entering the steamy bathroom and seeing her slender back through the clear glass shower brought his prick straight to attention.

She didn't look up as he entered the bathroom. The thickness of her silence warned she'd retreated to that cave she'd been hiding in for years. He had a few ideas on how to drag her out again.

Dropping the rest of his clothes on her tile floor, he joined her in the spacious shower with its double showerheads. She kept her back to him. He helped himself to the Irish Spring, grateful she didn't use one of those perfumed soaps that would leave him smelling like a bordello.

Oz sudsed his hands, reached around her, and began bathing her breasts. She jerked in startlement. Before she had time to fight, he pressed his arousal against her buttocks while soaping the pert nipples begging for notice.

"Yesterday, I let you take charge," he murmured, rubbing the soap lower. "Tonight is mine."

"No, I can't. *We* can't." She whipped her head back and forth, wriggling in his embrace.

"Tell me that again later. Right now, your brain is so full of boogeymen that you won't sleep anyway. Let's just relax and see where this goes." He dipped his hand between her legs, and she groaned, threw back her head, and opened for him.

Pippa cried out in frustration after Oz teased and aroused her into acceptance and then stopped his lavish attentions to turn off the water. She pounded his back when he played Neanderthal and hauled her into his arms to carry her from the steamy shower fantasy.

"What are you doing? Put me down, you lumphead." She grabbed at a towel as they passed by the bar.

"Pardon me for thinking of your comfort, but a tile wall does not constitute a soft mattress." He strode the few yards to her bed and dropped her on it.

She'd only lit a small bed lamp earlier, but it was enough to highlight the powerful planes of Oz's torso and thighs as he remained standing, gazing down at her with smug male satisfaction.

She wanted sex, not admiration. She scrambled up, intent on stripping the quilt back to the sheets. Oz reached for a bottle of expensive moisturizer she kept beside the bed.

Eyes widening, she pushed the cover off with her feet and retreated against the pillows propped on the wall. "That's for my face," she warned.

His grin was wicked and sexy beyond measure as he poured the cream into his palm. "So I'll rub your cheeks. Turn over."

"No! I hate massages." She didn't know why she was being so obstinate except she hated taking orders and not being in charge. Which was his point, apparently.

His erection could compete with a stallion's. What did the damned man think he was doing by slowing down what could have been a great slam-bang moment? "I don't like people touching me," she warned.

"Tough." He wrapped a big arm around her waist

and flipped her over before she could believe he would dare. Kneeling over her thighs, he prevented her from rolling off the other side. "My turn, remember? I get to call the shots."

He pressed the heels of his hands into her shoulder blades, pinning her to the bed. She could throw him. She knew how. But he began spreading the warm lotion over her back, kneading knotted muscles, and she couldn't summon the energy to continue their power struggle.

"No going to sleep on me," he warned, rubbing circles at her lower back, then slipping lower. "We're just getting started here."

Pippa buried a moan in her pillow as he stroked and teased her buttocks with deft hands. She was damned ready to fall apart, and he hadn't done anything except *touch* her. She'd never been this easy.

When he began massaging her thighs without touching where she ached, she bit the pillow in growing frustration.

"You're too quiet," he chided. "You don't have to be quiet for me. Scream, if you like. It's music to my ears."

"You bastard—" She flipped over so fast, she nearly tossed him off.

He recovered his balance rapidly, shoving his knee between her legs and holding her shoulders down while he leaned over and covered her mouth with his.

She grabbed his surfer's locks, swearing she would pull them out. Instead, she merely gripped his hair and let his tongue possess her mouth so thoroughly she couldn't have screamed if she'd wanted.

She arched into him, demanding satisfaction, but he took his time. The delicate rose fragrance of the lotion wafted around them as he stroked her face and buried his hands in her hair. She could taste the coffee on his breath and feel the stubble scraping her face, and still she struggled for more.

She *needed* his touch, this reality. She needed whiskers and coffee and lumpy knees and creased sheets and the musky scent of sex. The play of powerful biceps when she grabbed them. The surge of male arousal between her legs.

She sang out her need when he turned his greedy mouth to her breasts. She pleaded and gasped and writhed and came alive. The cotton batting she'd wrapped herself in fell away. Oz was *real*. Solid. He didn't live only in her head. He wouldn't dissipate with the dawn.

He flipped her to her stomach again, raised her on her knees, and shoved so deep inside that she felt him rub her belly from the inside out.

And she shattered. With a wild cry, she came apart in one stroke. She shook and sobbed as he moved inside her, teasing her with his fingers, driving her higher, until she keened with desire and followed him to the stars again.

He came then, driving deep and bellowing his release as her muscles gripped him with her climax.

Before she passed out, he rolled them to their sides and spooned her securely in the curve of his big body. She didn't need the cushioning of fantasy with male muscle securely wrapped around her.

They made love again at dawn, with the birds singing their mating songs outside the window. Made love, tender love without the power struggle of sex, just two human bodies coming together naturally for comfort and pleasure.

Pippa feared she could become too used to that. She was a grown-up now. She knew desire did not equal love, that need was no foundation for a permanent relationship. But she had been denied human touch for so long that she craved it with the desperation of the starving. And Oz was apparently the only man in the world who could withstand her Voice.

He protested when she rolled from the bed later. His bronze shoulders and big body took more than his fair share of her double bed. His feet hung off the end. His hair stuck up in a cowlick in back, and she grinned. Perfection had flaws.

She locked the bathroom door behind her, removing the opportunity for any more seduction. She needed a clear head to face the day.

She showered again, donned her robe, and left him to stagger out of bed while she squeezed fresh oranges in the kitchen.

The day was going to be a warm one. She wandered out to the pool, sipping juice and soaking up the sunshine. She wondered what her mother was doing.

Her *mother*. She played with the word, mashing it around in her mind. Pippa's foster mother had encouraged Pippa to call her "Mother" when she'd gone home with them as a toddler, but she never had. She hadn't been a very loving child. She didn't think that would change now that a stranger had walked into her life claiming birthrights.

But things *had* changed. She knew someone with eyes like her own now. She was officially no longer weird. She let her mind wrap around that, absorb it, and let it settle comfortably. She wasn't a space alien. Other people had turquoise eyes. Her *family*.

Oz trailed out wearing half-buttoned jeans and no shirt, chugging the juice she'd left for him. If he thought their half-dressed states meant more sex, he was about to be disappointed—even if he did look like a wanton sun god with his burnished bronze torso and gold-streaked hair. She couldn't afford too strong an attachment.

"Singing the seal song will not return Donal," she told him, shattering any harmony that might exist between them.

"Good morning to you, too. Do I push you into the pool now?"

She couldn't stop her lips from quirking upward. "Nothing fazes you, does it?"

He gave that some thought. "All things are relative. I don't think *fazes* is a good word to describe my usual response to obstacles, so no, things don't faze me."

A man who not only looked good at dawn and gave good sex but could talk intelligently too. Pippa wondered if there were any more like him out there and where they'd been all her life.

"Have you called Conan yet?" she asked neutrally.

"Nah. He's got to sleep sometime, unlike us, apparently. He'll let us know if he finds anything. Breakfast at the café?"

His ego didn't seem deflated just because she was giving him the cold shoulder. That was good. They could maintain a safe distance.

"I can fix whole wheat waffles and strawberry compote. No bacon though. Greasy eggs or healthy food?"

"Whipped cream?" he asked hopefully.

She arched an eyebrow, turned on her heel, and returned to the kitchen. *She* wanted waffles. He could do what he liked.

Oz figured he could endure crunchy bread and syrupy fruit if it meant enjoying sunshine and Pippa's hidden smiles.

She was a real piece of work, but he was enjoying her company, perhaps a little too much. He tried to define why a prickly string bean appealed to him, but it was like trying to describe admiration for a sunbeam caught in the prism of a raindrop. He apparently had an appreciation for subtle jewels. Who knew?

They were by the pool, cleaning the last of the strawberries from their plates—Pippa had found cream cheese and sweetened it for him—when his phone rang. He'd given Gloria his number.

He checked the screen, and Thank you texted across it. The Librarian. He held the screen up for Pippa to see. Her smile dimmed a little, but she nodded understanding.

They'd done what some anonymous manipulator wanted and received gratitude in recompense. Oz wondered if there was a screenwriter in the world who could make an audience suspend disbelief for a plot this absurd.

"Do you think she's still here?" Pippa asked in that neutral voice she'd perfected to hide her fears.

"Who, Gloria? I think we're her best bet, and she's not a fool. We don't know how long she's been running and hiding. She needs her rest. Besides, the old lady at the inn is probably talking her ear off."

Pippa blessed him with another of her smiles. He liked to believe they were coming with more frequency.

"We may have to rescue her again. Amabelle doesn't know when to shut up." She carried her plate into the kitchen to rinse it off.

Oz followed, wondering if there was still some chance of getting her back in bed. Sex would take his mind off all the questions no one was answering about Donal.

That his son might still be alive was such an immense relief that he didn't dare consider it yet, much less try to believe it. He couldn't trust a crazy old woman and an anonymous messenger. It could be a scam. At some point, he'd even given up prayer. He would just keep scraping away the dirt, as always. Action was all he had.

So, what action did he take next? Sex was good but didn't find Donal. Call Conan and have his sleep-deprived brother hang up on him? Or hunt down the dotty lady at the B&B and drag information out through her tonsils? That might work.

He wasn't sure how Pippa stood on the subject of dotty ladies who might be her mother. Probably as ambivalent as she was about singing the seal song to find Donal. Which meant he had his work cut out for him.

Pippa's cell rang. He watched in curiosity as she fished it out of a pocket of the miniscule bag she'd left on the table.

She raised delicate eyebrows as she listened to the overexcited voice on the other end. If he could hear it across the room, she must be getting an earful.

When she closed the phone, she gave him a look rich with implication.

"That was the pastor of the church. It seems your crew is measuring the auditorium. And oddly enough, this is Sunday."

Chapter 24

FINISHED WITH THE DISHES, PIPPA FOLLOWED OZ outside to the pool while he employed his masterly phone skills in connecting all the right people to pull the clueless crew out of a church about to fill with Sunday morning parishioners.

He'd retrieved his suitcase from the car and donned a white, open-necked, pullover linen shirt, very Hollywood, before breakfast. It was probably meant to be tucked into slacks, but he'd stuck with his jeans, so he had an L.A./surfer look happening. Business professional to good ol' boy in ten seconds flat. She wasn't certain where the real Oz fell on that spectrum.

He just looked so spectacularly at home that she couldn't help sitting back and admiring. So she adopted her lotus pose and attempted to find her center while he paced back and forth.

She wasn't too successful. Somewhere over the last few days, she'd lost her center. She felt as if she were floating in outer space, or maybe cyberspace, untethered. Everything she believed was no longer true.

She'd used her Voice, and Oz hadn't keeled over dead. She'd actually used it to *help* a little. Such a leap shattered the world she'd built around herself without adding all the other complications.

She had a mother. Maybe. And more family, somewhere. Pippa wasn't too clear on how Oz's son was involved.

Or why she hadn't been killed in the accident. But she was very clear that some wretched stranger had access to her musical library, her thoughts, her soul. And apparently her pain hadn't killed anyone who had listened to her songs. Which put her right back where she started—was she wrong about her Voice?

Oz shoved his phone back in his pocket and watched her warily.

"Now does one of us throw the other in the pool?" Pippa asked with curiosity.

He grinned, the masculine angles of his face lightening as if the sun came from within. "There are better things to do in a pool besides fight."

"I don't suppose you're talking about swimming?" She arched an eyebrow, if only to fight back the butterflies swarming in her midsection when he looked at her like that.

"Is the pool heated?" He strode over to the pole with the pool's electrical equipment box.

"Nice thought, Oswin, but we have more important things to do with the day. Did you pull your overeager techies out of the church?" The butterflies were most likely because she had a sinking feeling that now that Oz had found her mother, he expected her to go on a stage and read books and sing in front of an audience. And it wasn't happening.

But she'd promised... She didn't have real, official proof that Gloria was her mother, but she knew in her heart—*she had a mother again*. She was trying to be wary, but joy and excitement kept intruding. Gloria believed in her Voice. Or she was scamming her.

Whatever. Oz had found her mother, and he deserved

to have his son back in return. Pippa didn't know how to fix that. Or if she even ought to believe Gloria that Donal was alive. Mixing cynicism with hope was a Molotov cocktail for sanity.

"The crew has been unemployed for a while," Oz said. "They're eager to do a good job. I've sent them scouting the town for possible set design. You don't turn the pool's heater on?" He flipped a switch inside the box and strode back toward her with a decidedly heated look.

"Wastes energy." Rather than waste more of hers, Pippa swung her legs over the side of the lounge, stood, and strode for the house. "I want to talk to Gloria. There are no cliffs near Bakersfield. I was abandoned in Bakersfield."

She might not have found her center, but she had her focus. She didn't want Gloria to be a liar, if only for the sake of Oz's son. But it was better to find out now, before their hopes climbed.

"Drive or walk?" he asked as she grabbed her purse and headed for the front door.

They were on the brink of a showdown every minute he believed she would let Syrene stand in front of a national audience, much less use her Voice.

There had to be some other way of finding his son. And Gloria had all the clues.

"Let's walk. It's only half a mile into town. Your legs won't fall off." That was snarky. He'd been walking back and forth without showing a bit of effort, but she needed distance.

Oz fell easily into stride with her, shortening his loping gait to hers. It felt extremely odd—almost intimate—to have anyone accompany her up the garden path and into town. She was used to being alone.

It felt even odder that he was tall and wide and formidable. She could see where women would fall into the fallacy of relying on big men to take care of them. She knew better these days.

She just needed to realign her thinking. He was there for his son. She was simply an impersonal cog in the wheel of his search. She could live with that.

They found Gloria sitting at an ironwork table on the B&B's stone terrace, her hands folded in her lap as she gazed at the pots of blooming daffodils and tulips Amabelle had gathered on the wall. Or perhaps she listened to the blackbirds arguing in the evergreens.

She looked up and smiled at them, although the smile didn't quite reach her eyes. Pain was still etched too thoroughly there, although Pippa thought she saw excitement too. Or maybe Gloria simply reflected Pippa's confused feelings.

"I didn't want to disturb you," Gloria said in a warm contralto. "I've disturbed your weekend enough as it is."

"Disturbed?" Pippa said, waving off Amabelle who had appeared at the back door bearing a tray. "I've possibly found my family and been told we could be an endangered species, and I'm so far beyond disturbed that I don't think there's a word for it."

Oz pulled a chair out for her. "You could sing about it," he suggested, his voice warm with humor.

"Don't even go there." Pippa took the chair and scraped it across the stones to the table. She was becoming too bold about expressing herself around him. She moderated her voice with a sigh of impatience. "I'm sorry. This is an impossible situation, and I'm not used to dealing with people much anymore."

Gloria studied her with warm concern. "For years, I lived with the grief of believing you had died with your father. I isolated myself as much as the nursing home did. My hands and legs were so useless that it was easier to lose myself in audiobooks than bother with the outside world. I missed your teenage years.

"Living in Mexico these past six years after my release from the home, I didn't immediately pick up the habit of listening to TV or radio, not until I'd refreshed my Spanish. Several times, I caught hauntingly familiar refrains, but the memories were too painful to consider. I'd last heard you as a toddler, so I convinced myself I was imagining things. Your range is so much more mature now! I preferred to think I was hallucinating. Not until about four years ago, when the Librarian sent me a few of your recordings and a picture did I dare believe, and by then you'd completely disappeared. We both may need sedatives to survive this."

Pippa ran her hand over her shorn hair, tugging at the roots to stay grounded. "I was found in Bakersfield. There are no cliffs in Bakersfield. I may not be who you think I am."

Gloria smiled and gently patted Pippa's hand. "Your grandmother christened you Siren after we discovered your talent. You had a voice so crystal pure that it made grown men weep."

"Siren," Pippa half-laughed at the irony. "I told the firemen my name was Philippa Siren Malcolm, not Seraphina, right? And they misunderstood. There's nothing seraphic about me."

"I'll never admit that your voice is anything short of angelic," Gloria said, "although I'll agree that you could scale the hide off a bull when angry. And if you didn't get your own way, you became very angry. I wish I had been there to help you learn how to deal with your passions. Your foster parents had their hands full."

Pippa buried her face in her hands. Having planted his chair close, Oz rubbed her shoulders but blissfully stayed out of this. He had to be bursting with impatience, but he put her needs first, understanding she needed reassurance. Because he was *empathic*? If Donal was a Malcolm, did that mean Oz was a weird Malcolm too? She was avoiding the topic.

"I should probably give the Jameses awards for patience," Pippa agreed, weary from information overload. "But they took half of everything I made, so they didn't come out too badly."

"Half?" Oz jerked as she hit on one of his business buttons. But he pulled back, muttering something about *greedy bastards*.

She didn't even bother glancing at him for fear of distraction. "I can see the flames of the car crash in my head. I don't see how anyone survived. Where were we?"

"On the coast highway." Gloria pushed her water glass around, creating a wet circle on the table. "Mountain on one side, rocks and cliff on the other. Jordie hung on as long as he could, until we were almost past the worst of the cliffs, where the slope was more gradual."

Pippa wished she had somewhere to put her hands. She shouldn't have waved Amabelle away, but she hadn't wanted anyone around, either. She dug her fingers into her scalp and tried to keep it real. Her father's name was *Jordie*. Jordie Malcolm.

"Twenty-four years ago, air bags weren't what they are today. I don't know what happened to his seat belt. He tried to keep the car from overturning as we went down the embankment, but when we smashed into the rocks, he went through the window." Gloria looked wistful. "He was a brave, wonderful man. I wish you'd had more of a chance to know him."

Tears leaked down Pippa's cheeks at the horror described. She rubbed them away, but she didn't dare speak.

As if understanding, Gloria continued. "You were screaming. The car was crumpled all around us. I couldn't move my legs. The semi must have gone on, but I don't remember. I told you to get out of your seat. And you must have."

Pippa kept shaking her head, not recalling any of this, grateful that she couldn't. Oz squeezed her knee beneath the table, reminding her that he was there, that she could fall into his arms and scream later. That helped.

She ought to go to her studio and let all the pain and confusion loose and not rely on Oz. But she needed the comfort of his steady strength just to survive this moment.

"I don't know how I crawled out of the car, but I must have," Gloria continued. "I remember it bursting into flames and screaming my voice raw. My legs were burned. I didn't know if you'd escaped. I couldn't see you. And then I passed out. The next thing I remember is the hospital and being told my husband was dead and that I'd been comatose for months."

"Months?" Pippa asked weakly. She tried to picture it all in her head, but she had no memory of being removed from that flaming scene. Cars must have stopped. The PCH was a busy highway. Someone had to have seen the fire. The ambulance would have come much later. By then, had she been spirited away? Why?

"When I woke up, I wasn't in a mental state capable of more than surviving," Gloria said softly. "I regret that. Maybe if I'd been able to ask questions, demand to know what happened to you, the police might have looked harder. But I was heavily sedated for so long... I don't even know how long. I was living off the state. If we had insurance, it expired before I was even aware enough to question. Sedation is the medication of choice in those places. It was years before I finally received disability, moved to an assisted living center, and regained enough sense to begin looking for answers. But I was still partially paralyzed. Communication was difficult. And so I cut myself off from the world—and you."

Pippa fought the sobs. She was good at fighting pain, but this was too raw, too real. Her mother had been alive all these years, alive and suffering while she'd been taking a road to glory. And self-destructing.

Oz returned with tall glasses of tomato juice. She hadn't even known he'd left. He set one firmly in front of her. "Drink. The past is done. Let's figure out the future."

"No alcohol," she warned, afraid to accept his offering.

"No alcohol," he agreed. "Herbs, seasonings, maybe some fizzy water. Anything to make tomatoes potable." He wrinkled his nose in distaste.

Pippa tasted the celery stalk and nodded approval. Gloria looked exhausted and as if she needed vodka, but she gallantly sipped the juice.

"How can we figure out the future if none of this makes sense?" Pippa demanded, relieved to be released from the spell of her mother's tale.

Oz looked grim as he turned to Gloria. "Did you hide because of drug dealers or because of the Librarian's warnings about that website?"

"Both," she said wearily. "Toward the end of my stay in the home, when I finally summoned the ability to learn the computer, I checked that website. Shortly after, a man showed up, asking questions. And the Librarian sent me an email telling me to get out."

"Then, if we want to believe that someone is tracking Malcolms," Oz said, "they should be coming after me and my family. Half the family tree is Malcolms." He threw back a gulp of his juice.

Pippa assumed he'd added alcohol to his concoction, and she couldn't object. Her horror was magnified by his confession—*Malcolms* were the missing link between her and Donal?

He set the glass down and resumed his seat, sitting forward and suddenly taking charge of the conversation. "You said you've known about Pippa for four years. How did you find out?"

"The Librarian, dear," Gloria said gently. "After I called you to come get Donal after your wife died in Mexico, the Librarian rewarded me by sending me Pippa's songs. She apparently believed Syrene might be my missing daughter, and she stole your recordings somehow. I recognized the seal song immediately. I gave you a stuffed seal when you were only a baby and told you about the selkies. It was one of your favorite stories."

Pippa's brain went into overload. Gloria had *called*

Oz? Her mother had been the mysterious woman who had saved Donal the first time?

Pippa shoved back her chair and stalked away.

Oz pulled out his BlackBerry and began punching buttons.

Looking bewildered, Gloria sipped her juice.

Chapter 25

WHEN CONAN ARRIVED AT PIPPA'S HOUSE TO RETURN her computer, he walked in the front door as Oz had instructed. Buzzed by his brother's story of Malcolms and sirens and a mysterious connection to their family, he was ready to sit through operas if necessary to find out more. Unlike Oz, he had a secret obsession with old wives' tales about families with superpowers, for reasons he wasn't about to divulge to his cynical older brothers. He set the server box down on the kitchen counter and wandered to the glass doors leading to the pool where everyone had gathered.

Oz was striving to look relaxed and unconcerned, lounging in one of the chairs, sipping water with lime, and pounding on his laptop. But Conan had learned enough this past year to read the tension in his brother's stance. Oz was on full storm-warning alert, his formidable brain processing faster than a computer. If anyone made a wrong move, he would take them down before asking questions. Conan considered throwing a ball at him just to watch him go.

But the rest of the guests kept him in line. Sitting next to Oz, Pippa—Syrene—appeared as fragile as an old church window, and in a bright orange halter top and yellow capris with the sun glinting off her orange-red hair, more colorful than any dull church glass. Conan didn't have Oz's sensitivity to people, but even he could see that she wore clothes as a line of defense, letting the bright colors blind anyone from seeing the person wearing them.

She was cuddling a dirty, gray lump that might have been a stuffed animal once but lacked shape, form, and most of its fur now. The offensive bitch had a soft, vulnerable underside. He enjoyed puzzles, and she was a fascinating enigma.

Sitting under an umbrella at a table facing Oz and Pippa, an older woman with fading blonde hair and tired eyes watched Pippa with love and maybe disbelief. Conan wanted to hear her story too.

The other pair were just a couple of Oz's studio jerks, trying to look cool around the boss. He didn't know why they were there. Logic 101—he'd not hear any stories while they were around.

Conan pushed open the patio doors to make his presence known. Only Oz noticed, lifting a hand from the keyboard to signal the ice cooler. Score one for the man.

Helping himself to a bottle of water, Conan unscrewed the top and stood in the shade near the house while he got his bearings.

They were discussing set design. They'd dragged him up a mountain on Sunday morning to discuss cardboard cutouts? No effing way.

He considered flinging bottles of water into the pool until someone acknowledged his presence, but that was boring, and he wanted the minions out of here. And he knew just how to do it while setting the storytelling in motion at the same time.

Conan pulled out his iPod, selected a song, plugged it into his pocket speakers, and turned the volume up.

"The Silly Seal Song" tinkled from the miniature speakers. Even without amplification, Syrene's crystalline voice soared like birdsong at dawn.

Pippa, the old lady, and Oz sat up and spun around as if on wheels. The other pair only looked mildly puzzled.

Both Pippa and Oz dived for him. Conan dodged, but two against one wasn't fair. As he leaped across a lounge chair to avoid Pippa's full frontal grab for the iPod, Oz brought him down from the back. Pippa snatched the player, speakers and all, and flung them into the pool.

Laughing, Conan didn't struggle when they teamed up and tossed him into the water after his equipment.

It was good to see the old Oz back. Maybe now they'd see some action.

"No one keeled over screaming," Oz argued while Conan sprawled in a pool chair like a lizard on a rock. Pippa wanted to dump him in the water all over again, the rat-fink bastard.

The set designers had toddled off on their business. Gloria was sketching ideas for Oz's production. And Pippa paced uselessly up and down the pool tiles, feeling as if a whirlwind occupied her insides.

"He played my song! I told him not to open those files!" She picked up the towel Conan had used and swatted him with it. The rat merely opened one eyelid, gave her the evil eye, and closed it again. She hit him a second time and then threw the wet towel over his soaked khakis.

"I'll throw him in the pool again if it helps, but that's

what he does—experiments. And it worked. Your song hurt no one."

Pippa wanted to hit Oz, too, but she was rational enough to know it wasn't his fault that his brother was an interfering jackal. "We're *adults*. The song is geared for children. We don't know what effect—"

"It's a children's song, Pippa. Quit overthinking it," Gloria scolded mildly. "Be upset because he broke your trust, if you like. He deserved dunking for that alone."

"Unfair, Gloria," Conan protested from under the towel he'd placed over his face. "You've played those songs and didn't die. I want to hear about you, Mexico, Donal, and Alys."

Pippa glowered, but he had the right to hear the story if he was supposed to be investigating the case, although he didn't appear to be doing more than drying out at the moment.

"There's not much to say, dear. As soon as I was mentally and physically recovered enough, I tried to look for family on the website, and the Librarian warned me to run, that I was supposed to be dead."

Pippa had heard this once, when Oz had forced the information out of her mother earlier, but she still couldn't quite process it all. The Librarian had known who Gloria Jean Malcolm was, knew Syrene and Gloria were related...

But the all-knowing Librarian hadn't known where Syrene went. She didn't know Pippa. Or hadn't. She probably did now. Did the Librarian want to reveal Syrene's location, or was she simply trying to help Gloria find her?

"So I paid cash for a clunker," her mother obediently

continued the story, "found a driver, and moved to Mexico. I could live there on my disability checks. But I kept the email account I'd established earlier and checked it every once in a while. That's when I found the note that the Librarian was sending someone to me for protection."

"How come she could say that much to you and she can only send me Twitter notes?" Oz asked in disgust.

"These weren't long missives. Several had gathered by the time I read my mail. One said *need help*. Another later gave an address, just as you say she's done for you. It was a miracle I opened them in time."

"I don't like it," Conan said from beneath his towel. "There's too much left to chance."

"You're the expert," Pippa said, not bothering to keep the edge from her voice. "If someone's computer messages can be monitored, how much can they send without being discovered?"

"None," he said succinctly. "But if the Librarian spends all day at a computer under supervision, she may simply be sending hasty messages when someone's back is turned. I still don't like it."

Oz threw an empty water bottle at him. "We don't care what you like. The whole thing stinks."

"I failed poor Alys," Gloria said, ignoring the byplay. "I'm terrified I'll fail Siren and Donal as well by not giving you what you need to protect them."

"You saved Donal," Oz corrected. "I'm the one who lost him. What happened to Alys was completely accidental. I had her death thoroughly investigated. She was a victim of bad luck and bad driving."

"And panic. She wasn't thinking very clearly,"

Gloria admitted. "She was afraid you might be the one endangering Donal, so she didn't dare call you. She was almost hysterical when she left Donal with me. She didn't even know whether to call her family."

Pippa stopped her pacing to squeeze Oz's shoulders when he tensed. He'd already had to endure one hysterical woman in his life, one who had endangered herself and his son. He certainly didn't need a neurotic female like her around, but they were stuck in this together.

"We all react differently to danger," she murmured. "Alys tried to do the right thing."

"She should have trusted me," he said grimly.

"Like you trust others?" she asked, causing him to turn and glare. Had Alys been a passive wimp afraid to confront Oz the bully? Pippa was betting yes.

"So, how did you communicate with the Librarian?" Conan demanded, riding over the emotional interference with pragmatism.

"I didn't, dear," Gloria said, returning to her sketching. "She sent me a message akin to 'Siren lives' and attached songs, and I simply did what she asked without question after that. My daughter's voice is rather unique, you'll have noticed," she said dryly. "Once I recognized the seal song and realized I wasn't hallucinating, I couldn't deny her voice."

"Which probably means the Librarian has heard Pippa's recordings, too, and hasn't died from it," Conan asserted. "Just as millions heard them when she was a kid. All I've done is prove the new song is harmless."

"No, you didn't," Pippa said sharply, hoping he'd cringe. He didn't. "All you did was prove *some* people are immune. I already know Oz is. You may be too. My mother has taught herself to tune me out. And the set designers are adults. Until you play the song for children, you know *nothing*."

"I know the computer store where the Librarian probably stole the songs is owned by Adam Technology," Conan said, apropos of nothing.

That stopped Pippa's pacing. Even Oz quit typing to stare.

Conan lifted the towel to peer out. "Anyone heard of them?"

"Can't say that I have, dear." Gloria held her sketch up to the light to examine it and then passed it on to Oz.

Pippa wanted to jump up and down in frustration. "I will start detesting you shortly," she warned Conan. "Loathing isn't far behind."

He covered his face again. "Adam Technology also owns the website of Malcolm genealogy and the server to which you're backing up your files. Very busy people. Lots of moola. Connected to every cyberspace corporation known to mankind and maybe some I can't track on Mars, which may be where the owners live. It's not a public company, and I can't find the owners, but I'm betting your Librarian has access to their servers."

Even Gloria and Oz were staring at him now. Pippa grabbed a bottle of water, took a chair, and settled into a lotus position. Conan apparently liked attention. Oz should give him his own show. She refused to rise to his bait.

"The dates line up," Conan continued from beneath the towel. "Gloria's accident was in the news twenty-three-and-a-half years ago, to be precise. Seven-day wonder, before a missing hiker and a wildfire took over the headlines. Driver dead at the scene. Woman paralyzed and comatose. No family members to contact. No identity."

"My grandmother was a Wainwright and lived in Texas. She was old and frail, and I didn't list her as an emergency contact, so even if my purse didn't go up in flames with the car, no one would know to call her," Gloria said, returning to her sketching.

Pippa sighed and asked the obvious. "Your grandmother wasn't a Malcolm? So how did she know about my Voice?"

"Oh, she had Malcolms on her family tree too. That's how she knew you were a siren. You got it from Nana's mother. I met Jordie at a Malcolm reunion when we were both teenagers. He didn't have an ounce of talent, but he had excellent instincts as a cop."

"And your parents?" Oz asked.

"We moved to California when I was a baby so they could work with South American archeologists. They went on an expedition when I was ten and never returned." Gloria sounded ineffably sad. "I was too young to see the pattern then, but I wish I'd seen it later, when I learned Jordie was an orphan too. I didn't start making the connections until I started recovering, years after the accident—too late for everyone. Our family is disaster prone."

"Just because your accident was deliberate doesn't mean they all were," Oz said.

"Besides, how could anyone track Malcolms before there was an Internet?" Philippa protested, unwilling to believe anyone would deliberately target a widespread family, no matter what inane reason.

"Want to bet that if there is an evil villain, he's someone who knew Gloria's family, maybe even someone at one of those family reunions?" Conan asked idly. "There's always one troublemaker in every family."

"He's talking about Moron, our middle brother," Oz said, striving for humor to ease the pall.

"Moron?" Philippa had to ask. Dylan and Conan were bad enough. She couldn't imagine naming a child Moron.

Conan laughed. "Magnus. Our grandmother was nuts about using family names. She wanted to call him Mervyn. Dad had to draw the line somewhere."

"So we all have nuts on the family tree," Oz said. "I still think the pattern is random. I'm not saying I believe Malcolms have mysterious abilities, but people with talent attract attention, some of it adverse. My competitors would probably love to kill me. Pippa's managers used her talent to get rich. Jordie might even have had an empathic talent," he said that with skepticism, "that made him a good cop and got him killed, but that's all I'm seeing here. Talent has a tendency to take risks others don't."

Pippa couldn't find her center with a painful conversation like this flowing around her. Even humming wasn't helping. She could hear Oz's pain through his logic. "The news reports didn't mention me?" she asked, to divert his anguish and place it back on herself.

"Ah, she speaks to me again." Conan threw off the towel, sat up, and looked about brightly. "Does this mean your beastly Voice has freed me from its spell?"

Pippa flung her water bottle at him. He ducked and let it bounce off the wall behind him.

"I'll quit paying you, bro," Oz said ominously.

"Now there's a voice I respond to." He stood up and circled the pool to take the laptop from Oz. "You've seen the news stories. You know they don't mention any wandering toddlers at the crash site." He keyed a code in and set the machine on Pippa's lap. "But the date from the Bakersfield crap sheets report an abandoned toddler twenty-four hours after the *Times* reported the accident on the coast."

"Someone grabbed her from the side of the road?" Oz suggested as Pippa read the dates on the articles Conan had summoned. "Maybe the guys in the semi came back to make certain they'd done the deed, saw her, and didn't want any evidence wandering around."

"And she probably screamed them into letting her out a few hours down the road," Gloria said wryly. "If we could find the Librarian, we might find some answers. I don't suppose you have any magic for conjuring the invisible?" Gloria asked wistfully.

Pippa watched with suspicion as Oz's lanky brother grinned. Conan was almost as good-looking as Oz, in a more angular way, but his robot mind robbed him of Oz's personality. On Conan, a grin seemed ominous.

"I've planted my own bug in their dirty little cloud," he announced. "They're transmitting from a server in Utah. The feds are circling as we speak."

Finally, good news! Pippa tried not to get too excited, but locating the Librarian seemed essential. "Then the Librarian can lead us to Donal."

Oz looked skeptical. Pippa caught his hand, and he squeezed her fingers. To her surprise, he was the one who responded, not his attention-grabbing brother.

"The server is just a host," Oz explained. "The Librarian could be in China. Probably is, or Conan would be collaring her now. All the feds can do is check the server's records and try to trace the customers using their facilities. Even if Adam Technology owns it, they can't be blamed for what their clients are doing."

With despair, Pippa verified his explanation by the smile disappearing from Conan's face. His expression was grim. She cuddled her poor stuffed seal.

"It's only a start," Conan agreed. "The feds can trace the satellite and work from there, but most of these virus-wielding creeps are out of our reach. We can shut down their access to the server, but they pop up again somewhere else. We call it whack-a-mole."

"I really think the Librarian is trying to help us," Gloria insisted. "I'd rather you not do anything to cause her harm. She's the only connection we have."

"She may be our mole in the enemy camp," Pippa suggested. "If there is an enemy."

Oz seized on her suggestion, turning to his brother. "Can you get a message to the Librarian through your bug?"

Conan nodded warily. "Possibly. Since we have no idea what we're working with, it would have to be innocuous if we're trying not to endanger her or Donal."

Pippa didn't like the satisfied look on Oz's face before he spoke.

"Tell her we'll have a live audience for Pippa's first rehearsal in a week, as soon as we find a location."

Chapter 26

PIPPA GRABBED HER GRAY BUNDLE OF SEAL-SHAPED fur, stalked through the back garden gate, and slammed out of the pool enclosure.

"Where's she going?" Conan asked from the lounge chair he'd returned to after Oz's announcement that rehearsals were scheduled.

"To her studio, to keep from throwing me into the pool." Oz supposed he was lucky they had progressed from physical combat to the silent treatment. But if Pippa was still afraid he'd drive off a cliff if she yelled at him, he understood her silence. What he didn't understand was why she was angry.

The damned woman *knew* what they had to do. She couldn't still be objecting to singing one silly song. "I probably ought to carry the computer down to her." Oz stood, heading toward the house.

"I wouldn't, if I were you," Gloria said placidly. "She never liked being told what to do. You played that badly."

"I shouldn't have to play her at all!" Oz objected.

"You're bullying her, not leaving her any choice. Did you ask what she thought?" Gloria's placid tone took on an edge reminiscent of her daughter's.

"It's not all about you, my lad," Conan agreed mockingly.

Oz grabbed the back of his brother's lounge chair and lifted. Cushion and Conan slid straight into the pool.

Conan popped back up, flinging his soaked hair off

his brow and grinning. "It's warm in here. I think I'll stay awhile."

Flipping off the pool heater switch to cool off his know-it-all brother, Oz took the path around the house toward the day care parking lot. He didn't have to deal with a woman who drove his protective instincts into overdrive while his mind was crazed with worry about Donal. Conan had obviously retrieved Pippa's music from her computer. They could broadcast the stupid seal song if they wanted. Not that he could figure out how that would lure Donal from his kidnappers—not any more than he knew how Pippa could.

He just wanted to fix things, *now*.

And he couldn't. He couldn't do anything. He'd been helpless for a year, and just when he thought he might have a handle on things—

Damn. He still had nothing. He'd simply added Pippa to his mucked-up head—and he couldn't do shit about anything.

They were politely sitting around pools, discussing inanities, when his boy could be suffering. He needed to punch someone. Maybe he needed to let Pippa scream for him. Even a scream that shattered tall towers wouldn't be sufficient for his current rage.

He strode into town, looking for his set designers. Or trouble, whichever came first. If Pippa wasn't going to cooperate, he had no good reason to keep his crew up here. They could all go back to L.A. and their air-conditioned offices and decent restaurants. He could film at a real studio.

He'd thought Pippa understood the urgency of the situation. How could she hold out now, after hearing her mother's horror stories? After Conan had proved her songs hurt no one?

Except—Oz had seen her sing a drunk to sleep. And lure a little boy from the desert. Improbable, but he wanted to believe she was magic and could save Donal too. He wanted to believe there was something mystical about that stupid song.

He was grabbing at straws, and that frustrated him even more.

What few shops existed along the main drag were closed on Sunday. Oz strode down the street, still simmering. It was past noon, and the café was humming with after-church customers. Maybe the tavern wouldn't be busy. Chet and Jake were more likely to go for a beer than join the Sunday crowd.

"First customer of the day!" Lizzy called cheerily as Oz entered the dingy Blue Bayou.

Except it wasn't quite as dreary as it had been the other night. He glanced around, trying to pinpoint the difference. The black curtains were gone, and sunlight streamed across the scarred wooden floor and tables. Not necessarily an improvement but a more cheerful aspect, at least.

"Pizza?" she asked, when he simply stood there, wondering why he was there. "I've got a new menu!"

With nowhere better to go, he took a seat at the counter and glanced at her new menu. She'd printed it on fake antique vellum. The formatting left a lot to be desired, but it was a menu. He pointed at the pizza with the most meat on it. "I'll try this one. How's business?"

As if he couldn't tell. He turned the stool around and leaned against the counter. The window had been washed until it gleamed. The floors didn't have enough wax to sparkle, but they were peanut-shell free. Someone had put a lot of work and hope into a crappy hole-in-the-wall.

He was supposed to be bringing customers up here. Lizzy—and a lot of other people—were pinning their expectations on him. And Pippa.

It wasn't all about him. He hated it when his brothers were right.

"Business isn't bad," Lizzy said tentatively after calling the order to someone in the kitchen. "When are your people showing up?"

Never, was his ornery response. But he kept his anger to himself, unlike a certain redhead who let her displeasure be known with slamming doors and gates. Why in hell should he listen to her if she never listened to him?

"Director will be here tomorrow," he said noncommittally.

"Pippa is freezing up, isn't she?" Lizzy said, grasping his problem with surprising insight. "She hates being in the spotlight. She'd be great in our little theater, but she won't even come in and watch."

"If you know her that well, then you know she has her reasons," he said grumpily.

"Introverts don't like attention," Lizzy concurred, polishing the bar.

So even Pippa's best friend didn't know who she really was. How could she possibly hope to hide her identity and still help the town?

She hadn't expected to have to live up to her part of the bargain. She hadn't believed he would follow through on his promise to find her family. She'd meant to bow out and leave him with the books and the production and no star. He'd known that going in. He hadn't known the depth of her problem then. He still didn't grasp the whole of it, but he understood better.

Pippa really didn't want her face on television. Chances were excellent that even if he didn't use her stage name, some media bozo somewhere would recognize Syrene all grown up. Oz couldn't make any promises to the contrary. He couldn't even be certain he wouldn't use her stage name if that would get Donal back.

"Can I get you a beer?"

"Yeah, whatever's on draft." A strong one, if he had to sit here and muddle out where he was going with Pippa. He'd starve and go thirsty if he wanted any kind of relationship with a vegetarian opposed to alcohol.

Did he want a relationship with a temperamental, neurotic former child star?

A week ago, he would have said *hell, no*.

Right now, he didn't know what he wanted, except to punch someone or something. He glared at a tilting wooden booth and wondered if he could hammer it into place with his fists.

Lizzy pushed a frosty glass across the bar. "Want me to talk to her? Her heart is in the right place. She wants to help. But I think someone hurt her badly, and now she's afraid to come out of her shell."

A whole lot of someones had hurt her from what he could tell. And Pippa still fought back like a wildcat. He'd known that too. But after a few nights of great sex, he'd thought he'd tamed her. He was an idiot.

He didn't want her tamed. He wanted to unleash her

on the world as she was—brilliant, captivating, talented, and moody as a bitch. He could live with that. Pippa would never in a thousand years sneak around behind his back, steal his son, and run off to Mexico.

She was far more likely to hire the county police force, buy AK-47s, and go after the bastards on her own, without consulting him. Oz almost grinned at that.

There was his problem. Pippa didn't play well with others.

And they had opposing views on a shitload of things, but he was the negotiator. He just had to remember that she wasn't Alys. Alys had been weak and had never really accepted him as more than an ATM. She'd had her friends. He'd had his. There had been no connection on which to build trust.

He figured he could trust Pippa, but he couldn't ignore her as he had Alys, or she'd hit him upside the head. That would take some getting used to.

"Give me a hammer," he said.

Looking at him oddly, Lizzy opened a toolbox under the counter and did as told.

Setting his lips in satisfaction, Oz pounded the tilting booth back into place and looked around for more things to smack.

Without all the background music from her computer, Pippa could do no more than scream into the microphone, unleashing the Beast in all its fury.

Except this time, singing couldn't help.

Her *mother* was sitting by the pool, alone. Who knew what Conan was doing? And Oz... She strangled the wire and shrieked into the microphone until even Mars ought to hear her.

The damned man needed a golf club taken to his head. Or a baseball bat. How could he possibly expect Syrene to go on stage?

He *knew* what she could do with her Voice. He'd seen it for himself, even if he couldn't hear it. Did she need to make his crew crawl before he'd acknowledge that she really was dangerous?

How could he even think that it was safe to set her before an entire audience in some vague hope she might possibly be heard by his son, somehow, someway? It was ridiculous. Why didn't he just set a bomb in the road and see if it found Donal?

Why should she risk everything and everyone in a futile endeavor?

She knew why, but she couldn't admit it, so she screamed into the microphone until her voice was raw.

Her familiar—safe—routines were gone forever. She had a mother. And responsibilities. And "Fail" signs blinked everywhere she walked.

Dropping to the floor after half an hour of gyrating to her own music, sweat pouring from her forehead, Pippa sipped cold water from her cooler and tried to find a center of peace, but she was still off-kilter.

Shit. She held the cold bottle to her forehead to cool off.

She'd sung in concert with the best voices of her time when she was twelve. She'd filmed her first video at thirteen. She'd been on television at fourteen and touring at fifteen. She'd traveled the world.

Surely she could do one small television show

without killing anyone. Except maybe Oz. After all, she didn't have to *marry* him. So maybe she wouldn't drive him over a cliff. Just drive him to drugs. Like Robbie.

With a sigh at her own fatalism, Pippa finished off her water, threw the bottle in the recycle container, and stretched.

Oz had found her mother. The miracle had scarcely begun to sink in. She had a real *family*.

She would be an unforgivable bitch if she didn't help the man who had found her family.

She might be a murderous one if she lost control. So she couldn't afford to lose control. For an extended period of time, exposed to multitudes of strangers, she had to resist stress and find perfect inner peace.

He might as well ask her to solve world hunger.

Bearing pizzas as a peace offering, Oz returned to Pippa's house to find a local furniture delivery truck parked in the lot. Wondering who made deliveries on a Sunday and why, he warily strolled down the path, looking for explanations.

A muscular man with a clipboard emerged from the courtyard, nodded, and hiked back up the trail as Oz entered.

Inside the house, he nearly stumbled over a desk that hadn't been in the front room before. An unplugged computer sat beside it. Voices traveled from the bedroom hall.

Oz knew he wasn't going to like this. Setting the pizzas on the table, he shoved his hands into his pockets and wandered back to the bedrooms as if he belonged here.

He wanted to belong here. Like Ronan the Lonely Seal, he was searching for a home. That thought ought to jolt him, but he'd had enough jolting for one day.

Hands in pockets, he stopped at the first door in the hall, the room that had once been Pippa's business office. The shelves of books were still there, but now, instead of a desk and computer, she'd set up a brand new bed and mattress.

He was pretty certain they weren't for him.

The women were making the bed. They looked up when his shadow fell across them.

"My mother is moving in with me," Pippa said, almost defiantly.

He couldn't very well say, *What about me?* He was pretty certain she was throwing up a wall between them. But he couldn't argue that she needed to know her mother and that leaving the injured woman at the B&B was cruel.

He had a place in L.A. to go to. Her mother didn't. Yeah, he got that.

"You think this is safe?" he asked, turning to Gloria, who looked a little overwhelmed.

"I have no idea what I've done by coming to this town," Gloria admitted. "I really don't know if anyone cares if I exist anymore. The drug dealers are probably long since dead."

Oz nodded. "I may have caused more problems by finding Pippa in the first place." He turned to Pippa. "Should I call you Siren now?"

Her turquoise glare turned him on. Everything she

damned well did turned him on. He wanted to drag her into the other bedroom and settle this in the only way they knew how.

"No, I don't think that's a good idea," she said in response to his question about her name, but it was the right response to his thought about settling arguments in bed too. They needed to learn how to communicate.

"Are you staying at the B&B tonight or going back to L.A.?" she asked.

Good question. Excellent question. He'd thought he'd be staying here, with her. With the damned woman who had sucked him into her crazy psychedelic world and taught him to hope again.

"I'll see you after story hour tomorrow," he decided. "We won't be using the Syrene name in this production, if that's what's bothering you. I left pizzas in the kitchen."

Without knowing where he was headed, Oz walked out.

Chapter 27

"I REALLY DISLIKE DISRUPTING YOUR LIFE... PIPPA," Gloria said diffidently, staring at the pizza she'd placed on her plate but hadn't eaten.

"Disrupting? You're giving my life back to me!" Oz had disrupted it, Pippa thought as she bit into his peace offering. She ought to be feeling guilty that he'd come here to make amends and she'd effectively thrown him out, but Oz needed to back off. If she had to adjust her entire way of life, she needed her space to figure out how.

He was relying on Conan's message to reach the Librarian, not her stage name. He was hoping her song alone could lure Donal. That was a concession so huge, she wasn't certain how to take it. Relief and fear and indecision roiled into one big mass of confusion. And that was before she gave thought to sex with a man who wasn't afraid of her.

Gloria's smile was tentative. "I'd like to hope that I can be useful, dear, but I've learned to live from one moment to the next. That doesn't leave much room for dreaming."

"I'm rich," Pippa said carelessly. "Stinking, filthy rich. I'm supposed to be able to do anything I like. I haven't tried irresponsibility since I was a kid, but if wanting to get to know my mother is irresponsible, I'll live with it. Maybe we can have Conan set you up with a new identity so you can feel safe. We can do anything we like. It's a good feeling." She didn't have good feelings often, so when they happened, they were quite clear. Having her mother in her home made the world right, provided a balance she'd been missing. The connection between them was amazingly strong.

"And have you been feeling good about what you're doing?" Gloria asked, tasting a small bite of the pizza.

Pippa thought about that. "I don't feel bad about it," she concluded. "I felt really rotten about my life before I threw away Syrene and learned to be me."

"But are you really being you?" Gloria inquired, apparently forming her words with care. "I don't want to be a pushy mama before you've even come to accept I'm real, but I can't help wanting my only baby to be happy."

Tears leaped to Pippa's eyes. "Even if there's some crazy mistake, you can still be my mama. I don't think anyone has ever cared if I'm happy or not."

"I think Oz does, dear. He's as worried about you as he is about his son, but I think he's trying to give you... space?"

Her mother was a mind reader. Great. Pippa angrily chewed her pizza, trying not to make hasty judgments, but she was still furious with him for not consulting with her first about where and when and how she would perform. "Oz has to try to give me space because his natural state is hovering bully. I had those types running my life for years. No more."

Gloria adjusted her injured hip to a better position, and Pippa resolved to find more comfortable chairs. She might have to consider buying a house closer to the road. She couldn't expect her mother to regularly walk that uneven path.

The thought of giving up her sanctuary didn't set well. She glared at her hapless pizza and picked off a mushroom to pop in her mouth.

"A child is easily bullied. I doubt that Oz or anyone can bully you now," Gloria said with a degree of confidence. "I watched the two of you argue earlier, but it wasn't one attempting to coerce the other. It was more an exchange of ideas and opinions. When necessary, you instantly united to fight a common foe. It was fun to watch."

Pippa smiled, remembering flinging Conan into the pool. That had felt good, even if she'd been so furious, she could have let him drown. Speaking without monitoring her Voice had felt good too.

Singing would feel even better. Except she couldn't unleash Syrene in public.

She was treading dangerous waters now. "Have you listened to all my music?" she asked with wary curiosity.

Gloria sipped her iced tea. "Nine years ago, when you disappeared from public view, I was barely aware of the world outside my room. I missed watching you grow up as a child star. I've bought your CDs since then and listened to your anguish in the unpublished songs the Librarian smuggled to me. You harbor a lot of anger, although I suppose you don't need a meddling old woman to tell you that."

Pippa leaped up and hugged her mother in the first spontaneous gesture she'd offered in so long, she wasn't entirely certain she remembered how. "You will have to learn to be who you are meant to be too! You're not a meddling old woman. You're a wise, wise woman, and I desperately need you around."

Humor tinted Gloria's reply as she awkwardly hugged Pippa back without trying to stand. "You only need me around until you decide whether to accept Oz or drown him. If you choose drowning, you might need me a little longer."

"I can't accept..." But she could. Her Voice didn't affect Oz, so anything she said, he was taking at face value, not under some hypnotic influence. It was a liberating experience, knowing he was responsible for his own actions, not her.

Yes, he was an insufferable bully, but if her mother was right, if she was strong enough to fight back... why should she throw away the one man who could actually hear her?

Because she couldn't give him what he wanted. Not now. Not ever. Even if they got past the TV show, she couldn't live in L.A. Couldn't entertain his guests. And would avoid the paparazzi-filled world that he thrived in.

She sat down again and met her mother's eyes across the table. "If you heard my pain, did you listen to my songs without whatever shield you erect when I speak?"

"I tried, but sometimes it simply hurt too much," Gloria admitted. "I cried for a week after hearing the seal song, but that could be because I remembered telling you the story. Some of the later songs the Librarian sent were so raw, even a shield couldn't prevent your pain from seeping through."

"But the pain didn't cause you to act oddly?"

Gloria shook her head. "They made me cry or smile,

like any good music does. I was desperate to find you, but the Librarian didn't know where you were."

"She wasn't trying very hard." Pippa thought about that as she finished her pizza. "I used Philippa James Henderson on all my IDs after I left the music business. I dropped Robbie's name before I signed the book contracts, but I was always known by my adopted parents' name of James. Oz found me."

"Perhaps..." Gloria wrinkled her forehead, trying to work it out. "The website simply tracks the name Malcolm, and you quit using it."

"Possibly, although I still don't understand that site. You said you used your Voice to help my father? Did you fight evildoers like in the comic books?" Pippa asked with a smile, because the whole idea was too much like one of her children's stories.

"Nana did her best to develop my skills, but at most, I have a slight siren talent and some empathic abilities." Gloria didn't appear particularly bothered by the lack. "I warned Jordie when I overheard the drug dealers closing in on him. I used my Voice to distract them so we got away. But I was mostly a threat because I knew too much and because they saw me as dangerous. I doubt that they feared I'd pass Nana's lessons on to you, but that's what hurt you most. Without my training, you were lost and scared when you could have helped so many."

Pippa scowled. "You think I can use my gift for good if I'm trained?"

"There's no reason you shouldn't be able to direct your talent once you learn how. Right now, you're like a person with linguistic gifts who grew up in a world with only one language."

"You don't really believe anyone is deliberately seeking us out, do you?" Pippa tried not to sound alarmed. "Because if by some freak chance we found Donal..."

"If he has any extra abilities we could teach him to use, he might be in danger all over again," Gloria agreed sadly. "I have no idea."

"Damn, I need to talk to Oz." Dumping her plate in the dishwasher, Pippa went in search of her phone.

Bakersfield the Librarian's text read. Oz glared at the screen.

Was this her response to the message Conan had implanted in the server? If so, it told Oz so much that he had to collapse on his couch to absorb all the parameters. Bakersfield, where Pippa had been found. Bakersfield, where the Librarian wanted him to have Pippa sing the seal song? *Where Donal might be held?*

He wanted to race across the mountains and tear the town apart, but unlike Santa Domenica, Bakersfield was a sprawling city with nearly a third of a million people in it.

If he ever found Donal, he was implanting a GPS signal in the kid. Oz dropped his head in his hands and tried to focus.

After leaving Pippa, he had returned to L.A. to refresh his wardrobe. The stark white walls of his condo pressed in on him now. Even opening Donal's nursery and wrenching open every hole in his heart couldn't firm his resolve. Focusing was out of the question when every nerve was set on full alert. He needed action, but it needed to be the *right* action.

If he persuaded Pippa to sing in Bakersfield, was he drawing her into a trap?

Thinking like that was unproductive. Pippa was stronger than a five-year-old boy. He could surround Pippa with bodyguards.

First, he had to persuade her to appear on a stage. She'd grown up in Bakersfield. People there were more likely to recognize her than anywhere else. He didn't like that any better than she would.

His phone rang just as he was wondering if he dared call her. To his amazement, caller ID brought up Pippa's number.

"Is everything okay?" he asked in alarm.

She didn't seem startled by his abrupt response. Hers was equally blunt. "If there really are madmen after Malcolms, we're all in danger if we put a show together where they can find us. You don't want Donal anywhere near me. Or maybe even you. That could be why Alys took him and ran."

"Putting us all in one place may be what someone is after," Oz reluctantly admitted. "I just had a message from the Librarian. I think she wants us to do a show in Bakersfield."

Oz imagined he could hear the curses in her silence.

"I want to take the kidnapper down," she finally replied.

"After we get Donal out," he warned.

"How? How are we supposed to lure Donal from his kidnappers by going to Bakersfield and singing a stupid song if we don't use my stage name?"

"I don't know, but I'll do everything in my power to make it happen if you're on board. I'll start talking to my PR people as soon as you give the word.

I want the whole damned town to know the famous children's author Philippa James is filming a TV show about seals."

"Then I can wear a disguise and read a book while the song is played in the background?"

Oz rumpled his hair in indecision. "I just don't know. She sent me after Syrene. Or maybe... She wrote Syren, with a *y* and no final *e*. I'm hoping all that matters is that it's you. Will your adopted parents recognize you? Maybe the Librarian knows them? It's all coming together too fast. My God... Bakersfield?"

"Hell on earth," Pippa concluded. "My adopted parents moved to Seattle after I split the music scene. They're not a problem. But I went to school there."

Oz waited, heart in throat.

"If the Librarian doesn't know I'm Philippa James, I don't see how this will work," she finally said with a weary sigh. "Maybe you ought to start hunting Malcolms while you're at it, bring the whole clan to town, see if any of them are psychic. I'll see you tomorrow."

She hung up. But Oz smiled. He wanted this woman with her intelligence and courage. He wanted her enough to chase her to the ends of the earth. He didn't think that had ever happened to him. He was a persistent bastard and had worn Alys down, but this was different. He wanted Pippa to want him, too.

That might take a miracle, he acknowledged. He had nothing whatsoever to offer her except grief.

Monday morning, Pippa didn't know whether to fall down laughing or go looking for a baseball bat when she walked down her garden path and discovered a house-size RV parked in the day care's lot—with Oz sitting at an outdoor camp table, sipping coffee.

He waved at her and continued reading his newspaper.

The man was downright uncanny. She wanted to jump his bones right then and there. *He understood.*

She could walk past him without a word, and he wouldn't be offended. What would he do if she...?

Rather than wonder, she walked over, took down his paper, leaned over, and planted a big one on him.

He was right there in an instant, cupping her head and applying his tongue full throttle. He tasted of coffee and smelled of shaving cream, and he nearly melted her knees with the strength of his desire.

She pulled back before he got any ideas of dragging her into that sardine can before she was ready.

"Practical solutions," he said smugly, sitting back and admiring the green stripes she'd applied to her hair to match her green sundress and blue face paint. "The crew will be assembling shortly. Will your mother mind if we work around your pool?"

"Unlike me, I think she'll enjoy the company. She's been alone for too long. I forgot to thank you for finding her for me." Pippa wiped a smear of her lipstick off his mouth. Her heart pattered too fast to be sensible. She liked that he'd found a compromise that worked for both of them. He was *good*. She wasn't certain what to call the humming vibrations he set off inside her, but they balanced her world in ways she could love.

Oz captured her hand and licked her finger before she could retrieve it. Sheer lust shot through her so quickly, she actually contemplated the damned RV. She yanked her finger back. "Slow down, Oswin. Gratitude does not mean I want to get dressed a second time this morning."

He chuckled. "But I made you think about it. And kept you from remembering the Librarian and that your mother found us rather than the other way around. But maybe if you're thinking of me, you won't be thinking about Bakersfield."

"That's not happening. Better that you give me a picture of your son so I can keep his image in my mind while you're torturing me."

His smile disappeared. "I've already given posters with his photo to the Bakersfield police. Go read to the kids. I'll be here when you're done."

She nodded and walked away even though every cell in her body cried out for sweaty naked skin contact.

She'd learned to separate need, want, and reality. More than ever, she had to practice what she'd learned so she could move forward.

Chapter 28

WEARILY, PIPPA RAN HER FINGERS THROUGH HER HAIR, knowing that she had it standing straight up after working all afternoon with Oz's crew. At least they all seemed to take her at face value as no more than a children's book author.

In the growing dusk, Oz lit her citronella candles while his director made notes in a hastily scribbled script they'd patched together.

Some of his crew had already returned to the city for the evening. Gloria had retreated to the house hours ago. Only the scriptwriters, the director, and a few flunkies remained, although Oz spent half his time on the phone with the missing members of his staff, arranging this impromptu rehearsal. Or show. Marketing wanted to tape with a live audience.

It seemed ridiculous to go to this much trouble for what was essentially no more than a reading—something she did every day. But this was Oz's job—producing a marketable production. With a live audience to test it on, he couldn't scorn the opportunity, even if not knowing whether it would lead to his son was killing him.

Pippa watched the tired lines on his face as he returned to the lounge he'd claimed as his. She knew he simply wanted to go to Bakersfield and let her loose, but if they didn't use her Syrene name, then they had to drum up publicity or she'd have no audience. So they had to plot and plan—without telling his crew what he hoped to accomplish with this rushed production.

She wanted to help, but she was relatively useless at this end of the business. So she'd worked at rewriting the Ronan story with her new experience as a writer rather than with the heartbreak of a lonely teen. Passion needed grammar and structure.

Conan had just arrived a little while ago. She didn't know why he was here, but she kept an uneasy eye on him while he worked the tiny keyboard of his netbook.

Boxes of Lizzy's pizza were scattered everywhere. Gloria had prepared raw vegetables and a salad. Half-eaten bowls of lettuce were still strewn about. Oz grabbed a handful of carrot sticks and scooped out the last of a veggie dip, but Pippa figured he was ready for a steak.

She wished she knew what she was doing. He'd handed her a framed photograph of his smiling toddler when she'd returned to the house at noon. This one was better than the one she'd seen in his condo. The boy had huge heartbreakingly cinnamon-colored eyes just like his father's.

Oz dropped down on his chair and gestured toward her with his carrots. "Your turn, Pip. Let us hear what you've got." He crunched off the ends of the handful of carrots as if he were biting off someone's ear.

He was as nervous about this as she was.

"It's a children's story," she warned when every head turned in her direction. She'd tried to remain unobtrusive, but she knew they had been studying her, wondering if Oz was going to all this work for some bimbo he wanted to boff. If any of them had recognized her as Syrene, they showed no sign of it, which gave her a small measure of confidence. "The book Oz wants me to do hasn't been edited or published yet, and we have no illustrations."

She was stalling. They all waited patiently. With a sigh, she scrolled to the opening of the document and began to read about Ronan the Lonely Seal who imitated everyone he knew in hopes of making friends with them, but no one loved him—until he barked. Ronan had the best, the loudest, the most musical bark in the entire Pacific.

She read as she did to the children, with only a fraction of her Voice, just enough to hold them still and enraptured with the story.

A production assistant was wiping her eyes and sniffling by the time Pippa stopped reading. The men looked a little stunned—sitting silently, as if in deep meditative thought about a stupid story.

Oz crunched his carrots and watched his crew's reaction. Looking up from his computer, Conan stared at them, mystified.

She'd mesmerized everyone but the Oswin brothers—who had Malcolms in their family tree. Interesting.

Enthusiastic applause finally broke out, and Pippa blushed. It had been a long, long time since she'd last heard applause. She still wasn't ready for a theater audience, but at least her recitation hadn't harmed anyone. She hoped.

"Brilliant," Oz declared, kissing the back of her hand—the first intimate gesture he'd made since she'd returned from the day care. "We're gonna do this, folks. We've got a winner."

Taking that as a signal, the remaining crew began packing up.

Conan ambled over, removed her laptop, and replaced it with his netbook. "I hacked the genealogy site. I've left open the page from the early nineteen-hundreds where your California Malcolms divided from our East Coast Ives branch. Looks like our umpteen-great grandpappy Ives had wanderlust and took off with his California Malcolm wife for the Far East. Since then, his descendants have scattered around the world, leaving them relatively unscathed. Your branch stayed here, to disastrous effect, since the late fifties."

"The fifties, when people began moving to California in droves?" Oz asked, forgetting to crunch his carrots.

"When Disneyland opened," Pippa suggested.

"When Elvis was king," Conan added dryly. "All probably irrelevant."

"So, why Donal?" Oz demanded. "Different century, different family tree."

"My guess, as far-fetched as it sounds, is that we're dealing with a computer-oriented generation of California geeks who know Malcolms are different and are trying to tap into their differences." Conan leaned against the wall, sipping his water and watching the sun set.

Did that mean Conan actually *believed* Malcolms were different, or was he humoring her?

"California Malcolms are more likely to learn about the website by word of mouth as Pippa did," he continued. "The site has gone viral. Until Alys—someone who lived here all her life and heard about the site— our branch has been mostly too scattered to know of the website's existence. The East Coast lot probably doesn't even know about the Malcolm connection and have never ventured near the family tree. Yet. That website is one sticky web. Who hasn't tried to look up their ancestry just once? And once someone visits, the site's bug crawls into their computer and checks them out."

"This is all ridiculous speculation, you realize," Oz said, removing the netbook from Pippa's hands to study it. He waved his farewell to the last of the departing crew without lifting his gaze from the screen. He snorted in amusement. "Looking at these biographies, you'll notice no one on our side of the family has an iota of talent. No singers, dancers, or artists. Our grandfather, the senator, is listed with the name of his wife and children, but Aunt Bessie's marriage isn't listed because she married a grocer and never makes the news. Our father owned a chain of hotels, but we grew up in half a dozen cities so the site doesn't record where we live. Magnus lies low, so they only have his name. Someone may have used a clipping service in the past to follow Dad and found our names that way but not birthdates or other vitals."

"It's kind of fascinating," Pippa said. "I had no idea I was related to so many people."

"Damn good thing we're distant relations," Oz muttered, scrolling back to their shared ancestry. "What does this make us, cousins eight times removed? This screen is too small to get the whole picture."

Conan took back his fancy toy. "Reading through the bios on Pippa's extended family, they're mostly teachers. They're talented in many ways, they have fascinating if not wealthy careers, and then they settle down in California, near their families, produce children, and teach. Until or unless they meet untimely ends. You have cousins with birth dates listed, no deaths recorded, and no bios. They've simply disappeared."

Gloria arrived bearing a tray of drinks. She set it on the table between Pippa and Oz and held out her hand for Conan's toy. "We're educators because of the empathic factor," she explained in the tone of the teacher she must once have been. She studied the list of her ancestors. "It's difficult to become rich and powerful if we're more interested in improving the lives of others than in acquiring material things. That's where Pippa was led astray. Had I raised her, she would no doubt be a music teacher, singing in local repertory musicals."

"And much happier," Pippa agreed. "No offense, but wealth and power don't ring my chimes."

"Whereas that's what Oswins live for—ringing other people's chimes." Conan chortled. "It takes all kinds. But if we have a killer on the family tree, he's an idiot for taking out harmless teachers instead of some of the power mongers on the East Coast."

Gloria smacked the netbook back into his hands. "Teachers are the most powerful tools we have for steering the future and the minds of entire generations. Don't ever underestimate the power of education."

"Want us to throw him in the pool for you?" Oz asked helpfully.

"Power has its uses, when wielded wisely," Gloria conceded. "I'll hope your mother taught you well. I assume my grandmother escaped unscathed because she moved to Texas, so as much as I hate to admit it, you may be onto something. Are there any California Malcolms left who could be selling our family secrets?"

"Scattered, but yes. Shall I send them invitations for a family reunion?" Conan suggested.

"I doubt that a kidnapper would take Donal to a family reunion," Pippa pointed out. "Catching an imaginary villain is secondary to finding Donal."

"And secondary to keeping Pippa safe," Oz added. "Have you got a plan for that?"

"I will once you give me the details," Conan said. "The Adam Technology lead is taking me nowhere. The computer store is irrelevant. Some geeks bought it from one of the many, many divisions of Adam. I've checked, and they are genuinely repairing old computers for charities. If they know your Librarian, all she had to do was tell them a charity needed Pippa's old hard drive, and they would hand it over, no questions asked."

"With my data still on it?" Pippa asked in disbelief.

Conan shrugged. "So maybe she planted an employee who copied it. Things happen. I doubt we'll ever know. But if all the Librarian did with the drive contents was send them to your mother, I can't call that evil."

"She did something for the Librarian, so the Librarian returned the favor. Balance. Very Zen." Pippa crossed her legs and pressed the heel of her hands into her eyes to ease the ache. "Let's just do this."

She didn't see Oz rise, but she felt him looming over her. Before she could uncover her eyes, he'd scooped her off the lounge. And she was grateful he was carrying her away from all this. Her arms circled his neck, and she buried her face in the enticing male scent of his hard chest and hoped he could make the world go away.

"Get your crew lined up, bro," Oz ordered. "We've

got the largest auditorium we could find in Bakersfield signed up for a week from today, after school. The PR people are already on it. The six o'clock news will have carried it."

Pippa wished she could cover her ears as well as her eyes.

A week. He wasn't giving her much time to rethink this.

Restlessly awake at dawn on Saturday, Oz tried to stretch in the narrow RV bed but succeeded only in crushing Pippa into a corner. She'd slept with him out here all week. He would not attempt to delve into her psyche to determine why it was okay to sleep with him in an RV and not in her bed.

He simply wasn't letting her too far out of his reach, even if it meant living in a tin can. He had no idea where this relationship was going, but he was grateful she wasn't shutting him out until they worked it out. He needed her with a hunger he'd never known, a passion that made him come alive again.

He rolled over and covered her with his body as the birds began their dawn chorus. Naked, she circled his back and accepted his stubbly kiss with as much eagerness as he applied it.

Sixty hours and counting until the live rehearsal. Hours until he learned if all their planning and scheming would produce results.

She had to be as terrified as he was, but they'd spent these past nights learning the best ways of distracting each other. He'd discovered it was possible not to think at all while he had Pippa in his arms. He cuddled her closer and explored her perfect breasts. She responded by kissing his throat and wiggling into his arousal.

Once these next few days were over, once he'd played his hand and won or lost, he would have to figure out how to keep his elusive elf in his life. She was too good to throw away like the other women who crossed his path.

She grasped his butt and urged him on without any fuss about morning breath or needing a shower or coffee. Oz obliged, loving the hum of arousal she emitted.

Pippa's warbling cries of ecstasy brought him to climax before he was ready. He didn't want her to leave his bed today.

Donal needed them.

"You're doing everything you can," she whispered near his ear, apparently sensing his tension. "Not hearing from the Librarian is *good*. It means we're doing the right thing."

"For whom?" he asked bitterly, rolling back to the narrow mattress. "I want to lock you up in a bulletproof box."

She giggled. "Clear glass. I can paint my face white and mime trying to escape. The kids will love it, but mimes don't sing."

Disgruntled, he rolled off the bed. "I like that. I'll call a set designer and have him order it up."

She flung a pillow at his departing back. "You're ridiculous. I'm going to the house. Come down when you're ready."

Despite her prickly exterior, Pippa was too trusting. For all she knew, her damned mother was the Librarian. And Pippa was leaving Gloria in complete possession of her household while she spent the nights in the RV and half her days at the day care.

Which was why Pippa would never use her wealth for control and power. For her, it was natural to trust and share. The defensive shield she'd built over these past years was as unnatural as it was necessary.

Oz pounded his head on the tiny closet door as he pondered this unwelcome insight. She'd damned well nearly seduced half his staff just reading a kid's book with her mesmerizing Voice. They hadn't been able to stop talking about the story since. They would probably walk on water for her.

He'd tried playing "The Silly Seal Song" for them while Pippa was away, using Conan's computer files— and they'd responded with shrugs. Oz was afraid that might be a problem.

Like Pippa's eyes, her siren Voice might not translate well into artificial mediums. Or maybe, as she had warned, the song's message could only be heard by children.

He was trying very hard not to consider the ramifications if her book reading and a recording didn't lure Donal out of the audience.

Setting Syrene loose on a stage wasn't happening. Even he couldn't ask that of her.

Chapter 29

PIPPA WAS STIRRING GRATED MOZZARELLA INTO scrambled eggs when Oz walked in carrying his travel mug of coffee and aiming for her shower. With only a water tank for his RV, he'd commandeered the use of her facilities all week. She wasn't surprised by his appearance now—except for the way his jaw had set with determination.

When he emerged from her bathroom, hair still wet from the shower, he was wearing his earring—apparently a signal that he was off duty. Judging from the faded jeans and Metallica T-shirt, she assumed his mulish mood had nothing to do with business. Which meant he'd set his stubborn sights and productive mind on her. Interesting that she had begun to understand him so well.

"Good morning, Gloria." He acknowledged her mother setting the table for the three of them. "Do you mind if I borrow Pippa for the day?"

"No, of course not, dear. I had assumed you would have plans for the weekend. I am quite capable of entertaining myself." She straightened the colorfully striped placemats, removed a wilting daffodil from the vase on the table, and began setting out glasses of orange juice.

Pippa loved sharing the beauty of her few carefully selected possessions with her mother. Oz, on the other hand, had a tendency to crash through her fragile existence with the carelessness of the proverbial bull.

She eyed him skeptically now. "I didn't know we had plans."

"Big ones," he said in satisfaction, refilling his mug with the coffee Gloria had made with the pot he'd provided. "We're going to ride a Ferris wheel, maybe a carousel. Do you Rollerblade? Bicycle?"

Pippa set aside her skillet and gaped at him. "Whose plans are these? I don't remember making them."

"Do you want to sit here and fret all weekend? I don't think the set crew would appreciate it if we arrived to help them paint backdrops."

Ferris wheel. *Santa Monica*. He had no work left to do and wanted to take her to his place for the weekend to keep him occupied. The beginning of the end, though, Pippa knew. After Monday, their relationship—or whatever it was—would be over. There would be no more reason for Oz to travel up here once production was in place.

And she would have to show him that she could not exist in his world. She'd hoped for just a little more time...

She'd survived without a man in her life all these years. She could do it again. Might as well make the break clean.

"I bicycle. I Rollerblade. I haven't done either in years. What about you?" She scooped eggs on his plate, added Oatnut toast, a hydroponically grown tomato, a slice of mozzarella, and a fresh basil leaf.

"Not in years," he agreed, studying the selection while taking his seat.

His seat. He'd already carved a niche in her home. He'd bully his way deeper if she wasn't careful. Oz *used* people, she reminded herself. He was an exploiter. And he was using her now, but she understood his need and sympathized. It had to be hard, surviving these next few days, praying and hoping he'd find his son at the end of them.

"I just thought we could start in the hills and work our way down to the pier," he continued nonchalantly, taste-testing her Italian breakfast.

Start with uncrowded trails and work their way down to the mobs, he meant. Pippa ladled eggs on the remaining plates and placed her pan in the sink to soak. Steam hissed from the hot metal as the water hit it.

"I'm not afraid of people," she said. "It's irrelevant where we start."

"Fine. I'll arrange for bicycles. Maybe concert tickets for the evening. Bring an overnight bag." He blithely bit into his toast.

Oz's dark eyes taunted her, challenging her to back down. Pippa wanted to bop him over the head with the skillet. "Fine," she retorted in the same tone. "Arrange for an ambulance and police cars while you're at it. And a better getaway vehicle than a bike."

His grin had an edge to it. "Think highly of ourselves, do we? I won't let anything happen to the talent. I'm not forgetting we have a show to do."

Of course he wasn't. He was simply looking for a way to stay occupied, and he'd chosen a high-drama method to keep the adrenaline flowing.

She just nodded, chewed her toast, and worked out an appropriate disguise for the death of a relationship.

Pippa wore black, not a California color even in March. Oz assumed there was some significance to her choice, but he'd rather admire how she fit into spandex. The bike shorts featured a yellow racing stripe down the sides that matched the Tweety Bird image on her loose black T-shirt. She'd inked glare-preventing streaks beneath her eyes as if she were a ballplayer and carted a black bike helmet under her arm. He'd almost bet she had goggles in her backpack.

"Don't want to get noticed much?" he asked sardonically as he shouldered the backpack and led the way through the courtyard.

"This is me being me," she declared. "If you don't like it, you can leave me here."

Okay, he got that message. "That's Syrene hiding behind an attitude," he retorted. "I'm betting Pippa never went to the pier."

"Pippa grew up in the desert with a couple who couldn't afford to adopt her until she earned enough money to make it worth their while. Of course she didn't go to the pier. And even after we moved to L.A., Pippa didn't have time to play."

"Then it's time Pippa reclaimed her childhood. Pretend we're sixteen and dating."

"Robbie and I didn't date," she informed him as they traversed the walk to the parking lot. "We hung out together on a concert tour, worked at the same studio, and got married in Vegas when we had a couple of hours to spare. I have no idea what one does on a date."

"We look for places where we can make out," Oz said, leering, when he really wanted to take all the people in her life and slam their collective heads together.

"You're not thinking sex right now," she perceptively countered. "Your eyes go almost black like that when you're ready to lay someone flat."

"I don't go around laying people flat. Except maybe you, but I like to think that's consensual." He gripped her elbow to steer her over a rock outcropping and because he wanted to touch her.

Despite her tough attitude, she still seemed frail to him. He had difficulty juggling his need to comfort the little girl she'd never been and to back off from the prickly woman who would remove his testicles if he encroached too far. She kept him on his toes, at least.

"Maybe we should just have a sparring match and whoever remains standing gets to make all the decisions today," she suggested, echoing his thoughts.

"I like that idea. Let's remember it for the future. No matter how it plays out, I can't lose." He'd had his assistant deliver the Porsche after he'd driven the RV up here. He opened the door and helped Pippa into the passenger seat and then dropped her backpack in the trunk. He was hoping she'd packed something silky and sexy in that ratty old bag.

"You're on," she agreed when he took his place behind the wheel.

Despite the ugly costume, she smelled of the subtle rose lotion he'd learned she used on her face. And he'd used on other parts of her. He smiled, gunning the engine. He needed to replace her supply. And see if they made oils in the same scent.

If he thought about sex, maybe he wouldn't have to think about what he was really doing—falling for a woman who hated his life.

"I choose to live in the hills because I don't like the city, you realize," she said, reading his mind as she had a bad habit of doing. "I don't like crowds or traffic or designer clothes or shopping."

"You're not Alys, I get that," he agreed, steering onto the narrow two-lane mountain road that kept her home isolated from the city. "But the city has other attractions. I'm just showing you a few. We'll have fun."

He didn't turn to catch the knowing smile he knew was flirting around that luscious mouth of hers. Practically living together for two weeks had to be about the same getting-to-know-each-other rate as months of meeting in restaurants and falling into the sack for a quickie before running to make a morning meeting. He *knew* the damned woman and how her mind worked.

And he'd never know all of her. Pippa held secret facets that fascinated him. Every time he thought he had her pinned, she hit him with a new surprise. And he liked that, which amazed even him. Had anyone asked, he would have said he preferred routine. And he would have been wrong.

"I promise to have fun," she said solemnly.

He punched the CD button and let a rap song fill the interior. She leaned over and hit Skip, changing the CD until it returned to the Anonymous Four she'd heard the first time he'd taken her off this mountain.

Oz opened the console, revealing his CD selection for her perusal. She purred with delight and began rummaging through his titles. Before long, she had an entire repertoire of beach music filling the rack.

"Mood music," she declared.

"You really haven't listened to music all these

years?" he asked with incredulity when she slipped into a blissful fugue as the car filled with an old rock beat. "Not even an iPod?"

"I hear music and I sing," she said with a shrug. "It's like falling into water and swimming. I can't not do it—unless it's that ugly stuff you had in there. Rap may be poetry, but it's not music. I need melody."

He fretted over that all the way down the mountain—while she merrily harmonized with surfing songs. He wasn't certain that she wasn't happier singing than having sex. She beamed and glowed as if she contained her own private sun. And the music filling the car had more life and soul than a choir of angels accompanied by a gospel chorus.

He wanted to take her home and make love to her all day and night. He wanted to put her on a stage and make the world a better place. He wanted to bicycle recklessly down a mountain, singing beside her.

She was a siren. And he was supposed to be immune.

He'd closed his heart, and she made him see what a cold place he'd lived in. He wasn't as immune as he'd thought. How must she affect others?

Oz thought he ought to bang his head against the steering wheel, but that would merely convince Pippa she was right, that she was dangerous. And he had to admit, she was damned dangerous. People would weep if they couldn't have what she offered in her Voice. The power and beauty of her music could melt rocks. He'd bet that keeping her Voice undercover all these years had merely increased the power of it. She'd cause riots if she used it now. And singing was as natural to her as breathing.

By the time he parked the car in the lot at the foot of the biking trail, Oz couldn't restrain his need to kiss her. He dragged Pippa halfway across the console and, despite the awkward position, claimed her mouth, her tongue, her kisses until his head spun with desire and she was practically yanking him back across the console into her lap.

Someone rapped the hood of the car, jarring them back to reality. "Sixteen," he muttered. "We really are adolescents."

She snickered. "Necking, and it's not even dark. Shame on you."

"It's not your Voice," he warned. "It's you. Your Voice is you. I hear *you*. I want *you*. So don't give me that siren crap."

"Yes, sir, wouldn't think of it, sir," she agreed with a laugh. "Is that your bicycle person waiting for us?"

Still shaken by his uncharacteristic desire to show the world this treasure he'd discovered, Oz climbed out of the car and met the bike rental guy. He'd wanted a distraction until they could drive to Bakersfield. In Pippa, he'd found it. He couldn't even think right now.

He wasn't thinking much better a little while later as they biked into the hills of the Canyon. Watching Pippa's slender hips pumping in tight shorts was sufficient to spin his head around backward, and he thought the image of her ass might be permanently emblazoned on his brain. He was trying to bicycle with a boner! She hummed as she biked, occasionally breaking out into one of the songs she'd heard in the car.

Oz watched as other bikers raced toward them, came in range of her Voice, and toppled into the sagebrush, unable to pedal straight while turning to stare. After each incident, she'd shut up for a little while, until they were on a clear stretch, and then she'd sing out her joy again. Until some fool raced over a hill and nearly plowed into them.

"There are too many people here," Oz griped after the spectator righted himself and pedaled off in embarrassment. "We should have started earlier."

Pippa pulled the bike to the side of the trail and gave him her wise woman look. "Or I can stop being me, or I can live where there aren't any people," she reminded him.

"You're doing this on purpose, aren't you? You're projecting something with your Voice that I can't hear but everyone else does."

"I'm not projecting anything. I'm simply not holding back. I'm singing what I feel. Right now, I'm singing my happiness. I've never had a chance to bike these hills and always envied those who were free to do so. Thank you for bringing me here."

"Then why are these idiots falling all over themselves?" Oz asked, glaring at the next set of cyclists coming up the path. He nodded in their direction as they raced past. "Most of the cyclists here are experienced. This morning, I feel like I'm in rush-hour traffic on a rainy freeway during a full moon when they let all the zanies loose."

The smile slid away from her face, and she gazed at a patch of flowers just opening their buds. "Maybe people don't recognize happiness when they hear it. Or maybe they do, and they're trying to find it. Mostly, I guess, I'm a distraction." She crouched down to pet the tender bud.

"You're not still believing you're a siren luring the stupid to their deaths?" he asked warily, not knowing whether she was avoiding his eyes or simply exploring new territory.

She shook her head. "Not with happiness. I sold a lot of concert tickets with happiness. The bad part comes later, when I'm frightened or angry."

Damn, how could he prove she was wrong when all signs pointed in the opposite direction?

Could she literally *kill* people with her Voice? He didn't want to believe it.

Chapter 30

THEY ATE LUNCH AT A SEAFOOD RESTAURANT ON THE pier overlooking the bay.

Pippa washed the black streaks from her face and tucked her helmet into her backpack, daringly walking into Oz's world with only rose-tinted glasses to disguise her turquoise eyes. Of course, using no cosmetics, with her hair short and back to its natural red and wearing clothes similar to those of every other grubby tourist on the pier, she hoped she bore little resemblance to a wealthy rock star.

So far, people only glanced at her when she spoke.

So, for Oz's sake, she kept her Voice neutral while expressing her appreciation in other ways. She really was enjoying this day of escape. Since he was trying so hard to give her a good time, she would do her best to prevent it from turning ugly. Besides, she was having a blast pretending to be normal for a little while.

She'd happily hugged Oz's arm when they'd entered the restaurant and then reached across the table to press finger kisses to his cheek while they ate. He had looked a little perturbed by the biking experience, but he started to relax when he realized she wouldn't have every customer in the place lining up for an autograph or falling in his oyster stew.

Pippa loved her newfound anonymity. She loved that she could talk to Oz without restraint, as long as they weren't in public. And she really loved that he responded to her touches as eagerly as others did to her Voice. As she responded to his heated looks.

Definitely very adolescent of them.

The peaceful interlude couldn't last forever, she fully realized. This was just an escapist moment of avoiding the black hole of Monday. She feared failure to find Donal would be a blow from which Oz wouldn't recover. She was fairly certain either way, it would end their relationship.

But she appreciated that Oz had thought of a wonderful way to play and that he wasn't telling her what to do, as he bossed everyone else around him.

With his overlong sun-streaked hair, earring, and T-shirt, he should fit right into the crowd, but he couldn't disguise his brawny shoulders, arrogant stride, and aura of privilege. Women turned to stare at him as much as the bikers had turned to stare at her singing. When a waitress leaned over to clear the table, flashing too much plastic cleavage, Pippa decided he'd had enough attention and began humming. The woman scampered.

Oz eyed her with suspicion, and Pippa offered her best evil smile in return.

"You have a hum that scares people?" he inquired without inflection.

"Something from Tchaikovsky. My music teachers insisted that I listen to the classics. 'Peter and the Wolf' has some lovely dark notes."

"And you learned to use them how?" He handed over his credit card to pay the bill, and Pippa noticed the waiter did a double take, recognizing Oz's name on the card. A wannabe actor, she suspected. And Oz was one of the important players.

The server glanced at her with envy, and Pippa began humming under her breath again, not answering Oz until the waiter ran away.

She shrugged. "That was a test run. When I got bored with the classics, I used to scale my Voice to the notes of the symphony. I learned the teacher would abruptly shut off the music or switch it to a happier tune when I did that. I discovered later that the notes were good ones for releasing my dark feelings. I use them in several of my songs, the angstier ones."

"So you can use your Voice as a weapon," he suggested. "Like a porcupine raising his quills, at the very least."

"If I'd been trained, probably. But my knowledge is entirely accidental, and experimenting can be dangerous. If a few minor notes can chase people away, I don't want to know what would happen if I really unleashed my anger." Actually, she knew what happened. They turned to drugs and drove off cliffs.

He signed the receipt and tucked his card back in his pocket, ignoring the murmurs and glances of the wait staff as he assisted her from the booth. Oz had his own shield of oblivion, Pippa realized with envy. He strode through the world, assuming people noticed him and expecting them to keep their distance. She wished she'd learned that technique.

Oz could teach her. He'd already taught her that she could come out of hiding if she was careful.

"If you weren't actually angry, but just wanted to project anger, could you control the effect of your Voice?" he asked with interest as they strolled back into the sunshine.

"I've only practiced control these past years. I can keep my Voice neutral, and I can use the mildly hypnotic tone you've heard when I read. Sometimes I can project soothing sounds, like with the drunk. This is the first time I've attempted to warn anyone away. Beyond that, I don't know."

She was relieved that he finally accepted that her Voice was more than just sound but an instrument or weapon that could be used. She wasn't certain she liked the direction of his questions, though.

"Carousel or Ferris wheel?" he asked, leading her through the crowds in the direction of the park.

"Much better question. Carousel. And cotton candy." Holding Oz's hand, swinging it, Pippa rejected their earlier conversation in favor of returning to their date with fun. "And then I'm going to beat you at every game on the midway."

He threw back his head and laughed. She admired the long brown column of his throat—as did all the women around them. She sighed with contentment, absorbing these moments to pull out and remember when she had to return to her loneliness.

But she wouldn't be lonely any longer. Thanks to Oz, she had a mother now. She prayed she could save Donal so she could return the favor.

She'd eventually get over the heartache of missing Oz's vibrant energy in her life. She hoped.

Despite every hair on his head slowly turning gray while he worried over Donal, Oz enjoyed the distraction that was Pippa.

She wasn't so good at the water gun games, which he won hands down, thanks to his video game practice, but she had a deadly aim in the games involving throwing balls, beanbags, and other assorted oddments. Her focus was almost frightening. He'd spent his wayward youth on the pier and knew how the games were rigged and could direct his throws a little off center, where the hit really counted, so he could still match her. On whack-a-mole, however, she won, with a stunningly fast lead.

"I'm never letting you come after me with a mallet," he announced as they emerged from the midway with a stuffed monkey wrapped around his neck and a heap of cheap Mardi Gras beads layered over Pippa's Tweety Bird shirt.

"I think I have a new profession. I'll hire myself out to whack moles. It could be fun," she decided, grinning happily.

Oz wished he'd spent days like this with his son and vowed he would spend every weekend enjoying Donal's company if only he could have the boy back. He watched the other parents with envy, trying not to crush Pippa's hand when he saw a towheaded kid who might be his.

She hummed a soothing song, and he yanked her hair in retaliation, proving her Voice didn't work on him. She was brilliant and talented, and her animation could make him feel joy and happiness as he hadn't in years — but she couldn't remove his anguish and fear, no matter how she tried. He almost wished he could be one of the poor saps she could tease and seduce so he could spend these next days in a hapless stupor.

They'd decided to save the Ferris wheel for last,

hoping the lights would be on before the concert began in the park. Except as the afternoon wound down, Oz doubted the wisdom of their plan. Even looking like an ordinary tourist, Pippa was incapable of blending in with the crowd. She was tall and distinctive, and she kept adorning toddlers with necklaces from the gaudy stack around her neck. The children loved her. And she obviously adored them. But people turned to watch, and he felt stares follow in their wake. This was L.A. People were always stargazing, and Pippa possessed star quality.

They ate junk food from the stands for their supper, and Pippa hummed over a damned tofu chili dog. She hummed when she was happy, and Oz loved hearing the sound. So did everyone else in the vicinity. Heads turned again. Remembering the bicyclists, he tensed up.

He steered her between two stands, over an alley of electrical cords, and into a crowd on the other side when he recognized that puzzled *I-know-her-from-somewhere* look in the eyes of several couples who'd turned to look and listen. He'd been around enough to know when people recognized their favorite actor passing by—even when the stars were dressed in shabby jeans and a two-day beard. Some people were just good at faces.

He bought her an overpriced ball cap at the next stand and yanked it down over her eyes. Pippa blinked and caught his concern immediately, checking over her shoulder.

"Just in case," he said easily. "Let's hit the Ferris wheel now. We'll be far above the masses and out of sight."

She nodded, and they stood in line, but Oz's back itched, as if there were a target there, drawing stares.

She'd have him believing he was actually empathic. Pippa switched uneasily from foot to foot, as if she felt it, too.

"We should leave," she whispered.

"And not ride the Ferris wheel? You'll let a few freaks spoil your fun?"

"I think I may know the short guy," she said, not hiding her annoyance. "This really is a small town, and I worked with a lot of people."

"So, he asks for your autograph. Will that hurt?" He didn't want her to run. He wanted her to stand up to her fears. She was no longer a timid, frightened teenager.

The glow of joy left her eyes. She stiffened and faced straight ahead. "Whatever happens is on your head."

Too late, he remembered she didn't like being ordered about, as if her opinion had no relevance. Before he could change his mind, a little girl with a long braid ran up to Pippa, holding out an advertising flyer. "My daddy says you're Syrene. Could I have your autograph?"

He couldn't blast a kid who wasn't even old enough to know who Syrene was. Oz threw a cold glare over his shoulder but couldn't find the parents who had put her up to this.

"Your daddy is mistaken," Pippa said, calmly leaning over to take the flyer and pen. "But maybe you'll know this name." She used Oz's back for a writing desk. He could feel her signing Philippa James.

The little girl looked at the autograph with puzzlement and then brightened. "I read your book at the library! Wow!"

She scampered off into the arms of a perfectly innocuous couple who led their excited daughter away without incident.

"Good move," Oz murmured. "If you want to leave, I'll take you."

"I'm still recognizable," she growled, not leaving the line as they moved closer to the ride. "You know what will happen at the reading Monday?"

"Conan will have bodyguards there. Nothing will happen," Oz assured her. "Even if someone happens to recognize you, they can't reach the stage, and we'll have a car waiting outside so you can get away quickly."

She took off her ball cap and smacked his arm with it. Several times.

He deserved that. If people thought Philippa James was Syrene, she'd never have peace again.

And still he wouldn't back out. A terrified little boy came before a woman whose narrow life was about to publicly explode.

They were at the top of the Ferris wheel, staring into the sunset, with lights popping on all over the dusky landscape below, when Pippa remembered that the Santa Monica Pier was the end of Route 66, the road that had carried war-weary soldiers and their families across the country to the land of milk and honey.

The road that could carry her out of California, into the wilderness where no one would know her. She should never have settled so close to L.A. It had been foolishly sentimental of her.

She would have to leave behind all she knew and loved—her studio, her friends in town, her day care kids—Oz.

Real tears slipped down her cheeks, but she

understood what it was like to be hunted and stalked far better than Oz could ever imagine. Her life was about to become hell. And if madmen or power mongers really were hunting Malcolms, then it only made sense to take her mother and hide.

It made even more sense than trying to fit into Oz's world, where she would be a danger to him and his son and the rest of his family, even if she wanted to live in the city. Which she didn't.

Silently, she said farewell to the ocean, to the mixed-up, crazy world she'd loved for a while, to the relationship she could never hope to have.

Flinging her arms around Oz, she kissed him as the wheel rotated, kissed him with all the love and passion she would never share again.

Chapter 31

SAFELY ENSCONCED IN OZ'S BIG BED, FAR FROM HER sanctuary, Pippa dreamed of Oz's kisses and snuggled closer to the furnace of a man spooning her. She dreamed of his hands stroking her breasts into arousal, and the need to caress him in return was as natural and instinctive as coming home. She caught his big hands and guided them, enjoying this moment of possession, the human contact she thought never to know again.

His erection prodded her thighs, and she adjusted herself to his need, trusting the solace of his familiarity, the security of his strength.

He murmured something insensible in her ear and rubbed against her. The piercing sensuality woke her from her dreams.

And Oz was still making love to her. She was humming happily as he stroked, and she wasn't entirely certain he was awake, either. She reached over her shoulder to rub her hand over his bristly beard, and he growled and thrust with more direction.

"Yes," he said in triumph. "Mine. I like waking like this."

So did she. This time, when she arched backward, he took what she offered. Their bodies recognized each other's so well that they knew what to do without conscious thought. It was better without thought, without fear. Pippa threw herself into the exertion with joy. She could almost see fireworks when they climaxed together.

She relaxed and fell asleep in his arms again.

Sing.

That's all the Librarian's text said on Sunday morning. Oz wanted to chuck the phone across his bedroom.

Pippa was singing in his shower—probably with the dark notes she'd told him about yesterday. Her glorious voice echoed off the limestone tiles and danced across his ceiling. He didn't need artwork if he had her voice. He could never tire of hearing her. Which did not bode well for the future, but he couldn't think beyond Monday.

He was fairly certain this message meant that the Librarian wanted Pippa to sing at the reading. He couldn't allow that to happen. After yesterday's near fiasco, he couldn't let the entire world know that Philippa James, the author, was the missing singing sensation Syrene.

He'd fooled himself into believing that no one would recognize her. He'd made believe that a recording would suffice. He'd bullied her into an impossible situation. And for what? The possibility that Donal was still alive? It wasn't as if the Librarian had offered any hint of proof.

Yesterday had confirmed Pippa's worst fears—she was recognizable, no matter how she disguised herself. And they would be in Bakersfield, where she'd grown up. There were probably posters of Syrene hanging all over town, even after all these years. For the filming, Oz might bring in Audrey, the skinny actress understudy Nick had suggested, but he had to ask Pippa to go on stage this one time. He was praying her presence was all the siren call needed to lure Donal from hiding.

They hadn't gone to the concert last night. People had been standing around the Ferris wheel when they got off, whispering and nudging one another and staring at Pippa. She'd hummed her off-putting tunes, but Oz had felt her fear building, even if he couldn't hear it in her voice, as others must have. The entire crowd had started backing away before he'd hurried her into the darker corners of the park, out of sight.

He'd had the shuddering notion that if she'd been any more scared, she would have projected her terror, and the happy holiday throng would have mushroomed into a mob scene.

Syrene had once caused a riot. With her Voice? He understood her fear better.

He hoped they were safe in the condo, that her Voice didn't project beyond his walls. He didn't know what she was channeling this morning, but despite their ecstatic lovemaking last night, she didn't sound happy.

Rather than risk taking her to a restaurant, Oz ordered up stuffed bagels and made his own coffee. He rummaged in his cabinets until he found tea bags someone had given him, probably in a company Christmas basket.

He had plates on his glass table and wished he'd ordered a bouquet by the time Pippa emerged, dressed in a long, flowery sundress with a sleeveless turquoise turtleneck beneath.

He had a feeling the turtleneck was a symbol of her drawing back into her cave.

After the rapturous midnight sex, their lovemaking

this morning had felt like a farewell. Pippa had cuddled and held him instead of playing games and teasing him or driving him to new heights of passion. Oz wasn't at all surprised when she dropped her little bomb this morning.

"I think I need to go home today and get ready," she declared. "You need to work with Conan and his team on ways to locate Donal in the auditorium and make certain he escapes safely."

She serenely poured hot water from his kettle over the tea bag in her cup as if she'd simply said, "Good morning."

"What do you have to do to get ready?" he asked irritably. "We have dancers and magicians to fill the opening acts. All you have to do is walk on, read, and walk off while we play your recording. Conan is in control of whatever happens next."

"Overstimulation," she said vaguely. "I need to clear my head."

"Bullshit," Oz said bluntly. "You're running away. I don't have time to put a security guard on your tail."

She shot him a turquoise glare. "I promised to read on Monday, and I will be there. You don't need to lock me up. I've had quite enough of that kind of security before, and I won't suffer it again."

"Figurative running away, then." He bit fiercely into his bagel so he couldn't say more.

She sipped her tea and studied the breakfast selection. Definitely retreating. This was Zen Pippa, no confrontation.

Yesterday had disturbed her as much as it had him.

"I'll take you home," he agreed, "but you need to get used to the stares. You're an attractive woman. People stare."

She offered a wry smile, chose the Asiago cheese bagel, and nibbled the edge.

Damn, he hated when she did that. He wanted her to be the Pippa singing her way up the mountain—or roaring her displeasure, which she had yet to do.

"We're not adolescents any longer. You cannot spend your days surfing," she said gently. "I can only follow my bliss within limited conditions. I've accepted that. You must too."

She was right, and he hated that too. "I like my work as much as surfing," he muttered.

"So do I. Writing suits me better than performing. You've showed me I don't have to give up music entirely. I simply need to keep it to myself. I'll study on how I can do that more often, without acoustic walls around me."

There it was again, that note of farewell. Oz scowled at her. "I still don't want to let you out of my sight."

She offered an enigmatic smile and chewed her bagel, apparently savoring the flavor.

"You can't get bagels like that in the hills." He had to make her see that they could share their different lives. He didn't want to give her up.

She nodded agreement but said nothing.

He was Oz. He never took no for an answer. He wouldn't let her run back into hiding, not now, not when he'd finally found a woman he actually wanted in his life.

Even if she was Syrene and a royal pain in the ass. If anyone knew how to take care of neurotic performers, it was him. She *needed* him.

As much as he needed her. He ripped off more bagel and kept silent.

Pippa sighed in relief and regret after Oz finally sped away in his tiny sports car. He was too much man and too overwhelming, and she definitely needed space to clear her head. His RV loomed large in the parking lot, promising he would be back, but she wouldn't worry about that.

Gloria looked up with surprise and concern when Pippa walked in and immediately started examining the contents of her storage cabinets.

"We need to leave California," Pippa said, not waiting for questions. "Tomorrow is a trap, and we need an exit route."

"Yesterday did not go well?" Gloria asked, pushing up from the couch with difficulty.

"Syrene is still recognizable. I don't know why the Librarian wants the world to know that Syrene and Philippa James are the same person, but that's what will happen. Even if we rescue Donal, he'll be in danger as long as I'm around. It's best to make a clean break."

"But Oz..." Gloria looked at her with sadness.

"Oz will survive. I hope he gets his son back. I don't know what I'll do if the reading doesn't work. I just know if it does, and we find Donal, I have to leave. Conan proved that California isn't safe for Malcolms. I won't lose you again."

"But the town... I thought you and Oz had an agreement to help El Padre." Gloria opened the closet containing the suitcases.

"I'll hope he honors it anyway. He has to understand what I'm doing. I'll leave him a note. Eventually, I'll have to sell this property. He has the film rights to my books. Maybe the show will be a great success, and Oz will know people who will want to live here. I don't know. I don't know anything."

Pippa fought the cry in her voice, but she feared her mother heard it. She didn't want to leave her cozy cottage. It was the first real home she'd ever known. She didn't want to leave town. She didn't want any of this to happen. But she couldn't blame Oz for making it happen. She wanted to find his son as much as he did. And she longed with all her heart to be there when it happened, to hold him in joy or sorrow, but she was a walking target for disaster.

"If you're doing this for me, don't," Gloria said carefully. "I don't think anyone sees me as dangerous anymore, but I know how to hide. You shouldn't have to give up your home."

"I shouldn't, but I have to, for me, for you, for Donal. Even *strangers* know me in L.A. But I bet I could move to Omaha and be virtually invisible because no one would believe Syrene lives in Nebraska. I could live almost normally anywhere else." She wanted that. She wasn't running away. She was running toward a goal, she told herself.

Gloria nodded and began to fill the suitcases with the treasures Pippa pulled from her cabinets, the ones she couldn't bear to part with. She may have disliked what she became, but she'd enjoyed working with music professionals and had CDs signed by her backup band, friends, and people she'd toured with. Artists had given her autographed originals of the illustrations in her books. She knew what was really precious.

"Do you have a car, dear?" Gloria asked warily.

"I can rent one." Pippa looked up from sorting through the next cabinet. "I need Conan to make new identities for us. Do you think he will without telling his brother?"

"I cannot imagine it, but I suppose it can't hurt to ask."

"I'll ask him to make one just for you. With a driver's license. That won't seem odd to him. And then we'll rent the car under your new name." Pippa dived back into the cabinet, letting adrenaline take over so she didn't have to think about everything she was giving up, the life she had so carefully built, the one so eminently suited to her handicaps.

She could do it again. She simply didn't know if she had the heart for it.

She could very well be leaving her heart here. With Oz. It wasn't doing her any good anyway.

Sitting in the dark cave of his front room, Conan hung up the phone and stared at the programming code scrolling across his monitor.

Gloria Malcolm wanted new ID. Good thinking, given the drug dealers in her past, but he had to wonder about the timing. Pippa's performance was tomorrow. Was she preparing to make a break afterward?

He would, if he had any Malcolm talent. California wasn't safe. The evidence of that was scrolling across his screen right now.

Oz would hate it.

Conan stared at the code and then back to the photo

of a towheaded toddler taped to the corner of the big screen monitor. He hadn't paid much attention to the kid when he'd been around. Munchkins lacked higher communication skills, so Conan couldn't talk to his nephew. But he'd watched the kid out of curiosity on the occasions they'd crossed paths.

Donal had been a destructive tornado with an infinite capacity for discombobulating every mechanical item that caught his attention. Oz had laughingly given him a toy toolbox for Christmas after his son had unerringly located Oz's prized pocket knife to jimmy open the television remote. Donal had immediately used his toy hammer to smash open the toy computer to see how it made sounds. The kid wasn't dumb.

What if…?

Conan shook his head. There was no arguing that the Oswin/Ives branch of the family had some power brokers and geniuses, but that was brains, not woo-woo abilities. If he wanted to find a powerful Malcolm—he'd go after the influential side of the family before he'd go after singers.

Which is what someone had done—gone after Donal.

If even his logic fell down that foolish path of wanting to believe Donal was *special*, Conan would bet the women really believed the kid had been kidnapped because he was some magical Malcolm genius. In which case, they might believe they were protecting him by leaving. Oz wasn't going to like that either.

The question was—did he tell Oz because his brother ought to be warned? Or did he keep his mouth shut because he thought the women were doing the right thing?

He supposed it depended on what happened

tomorrow. He couldn't bring in the FBI on the basis of a few simple text messages and a woman's hysteria. The program code he was reading from the website was merely a targeted virus that the police wouldn't take seriously.

It was up to him and his team to keep Pippa safe and scoop Donal out of a crowd of youngsters and their mamas. He was a geek, not Special Ops. But this was California. He could find what he needed with the punch of a few buttons. It was just knowing what he needed that was the challenge.

Thinking like a kidnapper had never been one of his talents.

Chapter 32

Pippa woke up Monday morning to a pillow still damp from crying herself to sleep. In irritation at her weakness, she punched the feathers, checked the time, and forced her feet to find the floor.

She hated sleeping alone. One of the best parts of marriage had been having Robbie there to comfort her when she woke up with stress-related panic attacks. Until the nights when Robbie hadn't been there and her life had fallen apart.

She missed having Oz's broad back in the bed beside her, providing the physical security she'd never had and the sexual tension that she relished. She missed his husky murmurs and his arm reaching to drag her back, telling her without words that he needed her.

In a few short weeks, she had grown far too dependent on an arrogant man who wanted to rule her life.

Even she knew that argument was full of holes. So she stood in the shower and soaked her head.

Conan had sent someone with a rental car and Gloria's ID last night. The man was uncanny. Pippa fretted that he'd tell his brother, but so far, a furious Oz hadn't shown up on their doorstep. Maybe Conan could calm him down and explain once they were gone.

If she thought Oz really needed her, this would be harder to do. But once he had Donal back, he'd return to his old self, and he'd be fine. He needed to get back in sync with his usual business. Putting up with her idiosyncrasies would only hold him back.

She wasn't entirely certain what she would do if they didn't find Donal. It would be cruel to desert a grieving father, but maybe Oz would prefer that any reminder of his failure went away. She simply didn't know what was right in that case.

Maybe it would be healthier if he accepted that Donal was gone and move on. She just didn't think Oz knew the meaning of *give up*. And she couldn't be Syrene for him. She feared that's what he would want—for her to go on singing, in his hope that somehow Syrene could find Donal. She wasn't that scared teenager any more. She couldn't go back to what she hadn't wanted to be in the first place. She liked who she was now. Mostly.

She finished packing her suitcase with last-minute items and then studied herself in the mirror. She was older and wiser than her teenage self, but her cheekbones and eyes couldn't be disguised. She dragged on Oz's ball cap, set her rose-colored glasses on her nose, left off lipstick, and made herself a little bit invisible. But she couldn't wear the disguise on stage while reading for the cameras.

With a sigh, she took off the cap and glasses and shoved them into her overlarge shoulder bag, added her stuffed seal to her suitcase, and zipped it up. She glanced around at the sunny bedroom she'd decorated in crisp whites and soft blue-greens, drew her fingers wistfully over the smiling flowers she'd painted on the wall by her mirror, and said her farewells.

She'd lived here longer than she'd lived anywhere. She knew how to move forward.

Gloria was garbed in her usual long peasant skirt that concealed her twisted hip. Her eyes looked shadowed as she glanced up at Pippa's entrance. "Good morning, dear. Do you have someone who can empty the refrigerator if we don't return?"

"I'll call Lizzy. She has a key. Park will help you with the bags after Oz and I leave. You'll like him. He's a lovely man, with tons of grandsons who can pick him up in Bakersfield."

"I'd rather go with you now." Gloria still wasn't completely happy with their plan.

"I'll be more comfortable doing what I have to do if I know you're safely in the car waiting for me. I really don't expect an audience of mothers and kids to be a problem. It's not a concert, after all. I'm just worried about what happens if Oz grabs Donal and runs. Maybe I can have someone send us a video of the show later so you can see it."

"Maybe we can watch it on the TV news," Gloria said dryly. "Producer kidnaps his own child. Syrene comes back to life and disappears again."

The potential for disaster was enormous, but she refused to worry. "I kind of like that headline." Pippa rummaged through the fruit, looking for some they could take with them in the car. "I'm liking the idea of a road trip too. I haven't done this in a long time."

"Do you remember how to drive?" Gloria sliced an orange with a sharp clank of her knife against the counter.

"Like riding a bike. I did that just fine too. How good are you at navigating?" Pippa was thrilled to see that Gloria was perking up enough to argue with her.

"I'll need more than your old atlas," her mother warned.

"We can pick up maps at welcome centers. It will be fun, honest. Start thinking about where you'd like to live next."

Pippa was still telling herself that a few hours later when she strode up the walk to meet Oz.

Oz watched Pippa hurry up to the parking lot, swinging a huge shoulder bag, as soon as his car pulled in. He had to hurriedly finish his phone call over last-minute preparations so he could climb out and greet her. She must have been waiting for him.

She looked spectacular in a tie-dyed twist skirt that hit right below her knees and showed off her ankles in high-heeled wedge sandals. The strappy peach camisole revealed as much as it concealed, forcing him to check out the goods before giving her a happy smile. He hoped the bare skin was for him.

He caught her waist and kissed her thoroughly before she could say a word. To his relief, she threw her arms around his neck and kissed him back as if she hadn't seen him in eons. He loved her enthusiasm and enjoyed the blush of color on her cheeks when he finally set her down. He liked even better that she didn't shove away but lingered in his arms to lean against him. Maybe she'd recovered from Saturday's debacle.

"I missed you," he said in a scolding tone. "You better have had as bad a night as I did."

"Worse," she admitted with a shrug, finally pushing back. "We'll survive. Is your crew on the way? No glitches yet?"

He opened the BMW's passenger door for her.

"Moving like clockwork. I followed the set truck until the exit up here. The school will keep the entire stage area cordoned off, so we can move about freely. Costume and makeup will be there after lunch. It's a go."

She glanced in the back. "No child seat?"

The vise around Oz's heart tightened, but he tried to keep it light. "In the trunk. Are you sure your mother doesn't want to go with us? There's room."

"She's afraid her limp will hamper us. I told her you'd send a video. She's manning the phone, just in case." She produced her cell phone. "I can call and tell her I'm fine."

He was oddly reluctant to close the door and take his seat. He didn't want to involve Pippa in this. She appeared completely unconcerned, but he knew better. She'd learned to maintain calm in the face of the storm. That didn't mean a storm wasn't raging inside her. He knew so much more than when he'd brashly walked up to the day care and told her he wanted her on his show. She was shutting out the world right now, and that included him.

He wanted the real Pippa back, but Donal came first. If she needed to be Zen Pippa to do this, he could take it.

"The minute you feel uneasy, I want you to walk off the stage," he ordered, starting the engine. "Conan is meeting us there. He'll have someone backstage who can hustle you out."

She waved at an elderly Asian dude stepping out of an old Corolla. The man bowed back. The martial arts instructor, Oz remembered. Gloria wouldn't be good at kickboxing, but maybe she could take up karate.

Pippa was as good at organizing and manipulating as

he was, just more subtle. She'd found a way to keep her mother occupied.

"I don't think there will be any problem with the performance," she said serenely, folding her legs in the seat and adopting a yoga pose. "What's with the beach clothes?"

Oz glanced down at his Tommy Bahama shirt and jeans, and it was his turn to redden. "Donal saw me mostly on weekends when I was wearing casual clothes."

He didn't explain further, but Pippa nodded, understanding that he hoped the clothes would help Donal recognize him.

"You have the hard part, looking for Donal," she agreed. "I'll have the lights in my eyes and won't be too helpful there."

There were too damned many ways for this to go wrong.

"I'm hoping the song is some kind of signal to the Librarian, maybe to let the kid loose. But he'll be confused. I hate this." Oz pounded the wheel.

"It's just as likely the song will be a signal to start a riot or a fire," she said with a trace of humor. "We'll have to hope my mother is right and that it's a siren song for kids. We really can't predict the results. We simply go in there and stay alert. Once I start reading, I think I can keep the crowd quiet. Maybe it will take time for them to recover before whatever happens, happens."

He hadn't told her that the Librarian wanted her to sing. And he didn't intend to. The recording would have to be enough. He'd learned his lesson about pushing too hard when Pippa said no. He had to trust her instincts as much as he did his own.

"You're right." He punched the CD button, and

Saturday's beach music filled the car. "I put more disks in the console and in the backseat, if you want to look at them."

Pippa flipped through the console and the ones he had in a case in back. He'd come prepared to feed her music cravings.

He almost lost it when she chose the one with the children's songs on it that he'd brought for Donal. His fingers clenched the wheel until his knuckles turned white. Would Donal remember singing those songs?

Oz didn't know what vibes he was giving off, but Pippa immediately shut off "Wheels on the Bus."

"I'm sorry," she murmured. "It's been so long since I heard children's songs; I thought maybe they'd be good to know…"

"It's okay. You're right. Singing a kid song might be needed for crowd control. I don't want that to happen, but it's better to be prepared. You just caught me by surprise."

She reached over and squeezed his thigh, which drained the blood from his brain to other parts and let him release his iron fist around the steering wheel.

He refused to sound weak and say he needed her to stay in his life. He'd tell her that later, when they were both standing on firm ground again. He reached over and punched the CD on, but he skipped past the damned bus song.

They arrived in Bakersfield before lunch. Pippa studied the sprawling desert town with adult eyes, flinching at the rusting trailers, cars up on blocks, and old sofas sitting on front steps in the part of town where she'd grown up. Her adopted father had been a bus driver, a perfectly respectable working-class man. Her adopted mother had baby-sat and taken in foster kids.

They'd made ends meet, just like everyone else in the neighborhood. But living paycheck to paycheck... things happened. She had never blamed the Jameses for taking the opportunity to get rich when it had arrived. They may have taken in kids for the money, but they'd been kind and provided a home, which was more than the wealthy had done.

Pippa hoped her adopted parents were enjoying life now. They'd made it clear that they were happy to be rid of her and to move on, and she wished them well. They'd never really known what to do with the cuckoo in their nest, and she'd pushed their endurance to the limit.

The school was situated in a modest suburb of neat stucco houses and tiny yards. The small parking lot was already half full. She didn't know how many people would actually attend a television rehearsal with only a children's author as a draw. Depended on what else was happening that day, she supposed. Did they have ball games on Mondays?

Oz pulled up next to the sound truck. The set crew was still unloading the back of the van. Pippa felt a shiver at this familiar routine. But it was broad daylight, she wasn't arriving in a chauffeured limo with bodyguards on both sides, and this was an elementary school full of little kids, not a riot of screaming fans. She could do this, one hand tied behind her back.

"I wonder if the Librarian is watching," she said quietly, opening her door without waiting on Oz.

He turned his headset back on and shook his head. "Want to check out the school library, just in case?"

"Let one of Conan's men do it. Or women," she added, watching what appeared to be a teenager crossing the lot, ponytail swinging. Except Pippa knew how to spot body armor and weapons beneath the hoodie. She bet the school wouldn't like that if they knew.

Oz's headset buzzed as he held her elbow and escorted her across the lot to the rear of the school. She figured he was better off keeping his mind on the production and not whether his son was inside somewhere.

A mob of little kids raced onto the playground, and Oz froze, swinging around to watch. The kids looked a few years older than Donal would be.

They had no way of knowing if his son attended this school or any school. He'd only be in kindergarten. The school had been chosen because of its availability, not from anything the Librarian had told them. There was no reason to believe the boy was on the grounds.

There was no real reason to believe the boy was alive.

Pippa set her back teeth and tried to keep a rein on her nerves. This would be far easier if there weren't so much at stake.

Half of her wanted to stand in the middle of the parking lot and sing until the whole town showed up. The other half wanted to hide and pray all she had to do was read a book.

Park and her mother wouldn't arrive until it was almost time for the performance. Until then, Pippa had a strange desire to look around, to see if she recognized anyone, but she accepted Oz's wisdom in hastening into the dark recesses backstage where she was surrounded by his people. There was strength in uniting and circling the wagons in a defensible position. She almost wished she hadn't left Gloria behind.

Conan didn't even acknowledge them when they entered. He was going through a PDA checklist with a burly guy who kept nodding and barking into his headset.

Pippa peered around the curtain to the empty auditorium, with chairs stretching movie-theater style to the back. This was a better school than the one she'd attended. There was even a small light and sound system overhead. Oz's crew was already playing with it.

The set under construction was simple—they'd decided on an ocean theme to go with the seal story and song. Rocks adorned by big purple cardboard seals filled the background. Oz was hoping that advertising the theme and song would be enough for the Librarian to get the significance of their arrival, along with Conan's implanted messages. They'd debated putting Pippa in a lifeguard's stand but decided she could escape faster from a beach chair stationed on what was supposed to be a grassy hillock on the side of the stage. Most of the stage was left open for the real performers.

The lunch truck and its catering wagons arrived. Pippa stood in the shadows, straining to recognize faces of the local catering staff, but it had been too long, she realized in relief. Elementary school kids changed too much. She'd left Bakersfield when she was ten.

While Oz signed off on invoices, Conan cornered her, stuffing a packet into her shoulder bag. "I can find you, wherever you go. Don't do anything stupid."

He walked off, leaving Pippa chilled to the bone.

Chapter 33

Oz watched Pippa turn pale and cursed Conan. His brother, the geek, had never learned to employ a modicum of finesse. What the hell had he said to her?

The caterer shoved an invoice in front of him, and Oz quickly perused it while listening to Nick, the director, shouting through his headset about a dancer who'd flaked out. It was impossible to rush to Pippa's side. She wouldn't want him to.

Oz's assistant signaled from the sidelines, where she stood beside a woman who looked very much like a school principal in neat navy blazer, dumpy blue dress, and comfortable shoes.

He didn't dare believe the Librarian would actually make an appearance, but he wouldn't take chances. He cut off Nick, signed the invoice, and worked his way through the tangle of cords and crew milling around the buffet tables.

"Mrs. Lillian Thompson, the principal," his assistant said as Oz strode up.

"It's a delight to have Ms. James here today. The children are all excited," the principal said with a good-natured twinkle in her eye. "I'm hoping most of them will be able to stay after school for the show. Anything to encourage them to read has my approval."

Harmless and most likely not the Librarian was Oz's instant appraisal. His headset buzzed, and he ignored it to shake the lady's hand. "I appreciate your willingness to lend a stage on such short notice. If this experiment works, we may be able to travel from school to school, encouraging reading. And of course, your library will receive a substantial donation from our sponsors. Would you like to meet Ms. James?"

Silly question. But Oz figured Pippa would be more relaxed if she knew someone here and was more connected to the good they could do. He signaled his assistant to lead Pippa from her hiding place, but a problem with security had him saying farewell before she arrived.

Vowing to make it a point to know every damned person on the set or anywhere near it, Oz jogged down the steps and into the auditorium. This might be his last chance to find his son, and he wouldn't risk blowing it.

Pippa invited the principal to join the crew for lunch. They discussed children's literature, which was a cathartic experience. She'd never had an opportunity to actually talk books with readers, to learn what children outside the day care liked or what their parents wanted. Mrs. Thompson told her of a local writers group that included several children's book authors, and Pippa wondered what it would be like to discuss writing with them.

She'd been isolated for so long…

For good reason. Driving into L.A. for intellectual discussions would have been dangerous, especially before she had control of her Voice. Maybe now that Oz had shown her she could achieve some normality, she'd look for a town with other writers in it.

After lunch, the musicians and dancers began warming up, and Mrs. Thompson excused herself and departed. Pippa slipped into the restroom that had been cordoned off for the day and checked the papers Conan had shoved into her purse.

An Oklahoma driver's license in the name of Sarah Wright—borrowing from her mother's maiden name of Wainwright. The license he'd had delivered to Gloria last night had given her name as Jean Wright. He'd provided identical addresses in Oklahoma for both of them.

Conan knew she was leaving. Oz's brother might be blunt and rude, but he understood security. Maybe she wouldn't throw him in the pool the next time she ran into him. If there ever was a next time.

Shoving the knifing pain of departure deep down inside her as she'd eventually learned to do after she'd left the music business, Pippa breathed deeply and evenly and regained some of her Zen calm. Oz had bent over backward to make this easy for her. He didn't need her to fall apart at this crucial moment.

She found the makeup person and submitted to being plastered with a foundation color darker than her natural vampire pale, one that would look better in TV lights. She wanted to suggest purple teardrops and bright green eye shadow, but the cosmetician was trying to make her look like a lovable author, not a clown. Pippa's only insistence was that the lip color be kept to a bright red. Platinum Syrene had been known for pale pink.

Not that Pippa had any intention of revealing her face on camera if it could be avoided. She'd discussed this with Oz and the director, and they'd found a solution that suited her.

She met the costume technician who had a loose linen beach shirt and pants ready for her. Fit wasn't a problem with the drawstring waist. A huge gaudy necklace of bright-colored beads and shells added sparkle to the neutral vanilla of the shirt. The pièce de résistance was the big floppy beach hat with a band dripping with beads and shells to match the necklace. The bright red straw matched some of the bigger beads. Best of all, the broad brim could be drawn down and tilted to conceal most of Pippa's face.

Oz came over to check on her as the set director arranged her in the beach chair, and Nick Townsend ordered the light crew to make adjustments.

"Are you okay?" he asked in low tones so the people rushing around them couldn't hear.

"Not totally centered, but as close as I can get," she replied, trying to reassure him. "Does Conan's security team all have pictures of Donal?"

"Age-enhanced," Oz said grimly. "They've been on this case for a while. They're so jazzed, I can only pray they don't grab the wrong kid."

"Praying is all there's left for us to do." She squeezed his hand—she wouldn't acknowledge that it might be the last time—and then returned to professional mode, adjusting her hat according to someone's shouted command.

Oz stalked off to settle another crisis while the sound crew adjusted her microphone and cursed the floppy shirt and the beaded necklace. With the ease of experience, she clipped the mic to her necklace and shirt to avoid rattling noises and anchor the clip's weight.

Frightening that even after all these years she had as

much experience as the technicians here today. It made her feel like an old wise woman before her time.

She slipped into her zone to pray that she would do the right thing when the time came—whether that time was failure or triumph.

Trying for Pippa's Zen calm and failing, Oz paced at the end of the stage behind her, where he could peer from behind the curtain at the audience and keep an eye on Pippa and the performance at the same time. It wasn't a big stage. He should be able to react quickly at the first sign of trouble.

He told himself that the production would move smoothly and there would be no revelations, but hope had wiggled its way out of the steel box he'd hidden it in for so long. He blamed Pippa for that. Despite her laconic attitude, her magical talent had given him reason to believe that there was a greater plan behind the void that had become his life.

He had Donal's favorite Transformer figure in his pocket. Would a kid remember his favorite toy after a year?

Oz's brother slipped out of the shadows and jerked the curtain back to observe the empty auditorium. "They're about to let the crowd in," Conan said. "The crew has checked everyone in line against the photos of the nanny and Donal. We're not finding matches. I have people stationed at every entrance."

Okay, so his son wasn't here. Oz tried to breathe and couldn't. He nodded and double-checked on Pippa. At least he had Pippa. He hoped. He wasn't sure if he could keep her, but he wanted to. That might be the wrong part of his brain talking. He'd straighten out his thinking later, but he was pretty damned sure Pippa with her eager kisses, creative mood swings, and blunt honesty was exactly what he needed to stay sane.

He held onto that thought as the audience filtered in, chattering happily. He couldn't tear his gaze away from the kids to look back at Pippa, but he knew she was stationed in her chair yards away, waiting for the curtain to open. She'd been trained well. No last-minute hysterics from his star.

The auditorium wasn't well lit. He could see dozens of towheaded children, but the kidnappers could have dyed Donal's hair. He needed to see faces, eye color, his son's determined little chin. His animated expression when he tore apart his Transformer toy.

Maybe Donal had outgrown Transformers and children's songs.

Maybe he was dead.

Oz clutched the curtain and continued to scan the audience, this time looking for the nanny. The place was filled with young women and their children. Heidi had been in her twenties, with long blonde hair, blue eyes, and a kind face. She could have cut and dyed her hair, so he stuck to faces. Most twenty-somethings had kind faces. Or bland ones. None of them had Pippa's character. He was obsessing. He clutched the curtain tighter and focused.

As the last of the audience wandered about, looking for seats, Oz cast a glance over his shoulder to Pippa. She was watching him. Even he could scarcely recognize her in that boringly neutral loose outfit. She could be eighty in that thing for all anyone could tell. He leered at her anyway, and her lips tilted upward in acknowledgment before she turned back to watch Nick's signals.

She was nervous. She wouldn't be paying so much attention to orders if she wasn't unsure of herself. *Breathe, Oz.*

Announcer. Greetings. Lights down. He couldn't see faces at all now, only movement. A few stragglers located seats. Kids giggled, parents murmured, until the curtains opened and the magic began.

Dancing purple seals caught their interest. *Stick to business*, Oz reminded himself. The mechanical gulls caused a wave of laughter. Excellent.

He glanced back at Pippa, but she faced the stage, and he couldn't tell if she was enjoying the production based on her story. They probably needed her reading throughout the show, but for this attempt, they'd decided to let her read the whole story last. Right now, she was merely a shadow on the sidelines. The dancers and singers had the spotlight.

Latecomers began lining up along the walls and crouching down in front. Bad for fire safety, Oz suspected. If they did take the production on the road, he'd have to add an audience limit. Today, he wanted everyone here who wanted to be here.

There had to be five hundred people out there. Donal could have slipped past Conan's crew. Wiggling, giggling kids weren't easily identified in mob scenes, not by strangers, anyway. Oz wanted to walk down there with a flashlight and scan every face. After all this effort, his son had to be out there, if only he could get close enough to see him.

He couldn't believe he was actually trusting a text message—as Alys had. He had to forgive her for that. He had to let it all go and simply hope.

The production was scaled to a half-hour television format, which meant it was less than twenty-five minutes long. The spotlight fell on Pippa before Oz was prepared.

Calm and crystal clear, her voice captured the audience from the first line: "Ronan was a lonely seal who only wanted a friend."

Straight to the heart. The purple seals on stage turned their back on the speckled one—the newcomer just appearing on stage. As Pippa read her story, the dancers formed circles, excluding the speckled seal, who retreated to his lonely rock.

The audience fell into a trancelike silence. He'd seen this happen before, back on the mountain when she'd hypnotized her listeners until she'd lured an autistic little boy out of the chaparral. He knew the spell would end a few minutes after Pippa's voice halted. She wasn't applying any emphasis, didn't do character accents or raise or lower her voice for the different animals. She simply entranced with what she called the hypnotic sound of her Voice.

Conan's crew was trying to circulate, but the crowd filling the aisles prevented it. They should have gone for a larger stadium, but Bakersfield didn't offer a lot of last-minute choices. Oz fretted, but he couldn't change anything now.

Pippa was reaching the end of the story. Several of the kids sobbed, and a couple of mothers wiped their eyes.

The musicians struck up their tune as the speckled seal barked. Pippa had updated "The Silly Seal Song" to start out as a rap tune, with lots of rhythm. The seal pounded his flippers on the rock as if it were a drum. The dancer was really getting into the gig, and Oz almost smiled. Even without Pippa's voice, the song was a winner.

The other seals turned to watch the smaller, speckled one dancing on the rocks. Pippa closed the cardboard mock-up of a book, and the Syrene soundtrack began. The live musicians toned down to accompany the CD. Syrene's voice soared through the auditorium—and the seals began to dance together.

Silent now, Pippa didn't leave her post but stared over the audience, her hands clasped tightly in her lap.

Oz turned, too, praying a small boy would magically tumble out of the audience and run up to the stage, not knowing what to expect as the song played through its verses and the seals danced.

The ensuing silence wasn't the reaction they wanted.

Chapter 34

PIPPA HADN'T EXPECTED HER HYPNOTIC STORY READING to lure Donal from his keepers—if he was even here. She could only hope she had lulled them into complacence.

Like the color of her eyes on film, the full power of her Voice did not come through in recordings. She'd hoped enough of the siren quality of the seal song would survive on the CD, as the anger had on the recordings her mother heard, but a child's song was more subtle. It apparently needed to be live to work.

She had no idea what would happen if she sang. She'd never killed an audience, though. She'd caused riots, but drunken teenagers weren't the same as happy mothers and toddlers. The seal song might not affect adults at all.

As the final verses of the recording played, the audience remained captivated, but there was no sign of Donal. Oz's tension and disappointment, as well as that of Conan's search crew, practically vibrated the air.

Pippa had argued with herself for days. Weeks. When it came right down to it—she couldn't put all these people, she couldn't put *Oz*, through this intense event, this heartrending expectation, without giving all she had to give.

Even if it meant the end of her privacy and any hope of staying with Oz, Pippa couldn't leave a lost boy out there if she had the power to find him. For once, this wasn't about her.

Watching sharply for any movement in the crowd, finding none, she signaled the sound crew. Prepared, they lowered the recording, and Pippa began to sing into her microphone as she hadn't done for an audience in nine years.

She poured all her own loneliness and fear into her siren Voice. The song bled from her heart, soared through the room, transmitting her heartbreak and isolation directly to her audience.

After the first few minutes of astonishment, children leaped from their seats and raced for the stage, just as if she were the Pied Piper. Mothers shouted and chased after their toddlers. Conan's crew formed a security guard at the foot of the stage.

Someone shouted, "Syrene!" Pippa caught the flash of a camera. She continued to sing, searching for the one little boy who meant the most. Cell phones emerged, capturing the moment as children scrambled around the guards, leaving their mothers helplessly in the audience. Still no Donal. Would she even recognize him?

The film and the music would be instantly flooding the Internet. It wouldn't take long for rumors to fly. The media would be on it within an hour. Her anonymity was shattered.

Pippa continued to sing, unleashing her siren call with all the power in her, praying one of the children scrambling to the stage was the one they wanted.

She touched their hands as they gathered around her, studied their faces, tousled their hair, and pointed at the floor, where they obediently sat cross-legged. She continued scanning the last of the children escaping the audience as she sang, praying hard for the right one.

A dark-haired boy with suspiciously light roots and wearing heavy glasses fought through the crowd of mothers to race up the stairs. Pippa's voice stumbled upon seeing the familiar cinnamon-brown eyes behind the glass. Then the elation of recognition escaped, and her Voice soared with joy. She reached out to him, and he grabbed her hand with an Oswin smile. She shivered with triumph and rejoiced.

She hauled the boy into her lap and hugged him tight. She heard a frightened shout from the audience as she finished the last notes. Conan's security guards closed in on the foot of the stage. Pippa didn't look away from the little ones at her feet.

The boy wrapped his short arms around her as if he'd never let go. Her heart took him in, loved him, and sheltered him. He looked so much like his father! She wished she dared turn to see Oz's face, but she had to stay focused. Tears filled her eyes as she slowly rose with children clinging to her clothes and cell phone flashes popping all over the auditorium.

Wild clapping filled the air, filled her soul. The shouts were louder now, closer. Pippa briefly closed her eyes against the fear, but Conan's security guards were leaping to the stage to surround her.

The curtain dropped before the applause was done, and suddenly Oz was there, reaching out, crying his son's name.

The boy shouted "Daddy!" and almost leaped from Pippa's arms.

It was going to be all right.

Tears washing down her cheeks, she helped usher the children around the curtain, back to their mothers. She didn't know why these children had responded to her song, if they were lost like Donal. She couldn't linger to interview the parents, as much as she might like to do so. She wasn't qualified to choose who belonged where.

A loud argument and scuffle broke out in front of the curtains, warning she needed to flee. Pippa hoped Conan's security was capturing a kidnapper, but she couldn't wait to find out. Uniformed policemen rushed Oz and Donal backstage. Someone had called in official reinforcement.

Guards prevented curiosity seekers from slipping past the curtains. The crew was needed elsewhere. Left alone, Pippa calmly lay her hat on the chair. She unpinned the mic and removed the beads and then stripped to the peach tank top and biker shorts she'd worn under her skirt earlier. Producing her ball cap and glasses from her bag, she strolled through the mob backstage, unnoticed in the excitement, creating a bubble of invisibility with her tuneless humming.

Outside, when she was almost safe, a burly man rushed up to her, shoving a microphone at her face and shouting about Syrene. As Syrene, she would have panicked and shrieked until he'd groveled at her feet.

But that wasn't who she was now. Nearly petrified that she'd been discovered and would soon be mobbed, Pippa still kept her cool and didn't scream. Clamping her mouth shut, she used the self-defense tactics Park had taught her, disarming the microphone with the swing of her arm and then kicking sideways while her victim was off guard.

The man tumbled to the ground, holding his crotch. She wished she'd known that maneuver when the paparazzi had surrounded her. Heart pounding, she jogged for the street, scanning the parked cars for her mother's nondescript white rental.

She'd done it. She'd performed and escaped the mob without notice. She'd feel relief later, once the paralysis of fear wore off.

Police cars were still arriving. Trying to still her racing pulse, she hummed as she passed officers rushing for the entrance. Like the crowds on Saturday, they gave her a wide berth. Control was the key. *No panic, Pippa,* she told herself.

Spotting the rental, Pippa increased her pace. Oz would be tied up with police and the school and whatever was happening back there. She wished she could be part of it, could hold his hand, admire his gorgeous little boy, and hum them into relaxing. But she'd done her part. She wasn't needed here any longer. For everyone's safety, Syrene had to disappear again.

It didn't matter that it broke her heart to do so. Her love was strong enough to endure the pain.

Her mother struggled out of the front seat to hug her when Pippa reached the road. "Did they find him?"

Pippa nodded. "He's a beautiful little boy. They'll be fine. Let's go."

Gloria wiped the tears on Pippa's cheeks, studied her sadly, and then nodded. "I wish it could be otherwise," she whispered.

There wasn't anything Pippa could say to that. Leaving her heart behind, she stuck her key in the ignition and eased the car onto the road.

Holding Donal, letting him play with the Transformer while smiling like a demento and firmly rejecting anyone who suggested taking his son away, Oz searched the crowd for Pippa. He'd hoped she would be here by his side while he struggled with the police, waited for his lawyer, and reassured his crew. The terrified nanny had stopped screaming a moment ago.

He lifted a questioning eyebrow at Conan when his brother arrived, but the geek merely shrugged and insinuated himself into the crowd around the nanny his security held.

Facts and small details were beginning to emerge from Heidi's stumbling protests, but Oz wanted them all written up in a paper file he could study later. Right now, he couldn't concentrate on stories or guilt. He wanted to take Donal out of here and find Pippa and go home. He didn't care what home as long as it contained his son and Pippa.

When a newspaper reporter showed up at the same time that his son started searching for the pretty lady singer, Oz knew it was time to leave. Justice rolled too slowly. Pippa and his son were more important than kidnappers or revenge.

Cops objected to his removing the boy, but Conan's staff intervened. Oz's lawyer showed up right behind the reporter, adding another layer of security. Oz eased out of the crowd, placing Donal on his shoulders and telling him to yell if he saw the pretty lady.

The kid got into the search, but no one had seen Pippa.

Oz found her hat and shirt laying across the chair, and his heart sank. Like a chameleon, she'd slipped into new colors. She was gone. He knew she was gone.

Had known she would leave from the first shout of *Syrene!* in the audience. But he had hoped... She had given up her anonymity for Donal. He wasn't allowed to ask for more. He thought he might choke on his grief and fear for her.

Nick arrived to tickle Donal under the chin. "My boys are eager to see you again, kid. Glad to have you back."

Donal smiled shyly and buried his face in Oz's hair.

Nick grew solemn and removed a sealed envelope from his pocket. "Pippa said to give you this. Are you going to explain what happened here today?"

"Pippa worked magic," was all Oz said, trying not to stare at the note in horror. He tucked it into his shirt pocket, refusing to reveal his desperate need to open it.

"Don't give me that *Pippa* bit," Nick scolded in the tone of an old friend. "I've kept my cool and played with a straight face, but no one else in the world has that voice. With the hounds baying at the door, I suppose the note means she had an escape route planned? Was this Syrene's leap back to the limelight? Am I looking for a new reader for the next show?"

"I told you to have an understudy lined up," Oz said wearily. "Bring Audrey in. And no, this isn't anyone's leap back to the limelight. The exact opposite, in fact, so keep what you think you know under your hat, will you? I need to see that she's all right."

Nick scowled, but he stepped back, blocking all the other people crowding around with questions, allowing Oz to escape.

Pippa was tall and should be watching, preparing to make the break with him. He didn't see her bright orange-red hair anywhere.

"Where's Heidi?" Donal asked as they walked into the desert warmth of an almost-April day without any sign of Pippa anywhere.

"Heidi needs to talk to some people." And fight a kidnapping conviction. Explaining to his son what happened to the nanny might take creativity that Oz didn't possess. He needed Pippa's reassuring voice and presence. The letter burned in his pocket.

"Where's your favorite place to eat?" he asked as Donal's face began to crumple. The kid had already lost a mother. Losing the woman who had been his substitute mother for years would be devastating. Were five-year-olds too young for therapy?

The boy brightened again. "McDonalds!" he crowed. "I wanna kids' meal and a chawklit milkshake."

"I can do that, big boy." Vowing to eat a steady diet of Big Macs if that's what it took to make his kid happy, Oz set the boy in the back of the BMW while he produced the child's seat from the trunk.

He didn't have another nanny lined up. He would have to learn to do all these everyday things on his own.

His head was a whirl of giddy relief that he had Donal back and his son seemed to be fine, fear that he couldn't do this on his own, and distraction at Pippa's flight.

With Donal strapped into his seat and playing with familiar toys, the CD player turned on to his favorite songs, Oz stole a moment to rip open the letter.

It smelled of roses. It was as brief as Pippa was laconic.

> *I owe you for my life and my mother. I hope finding your son pays back some of what I owe. I can't repay you with the grief Syrene*

*would cause. Have a happy life and know that
somewhere in the vast wastelands of America,
a Malcolm loves you.*

Oz wanted to ball up the paper and fling it across the car. Instead, he carefully folded it and returned it to his pocket. Maybe it would make more sense later, when he was in better control.

A Malcolm loves you? The woman was crazed. But he'd known that going in.

His Bluetooth buzzed, and with a sigh, Oz clicked it on.

"The media is breaking down the door," his receptionist in L.A. cried frantically. "What does Syrene have to do with us?"

"Nothing. Absolutely nothing. Tell them they heard an old recording. Tell them I'll be available for interviews tomorrow. Tell them I've found my son and that's today's news."

His receptionist cried in joy but was cut off by loud voices in the background. Oz decided it would be best not to return to L.A. until after dark.

Pippa was right. All hell was about to break loose. She was better off disappearing if she didn't want to return to that life.

He'd need the nanny's story to see if being a Malcolm really was dangerous. It might be best if he kept Donal hidden a while longer.

Not daring to turn off the phone in case Conan had an urgent message, Oz steered the BMW out of the lot, wondering where to go after McDonald's.

Wondering if he could find Pippa and have a

wonderful life with a hardheaded, slippery Malcolm or if he had to go on only half living.

He checked the mirror to see his son and verified that retrieving him was worth losing his heart and soul.

Chapter 35

GLORIA STOOD IN FRONT OF THE HOTEL WINDOW overlooking the carnival lights of Las Vegas and shook her head. "Disney World for adults?" she suggested. "I've never seen anything like it."

Which told Pippa of all the things Gloria had missed while trapped in a nursing home or hiding in Mexico. Her mother had lost half her life. That could be rectified, if she wanted it. Pippa set down their suitcase and looked around for the television remote.

"I'm not certain the people who need bright lights and noise for amusement are exactly adults, but close enough." Collapsing on the luxurious bedcover, Pippa flipped on CNN—the place where Vegas-like adults got their entertainment news, she figured.

Sure enough, there it was. Callers were giving their opinion on whether or not the mysterious singer for the new TV kids' show could actually be Syrene, the missing rock star. *Oh right, like that was earthshaking vital news.* The story came accompanied by tinny sound, blurry videos of her hat, and images of children clambering onto the stage.

The story shifted to the news that five-year-old Donal Oswin, the subject of a national search a year ago, had been returned to his father after being kidnapped by the nanny. Lots of Nancy Grace wild speculation as to the whys and wherefores of his appearing during the television performance, light on facts. Maybe the morning papers would tell her something she didn't know.

Pippa switched off the channel, smothering the ridiculous desolation she felt at seeing Donal's happy face flash across the screen. He had been riding Oz's shoulders, but the photo had only caught Oz's tousled blond hair and the crinkle of his brow—probably with laughter. She wished she could be a fly on the wall when they returned home. She wanted to share their happiness, if only for a brief few minutes.

"Call him," Gloria urged, turning away from the window. "There's no reason to break it off so abruptly."

Pippa gestured at the television. "I'm the subject of national speculation right now. You want Oz to lie in front of Nancy Grace and tell her he has no idea where I am? Or worse yet, why Donal came running when I sang?"

"We need to hear the nanny's story," Gloria persisted. "Maybe there's a simple explanation, and you can let him know you'll return as soon as the uproar dies down."

"Syrene will never be invisible," she reminded her mother. "I'll get in touch when they've had time to sift through facts and lies," she promised. "In the meantime, want to explore Vegas nights or wait until morning?" She tried to sound upbeat, as if this were only a temporary break, a vacation.

But even she doubted her decision to leave. Was running away the right route for the person she was now? After driving across the desert, weeping inside, she didn't feel in the least triumphant for having escaped again, like she had the first time. She had a nagging suspicion that running away wasn't helping at all. She simply knew that Syrene couldn't lead a normal life, and Donal deserved one.

Syrene hadn't crippled the obnoxious reporter. Pippa had. That had felt good.

"I don't think Vegas is my kind of place," Gloria said with a sad smile. "After all these years, I don't know how to roam. Let's figure out where we're going tomorrow."

Tomorrow and tomorrow into eternity. Pippa guessed it was better than the alternative, but she was starting to question that—for both of them. Her mother needed a home, a place she felt safe. Pippa had a home she loved and didn't want to give up. Did abandoning those out of fear make sense? Was hiding from those she loved what she wanted?

It had been the right thing to do when she'd been eighteen, terrified, rootless, and heartbroken. She wasn't that abandoned child any longer. She was strong now. She was learning control—of herself and those who would harm her. She had friends who were counting on her and who would keep her from harm if they could.

She would be an idiot to run away from the only man she could be herself with.

Pippa didn't want to be a helpless, terrified idiot again. Hope wiggling its way into her heart, she switched to another station and saw Oz staring right into the camera while hugging his son. The stunned, grieving look behind his smile twisted a knife to her heart. She was an idiot.

She dragged out her laptop and turned it on. First, she needed to know her mother would be safe. That knowledge warmed her with joy. For the first time in her worthless life, she realized she wasn't alone, that she had people she could trust, and that she was needed.

Lizzy glanced up in surprise when Oz stalked into the Blue Bayou the next morning.

"I need to use your bar for a news conference. Is that okay?"

She wiped the bar and watched him warily. "Where's Pippa?"

"Running away. I need to get her back." Oz scanned the setup through his producer's eyes and began shifting tables and chairs as if Lizzy had already agreed. "The media will be arriving shortly. Get pizzas ready."

"If this is how you talk to Pippa, it's a wonder she hasn't flung you off a cliff." Lizzy put her rag back under the bar.

"Pippa knows not to argue when I'm desperate. You want my crew to keep working up here?" Oz straightened and glared back at her.

"Where's your little boy?" Lizzy didn't move.

"At the day care. I've got a security team working with them." He glanced out the newly sparkling window. "News vans can't park in this narrow alley. One's already pulling up on Main Street. Are you calling up the pizzas or not?"

Lizzy started to open her mouth, apparently saw the desperation in his expression, and turned around to yell an order at her cook. The cook yelled back, unprepared for an early lunch crowd. Oz ignored the byplay.

He opened the door for his sound crew, showed them

where they could run cable for their generators, orchestrated the production, and made things happen, as only he knew how. He wasn't an actor. He wasn't a publicity freak. He didn't give speeches.

To get Pippa back, he'd have to be all of the above. And be damned good at it.

He knew how to give sound bites, but this time, he'd promised the media an entire interview. He'd stayed up all night working with Conan and a speech writer. What he needed was a fiction writer, like Pippa. She could convince a bull to sit down and drink tea from a china cup, he was certain.

Convincing Pippa to come home might be equally difficult. If he had any of the persuasive talent of an empath, he'd best put it to use now.

Audrey, the understudy, arrived, along with Nick Townsend and the show's publicity director. They'd all been hastily coached this morning. Oz knew he should have waited until tomorrow to perfect the act, but he didn't want Pippa to get too far away.

He was running on hope and nothing more. He had his son back, but it wasn't enough. He was a greedy bastard, but Donal deserved more than an empty shell of a father.

"Am I serving beer?" Lizzy asked, bringing out mugs.

"Soft drinks, water. This crowd doesn't need alcohol at this hour," Oz said, scraping tables out of the way. "Charge me for renting the building for the day."

"Bring Pippa back, and the pizzas are on the house," Lizzy retorted.

"My wife concurs," Nick said dryly, holding onto a microphone while the crew set up a podium. "She wants to know if you were sitting on your head instead of using it when you let her go."

"Dammit all!" Oz shouted. "I've known her less than three weeks! What did you want me to do, put a collar and chain on her?"

A television crew walked in, cutting off any reply. Besides, Oz already knew the answer. He should have told Pippa he would run and hide in Outer Mongolia with her if that's what she needed to feel safe. She'd returned *Donal*. She'd given up her privacy and security for his son. He'd stayed up what remained of the night after his staff left, watching the boy sleep, just to be certain he was real. He'd cried. For the first time in his adult life, Oz had wept like a child.

He owed Pippa his life. And she thought she owed *him*? They were both nuts. Or incapable of relating on a normal basis, at least—but they understood each other at the most important levels.

What he was about to do wouldn't fix the way they connected, but he hoped it would fix a lot of other things he'd broken in his bullheaded haste to have what he wanted.

Publicity hung a blow-up poster of Donal waving at the camera. Oz wasn't about to subject the kid to the media, but the world deserved to see his happiness, to know that this year of searching and praying hadn't been wasted.

As the tavern filled to capacity with equipment and reporters, Oz gestured for Audrey to take a place behind Lizzy's bar. Audrey had had her hair cut short and dyed like Pippa's, not that anyone yesterday would have seen much underneath the hat. But he wanted the illusion out there, a public face that wasn't Pippa.

She wore Pippa's bright red lipstick and a loose sundress with a gauzy shirt over it. Pippa was about the same height and slenderness, without Audrey's breast enhancement. The camera couldn't tell through the loose clothing.

Oz wished Pippa was here if only to calm the noisy crowd. Reporters who knew him were already shouting questions. He shook his head and waited for Nick to test the microphone. Ignoring requests that he wait for cameras to be positioned or lights turned on, Oz stepped up to the podium as soon as Nick introduced him. He wanted this over. This was just one tiny inkling of what Pippa would endure should she return right now. He had to show her that he understood that.

He thanked everyone for coming, thanked everyone who had aided in Donal's search, referred to the handouts publicity had prepared with the facts about the kidnapping—the ones that were public information. He needed to talk to Pippa about the rest. The police didn't need to know about Malcolms and the Librarian, not yet.

With a solid ground of verifiable facts and information laid, Oz stepped into fabrication territory. "I'd like to introduce the star of our new children's show, Audrey Ephraim. Some of you may recognize her from the stage production last year of *Wicked*. She's a talented actress, singer, and dancer, and we're very fortunate to have her. Audrey, would you step forward?"

Questions flew. Oz could see the journalists didn't want to believe they'd been misled. Syrene returning would be a story they could work for weeks. Years. It would be like Elvis returning from the dead. When the questions got louder and more demanding, forcing

Audrey to give up and look to him, Oz did what he did best—made things happen.

He nodded at the sound crew, and the music from "The Silly Seal Song" began to play. Recognizing her cue, Audrey smiled and began to mouth the words. Another speaker fastened discreetly in the pocket of her shirt kicked in so it sounded as if Syrene's voice was coming from her. The reporters stood there, dumbfounded, as Audrey gestured like Syrene, lip-synching.

Movie magic.

Sitting in the Little Angels day care with Donal on her lap, Pippa smiled at the computer video Conan had hooked up to the press conference.

"Look, your daddy does magic too," she whispered in the boy's ear.

Most of the other kids had wandered off to finger paint, but Donal sat enraptured. "That's not you," he crowed, understanding without communicating clearly.

"Nope, I'm Pippa. I like staying home and singing. Audrey likes going on stage and singing."

"I like your song. Heidi played it for me. The Librarian gave it to her."

One more clue to her layers of knowledge. Pippa bounced him up and down. "I sang that song just for you," she said, reassuring the boy as best as she could over the loss of his nanny.

He puzzled over that while the reporters in the video began shouting about the previously unknown Syrene recording. Dogs with their teeth in a bone wouldn't let go, Pippa observed, marveling at how well Oz was dealing with the hounds, wondering how he intended to settle this little problem. Her life pretty much depended on him waving a magic wand and making Syrene disappear. If he couldn't, she'd have to consider running again. But she was trusting the man she loved to solve this problem. She'd been tragically wrong before. This time, she prayed her trust wasn't misplaced.

On the monitor, Oz replaced Audrey at the podium. "Ladies, gentlemen, if I had a good explanation for the song that started all this, I would give it to you. The truth is—*we don't know*. The recording arrived via an anonymous email that FBI experts have been unable to trace. We were told to play the song in Bakersfield. As you all know, that's Syrene's hometown. Perhaps it was an old song recorded when she lived there as a child. We simply don't know who sent it or why. Your guess is as good as ours." He waited a moment for the shouts to quiet.

"Originally, we'd hoped to have Ms. James, the author of the Ronan book, read her books for the show," he continued, "but once we had the song, she declined. She's neither actress nor singer, and we needed both for this performance. Audrey filled in perfectly.

"All I can tell you is that this song brought back my son, and I am eternally grateful to Syrene, if this is truly her work. Thank you for coming, and you may send any unanswered questions to my office. You'll understand that my son and I need some time alone, and I will be out of touch for a while."

Watching the webcam, Donal wriggled in Pippa's lap. "I missed my daddy," he said. "Heidi said he was dead like my mama. He's not going away again, is he?"

The poor kid thought he'd been abandoned. Pippa hugged his grubby, paint-scented little boy body. "I am one hundred percent, a-posititutely certain that he's not likely to let you out of his sight for far longer than you'll like."

She tickled him, and he giggled, tumbling from her lap, reassured even if he had no understanding of what she'd just said.

The conference ended, and the video connection snapped off. Pippa wanted nothing more than to run over to the Blue Bayou and fling her arms around Oz's neck and thank him for his wizardry. But she would ruin everything by appearing in public after he'd worked so hard to make her disappear, so she refrained.

Oz's RV was still in the parking lot. She didn't want to place any significance on that, but she hoped and she waited and she read to the children while Donal happily dismantled Conan's computer.

Hours later, Oz dragged into the RV feeling battered, bruised, and in desperate need of a nap or a drink before he rescued Donal from the day care. Between working on the news conference and staying up to watch over the kid, he hadn't slept all night.

An apparition in silky white floated out of the shadows in the rear of the vehicle. The scent of roses preceded her.

He wasn't so tired anymore. "Pippa?" he asked, unwilling to believe his eyes.

Long fingers reached around his neck to ruffle his hair, and a tall, slender form leaned into him, filling his arms with glorious warmth and curves. He could taste roses when he lowered his lips to hers.

He didn't want more questions. He didn't even want answers. He simply wanted Pippa. Without a word, he lifted her onto the narrow mattress that passed for a bed and covered her with his body so she couldn't escape. Or evaporate. Or whatever the hell the woman could do when she wanted.

"Don't ever do that to me again," he warned.

"I know," she murmured against his mouth, brushing kisses everywhere she could reach. "I'm sorry. I never would have done it if I hadn't feared I'd cause more trouble than I was worth."

Oz leaned his forehead against hers and took a deep breath, trying to settle his pounding heart before speaking. "You need to know that you'll never be more trouble than you're worth to me. I didn't tell you that before, so I can't blame you for running—although I still want to scream and holler and demand that you never leave me again. But I've learned from my mistakes, so I'm telling you now so you'll excuse the shouting later. I love you. I want you in my life. In Donal's life. Any way we can have you. If it's okay with you, I want to make love to you now."

"I won't throw you in the pool," she promised with laughter on her lips as she ripped at his shirt buttons. "And no, I shouldn't have waited for you to tell me anything. I'm perfectly capable of speaking for myself these days. But sometimes... I'm not perfect."

Oz laughed, rolled over so she was on top, and yanked her floaty gown over her head. To his joy, she wore nothing under it. "You're so absolutely perfect for me that you're terrifying. I don't believe in luck or magic, but I'm starting to believe in hope again."

"Soul mates," she declared, tackling his belt. "I can't hurt you with my Voice. You can't hurt me with your silly obstinacy. I'll tell you no when others won't."

"That works." He tugged off his clothes and rolled her under him again, and together, they launched their future.

Epilogue

Donal paddled happily in the pool while Gloria tossed balls to him. Fortunately the weather was warm, because Donal had dismantled the heating equipment and almost electrocuted himself before Oz flipped off the electricity. Gloria had recommended hiring an electrician to teach the boy. Donal's scientific mind was beyond her ability to teach—although she promised Oz a few lessons in empathy he could pass on should Donal develop any woo-woo Malcolm tendencies.

Oz had declined her offer—for now. Pippa had a feeling he might need to tune his natural empathic instincts once he realized Donal had more of Conan's scientific mind than anyone realized.

It had been almost a week since the news conference, but so far the media had respected Oz's request to leave him and Donal alone. That didn't mean the hounds weren't baying around Bakersfield in search of Syrene and Donal's story. Every minute of Donal's life this past year was slowly unfolding on the news, as was Syrene's childhood. And the poor nanny's involvement.

The guy Pippa had nearly unmanned outside the school had turned out to be a local reporter who was convinced he'd been taken down by the criminal mastermind behind the kidnapping. He was tearing the nanny's life apart in search of the connection. Pippa would happily kick every reporter she met if that was always the result.

But so far, journalists apparently had no reason to chase a children's book author too shy to appear on stage when they had lovely Audrey to question. Pippa's agent was fielding inquiries about her books and requests for interviews, but none were particularly persistent.

Under the umbrella, she poured more strawberry smoothie into her glass and snuggled closer to Oz on the double lounge while he checked his email.

"What has Conan found out about Heidi that the media hasn't?" she asked, unable to read the monitor at this angle, unwilling to sit up and lose Oz's arm around her. He was good at one-thumb typing.

He squeezed her to let her know he was as aware of her as his work. "It's a classic case as far as we can tell. Heidi's family was back in Austria. She didn't know anyone here. She was lonely. Her boyfriend ditched her. She lost a baby in a miscarriage. She's been taking cash jobs to support herself so she didn't need ID."

She watched Donal happily adjusting to her home and knew he'd been well taken care of over this past year. The nanny hadn't overtly harmed him. The story was plausible. "But she never attempted to let you know your son was safe. I'm not feeling the sympathy here."

"She says I didn't really care about my son." Pain etched Oz's voice as he scrolled down Conan's report. "She claims I was too busy to bother with Donal and that she thought she was doing the boy a favor to give him a loving family."

"She's making excuses. Don't believe her. Donal was thrilled to see you. That's not the behavior of a child whose father neglected him." Pippa squeezed his leg and handed him her smoothie. "What about the Librarian?"

she asked, and Oz sipped the healthy drink. He was slowly adapting to her diet regimen.

"That's the weird part," he said, frowning. "Heidi stole the file of Donal's birth and medical information from Alys's records. I'll give her points for planning ahead. But then she started hunting for Donal's genealogy, just like Alys. What's with women and genealogy?"

Pippa watched Donal climb from the pool to examine a security camera Oz had ordered installed to protect them from intruders. The boy couldn't reach the camera. Yet. "I'm betting they want to know if Edison or Einstein is on the family tree," she suggested with a laugh.

Oz gave her a puzzled frown and then looked up to find his son climbing on a hibiscus planter to reach the camera. Gloria was already rising from her chair to persuade him down. "He's just being a boy."

"You keep on believing that, honey pie," Pippa answered mockingly. "But Heidi went to the Malcolm website, and our Librarian nabbed her, right?"

"The police don't care about the hows or whys of the kidnapping, but Conan accessed Heidi's computer. He says someone calling herself the Librarian communicated with Heidi via email. She sent a copy of the seal song and told Heidi that scientific studies showed that children who learned the song were geniuses. As soon as you promised to come to town, the Librarian told Heidi that she ought to encourage Donal's interest in the musician. Someone played Heidi like a fiddle."

"She also played us," Pippa reminded him. "But strange as it seems, the Librarian might be our friend. So who in heck is she?"

Oz traced his finger down her nose and planted a quick kiss on her lips. "Conan is looking. Before I go any further, tell me first, do you think you can love me enough to marry me?"

Startled, Pippa swatted his finger and glared at him. "If this is a trick, Oswin, I'll remind you that I can fling you into the pool."

He grinned. "No trick. I'm just directing this production, and I need to know if I have my star before I sign any contracts."

"Impossible man." She leaned back against the lounge chair, refusing to fall for his manipulation. *Marriage*. She was barely getting used to having people in her life again.

"If I didn't love you, I wouldn't be sitting here," she answered the first part of his question firmly. This much, she'd had time to consider. "I'm trusting you with my heart, my home, my family. I'm granting you magic powers, Dylan Ives Oswin. How will you use them?"

"By moving up here," he answered instantly. "I've been talking to Bertha. She has big plans for her day care, and that old building out front isn't suited for them."

Pippa swiveled her head and stared at him through narrowed eyes. "Go on."

At her glare, he shifted uneasily. The man knew how to read moods. She didn't know if he was ready to accept that he was empathic, but it was obvious his ability to read people had made him the success he was. She could just about feel his mind shifting gears at her reaction.

"If you curl up and go all *ommmm* on me," he warned, "I'll heave you in the pool."

She stroked his thigh, causing him to hum in appreciation. "This works better than yoga," she decided.

When his brain reconnected, he still responded with care. "I don't want Donal living in the city where he's an easy target. I want to be available when he gets home from school, which means I have to work close to where we live. In this day and age of Internet communication, it's easy enough to operate my office from anywhere. So I thought I could buy Bertha's property and build a house up on the road, one that would be easier for your mother to access."

"Uh-huh, are you telling me or asking?" Pippa demanded.

She bit back a smile while Oz-the-bully thought about what he'd said, processed it through his blender of a mind, and came up with the right answer.

"I'm asking?" he said in a tone that implied he was humoring her but his mind was already made up. "You could keep your studio and use this place as your office. It would be even more private with a big mansion sitting up front with a wall around it. And Donal and your mother would be safer out of the city, surrounded by people who know them—people they'll learn to trust. We'd have a whole town watching out for them. If that's okay with you."

"And if it's not?" she asked, challenging him, although the idea appealed far more than she would admit. She hadn't wanted to give up her sanctuary, but she knew the garden path prevented her mother from going into town as much as she would like.

"Then I guess I'll take no for your answer and come up with another plan," he agreed with a grin.

She punched his bicep and kissed him at the same

time. "I love you," she murmured against his mouth. "I just wanted to be sure I got a say in your next production."

He caught her chin and heated the kiss to inflammatory. "Is that a yes, Ms. James?"

"That's an I'm-thinking-about-it-but-probably-yes, Mr. Oswin. Does all this planning mean that Conan has found the Librarian?"

He grimaced and removed his arm. "You're an impossible case, but I'll wear you down." He turned the laptop screen so she could see it.

He'd left the text message open. Circle the wagons, it read. Pippa glanced at the sender's name. The Librarian.

"Maybe she's psychic," Oz said to her questioning look. "Maybe she's predicting an onslaught of paparazzi. We'll have walls, security guards. We'll be fine. I'll build you a labyrinth so you can walk the paths if my crews get on your nerves."

"Malcolms," Pippa countered, glancing pointedly to Donal and her mother at the pool's edge. "People with turquoise eyes and weird abilities. Let's find our own kind and circle the wagons. We'll love the labyrinth. Let's do it."

Acknowledgments

Thank you to all the Magic series readers who encouraged me to write about the offspring but probably didn't expect me to go this far. And thanks to Deb Werksman for seeing the potential in a little contemporary magic!

About the Author

With several million books in print and *New York Times* and *USA Today* bestseller lists under her belt, former CPA Patricia Rice is one of romance's hottest authors. Her emotionally charged contemporary and historical romances have won numerous awards, including the *RT Book Reviews* Reviewers Choice and Career Achievement Awards. Her books have been honored as Romance Writers of America RITA® finalists in the historical, regency, and contemporary categories.

A firm believer in happily-ever-after, Patricia Rice is married to her high school sweetheart and has two children. A native of Kentucky and New York, a past resident of North Carolina, she currently resides in St. Louis, Missouri, and now does accounting only for herself. She is a member of Romance Writers of America, the Authors Guild, and Novelists, Inc.

For further information, visit Patricia's network:
www.patriciarice.com
www.facebook.com/PatriciaRiceBooks
www.twitter.com/Patricia_Rice
www.patriciarice.blogspot.com/
www.wordwenches.com

New York Times bestselling author

Merely Magic

by Patricia Rice

She has the magic as her birthright...

Ninian is a healer, but she's a Malcolm first and foremost, and Malcolms have always had a bit of magic—unpredictable though it is—to aid them in their pursuits. She knows she must accept what she is or perish, but then Lord Drogo Ives arrives, bringing the deepest, most powerful magic she's ever experienced and turning Ninian's world upside down...

But Drogo Ives has no time for foolish musings or legends, even if he can't seem to resist the local witch. Thrown together by a series of disastrous events, Ninian won't give herself fully to Drogo until she can make him trust and believe in her, and that's the last thing he'll ever do...

Praise for Patricia Rice:

"You can always count on Patricia Rice for an entertaining story with just the right mix of romance, humor, and emotion." —The Romantic Reader

For more Patricia Rice books, visit:

www.sourcebooks.com